MW01075091

FDR DRIVE

FDR DRIVE

A CRIME NOVEL

JAMES COMEY

THE MYSTERIOUS PRESS
NEW YORK

To the people of SDNY, past and present,
who are an enduring force for good

FDR DRIVE

Mysterious Press
An Imprint of Penzler Publishers
58 Warren Street
New York, N.Y. 10007

Copyright © 2025 by James Comey

First Mysterious Press edition

Interior design by Maria Fernandez

Library of Congress Control Number: 2024950315

ISBN: 978-1-61316-644-4
eBook ISBN: 978-1-61316-645-1

10 9 8 7 6 5 4 3 2 1

Printed in the United States of America
Distributed by W. W. Norton & Company

PROLOGUE

New Wave Pier baked in the early September sun. The occasional tongues of artificial turf that the New York City Department of Parks and Recreation had bolted down to create a "park" out of a long strip of concrete on the East River's edge were hot enough to burn exposed skin. Not that the joggers and stroller-pushing parents were tempted to linger. Here at Forty-First Street, the pier ended without warning and the choices were a U-turn or a dip in the treacherous river, chaotically reversing direction with the tide.

Today, the pedestrians made their turns long before the end, rather than approach the big black NYPD Emergency Service Unit vehicle idling loudly in the sunshine. The sanitation department had moved two barricades to open a gap in the fence so the BearCat could back onto the pier from the FDR Drive. The truck's air conditioning was working hard, which was a blessing to the seven ESU officers inside in full tactical gear. In the front passenger seat, Sergeant George Burrell stared out at the northbound traffic on the Drive and fantasized about not being a supervisor so he could be hunched in the back with the team, who were scrolling on their phones. *But I'm a boss now,* he thought, shaking his head. *Boss of this hot-as-hell little piece of concrete.*

"It's all about deterrence and perimeter," his lieutenant had explained. The big event at the United Nations was generating lots of threatening chatter on social media and NYPD was going to lock it down in concentric circles, which was why they were pulling his squad in from Staten Island. "Park near the FDR so the world can see you," he said. "Show the flag, and in the unlikely event the shit hits the fan, we got you in reserve. Easy time and a half for your guys."

Burrell couldn't say *I would trade the overtime for some action, sir. Great to be in Manhattan, but we don't wanna just sit here; we wanna do shit.*

But any shit to be done was over there, in one of the circles closer to the tall rectangle of the UN headquarters he could see through his door window. There were a bunch of ESU teams between here and there. Even FBI SWAT was positioned closer to the big rally. *I show the flag. They're in the fight.* He shook his head and looked down, glancing at his phone.

◆

He thought he might have imagined the faint *pop, pop* sound but he looked up just as an explosive shockwave rocked the BearCat, almost lifting the front wheels off the ground before dropping it down to bounce on the powerful suspension. Even inside the armored vehicle, the blast was loud, followed immediately by the sickening crunching of metal as cars were thrown against the FDR's barriers. Burrell shouted, "Go! Go!" as he jumped from the truck and began running toward a cloud of smoke on the far side of the FDR, right where Forty-First Street ended at the Drive. Holding his M4 rifle with two hands, he squeezed past a car with a crushed driver's side and weaved across the cluttered and suddenly still roadway.

At the corner of Forty-First, he saw something on the ground, mostly obscured by the gray smoke. Three steps more and there it was:

the lower half of a man's body—jeans and white sneakers with legs and feet still in them—lying next to a hole gouged in the sidewalk. He turned to see his squad behind him, charging across the FDR, then looked back toward a sound coming from the direction of First Avenue, in front of the Midtown Tunnel ventilation building. A woman was crouched beside a motionless figure in the middle of the street, shouting and holding something up in her hand. George sprinted through the dust cloud and leveled his weapon at her.

"FBI! Jessica Watson, FBI!" she shouted. He could see now that she was holding her leather credential case in the air. "Agent down! Agent down!"

Burrell was next to her now. He glanced at a very large man lying on his back, eyes closed. She was holding her hand against what looked to be a wound in his right chest under his arm, dark blood surging around her fingers with each beat of his heart as she begged with the wounded man. "Please, Benny, please, hold on. Stay with me." George had seen plenty of sucking chest wounds during his two tours in Afghanistan. "Doc!" he shouted to the squad's medic as the five operators came up behind him. "Officer down."

The medic knelt and tore open her kit. "Shrapnel?"

"Gunshot," Jessica answered as she moved out of the way so the medic could do her job.

Jessica turned to Burrell, speaking rapidly but calmly. "There were two. My partner was shot just before the first bomber blew up. Second is White male, thirties, six feet, black cap, green backpack." She looked up at him, then turned to point toward First Avenue. "It's gotta be another bomb. He's heading for the rally."

Burrell clicked his radio as he ran. "Dispatch, ESU Delta, ten-thirteen, ten-thirteen, Forty-One and FDR Drive. Officer down, officer down. Shots fired, explosion. In pursuit. Subject last seen headed to First Avenue."

He paused when he realized he didn't know the radio code for a bombing. "Possible bomb attack, UN. FBI says the guy has a bomb."

He was sprinting toward the corner as the dispatcher responded in the usual fashion, a flat voice requesting a description. He gulped for air and kept running, gasping out what Jessica had said. The emergency tones for all units sounded on his radio as he turned onto First Avenue. All he could see ahead were thousands of people walking north to celebrate global unity at the United Nations.

CHAPTER ONE

One year earlier

"So in college are you going to take me to class every day too?" Sophie asked as they walked along Eighty-Third Street not holding hands.

"This is different," Nora Carleton answered with a smile. "Sure, if that's what you want, but only if you promise to go someplace nearby."

"Hilarious. Look, Mom, I love you, but I'm in seventh grade now and I'm almost thirteen. Nobody my age gets walked to school anymore."

"Could be the other parents don't see the darkness in the world, Bug."

"Could be some parents see only the darkness."

Nora exhaled audibly. "Please give me a slight break since it's just the first week of school and change can be hard for parents, you know."

They walked several steps in silence before Nora spoke again. "Okay, I'll stop at East End. But then your friends won't get to see you model a deeply affectionate relationship with your mother, which is kinda sad."

"They'll survive," Sophie said, grinning. "Besides, they're raised by their nannies anyway."

They stopped at the northwest corner of Eighty-Third Street and East End Avenue, a block before the Brearley School, a private, all-girls

school that Sophie had attended since their move to Manhattan from
Westport, Connecticut. The school was down a dead end where the
Upper East Side met the East River, almost literally. The building itself
was older than the FDR Drive, which deferred to its elder by dipping
under Brearley and its neighbors so as not to block the view.

Nora opened her arms. "Nana will meet you after school. Gimme
a squeeze."

Sophie leaned toward her mother, but paused. "Can you ask her to
meet me here?"

"Of course," Nora answered. "And I will leave it to you to explain
that you are ashamed of her."

"Mom—" Sophie began, but Nora pulled her in close.

"Kidding, kidding. Can't believe how tall you're getting." Nora's chin
rested on top of her daughter's hair, which was straight, middle parted,
and auburn, just like her mother's.

"Should stop soon," Sophie replied. "I think I'm going to be average
height, thank God."

Nora pushed her back, her hands holding Sophie's shoulders, an
exaggerated serious expression on her face. "What, you don't want to
be five twelve like your mom? You've seen a lot of short WNBA stars?
And don't forget Taylor Swift is five eleven!"

Sophie smiled at their familiar banter and gave her mother a final
hug. "Nothing personal. Fine being you; I just want to be a *mini*-you,
and I prefer soccer to basketball. Also, I love you."

"Love you too, Bug." Nora released her and watched her walk
away, before calling out, "You know you can't choose height. It's in
the DNA."

Sophie spun in a circle with her arms out wide and smiled before
continuing the walk to school.

I am my mother, Nora thought, watching her. *How the hell did that happen so fast?*

◆

It was a short walk from Sophie's school to the subway. Nora could take the newer Second Avenue line downtown or walk two blocks farther to the ancient Lexington Avenue line. Because the Second Avenue Q train wandered in strange ways, both routes got her to the federal building in lower Manhattan in about the same time, so she alternated and tried to be random about it. Sophie was correct: Nora's work and life experience—especially now that she was the Deputy United States Attorney, the number two in the Southern District of New York—had indeed given her a dark view of humans. But she also knew another truth: patterns were a gift to bad people who might want to hurt you, so there was no harm in changing routes.

On the subway, Nora put earphones in to keep people from talking to her, but never played sound through them; that would obscure any threats around her. She would read on her phone and take calls if any came (and if she had enough reception), but she wouldn't be distracted by music or a podcast in a crowded metal box with strangers deep underground. *Yeah, maybe a little dark,* she thought, putting the devices in her ears. Still, her eyes swept the car at each stop and she wondered what voices some of those strangers were listening to.

Emerging from the Canal Street subway stop, Nora almost had to will her feet not to follow the familiar path to the United States Attorney's office. Her beloved and decrepit old building, which shared a brick plaza with NYPD headquarters, was getting its first overhaul since 1974, when the federal government originally built it next to the

Church of St. Andrew. The structure had been emptied and would be stripped down to the beams before being rebuilt, although it would end up substantially the same size and still be too small for the full United States Attorney's office staff. *Only the government would replace an inadequate building with a slightly nicer inadequate building.*

Instead, as she entered Foley Square, Nora turned toward the massive office tower directly across from the Thurgood Marshall courthouse—the Jacob K. Javits federal office building. But nobody called it that. To the FBI, which filled many of its forty-one floors, it was "26 Fed," short for 26 Federal Plaza, another made-up US government address in lower Manhattan. The tall windows of 26 Fed offered sweeping views in all directions. Now the Criminal Division of the US Attorney's office had those views—as a temporary tenant on two floors, just above the FBI. The space was fine—although the walk across Foley Square to court felt unnecessarily exposed—but Nora couldn't shake the feeling that they were unwelcome guests temporarily invading the FBI's turf.

The building's many federal tenants, including the perpetually busy immigration and social security offices, made it a crowded place during business hours, so Nora had to squeeze into an elevator for the ride to 38. There, the security guard greeted her with a broad smile and waved her around the X-ray machines.

"Mornin' boss," he said.

"You know you've got to stop with the 'boss' stuff, Artie," Nora replied, shaking her head. "You've known me for ten years."

"Only the day after you leave, which I hope is never," he answered.

Nora laughed and turned left down the long, narrow hallway. Prosecutors on the outside, with windows; support staff on the inside, no windows—sunlight reaching them only through the frosted glass walls of the lawyers' offices. She greeted everyone she saw, stopping to chat every few doors, trying to remember whom she had visited most recently.

Far down the hall, she could see the enormous figure of Benny Dugan blocking the sunlight coming out of her office. But she didn't hurry, hopscotching among office doors until she finally reached him and heard the Brooklyn baritone.

"Ms. Smooth," he said, using his longtime nickname for her, "you running for office or somethin'? Lotta baby kissing goin' on."

Nora smiled and looked up at the six-foot-five Benny, noticing for the first time, with the sun behind him, that his blond crew cut was turning gray. "I'm a *leader* now, Mr. Rough, as you too often forget. I'm the DUSA"—she pronounced it *doo-sah*—"and a leader needs to check in with the troops as often as possible. And I read somewhere that the CEO of a restaurant chain has to constantly taste the soup to know what's going on."

"Very leader-like," he replied.

"And unlike the crappy old building, where the DUSA only passed three offices on the way to her door, this monstrosity offers the DUSA a chance to taste a lot of soup along a single hallway."

Benny smiled. "And will the DUSA be referring to herself in the third person at all times now?"

"She is giving it serious thought," Nora said with a grin, pushing past him into her office. "And how may the DUSA serve you this fine morning?"

Benny followed her across the big office and dropped his two hundred and fifty pounds onto the blue faux-leather couch. "Your mom wanted me to remind you that she'll be home tonight—after she picks up Soph at school—and she's gonna make her ziti casserole. Asked if you could grab some bread and a bottle of Chianti on your way home."

Nora pulled her mouth into a tight line and stared at Benny without speaking.

"What, what?" he protested. "Just delivering messages."

Nora chuckled and shook her head. "I just can't get used to this life."

"What life?"

"You, Mom, an item. She didn't come home last night. I was worried sick."

Benny blew air out of his nose. "No, you weren't. You knew she was safe and sound in the arms—"

"Nope," Nora interrupted, "stop right there. Don't need any R-rated images of you and my mother in my head. No, thank you."

"Your mind," Benny said, shaking his head. "I was going to be entirely appropriate."

Nora laughed. "If my mom is making you *appropriate*, we may have a chance on global warming."

"Always the comedian," Benny mumbled.

"Will you be joining us to eat your girlfriend's famous ziti dish?"

"I wish," Benny said, "but I got a surveillance on the Buchanan case, which we're gonna brief Carmen on this morning."

"Oh right, what time are you meeting with Carmen and the DUSA?"

Benny paused and shook his head. "It's not working."

Nora laughed. "No, it's not. Was worth a shot. What time should I be there?"

Benny pushed himself to his feet. "Ten. Carmen's office."

As he walked to the door, Nora called after him. "Hey, just so you know, I actually like this new life. You're good for her."

Benny turned. "I'm not as good a person as you think I am."

"Did the DUSA say you were a good person?"

"The DUSA did not," he replied with a broad smile. "See you in a few."

CHAPTER TWO

"This nation's soul is at risk, y'all," Samuel Buchanan shouted, his mouth almost touching the pop screen on the microphone. "And a country loses its soul the way a man does, one tiny"—which came out *tah-nee*—"bit at a time"—*tie-um*. He was smiling at his two producers as he launched into the familiar riff, gesticulating wildly as sweat gathered on his forehead, but always managing to avoid the mic boom arm. He'd learned the hard way that a whack on the boom not only startled his live listeners, but also meant he had to rerecord the whole thing before they could release the show as a podcast; there was no way the sound guy could fix that "in post," whatever the hell that meant. His gravelly voice was deep Georgia; listeners could feel the Spanish moss dripping from the trees as the dogs—*dawgs*—napped on the porch.

Of course, Sam Buchanan was a long way from the Florida-Georgia line and had been since he left for prep school in New Hampshire forty years before—except for occasional visits south to hunt from horseback at a private plantation. He was in the sunroom of his Gramercy Park apartment in Manhattan, sitting with his back to a fireplace the co-op board had ordered sealed up long before a limited liability company bought the place for six million. On the mantle behind him were arrayed the hats and helmets of working people—mementos of a life dedicated to people he saw as real Americans, whose plight he had first become aware of during his undergraduate and law school years at Harvard.

Over the years, he had gained and lost any number of political consulting jobs, sales positions, and radio gigs—even marriages—but Buchanan had never forgotten the voiceless Americans of European ancestry, and now the combination of digital media and podcasting had given his own voice a power and range he had never imagined. The harder the titans of the corporatized tech world worked to silence him, the stronger he got. The fools didn't realize that their "content moderation" bullshit just made his followers hungrier for his words. Maybe his followers couldn't hear them in the usual channels now that Silicon Valley had worked so hard to throttle him. And maybe the advertisers had been scared away—except the commemorative coin and orthopedic shoe people, who understood what loyalty was. But the words still got out, streamed on messaging apps, watched on computer monitors, shared in clips by users on the very same platforms that had banned him. And now his new email subscription service was gaining momentum; it seemed there were a lot of Americans who understood that freedom was worth $29.99 per year. Of course, being banned from payment platforms made things harder, but he wasn't trying to reach people addicted to the opioid of Apple Pay or PayPal; *his* people were the Americans who realized what was at stake and wrote checks or mailed cash.

Buchanan was seated behind his desk, swiveling his Herman Miller Aeron chair side to side, which met his need to move, while keeping his mouth near the microphone. The headphones served as a sort of headband, holding back his unruly long brown hair. Senior producer Herbert Cusak sat on one side of a long table that was pushed against the desk to form a T. His job was to send Buchanan talking points and questions for politicians or commentators joining by Zoom, which was the usual way Buchanan hosted guests. Cusak's thoughts would appear on the laptop in front of the host. "Herb knows my mind," Buchanan liked to say; they had been together through various ventures since Cusak had graduated from Hampden-Sydney College and volunteered for a conservative Congressional campaign in southwest Virginia on which a young Buchanan was speechwriter. Now fifty-three, the never-married Cusak wore basically the same outfit as he had the day they met: white button-down dress shirt, hand-tied bow tie, and khaki pants with a nautical-theme belt. The only thing different about him was that his belly now obscured some of the nautical theme and his light brown hair was thin and combed over from a part, which sat just above his left ear. Cusak hated New York but saw little of it; he rarely left Buchanan's enormous apartment, splitting his time between the sunroom studio and the au pair suite on the far side of the floor, overlooking the back alley.

Across from Cusak, pushed back from the table with her laptop on her legs, sat the junior producer, Rebecca Hubbard, a recent journalism and mass communication graduate of the University of Wisconsin–Madison. Becky's job was to do instant research in response to electronic questions from Cusak or prompted by whatever Buchanan or a guest were talking about. She would feed her work product to Herb, who would decide what to put in front of the host. Becky loved New York and took the job after her college roommate's mother told her she knew of someone "in the media" who was looking to make an entry-level hire. She wore baggy clothes and oversized glasses, with her dirty blond hair pulled back in a ponytail, despite Buchanan's repeated suggestions that she "dress to impress," let her hair down, and get contacts so "the world can see your pretty self." She ignored him—he really didn't understand the younger generation, she told herself—and it didn't seem to affect her job, which paid very well.

At the far end of the table, a digital camera sat on a small tripod framed so only Buchanan was visible in the shot. Buchanan swiveled less when he knew they were filming. He was perfectly still now, glancing at the laptop and then up at the camera, his face glistening with sweat, which had run down his neck, darkening the front of his open-collar blue dress shirt.

"In my"—*mah*—"experience, the only thing necessary for evil to triumph in the world is that good men do nothing."

Becky quickly typed a message to Cusak: *Isn't he supposed to say that's from Edmund Burke?*

Ideally, but past it now, Herb typed.

Buchanan was indeed far beyond the supposed Burke quotation: ". . . and there is no doubt that what we face today in America is evil, plain and simple. There's no other word for the intentional, willful, *knowing* destruction of a culture established on this continent by the blood and sweat of our brave ancestors, a culture with roots much older than that, roots that stretch back to the words and work of our Lord and Savior two thousand years ago. And they want you to think it's not about you, that voices like my own are exaggerating the threat. They want you to stand there like sheep, silent bystanders to one of the great genocides of human history. In the words of a great poem:

"First they came for the children, and I did not speak out—because I was not a parent.

"Then they came for our privacy and I did not speak out—because I had nothing to hide.

"Then they came for gun owners, and I did not speak out—because I was not a gun owner.

"Then they came for me—and there was no one left to speak for me."

Wait, Becky typed, *that's not the poem and it's from the Holocaust.*

Whatever, came Herb's reply. *Good stuff tho.*

CHAPTER THREE

"Glad you moved the rug across the street," Nora said, standing in the US Attorney's reception area admiring the burgundy-and-blue Persian carpet that dominated the waiting room.

Georgene Jackson beamed behind the desk. "Be lost without that rug," she said. "Plus, if I left it behind, it'd be in a dumpster with the rest of the building."

Georgene gestured to a large, brightly colored painting of a tropical scene hanging over the couch and spoke in a whisper, combining, as she always did, the dropped "er" of a longtime "New Yorkah" with the lilt of her childhood in Trinidad. "But now that you remind me, I did forget to bring the big photo of all the White men from the office's two hundredth anniversary dinner at the Plaza. You remember the one, although you were in diapers when they had that party. It was on that old wall forever"—it came out *fa-ev-ah*—"so it seemed right that it stayed there and went down with the ship."

Nora laughed loudly. "Darn shame, but this is a reasonable substitute."

"It was a gift from my current boss—by a *Caribbean* artist," Georgene said, nodding her head toward the closed door to the US Attorney's private office. "You may recall your friend Ms. Garcia and I share that heritage."

"I do, I do," Nora said, deciding that being a senior leader meant not exploring whether Puerto Rico and Trinidad really did constitute a shared heritage. "She in?"

"She is," Georgene answered before adding, with a broad smile: "And she would want me to remind you yet again that you never need to ask, wait, or knock. The two of you are in charge of this place, baby girl, as shocking as that is to those of us who knew you when you were infant prosecutors."

"Imagine how we feel," Nora said, walking to the door and opening it as she called out in a loud voice: "Federal agent with a search warrant!"

"Never gets old," Carmen replied from behind her desk, not looking up from the computer.

"Morning, fearless leader."

"Morning," Carmen mumbled.

"You doing okay? I'm not getting the Time 100, woman-of-power vibe I'm used to."

"Really?" Carmen asked as she finally looked up, a reluctant smile creasing her face. "That's my vibe?"

"Well, not always," Nora said. "Sometimes you do a working-mom-making-bad-men-cry thing. But they overlap for sure."

Carmen stood and came around the desk, taking one of the armchairs across the coffee table from Nora. She was normally all energy and humor radiating from a face with the dark eyes of her native Puerto Rico. Carmen wore her thick black hair short and lived with her wife and their young son in the suburbs. "And, yes," she was quick to tell acquaintances, "there *are* gay Puerto Ricans; imagine the president's excitement at all the boxes my appointment checked."

"So what's grinding you down this morning?" Nora asked.

"Washington. They never stop trying to recover turf they think we stole in the Roosevelt administration or some shit. Teddy Roosevelt, by the way. And it's always on the civil side."

"What's today's turf drama?"

"Guns. Main Justice says they need to come argue every lawsuit involving a Second Amendment issue because"—she held up air quotes and deepened her voice—"these national issues need to be litigated consistently and by experienced counsel who aren't smart enough to carry the bags of SDNY Civil Division people."

Carmen dropped her hands and paused before adding, "That last bit about our people being smarter was something I added. Wasn't quoting them, but you know it's true."

"Of course," Nora replied, "and, for the record, you didn't say anything like that."

Carmen rubbed her face with both palms as she answered. "I did not. Because you convinced me that stuff like that being said for decades might be a big part of the reason they resent the fuck out of us. *Excellence is something you spray, not say*, was your turn of phrase, as I recall. Or was it *piss, not diss?*"

Nora could no longer hide her smile. "Either way, pretty great stuff, dontcha think?"

"It's not getting our people in the first chair on these arguments, so the jury's out, to be honest. But enough about my pain. How is justice in our sovereign district this morning?"

"She's blindfolded but somehow still getting it done," Nora said. "We have a meeting in a few about Sean's new project."

"Remind me?"

"The maniacs in NSIN—whom we love because they're *our* maniacs—want to do something about this right-wing podcaster/radio guy, Samuel Buchanan, and—"

Carmen cut her off. "We really do need to change that unit name, NSIN. Sounds more like something out of the navy than a terrorism unit."

"Sure, but we have to put *international narcotics* somewhere and having it in the name along with *national security* keeps DEA happy. And the unit needs the work anyway."

Carmen waved her hand. "Sorry to take you down that rabbit hole. Forget the name. So what's up with Buchanan?"

"Well," Nora continued, "he's a con man fraudster who makes bags of money by stirring up some awful shit—a bunch of people are dead or hurt because of his followers—but he wraps himself in the First Amendment. You know the drill: *I'm just asking questions; I never told anyone to attack anyone.* But Sean has a theory and he's talked the Bureau into supporting it—just NYO so far, not headquarters; the Director will be in his usual fetal position when he hears about it, for fear he'll have to testify on the Hill. Anyway, Benny's on it, working well with one of the Bu's domestic terrorism squads—Jessica's actually the lead. But I'll let them pitch it to you. I've heard a version and I think you're going to like it. Lemme run down the hall and I'll see you in a few with the team."

"Good. I like a little entrepreneurship, from time to time, especially if it keeps people from getting killed. And if the cost of doing the work is the FBI director getting yelled at by fools in Congress, seems a small price. Looking forward to it."

◆

Sean Fitzpatrick was wearing a suit and tie, which appeared to be making him itchy as he crossed and recrossed his legs on the waiting room couch, his collapsed black wool socks revealing pasty-white shins as he shifted.

"You got a funeral after this, Sean?" Georgene teased.

"Very funny," Sean replied, deadpan.

"You know she sees that you don't wear suits during the day, Sean, right? We're all on the same floor now; no hiding in your jeans up on nine like the old place, grabbin' a suit off the back of the door to run to court or see the boss. You know all this, right?"

Sean blushed visibly. "Guess so. Just feels weird to come see the US Attorney without dressing up."

A large figure interrupted from the doorway, booming a fake Irish accent. "Sean, me boy, you got a date after this?"

"I like *your* tie too," Sean said.

"Which I always wear, as you know," Benny said, dropping the accent, "because I'm a law enforcement professional."

"Yeah, without socks," Sean added.

Benny ignored the jibe, turning to the Black woman entering behind him and raising his voice. "Besides, I don't want the FBI thinkin' less of me."

"Never happen," the woman answered, squeezing past Benny to cross the Persian rug, where she extended her hand to Georgene. "Jessica Watson, FBI. I'm the acting squad supervisor on the case we're meeting with Ms. Garcia on."

"So nice to meet you, Special Agent Watson. I'm Georgene Jackson and I work every single day of my life with these fine White men."

Jessica paused and smiled politely, unsure what to say. She was saved by Nora's entry into the waiting room.

"Hi, all. Great to see everyone," Nora said moving toward Jessica with arms extended, adding, "but especially you, stranger." As they hugged, Nora noticed Georgene's confused expression. "Oh, Jessica and I go way back," she explained, stepping back. "Her first case was with me and Benny on Dominic 'The Nose' D'Amico and all that *that* turned into."

"Back. In. The. Day," Benny announced, punching each word before saying "when ships were wood and women steel."

They all turned to Benny. "Wow," Jessica said.

The office door opened. "Hey team," Carmen called, "come on in. Can't wait to hear what trouble you're going to get me into." She stood in the doorway and shook hands with each of them as they entered her office, putting a hand on Sean's shoulder to pause him at the end of the procession. "You look great, Sean, don't let them make you self-conscious."

The six-two prosecutor with short black hair and hooded green eyes—"the map of Ireland on his face" was an expression he had heard many times but never fully understood—had long been one of Carmen's favorites. Their stories couldn't be more different or any more similar, she had explained to Nora. Sean also came from humble roots, his working-class family emigrating to New York City from Ireland not long after Carmen's parents came up from Puerto Rico. Like her, his talent was spotted early in Catholic school. Where she was steered to the Convent of the Sacred Heart all-girls school on Manhattan's Upper East Side, Sean was recruited by the Jesuits to the nearby all-boys Regis High School, where every kid was on scholarship. The only thing the famously contrarian priests wanted in return, the joke went, was for the students to end up as successful, service-minded agnostics who contributed money back to the school. And it worked with Sean, in all respects except the money.

After Regis, he went to Amherst College, where he won school prizes in mathematics and economics by skipping classes and instead reading the course textbooks the day before exams. While other kids were in class, he was busy working as a janitor to pay his way through school or playing rugby. After law school at Harvard, which he approached in a similar way, he worked briefly at a law firm until he could apply to be a Manhattan federal prosecutor, where his slightly chaotic brand of intelligence soon became legendary. An early supervisor was appalled that Sean had simply piled the key documents he needed for a trial into a mailroom cart typically used to transport materials to court. The supervisor admonished Sean that the documents should be in folders and not just thrown into the cart. He returned to find each document in a separate, unlabeled folder, piled in the cart. Sean wasn't trying to be funny. He knew what was in all the documents, no matter how they were arranged.

In his fifteen years at the office, Sean had thrown himself into his work, almost literally. He spent many nights sleeping on the couch in his office and was so rarely home at his tiny Brooklyn apartment that he had never turned on the gas to his stove. The occasional visitor would panic at the sight of papers and empty pizza boxes piled on top of the burners. After Nora left the office to take a job in Connecticut—before her return as the Deputy US Attorney—Sean and Benny had become close partners investigating and prosecuting big cases, with Sean gradually convincing the older man that the biggest domestic threat was no longer Cosa Nostra but what the FBI called "racially motivated violent extremists"—and the most active of these were White people who believed that non-Whites threatened them and the continued existence of the United States of America. As chief of the National Security and International Narcotics Unit, Sean did very little chiefing; making cases was his passion.

◆

When they were all settled around the coffee table, Carmen turned to Nora. "Are we waiting on our Criminal Division chief?"

"No, he's on travel today, but fully up to speed." She nodded to Sean. "Tell the boss about the Buchanan case."

For the next fifteen minutes, Sean spoke without notes. He talked quickly as he described Buchanan's almost endless litany of sermons about the plight of White people in America, a predicament supposedly caused by a globalist elite bent on erasing the exceptional American culture that had once been the envy of the world. He explained Buchanan preached that an educated class of Americans actually hate their own country and want to reengineer it by replacing White Christians with waves of Latin American, Asian, and African immigrants, driving religion from the public square, blurring gender differences, and knitting the United States ever more tightly into a European Union–centered new world order. In Buchanan's view, Sean said, the culprits span the political spectrum—from the atheists on the left for whom climate change and gender fluidity are the new religions, to the corporatists on the right who want more brown workers to exploit.

Sean summed up by saying, "Buchanan prophesizes that, if left unchecked, these America-haters will allow babies to be killed, open the borders, ban fossil fuels, regulate the duration of home bathroom showers, take guns away, ban Christian holidays, and use schools to teach kids to be gay and androgynous while making two-parent families the exception. You and I may think it's crazy stuff, but people—lots of them—are into it."

When he paused for a breath, Carmen cut in. "Depressing, but I've heard a lot of that, and not just from him. Flavors of it are all over certain cable news programs and social media. But not our business, right?"

"Right," Sean replied, "if it stopped there. But it doesn't. Because Buchanan spends a lot of his time urging his followers to *do something* about it, and he doesn't mean organize and vote. Most of his calls to action are general, but sometimes he gets pretty specific, and then people get hurt and some die."

Sean handed Carmen a notebook. "Behind the first tab are examples of his general stuff. People who love America must do more than shout at the television, he says; they have to act, to stand up the way our forebears did at Lexington and Concord. Words will not save America, just as they wouldn't stop the British. What preserves freedom are patriots willing to risk it all."

He flipped to a page with a picture of a flag. "He talks constantly about Virginia's state flag, with Lady Virtue holding a spear and standing on a dead king, above the motto *Sic Semper Tyrannis*—'thus always to tyrants.'"

Sean waited as Carmen flipped through the pages of transcript excerpts. "Okay," she said when she was finished. "And then?"

"The next tab is the times he connected all this 'death to tyrants' stuff to specific people. Four times he identified a named person as a tyrant bent on destroying America. Their bios are there. Each time he named someone, he said, 'Something should be done' and 'They have to go.' All the targets were attacked within days. Two of them are dead."

After waiting for her to read the excerpts connected to each victim, he continued. "The last tab is a fold-out map of the locations of the attacks and, behind that, what we know about the attackers. So far we can't connect them to each other, but we *can* show they were all voracious consumers of Buchanan's bullshit."

Carmen studied in silence before quietly closing the notebook and looking at Sean. "And so what's our theory?"

"This is the Blind Sheikh with a twist," Sean said.

"I'm not tracking you," Carmen answered.

"The Blind Sheikh. Sheikh Omar Abdel Rahman. Our office prosecuted him for seditious conspiracy back in the nineties. Islamist radical cleric from Egypt who set up shop here and hammered at evil America in his speeches, telling his followers that being a believer required action, which he called jihad. They took him at his word and waged war on America, including the first attack on the World Trade Center and a plot to blow up the tunnels and bridges into Manhattan. He got life and died in federal prison. Never touched a bomb or a gun. He just inspired them and blessed their work."

"I remember now," Carmen said, "but isn't that last piece the key? Wasn't there evidence that they came to him with specific plans and he issued a fatwa blessing those? Seems different here, unless you have proof you didn't mention."

"That's right," Sean answered. "Rahman *did* know some of what they planned; not the specific targets in every case, maybe, but he knew from talking to them that they were going to attack. And we don't have that here. Yet."

"Okay," Carmen said, "which is why we investigate, right?" She swept her eyes around the group before adding, "So what do you need from me?"

Nora took that one. "We wanted you to know the investigation was underway. That's it. Info, not action."

"You think I need to tell Main Justice?" Carmen asked.

"Good question," Nora said, turning to Jessica. "I suppose it turns on what FBI New York is telling the Bureau in DC at this point. If the FBI briefs it to HQ, we don't want it coming across Pennsylvania Avenue without us giving Main a heads-up first."

"Don't know," Jessica said. "We try not to tell HQ much, but this is also the FBI, where we brief up visits to the bathroom. It was a miracle my brass agreed to your request that we keep this meeting 'skinny' or we'd have five more people from my chain in here. So let me find out and get back to you."

Carmen smiled at her warmly. "Okay, let me know, and if there are any ruffled feathers about some boss not being here today, I'm happy to call upstairs to your ADIC," she said, using the acronym for the Assistant Director in Charge. The New York office was by far the FBI's largest. Unlike most field offices, which were headed by a Special Agent in Charge, New York was led by an ADIC—pronounced, despite the irresistible jokes, as "a dick."

Again, she looked at the group. "The tighter this is held, the better, because—and I don't need to tell you, but I will—we're entering the political season again in this crazy, mixed-up, wonderful country of ours. Keep me posted. Thanks for coming in. Nora, could I chat with you for a second?"

"Sure," Nora answered. "Let me just show the team out."

As the group walked through the reception area, Nora caught up with Benny, who paused as the others walked on. "You were uncharacteristically quiet in there."

He smiled. "This is a different kind of mob and a different kind of bad than the Italians. Still sortin' it out. When I have somethin' worth sayin', I'll say it."

"I know you will; we're counting on you as usual. How's Sean to work with?"

"I like him. Reminds me of you, honestly, although he has even less of a life than you did back in the day. At least you had Sophie. Sean's got a *cat*, which I'm actually worried about because he never remembers to feed the poor thing. And I'm not a cat person, as you know, so that should tell you something about the kind of danger that animal is in."

"Well, I'm glad you're on this. Sure you can't make it for ziti tonight?"

"Can't. Gonna sit on this asshole Buchanan all week and see what I can see about his team. Tryin' to figure out where a weak link might be. Rain check, for sure."

Nora retraced her steps across the Persian rug and into Carmen's office. "What's up, boss?"

Carmen silently moved her hand to signal Nora to close the door. When Nora did, Carmen spoke quietly, her voice just above a whisper. "I've learned the walls they threw up for us here are pretty thin. Low bid, I'm guessing."

Nora smiled. "Which is how you knew they were teasing Sean about getting dressed up. Got it."

"Yup," Carmen said. "Hey, the reason I wanted to catch you is to ask you to stay extra close to this. I know that's not the DUSA's role, but I can see this becoming a big flaming bag of crap. Politics are always ugly, but now? Fuck. We make a case, the right goes nuts; we don't, the left says we're chickenshit. You know this. I would just feel better if you're on it tight."

"I get you," Nora said quietly, "but I worry that's going to rub Sean the wrong way."

"Maybe, but I also think he sees the potential shitstorm and he's smart enough to realize you can help him see around some corners. Plus, it's going to be really important how we manage DC on this; the last thing we need is the Main Justice Death Star trying to be helpful."

"Got it," Nora said. "Makes sense and it'll be fun to get back in the kitchen to actually *make* some soup."

Carmen scrunched up her face. "Do I want to know what you're talking about?"

Nora chuckled. "You definitely do not. I'm on this. Will keep you posted."

CHAPTER FOUR

"What was your best and worst, Nana?" Sophie asked as she reached for a piece of garlic bread.

Teresa Carleton beamed at her granddaughter. "Well, my best, obviously, is this dinner with my girls. My worst is that Benny couldn't be with us."

"What's yours, Mom?" Sophie asked as she chewed.

"This dinner, for sure," Nora answered, "and thanks to Nana for being a great cook. My worst is probably that I didn't get a chance to see the front door of the school today." With an exaggerated frown, she added, "Very sad."

Sophie laughed. "If that's your worst, your day's been pretty great. Nana didn't seem to have a problem meeting me on East End."

"That's because your grandmother doesn't love you the way I do," Nora replied, grinning broadly. "And your best and worst, my trouble-making daughter?"

"Dinner, of course," Sophie answered. "The ziti is amazing. And my other best—and, yes, I know because I'm in seventh grade that's a misuse of the word 'best,' but it's also a big part of our family culture—"

Nora and her mother exchanged wide-eyed looks as Sophie continued.

"—is that some kids at school told me about an indoor soccer club that they do; meets all fall and winter."

"Wow, that sounds great," Nora said. "Where is it?"

"At the old armory on 143rd Street."

"That should work," Nora said. "Send me the link so I can sign you up."

"Well, that brings me to my worst," Sophie said glumly. "They play on Saturdays and Sundays and I have to go to Westport to Dad's on weekends, so it's not going to work."

Teresa started to speak but stopped and glanced at Nora, who said, "Let me talk to your dad about it. You may remember that Vicki's family has a place in the city—just on the other side of the park—and maybe we could work something out where they come in to see *you* during the indoor season instead of you going to Connecticut."

Sophie's face lit up. "It's not that I'm trying to ditch them or anything. Now that Amelia's four, she's almost a real human being, so I like playing with her, and I still have a lot of friends in Connecticut, and Vicki seems happier now, and Dad, obviously, is my dad and—"

Nora interrupted, laughing softly. "Okay, okay, I'll talk to him and make sure he knows this is about loving soccer *and* loving them, all at the same time. But it's also his decision because that was our deal with him." Nora paused before adding, "And he's been a great dad."

"He has been," Sophie said quietly. "I mean, he *is*. And thanks for asking him."

They ate in silence for several minutes before Teresa changed the subject. "What's your favorite class so far? And I know it's early."

"Oh, that's easy," Sophie responded. "Social studies. We're talking about political polarization in America."

"Not really an ideologically diverse group of students, am I right?" Teresa asked.

"You'd be surprised, Nana. The teacher had us spread ourselves in the classroom—literally along an imaginary line—based on things like crime and policing or Israel and the Palestinians or taxes and spending. There were girls at opposite walls and spread out in between—on everything. It's probably all based on what their families think, but still."

"Where'd you end up on the line?" Nora asked.

"Somewhere near the middle, most of the time. I told them you're a rule-of-law social liberal and we're kinda moderate on most stuff, although Dad seems like more of a libertarian capitalist. The political culture of our family is unusual because my parents were never really together."

Nora and Teresa exchanged another glance as Sophie went on.

"The surprising part is how angry a lot of the girls seemed when everyone wasn't standing with them on every issue. As Ms. Johnson said, if people in our little bubble on the Upper East Side can't disagree in a thoughtful way, there isn't much hope for America."

◆

Sophie was down the hall in her room doing homework as her mother and grandmother cleaned up after dinner.

Teresa handed Nora a serving bowl. "So our little girl is now observing our 'family culture'? Wow."

"Yup," Nora answered as she added the bowl to the pile in the sink, "and it was definitely a mistake to make the move from best part of your day to best *and* worst."

Teresa smiled. "Your innovation, as I recall. Something about letting your child feel safe sharing disappointment and sadness as well as joy? I believe I was an advocate for all rainbows and unicorns."

Nora turned and began rinsing a pan, speaking quietly so her words stayed in their small kitchen. "Yes, I remember. But she has Nick *nailed*, don't you think? Personally, I might have gone with 'pile-of-gold conservative'—as in: 'my wife's family has a pile and we intend to keep it'—but 'libertarian capitalist' sounds better."

"Be kind," Teresa answered in a whisper. "Nick's turned out to be a reasonably good adult, and he's good to our girl."

"He is, he is," Nora said. "I just hope he'll help with her soccer."

"You think he will?"

"I actually do," Nora answered. "Despite my teasing, he's been a great partner on all of this. He's really grown up, our Nick."

"Some frogs do become princes," Teresa said with a smile.

Nora grinned and lifted her wet hands, palms out. "Okay, let's not go crazy with the prince stuff. He's a fine adult. But, let's be clear, I'm still glad we never got married. I got the best thing out of that relationship."

Teresa laughed. "Totally agree."

Nora reached back into the sink to scrub, adding, "And speaking of reasonably good adults, sorry that your boyfriend couldn't make it tonight."

Teresa smiled and ran a hand through her long, straight silver hair. "My *boyfriend*—and I'm using your term although we modern people don't put labels on love—is trying to keep this country safe. He doesn't give me details, of course, but I know he's out there doing good."

"Yes, he is," Nora replied. "And it's love now? Huh. Anyway, are you still going to see his family this weekend?"

"We are. Now that Calvin and Sheila have three little ones, they moved out to Hauppauge on the Island, to a bigger place, with a guest room. So we're gonna stay with them. I even think his son Kenneth is coming down from Boston, but he'll be at a hotel if he does."

"I still can't get over the fact that Benny has three grandkids. Amazing."

"And they worship him, Nora. It's just wonderful to watch."

With a smile, Nora said, "So he'll be sleeping on the couch while you get the guest room?"

"You're not the boss of me," Teresa answered with a grin, echoing a phrase from Nora's childhood. "Unless you want me to police where you stay in Westport after you drop Sophie at her dad's. Oh, did I say 'police'? Slip of the tongue."

Nora reached into the soapy water before lifting a wet hand to flick her fingers at her mother. "Fair enough. Mutual nondisclosure agreement."

CHAPTER FIVE

Senior producer Herb Cusak was standing in the open door to Buchanan's apartment, using his back foot to keep the door from closing. The elevator opened and a wiry White man with a shaved head and wraparound mirrored sunglasses stepped into the hallway. He was wearing a plain white T-shirt under a black bomber jacket, with green cargo pants and black Salomon boots.

When the elevator closed, Cusak looked confused. "Can I help you? You with Ms. Harmon?"

The man nodded and extended his hand. "David Lupo."

"Oh, hi," Cusak replied. "Nice to finally meet you. Good to put a face with a voice."

"Same," Lupo said, looking around the hallway.

Cusak paused, then asked, "Is she delayed or something?"

"No," Lupo said, looking past Cusak into the apartment. "She's in the car. This is what we call 'advance.' Need to check out the location before bringing the protectee."

"Oh, I see. Wasn't aware she had security."

When Lupo didn't respond, Cusak went on. "But no matter. We live in difficult times. Please do come in. Look wherever you'd like. Shall I wait here?"

"Suit yourself," Lupo said, brushing past him and into the apartment.

"Oh," Cusak called after him, "I suppose I should ask for some identification, even though I know your voice from the phone."

Lupo turned, with one corner of his mouth lifted in a half smile. "Glad you asked. Good security consciousness. Anybody just being able to walk in here was gonna be a major concern." He lifted a black leather credentials case with one hand, flipping it open in a smooth move.

Cusak peered at the laminated card filling one half of the case. "You're a *fed*? I had no idea."

Lupo flipped it closed. "Retired. That's what it says across the front in those little dots. But it's still me."

"Well, honored to have you here." He added, "After you," although the man was already ahead of him in the apartment entryway.

"Any threats or attempted entries?" Lupo asked without turning back.

"There've been a fair number of incidents involving some of Sam's followers and controversial people but nothing here, thank goodness."

"I've heard," Lupo replied.

"Still," Cusak continued in a sunny voice, "most of the people are okay and the nutjobs involved are literally that—mentally ill folks. Very sad."

Lupo started down a hallway but Cusak stopped him. "Oh, that's Sam's room. He's in there getting ready. Over here is our studio."

Lupo followed his gesture and leaned into the sunroom. He could see the back of Becky's head as she bent over in her usual chair, typing on her laptop. "Our junior producer," Cusak said quietly from behind as Lupo turned back toward the entry hall.

"All set," Lupo said. "Harmon will be up in a minute. I'll stay around the perimeter and meet her at the vehicle when she's done. Please see her to the elevator when you're finished."

"Okay, thanks," Cusak began. "I—"

The door slammed shut.

◆

Buchanan boomed his usual opening line into the microphone: "Good day, American patriots! Time to rise and shine and save our nation!" He nodded toward the image on his laptop of a tan woman in her seventies with short dyed-blond hair and gleaming white teeth and then looked up to see her sitting beside him. "We have a great show for you today. I'm honored to be joined by a truly great American—the next United States Senator from the great state of Arizona, Gwendolyn Harmon. Hey, Gwen."

The woman—and her slightly gauzy image on the computer—began moving, although much of the skin on her face remained immobile. "Hello, Sam. Thanks for saving our country, and for having me on your show."

"Always great to have you, Gwen," Buchanan replied. "Before we get to your campaign—and I do hope everyone listening or watching makes sure to contribute to your effort—I want to start with an emergency: The threat posed by the groomers looking to convince our children that gender is an illusion, that there are no boys or girls—we're all just fluid creatures who should sleep with whoever will have us."

"A great place to start, Sam," Harmon replied and then stopped. When Buchanan didn't pick up the conversation, she added, "And of course you mean . . ."

He rescued her. "Of course I mean the so-called 'Phoenix Pride' parade this coming weekend in your great state. Kids love a parade, but they're too young to know that this one isn't about celebrating the

Pilgrims with a Spiderman balloon; it's about indoctrinating them into a lifestyle that erases what God established when he took man's rib and created woman. It's about obliterating the bedrock of this nation—moms and dads, together, raising children with American values."

Harmon had it now. "I'm so glad you raised this, Sam, because I'm actually hosting a different kind of pride event Saturday at Deer Valley Park in Phoenix called Proud of America, where we'll celebrate just those family values. I don't think we have a Spiderman balloon, but we'll have a bouncy castle, face painting, and—"

Buchanan cut her off, speaking quickly. "Great stuff, Gwen, great stuff, and I'm sure the moms and dads and kids will have a great time at your event, but I want to talk about the threat from this Phoenix Pride thing. And, look, I'm not blaming the people who go to the parade or even those misguided souls who march in it. They're mentally ill. I feel sorry for them. I pray for them. But I *do* blame the people who take advantage of them, selling this nonsense that, so long as you call it 'love,' you can do whatever you like. Men, women, children, sheep. It's all 'love' so it's okay, right? No, it's not. It's killing this country. It has to stop."

He looked down at his notes before continuing. "I blame people like Carla Rodriguez—somebody I've talked about before on the show—the organizer of this thing. She—no, I'm sorry, she's not a she; she's a they/them or some woke crap. This Carla Rodriguez and her—sorry, their—ilk are the problem. They—and I'm not sure whether I mean they or them, so I'm just gonna use names—are the cancer eating this country from the inside. Carla Rodriguez thinks Carla Rodriguez can sit in Carla Rodriguez's little house on Camelback Court there in Phoenix and nobody will hold Carla Rodriguez accountable for attacking the morality of America's children? I got news for Carla Rodriguez: This country is full of people who are tired of watching America go down the drain, who are tired of the Carla Rodriguezes of the world attacking our families, our children, our nation. It must end now. Carla and her crowd have to go."

Buchanan was covered in sweat as he reached for his water. After an awkward pause, his guest offered a tight smile and filled the silence. "Thanks, Sam, I always appreciate your passion for America. As I said, I hope the good people of Maricopa County will come out to celebrate their pride in America with me this Saturday, and I hope all Americans will support my campaign to drain the swamp by making me the next senator from the great state of Arizona. And let me tell you about the campaign . . ."

After twenty minutes of back-and-forth, Buchanan bid farewell to Harmon. Herb Cusak walked her to the elevator as Buchanan continued his monologue about the Phoenix Pride event.

CHAPTER SIX

Friday was garbage day in Carla Rodriguez's Phoenix neighborhood of small one-story homes. So Thursday night after finishing work as a nursing home aide, Carla did what they—Buchanan was right that Carla identified as nonbinary and preferred ungendered pronouns—always did and rolled the plastic bin down the little cement driveway to the curb.

Carla didn't notice the headlights of a pickup truck parked just up the street, but they did hear the squeal of its tires after turning back up the driveway. The truck skidded to a stop by the can and a man wearing a cowboy hat and a black surgical-type mask shouted, "Hey, Carla!"

When Carla turned, the man leaped from the truck and swung a black metal telescoping wand. The first blow hit just above their right knee and sent Carla down hard to the driveway. Then the man was standing astride his victim, shouting about America and children while raining brutal blows on Carla's head and body. Before Carla lost consciousness, they heard another car skidding hard and voices shouting, "Police, police, drop the weapon!" Then the night went black.

◆

Benny's voice boomed through the speakerphone in Nora's office. "Appreciate the DUSA authorizing me and Seany Boy coming out here to the Valley of the Sun on short notice."

"Glad you're out there," Nora said, looking at her desk phone. "What'd you learn?"

"First, that the Phoenix FBI is scared shitless of this case. We were just there and nobody actually said it, but I get the feeling from their brass that they got a fair number of Buchanan fans in their ranks, or at least people who have a lot of friends who are fans. The ASAC over in national security told me the January Sixth cases caused, in his words, 'major divisions' in their office. Jesus. Seems the Bu got itself some dumbasses out here."

"Depressing," Nora said. "What about on the case itself?"

"The idiot they arrested standing over poor Ms. Rodriguez—"

Nora could hear Sean's voice interrupt in the background. "Mix," he said to Benny. "Nonbinary, so it's not miz or mister. Mx.; 'mix' is how you say it."

"Got it," Benny answered. "More opportunities for growth. Anyhow, the victim is gonna make it. Beat up bad, including major head trauma, but will pull through. Good thing the cops were sitting on the house, although woulda been better if they coulda sat close enough to stop the beatin' before it began.

"That's it on the victim. The perp, who is not among the most enlightened of souls in the Phoenix area, is a high school graduate, twenty-year-old Randal Staub, occasionally employed as a roofer but a full-time Buchanan fan boy. He's been telling everyone and his brother that he loves Sam, follows everything he says, heard him say Rodriguez needed to go, and so he tried to make that happen to save innocent children and whatnot. Says he had no contact with Buchanan except listening to him. Oh, and he's stupid as a stone. Drove right past the marked unit before he attacked. If this guy is the kind Buchanan is worried about being replaced by foreigners, Jesus, it'll be an upgrade. Anyhow, that's our report."

"Wow, that's a lot. Thanks for the update," Nora said. "Hey, you guys got a minute to talk next steps? I want to brief Carmen and I'm sure she'll ask."

"Sure, boss," Sean said. "What're you thinking?"

"Well, that's what I want to know from you guys, and of course we should have this conversation again with Jessica. But if our perp isn't giving us direct contact, what's our way into Buchanan-land? I know he has a new girlfriend, but I think she's a lawyer and that wouldn't seem like a good place to go overt. What do you think?"

"Benny and I actually talked about that on the way out here," Sean answered. "I'll let him tell you where we ended up."

"Motherless fuck!" Benny shouted. "How can he drive with his head so far up his ass?"

"I'm sorry?" Nora asked.

"Oh, my bad," Benny said quietly. "That wasn't for you. Some asshole just drifted into my lane."

"Where are you guys?"

Sean's voice came through the phone. "Not far from Flagstaff, headed to the Grand Canyon in an Avis white Cadillac with a red interior. Never felt more retro in my life. Sun goes down in ninety-three minutes and we're—let me check—one hundred and twelve miles from the South Rim. You gotta pick it up, man."

"Christ," Benny replied, "I drive any faster and this Caddy's gonna burst into flames."

"What're you two doing?" Nora asked. "The Grand Canyon is not in Phoenix."

"No, it most definitely is not," Benny said. "According to my navigator here, it is in fact two hundred thirteen miles due north of the FBI office. But neither of us have ever been, so we decided to check it out. What else are we gonna do before we come back in the morning?"

"I don't know," Nora said. "Maybe eat, drink, and sleep—like normal people. And it's going to be dark."

"Oh no, it won't be," Benny said, then shouted, "Get the fuck out of the left lane!"

"I'm going to let you go," Nora said quietly. "We can talk when you have less going on."

"No, we're good for a bit," Benny said. "Just cleared the last head-up-their-ass obstacle for a while and I can now see forever up ahead. So, yes, we definitely agree the girlfriend would be too aggressive a move. It would take us overt without much prospect of her helping us."

Sean's voice came on the speakerphone. "And to state the obvious: One reason we're so hinky about going overt is that it'll bring all kinds of political insanity into our backfield. Everybody up to the Attorney General will be dragged to Capitol Hill to explain"—he deepened his voice to sound like an echoing stadium announcer—"an unprecedented attack on free speech in America."

Nora laughed. "Yes, I know, and no matter that his listeners are being recruited to physically attack innocent people. Makes my head hurt just thinking about it."

The line was quiet for a few beats before Sean spoke. "And speaking of that, we should give you a heads-up that we, uh, called an audible today and interviewed Gwendolyn Harmon."

"The Senate candidate? You aren't serious."

Benny's voice came back. "Yeah, that's on me. One of the cops we talked to told us she likes to hang out at some fancy-pants resort just a few minutes from where we were—The Boulders—so we popped over. She was havin' lunch in some little tent by the pool—"

"Cabana," Sean added.

"Whatever," Benny continued. "With some wrinkly little dude who looked like her grandfather, name of Epps, although he didn't say much other than to ID himself."

"He did say how much he admired that we were giving taxpayers their money's worth," Sean added.

"Yeah, whatever," Benny continued. "She didn't say much either, except to make it clear she didn't appreciate us showin' up at her cabana or whatever in the middle of her fuckin' avocado toast."

"Oh, damn, you guys," Nora said. "That's probably going to cause some heartburn at Main Justice. Still, I guess I'm okay with the occasional blitz."

"Wow," Sean answered. "Good to know."

"*Occasional*," Nora added, with emphasis. "Meaning infrequent. So, other than cabana invasion, what else do you have in mind?"

Benny came back on. "You know I've spent a lot of time sittin' on Buchanan's place. My gut tells me our best way in may be through this young kid he's got working as a producer—Becky Hubbard. We dug into her and she's not an obvious true believer. Raised by a single mom, too busy to be political. Becky did regular college stuff in Wisconsin, no wacko clubs, no lunacy on social media. Honestly, she comes across like a nice kid. Not sure how she ended up with this evil bastard, but she seems our best chance of getting an inside view without risking some kinda Fox News breaking report."

"I agree," Sean said.

"Makes sense," Nora answered. "So we do what?"

"I'll keep sitting on her," Benny responded. "Look for an opening. When it presents itself, we'll know. And if it doesn't, then we start taking chances, probably starting with approaching her cold, away from her workplace."

Sean came back on, sounding concerned. "Hey, we got a bunch of cars up ahead. We better sign off so Lewis Hamilton here can concentrate on the racetrack."

"Okay, done," Nora said quickly. "Hope you get there in time. Also hope you don't die."

CHAPTER SEVEN

Two weeks later, Herb Cusak hurried out of the sunroom studio as soon as the day's show finished, mumbling something about taking a call. Becky was typing on her laptop, trying her best not to see Buchanan's postshow ritual, which involved him removing his sweat-soaked dress shirt and replacing it with a red silk kimono. She was still rattled by the show they had just taped, in which Buchanan had gone off on a rant about immigrants that finished with a recent target of his—Ashton Greenstone, a professor at the College of William and Mary in Virginia who had become a fixture on cable news shows arguing that America's detention of immigrants at the border with no due process was a human rights violation.

Normally, the day ended with Cusak and the kimono-clad Buchanan moving down the hall to the large living room to enjoy a cocktail while Becky finished up and slipped out the apartment door. But today, the kimono rustled next to her. "Don't know where Herb's gone off to. Join me for a drink, would ya?"

It wasn't really a question. Becky got up and followed him to the living room, where Buchanan gestured to a small couch and went to the bar. "What's your poison?" he asked over his shoulder.

"Sir?"

"Your poison. It's an expression, Becky. What do you want to drink?"

"Oh, nothing for me, sir."

"Where I come from, it's not polite to let someone drink alone. What'll you have?"

"Diet Coke?"

Buchanan sighed before dropping ice cubes in a glass and opening a soda can, placing both on the coffee table in front of Becky. As he did so, his kimono bowed open, revealing his large hairy midriff, and Becky darted her eyes toward the other side of the room.

After another trip to the bar, he returned with a glass of whisky and sat in a chair facing Becky, exhaling loudly.

"Woo, that was some show, dontcha think?"

Becky noticed that his southern accent was less prominent. "Yes, sir, there was a lot there."

"Pretty great, right?"

"Well, sure, sir, but . . ."

"But what?"

"Well, I'm just concerned about all the attention you paid to Professor Greenstone."

"Now why would that concern you? He's a bad man. Hates America. Every interview he gives is hurting this country."

"Well, sir, it's just that I've been reading about what your listeners have been doing to some of the people you talk about. The Carla Rodriguez thing. Stuff like that."

"Maybe he should have thought about that before he decided to betray his country."

"But aren't you worried that someone might hurt him?"

"Not my concern, darlin'. I tell it like it is. Sometimes the truth hurts."

"But *literally*, sir? You want that man to be *literally* hurt by the truth?"

Buchanan narrowed his eyes. "I'm not sure what you're gettin' at. I don't care if that man gets hurt, but *I'm* not gonna hurt him. I'm an entertainer. What other people do is their business."

Becky began tapping her forehead with the fingers of one hand. "I just, I just, I don't know, sir. It just feels, I don't know, *wrong* to me. Feels like you're telling them to go *do* something to him, like with the others."

Buchanan puffed his cheeks and then slowly blew out his breath. "Well, well, the wisdom of a twenty-three-year-old."

He leaned forward and put his drink on the coffee table, lifting one hand to comb his hair back. "Let me give you some of the facts of life, darlin'. We're a *business* here. To be a business, we need *paying* customers. To have paying customers, a business needs to provide something the customer wants. You make a shitload more than you would at some other first job out of college because our customers are happy with what we provide them—what *I* provide them. If you don't want to be in this business, you should find another."

Becky looked at her knees, her face flushed.

Buchanan paused, retrieved his glass, and took a drink. He continued, now holding the glass in two hands. "And we are lucky to be in a business where people pay us to tell them the actual goddamn truth. Because the actual goddamn truth is that the America-hating pieces of shit that my followers hurt deserve what they get. This country really is under attack, Becky, and there are too few people doing anything about it. I'm proud of my people, I really am. You should be too."

He stood and walked around the coffee table, dropping onto the couch next to Becky, who was still looking down. He spoke quietly now. "Hey, look at me."

She lifted her chin and he continued. "You're new and you're doing a great job. Just keep doing what you're doing and it'll be fine."

He took another drink before setting his glass back on the table and turning toward her. The kimono was open now, and she couldn't avoid seeing a thick channel of body hair running from his lumpy chest down to the sunken cavity of his navel. "And I've told you that you could do more to show your God-given self," he said, lifting both arms to reach toward her glasses. Becky jerked backward, leaving his hands in the air. He dropped them angrily.

"I'm just trying to help you," Buchanan said, grabbing his glass and sitting back on the couch, using his free hand to pull the kimono closed. "Appearances do matter in this world, and yours could be so much better." He looked down at her Crocs and then slowly lifted his eyes up her pant legs and hoodie until he met her eyes again. "Maybe it's not fair, but the world judges books by their covers. And your cover needs work. Easy to do. Shit, you seen the governor of Arkansas lately? That's a goddamn miracle is what that is. And you're startin' a lot farther down the track than that poor woman, who got whacked with the same ugly stick that hit her old man."

Buchanan lifted his empty hand and dropped it on her knee. Becky jumped like she had been tased. "I'm sorry, sir," she said, suddenly on her feet, "but I have to go." She hurried from the room, down the hall, and out into the elevator lobby. As the elevator doors closed, she began to shake. She crossed her arms to hug herself warm.

CHAPTER EIGHT

Benny sat in his aging Chrysler Pacifica, parked across the street from Buchanan's apartment building on Nineteenth Street. His colleagues liked to tease him about the dented blue van with the stickers he rotated on its tinted windows: Some days, there was one in the back depicting in stick figures a couple with three children and a dog; or one on each side warning about a baby on board; or sometimes one in the right corner of the windshield identifying an Uber driver. They also ribbed him about the rear wheel he occasionally used—a temporary spare "donut" tire. But Benny just smiled and said, "I know what works, and I know what I like." He knew from decades of doing surveillance in organized crime cases that nobody gave more than a glance to such a car, because no cop, especially a fed, would drive it. It obviously belonged to a mom or dad working hard to make ends meet.

Benny also liked the way the driver's seat in the Pacifica reclined and he especially liked that the middle row vanished after the seats were folded into the floor, allowing a big man to sit in the far back and stretch his legs as if he were watching criminals from a limo. "Plus, if you fools actually did the work, you would know there's a lot of in-car peeing in surveillance, and it's easier to pee in a jar when I can move around."

Benny believed in surveillance and had devoted years of his life to watching and photographing his investigative subjects. "Where they go, who they go with, and even how they stand tells you a story," he once explained to Nora. "And it's a story without the usual layers of bullshit people shovel." She had used his surveillance photos and related testimony dozens of times in her career. She never mocked the Chrysler. She also never drank from any container in Benny's car, ever.

Now Benny could see a story in the way Becky Hubbard emerged from Buchanan's building. She was hunched over, arms folded tightly across her chest, walking quickly up Nineteenth toward Third Avenue. She walked without a phone in her hand or earphones on her head, a rare sight in Manhattan. Something was bothering her. He waited several beats, then leaned forward and quietly slid the van's side door open. He had done this so many times that an observer would have been impressed with how easily the giant slipped out and began meandering up Nineteenth. But there were no observers.

Benny moved parallel to Becky, but slowed his walk as she crossed ahead to his side of the street near Third Avenue. At the corner, she turned south and stayed on the east sidewalk for two blocks before entering Follia, an Italian restaurant. She had gone straight there without looking around or checking her phone. Either she was meeting someone or this was a regular place for her. Benny pulled out his own phone and stood at Seventeenth and Third as if lost. He could see Becky had gone to the bar and was sitting alone on a wood-back industrial stool, facing away from him. She wasn't looking around for a companion. He dialed his phone and put it to his ear.

Nora answered on the first ring. "Hey, Mr. Rough. What's up?"

"You still at the office?" Benny asked.

"Yup, about to head out."

"Do me a favor," he said. "Meet me outside a place called Follia, Third Avenue at Seventeenth, on the corner. I got a hunch we may have the break we've been lookin' for and I need you to help me play it out."

"Sure, I'll jump in a cab now. Can you give me more?"

"Call me when you're in the cab."

During Nora's ten-minute cab ride, Benny explained his instinct that something was really bothering young Becky Hubbard and that, despite Benny's many charms, he was not the right person to approach her in the bar. "I think you should do the bump," Benny explained. "Jessica might also make sense, except this chick works for a crazy White supremacist, so it seems risky to send a Black woman for the first move. Soon as we hang up I'll call her to make sure she's not bent out of shape."

"I hate that I agree, but I agree," Nora said, "And Jessica will get it. I'm almost there. Lemme call Sean to make sure he knows what I'm doing."

◆

The cab stopped half a block past Follia, where Benny was leaning against a bus shelter. "Almost missed you," Nora said, stepping to the curb. "You blend, to my surprise."

"I will accept your backhanded compliment," Benny said, handing her a digital recording device. "As requested. We don't normally tape witness interviews, ya know."

"We don't normally have prosecutors meeting alone with a potential witness, ya know. Even Carmen might find it a bit out of line."

"Fair enough," Benny replied. "Appreciate you doin' this. Big move for the DUSA to go operational and all."

Nora smiled tightly. "I'm not parachuting into a firefight, for heaven's sake. Just gonna talk to a young woman. And it's the right play for the case at the moment. I trust your read that this might not come again."

"Yeah, somethin's wrong with her tonight. Watched her a lot of times. Never walked like that. Never went to a bar, and by herself."

"Where are you going to be?"

"There's a couple empty two-tops right behind where she's sitting. I've already asked the host to hold one for me. I'll be able to hear every word."

"Which will solve my problem with being alone with a witness," Nora said. "Okay, let's do this."

Nora walked down the block and into the restaurant. She told the host she was waiting for someone and would sit at the bar. Becky was scrolling on her phone when Nora slid onto the stool next to her, being careful not to hit her head on the rows of clean wineglasses hanging above the bar. Out of the corner of her eye, she caught Benny's enormous form moving into a chair at a high-top table. Nora ignored Becky, ordering a glass of red wine and scrolling on her own phone, catching up on news about Taylor Swift, one of the few things she and Sophie were equally passionate about.

Becky made an audible sniffling sound.

"You all right?" Nora asked, turning her head toward the sound.

"Yeah," Becky said. "I'm doing okay."

"Doesn't sound that way," Nora replied in a kind voice. "Tough day, I'm guessing?"

"Tough *months*," Becky answered. She moved her mouth as if to speak, but hesitated.

"Sorry, didn't mean to intrude," Nora said, lifting one hand. "I hope whatever it is passes," she added, looking back down at her phone.

Becky was still turned on her stool looking at Nora, who appeared engrossed by her Instagram feed. But Nora wasn't seeing any of the images. She was waiting and silently hoping. *Come on, Becky, come on. You can do it.*

"You like Taylor Swift?" Becky asked, before adding, "I'm sorry, I just saw your phone. I'm not a stalker."

"It's okay," Nora said, turning back to Becky and lifting her phone, before giving it a little shake. "Yes, I'm Nora and I'm a Swiftie and I'm the mother of a Swiftie in training. So I've got all the eras covered. What about you?"

"Of course," Becky said, a small smile appearing. "Becky. Sometimes it feels like she sees me more than I see myself."

"What song is she singing to you tonight?"

Becky looked up at the hanging wineglasses before answering. "'Look What You Made Me Do,' I think," Becky answered, before continuing with the lyrics in a singsong voice.

"Wow," Nora said, "sounds like a really bad day."

Becky nodded her head in agreement but didn't speak

Suddenly Nora was singing just above a whisper about getting smarter and harder in the nick of time. When she finished the line, she asked, "So did you?"

Becky didn't answer, but tears were now rolling down her cheeks.

Nora dropped an open palm on Becky's forearm. "I'm so sorry for whatever you're dealing with. You deserve better. And I don't want to pry, but I'd love to help you lift the load. Is it work or personal life?"

Becky paused, then said, "My job."

Nora let the silence sit until Becky spoke again.

"I work for someone who's a really bad person, I think. Took me too long to see it, but now I do and I have to get away from him. Bad things have already happened, so I guess it's not right to say I got smarter in the nick of time."

"But the important thing is that you got smarter," Nora said, her hand still resting on Becky's arm. "That's what matters."

When Becky didn't respond, Nora asked, "Did he hurt you?"

"No," Becky said. "He's a creep, but no." She paused before adding, "But he might ask his followers to hurt me if he saw me as a threat."

Nora exhaled audibly and withdrew her hand, shaking her head as if she wasn't sure this was a conversation she wanted to have. "What do you mean by 'followers'?"

"His listeners. It's a podcasting and radio thing. He's kind of a big deal in certain places. You may not have heard of him."

"I'm not sure it matters who he is," Nora said. "You need to get to a healthier place. You have your whole career, and life, ahead of you."

"It's complicated," Becky said, "because he's got a lot of people who think he's some kind of prophet or something. And they do bad stuff when they think he wants them to."

Now Nora took a chance: "Does he want them to?"

Becky breathed deeply before answering. "I think he does. I think he knows exactly what his followers will do if he points them at someone and says, 'That's a bad person.' They will hurt that person. I know that and I'm barely an adult. He *has* to know that. This is why I need to get away from him, from all of it."

"Do you have family you can go to? Away from here, maybe?"

Becky shook her head no. "Just my mom, and she's in Wisconsin with a new husband who I think probably listens to my boss. I can't go there."

Nora was quiet, trying to decide when to reveal herself to Becky. Then, with a slight nod of her head, she went at it directly: "Look, Becky, I think I can help you. I work for the government, and we know who your boss is and what he does to innocent people. You're right to worry that he might hurt you, but we can help you. We can protect you and help you move on with your life."

Becky narrowed her eyes, not quite understanding. "What do you do for the government? And what do you mean by 'the government'?"

"I'm a lawyer for the United States Department of Justice. I live here in the city with my mom and my twelve-year-old daughter."

Becky began shaking her head, as if trying to awaken from a dream.

"This isn't about you," Nora continued, "but you *are* on a tilted stage and you need to get away. I can help you do that. Please let me."

Now Becky turned her head slightly to look at Nora sideways. "Wait, did you come in here to talk to me? Have you been *following* me?"

Nora grimaced. "We've been really worried about what he's doing to innocent people, the violence he's causing. And that made us worry about whether you were safe. We've been watching your boss, but also wanted to make sure you're okay."

Nora gestured with her head toward Benny behind them. "One of my friends was outside Buchanan's place tonight. He saw you come out and he could tell you were really upset, so he asked me to come talk to you."

Becky turned on her stool to look at Benny, who smiled tightly and gave her a little wave with one enormous hand.

"This feels like a movie," Becky said, turning back to Nora.

"I wish it was," Nora answered, "but it's real. Buchanan's a bad guy and we really do want to help you."

"Am I in some kind of trouble with the government?" Becky asked.

"No, because you're doing the right thing, which means getting out of it and helping stop more innocent people from getting hurt."

Becky looked confused. "How am I supposed to do that? All I do is sit at the table and do internet research during his shows."

"Well," Nora replied, "I'm not sure, and that's something we can talk about."

Becky was looking down at the bar surface now, shaking her head. "I don't know, I don't know. I can't think straight." Then she sat up and said sharply, "Maybe I need a lawyer."

Nora shrugged. "Sure. That's okay. If you want to talk to a lawyer, that's totally fine. Sometimes it's good to talk to somebody like that. Do you know a lawyer you could talk to?"

Becky bit her lip. "I really don't."

"Do you want me to find one for you?"

"Would you do that?"

"Of course," Nora said. "I could get somebody tomorrow, somebody you could really trust."

"That'd be great," Becky said.

Nora paused for a moment, then said, "And would it be okay if I introduce you to my friend who was so worried about you?"

"Sure," Becky answered.

Nora turned and gestured to Benny, who got up and stepped to the bar, where he towered over the two women. "Becky, Benny," Nora said. "Benny, Becky."

Benny shook her hand. "Nice to meet you. And not to be rude, but would you two like to get a bite? Been doing surveillance all day on that creepster's place and I'm starving. Just smelling the food in here is killing me. My treat."

Becky smiled. Nora laughed.

◆

"So you're a real special agent, like on TV?" Becky asked, looking across the table at the large man devouring a plate of spaghetti pomodoro.

Benny finished sucking up a dangling strand of pasta before answering. "Kinda, except most of the shows are bull. I used to do Mafia cases—which is one reason I love this food—but now I work on sick fucks—excuse my French—like your boss. And, honestly, most of it is just surveillance and paperwork."

"So you're FBI?" Becky asked.

"No, I work with them on everything, including this, but I'm assigned to the United States Attorney's office. Really, all it means is that I don't have to fill out a lot of the forms FBI agents do. They're good people."

Benny expertly twirled more spaghetti into a large spoon and then lifted the fork to his mouth, speaking as he chewed. "Lemme ask you somethin'. I could hear part of what you and Nora were saying. You up for doing us a small favor on this?"

"Like what?" Becky asked.

"You think you could draw me a map of what the apartment looks like?"

Becky paused, then said, "I guess."

Benny reached down beside his chair and retrieved a notepad from his bag, sliding it across the table. "Nothin' fancy," he said. "Just a general lay of the land." He pulled a pen from his pocket and set it on the pad.

Becky hesitated before picking up the pen, but eventually began drawing a detailed picture of Buchanan's apartment, narrating the purpose of each space. She finished with the au pair suite. "This is where Herb Cusak stays—his senior producer. Strange man."

"The two a' them got somethin' going on—between-the-sheets like?" Benny asked.

"I don't think so," Becky answered. "I leave when I'm done and they live there all the time, so I really don't know, but I don't think they're lovers or anything like that. Sometimes it feels more like Herb is the boss of Sam."

"Got it," Benny said. "Hey," he added, "you really are doin' the right thing here. We're gonna keep this to ourselves. Nora will line up an attorney to meet with you tomorrow after work, like she promised. But, until then, you just go about your business."

"You mean, go to work?" Becky asked, wide-eyed.

"Yeah," Benny said. "Until we get a plan in place to get you to a new life, we don't want that creep knowing nothin'."

Becky darted her eyes to Nora, sitting next to Benny.

"I think that's best," Nora said. "It won't be easy, but that gives you the chance to plan something."

When Becky didn't respond, Benny said, "And you can be my eyes and ears in there. Like a special agent sort of thing."

Becky nodded at that. "Okay, I think I can do that. Kinda exciting, actually."

"Don't get too excited about it," Benny answered. "Not gonna last long."

"And call my cell when you're done with work for the day," Nora said. "I'll have the lawyer ready."

◆

Becky left the restaurant while Nora and Benny were still at the table. When she was gone, Nora turned with a smile. "Did you really just give her a junior special agent badge or something?"

"Hey," he replied, reaching for an arancini, "just giving her a sense of mission. No harm in it. God, I love these cheese balls."

"I can see that," Nora said, grinning. "And what's with having her draw the apartment? We already have the floor plan."

"Recruitment 101," he said, popping another rice ball into his mouth. "Have the subject give you something innocuous from their employer. It's a step across the line, and they almost never go back. It's the reason the Bureau spends so much time having foreign diplomats bring them an embassy telephone directory or some shit. Could get it on the internet, but once they hand it over, they're on our team—and they tend to stay there."

Nora arched her eyebrows. "You've recruited a lot of spies?"

"Cosa Nostra's just another evil empire, my friend, and my job was to get made guys to risk their lives and betray it. Once they bring me the private menu from the social club, they're mine. And speaking of recruiting, Ms. Smooth, you were slick at the bar there. You could do this for a living."

Nora shook her head. "Felt bad about it the whole time. Prosecutors aren't supposed to play games, be dishonest."

"Hey, you never actually lied to the woman, now did ya? That girl really does need help. And 'the game,' for prosecutors and low-life investigators like your hero here, is doing justice, as I recall. You should feel good about it."

"I suppose, but not something I want to get used to. I'd rather someone else do the undercover work."

"Fair enough," Benny said, "but I appreciate you stepping in during an emergency. You gonna finish that cauliflower?"

CHAPTER NINE

"You have any questions, Becky?" Nora asked the young woman.

Becky shook her head and then pointed to the man in the suit seated next to her at the conference table. "No. I had a lot, but Mr. DePippo explained it all to me. Basically, you promise not to prosecute me as an accessory or anything, and I promise to tell the truth and to help you if I can."

"That's right," Nora said gently. "You'll stay working for Buchanan and meet with us from time to time to talk about what you're seeing and hearing. And if he's ever prosecuted by us, you'll be available as a witness."

"I hope that doesn't happen," Becky said, "but I understand what you're saying."

"Good," Nora replied. "And we've promised in this letter that if we ever wanted you to record conversations with him or anyone else, we would discuss it with you and your attorney first."

"Okay," Becky said, lifting a pen from the table.

Nora reached across and put a hand on her wrist. "It's going to be okay. As the agreement says, if you're ever worried about your own safety, we will do everything we can to protect you, including relocating you. The most important thing is that you stay in touch with us and always tell the truth."

"I understand," Becky said. Nora lifted her hand so Becky could sign.

When her lawyer was gone, Becky turned to Nora and Benny. "This is both really scary and kinda exciting, like a movie or something."

Benny fixed her with a kind smile. "It's neither of those, Becky. This is just you doing what you've been doing and then calling me at night to tell me what's going on. Shouldn't be scary or exciting. Don't mean to disappoint."

Becky blushed and nodded. "I'm sorry. I'm just nervous."

"Don't be," Nora said. "It's important that nobody knows anything has changed, so just be yourself, do your work, and call Benny if you need anything. We'll always be just a call away. This is going to be okay. You're doing the right thing."

Becky sat up straight. "Yes, I think I am. And I appreciate you two."

"And we appreciate you," Benny answered.

Now Becky was on her feet. "Okay, I'm off to my secret agent career."

Nora began to speak, but Becky cut her off. "Kidding," she said, "kidding. I'll be in touch."

"Pretty funny," Benny said, smiling broadly. "Lemme walk you to the elevator."

◆

Sean and Jessica were already in the conference room with Nora when Benny returned. "I appreciate you two staying out of that," Nora said. "Kid's so nervous. Didn't want to do anything to spook her."

"Totally get it," Jessica said. "So now that she's signed up, where are we?"

Sean spoke first. "We need to charge Buchanan. After the Rodriguez thing, we just can't leave him out there any longer. Every day he's on a new target. He's gonna get more people hurt or killed."

"I agree," Nora said, "but charge him with what?"

"I think we go with hate crimes conspiracy, 18 U.S.C. 249."

"Explain," Nora said.

"It's a crime to agree with others to hurt or kill someone because of their actual or perceived race, religion, national origin, gender, sexual orientation, gender identity, or disability."

"Yes, I know *that*," Nora said patiently. "Explain how we would *make* a 249 case against some dude screaming into a microphone in his Gramercy apartment."

Sean looked embarrassed but went on. "He verbally attacks every victim because of who they are. All our victims fit in one of those boxes. It's all about retaliation for their identities."

"Got it," Nora replied. "And what's our proof that he knows he has entered into an unlawful agreement with his followers to hurt or kill people? Or even that he has induced someone to do it? That is, what's the evidence that he *intends* them to attack the people he criticizes and do it because of his words?"

"That's where we're a little thin," Sean said quietly.

"Oh, so only on that tiny part?" Nora said, not bothering to conceal the sarcasm.

"But I've got an idea," Sean said, going to the whiteboard and writing Buchanan's name before turning back to face them. "Seems strange to say, but the Blind Sheikh case was easier because they could prove the sheikh knew when he gave his blessing that his followers were planning to wage war on America and kill people. They told him what they wanted to do and he said, basically, 'Go with God's blessing.' FBI got a lot of it on tape. He also knew the identity of his key conspirators, because they were the ones coming to see him to get his blessing."

Benny scoffed. "I always thought that was a ballsy case, back in the day. Least that's the way the old heads talked about it. Now it sounds like a bit of a dunk."

"Not a dunk, for sure," Sean said, "but they had more of the traditional kind of proof than we do. We're in the age of what academics call 'stochastic terrorism'—statistically predictable, but individually unpredictable."

"Lost me," Benny said.

Sean nodded. "It's where a charismatic leader jacks people up but, through the wonder of the internet, avoids a direct connection to what comes next. *Stochastic* is a term from statistics that means you can estimate the likelihood of something happening, even if you can't predict who will do it and when and where."

Jessica lifted her hand. "So it's like when King Henry II got Thomas Becket killed simply by saying, 'Will no one rid me of this meddlesome priest?'"

Benny laughed. "Okay, now we're just makin' shit up. Kings? Priests? Stop. You guys have been drinking that Stolichnaya stuff."

Sean smiled. "*Stochastic*, Benny. Definitely not vodka. And Jessica is spot on. But the fuller story of Henry II and Becket is closer to where I think we actually are. A thousand years ago, Thomas Becket was the Archbishop of Canterbury—the head of what was then the Catholic church in England; this was hundreds of years before Henry VIII created the Church of England so he could get divorced. Anyhow, Becket and the king fought over all kinds of stuff. Got really ugly. I will spare you the details—"

"Which you know how?" Benny interrupted.

"Because I had an excellent Catholic education, thanks to the Jesuits at Regis. But I had to go look up the part I want to read you—what

Henry *actually* said in front of his knights, after which they ran off and killed the Archbishop."

Sean looked down at his notes. "Nobody was taping stuff on iPhones in 1170, but the most reliable version is that King Henry looked at his knights and actually said, 'What miserable drones and traitors have I nurtured and promoted in my household who let their lord be treated with such shameful contempt by a low-born clerk!' And the famous part was added about four hundred years later: Will none of these lazy insignificant persons, whom I maintain, deliver me from this turbulent priest?'"

Benny snorted. "So of course they go whack the guy. To the knights on his payroll, he's sayin' you're traitors and scumbags if you don't. That's about as close to an order as you can get. That's the way a Cosa Nostra boss would do it."

"Agreed," Sean said, "and we don't have anything that good on Buchanan. We could prove to a jury that King Henry *knew* they were going to go after Becket. He knew how the knights would react, given the way he spoke to them, which is damn good proof of his intent. But we actually can get pretty close to that here. I think we can prove—and no sheikh case pun intended here—that Buchanan is *willfully* blind to the individual attacks. He knows an attack will follow his words but he closes his eyes so he can say he wasn't part of it. Under the law, that willful blindness makes him as guilty as if he did the attack himself."

He turned back to the board and began drawing lines out from Buchanan's name, like the spokes of a wheel. "We can show five times he singled out someone, saying, in his words, 'They have to go' or 'They must be stopped.' Over and over again, he said that about a particular person—and within the overall context of 'Words aren't enough, people need to actually do something and take action.' And his listeners did exactly that—five times that we know of. Two deaths, three serious injuries, including Carla Rodriguez."

Sean next added small circles at the end of each spoke, putting an X in four of the circles. "In four cases, we've ID'd the perpetrator and can show the person was a *huge* consumer of Buchanan's shit. They considered themselves knights in his household, if you will. One actually wrote a manifesto before the attack and said Buchanan was his inspiration and God's messenger. Four of them made statements that they did it because he told them to on his show, including the Phoenix wing nut Benny and I interviewed. On the other one, we don't have a perpetrator yet, but it's a fair inference since the victim was one of Buchanan's named targets."

"But none of them ever spoke to him or connected with him directly, I'm guessing," Nora said.

"Correct," Sean answered, "but here's the part that could get us to willful blindness. As best we can tell, there's never been someone he focused on who *wasn't* attacked. Sure, he's criticized lots of people, but he's only *gone after* five people in his unique way—hammering on them, saying they're a threat and that they must go. When he does *that*, those named people are *always* attacked. I think we argue that means he knows for certain that his words will cause attacks; he intends for the attacks to happen even if he doesn't know the attackers. He knows there are knights out there somewhere and they will act. I think we could argue that makes him directly guilty, but at a minimum we get him on willful blindness."

Nora looked skeptical. "But doesn't your theory mean he's off the hook for the early attacks? Because he needs to see that his words cause violence before we can hold him accountable for causing it? And what's the point at which we can say that? The third attack? The fourth? And so he skates on the others? Seems weird."

"Yeah, that's a problem," Sean said, stepping away from the white-board and slumping into a chair.

The room was quiet for a moment before Nora said, "But that's okay. I don't think we need to base his intent on the perfect-attack-record thing. I think we just argue that he *had* to know his words would result in the attacks. He may not have known the identity of his knights, but he knew they were out there and would act on his words. So he just shouted that they were—what were the king's words? 'Miserable drones and traitors'?—if they didn't get rid of the people he named. He knew what his knights would do. That should be enough to prove he intended it to happen.

"And don't forget, we have someone on the inside who saw it all happen, and she believes he knew what he was doing and wanted it to happen. What did Becky say the other day? Something about Buchanan talks like he's motivated by the cause, but he's really in it for the increased donations after each attack? It all fits."

She looked at Jessica and Benny, who were nodding.

"Fuckin' A," Benny mumbled.

"Okay," Nora said, turning back to Sean. "Write it up. Carmen would approve without a memo, but you know she needs to go to DOJ Civil Rights on this. They can't order coffee without a memo. And we need Justice to authorize us not to seek the death penalty."

"Which we'd never get from a New York jury anyway. On it. I'll have a draft to you tomorrow."

"No," Nora said gently as she stood and turned toward the door. "Go home, feed your cat, get a good night's sleep. Next couple days will be fine."

She paused, then added, "You know, it just occurred to me that I never heard whether you knuckleheads made it to the Grand Canyon."

Sean laughed. "We did, but not in daylight. Benny got pulled over and it took so long to convince the trooper not to arrest him for reckless driving that we got there in the dark."

Benny smiled. "All true. But the stars were amazing. Like nothin' I've ever seen."

Nora shook her head and spoke as she walked out. "Upon these shoulders our democracy rests."

When Nora was gone, Sean tilted his head and squinted at Benny, who pushed himself to his feet and shrugged. "She must be a cat person," he said, clapping one hand on Sean's shoulder as he moved to the door. "See you tomorrow, big guy."

CHAPTER TEN

Benny brought his car to a stop in front of Nora's apartment building. "Thanks for the ride home, Benny," she said. "I'll take the food. You want me to wait while you park or should I meet you upstairs?"

"The parking process just ended, my friend," Benny said, turning off the car and reaching his hand up to the sun visor.

Nora turned her head to look back along the curb. "This is a bus stop. You can't leave it here."

"Maybe *I* can't," Benny said with a cheerful voice as he threw his Official Business parking placard onto the front dash, "but the United States of America sure can."

"How is this official business?" Nora asked, gesturing to the large paper bag between her feet. "We're going upstairs to have Thai food with my family."

"That's a mighty narrow view of things, my friend. As a federal law enforcement officer with a take-home car, I'm on official business until the moment I arrive safely home at my residence with America's car, which has not happened yet, which is why I can park here. Also, I'm hungry."

"Benny—" Nora began, but she stopped, shaking her head and smiling as she opened the passenger door. "Okay, let's not make a federal case out of it."

◆

Teresa and her granddaughter were at the kitchen table when Nora and Benny walked in, the butcher block surface covered in scraps of paper they were preparing to glue to a large poster board.

"Have no fear," Benny called in a loud voice, "your pad thai is here." He leaned down to kiss Teresa as Nora went around the table to hug Sophie.

"Art project?" Nora asked.

"Sort of," Sophie answered. "It's for social studies. I'm supposed to illustrate polarization in our society and Nana had the idea to find headlines on the same topics from different publications and put them on a poster in bubbles. To show how differently people see the same things."

"Your nana's smart that way," Benny said.

"And now thoroughly depressed," Teresa said, shaking her head. "The price of eggs falls and one headline is about how consumer prices are declining and another is about how Washington is waging war on chicken farmers."

"And that's the small stuff," Sophie said as she swept her hand over the pieces of paper. "There are soooo many examples of people seeing the same thing totally differently."

"Yeah, 'cause people suck," Benny said. "Been tellin' you that since before you could walk. Now, can we eat?"

Sophie smiled up at Benny as she began gathering the papers. "Mom says I should bring you in for show-and-tell, but they don't have that in seventh grade."

Nora turned from the counter, where she was unpacking the food containers. "Maybe as part of a lesson on the ability of strong-willed people to evolve their views? Your grandmother has had quite an impact on our friend here."

Benny smiled broadly. "In all kinds of good ways she's making me a better person, but I don't want my personal life on display in front of a bunch of rich brats." He paused before adding, "Present company excepted, of course, and no offense intended."

"See?" Nora said. "Just *that*. The concern about offending, limiting the scope of the insult. Wow."

"Okay, okay," Benny said, popping a dumpling into his mouth. "Enough about me. We gonna do best and worst?"

They were interrupted by the sound of the intercom buzzing. "You expectin' company?" Benny asked.

"As a matter of fact, yes," Nora said with a smile. "And, spoiler alert: It's my best." She took several quick steps to the door and lifted the receiver. "Yes, send her up. Thanks, Macio."

When Nora didn't return to the table, but stayed at the door looking through the peephole, Benny turned to Teresa and Sophie. "Okay, now I get it. Little slow on the uptake."

Before either could respond, Nora ripped the door open and a short woman with thick, wavy dark hair in a low bun leaped onto her. "Damn, I missed this tree—" the woman began, before noticing the dinner table over Nora's shoulder. Her heart-shaped face flashed pink and she let go, dropping onto the soles of her black Blundstone boots. "Oh, I'm so sorry. I didn't mean to interrupt *and* make a fool of myself."

Sophie's chair scraped back. "Demi!" she shouted, running to the visitor and giving her a hug.

"Girl," Demi said, kissing her forehead, "you're gaining on me. Soon I'll be looking up to *all* the women in this family, literally and not just figuratively. Hi, Teresa!" She crossed behind the table to embrace

Nora's mother, then turned to Benny. "And I'm having trouble placing this face."

"Captain Demitria Kofatos, I believe," Benny said with a broad smile as he extended his hand. "Not a hugger, as you know, but it's great to see you."

"You, too, Benny. Been too long."

"So, how's Westport PD treating you?" he asked.

Teresa laughed. "Could we get the poor woman a plate and a chair before the interrogation starts?"

◆

"If that's not hot enough, Demi, I can throw it in the microwave for a minute."

Demi stabbed a fork into a pile of noodles sprinkled with chopped peanuts and lifted it to her mouth. "Mmm, it's perfect, Mrs. Carleton—"

"Would you stop? It's Teresa, always."

"Or Nana," Nora added. "I've heard some couples go right to that, if they can, to avoid the awkwardness. And there sits grandchild number one, so Nana is ready-made."

"Great," Benny interjected. "You work it out however you want. I'll stay Benny, if you please. And can we return to my questioning of this law enforcement officer?"

"Right," Demi said, taking a swallow. "Westport PD is good. We think we got any bad apples out and there's almost no crime. So kind of boring, actually."

She nodded to Nora. "When I don't see *this* one for a few weeks 'cause I'm traveling, or she doesn't come out to Connecticut on the weekend, I go a bit nuts, honestly. So I came into town for some awesome Thai food and company. What's your report?"

"I'm good," Benny answered. "I'm in a healthy long-term relationship—"

"That's lovely to hear," Teresa interrupted with a grin.

"—and work is good, in the sense we have a lot more bad people than you do in Westport. I'm actually working domestic terrorism stuff with your significant other here. And Sophie just finished demonstrating to us that we're hopelessly polarized as a nation and objective truth is a myth. So I'm pretty great."

◆

"Let's walk down Eighty-Fifth," Nora said, turning west toward Central Park. "Quieter."

"Fine by me," Demi said. "I'm just the country mouse."

Nora reached for her hand as they walked and Demi interlaced her fingers in Nora's. "How come you don't like to hold hands when we walk in Westport?" Nora asked.

Demi was quiet for a bit before answering. "I'm not sure," she said at last. "It's not like they aren't both welcoming places. So I don't think it's fear of homophobia."

"Then what?" Nora asked gently.

"Honestly, I think it's job related there. There's something about the whole butch-cop trope that bugs me."

Nora laughed quietly. "But you *are* a butch cop."

Demi laughed back. "I know, I know. I'm not sure what it is. I'm the highest-ranking woman on the force and for some reason I feel the need to keep my private life private."

They stopped at the light on Fifth Avenue, facing the park. "You gotta do you," Nora said, "and I'm not pressuring you, just wondering. So do you want to do the reservoir loop or the Great Lawn?"

"What's the difference?"

Nora gestured, first to her right and then left. "The Jacqueline Kennedy Onassis Reservoir—she used to run there—has a crushed gravel track around it, about a mile and a half. Has some amazing views, but we have to watch out for joggers coming up behind us. The Great Lawn Oval is a paved thing that goes around the, well, Great Lawn, which is where a bunch of ball fields are. Fewer runners."

"Reservoir," Demi said. "Anybody tries to run you down, they've got to get through a butch cop first."

They walked around the reservoir counterclockwise, as required, holding hands and chatting as Nora narrated the buildings of the rich and famous, which were coming alive with lights as the sun faded. "There," she said, pointing west across the water, "all of those are apartments along Central Park West."

"We should get one," Demi said with a smile.

"Not in this lifetime," Nora replied, holding her pointed finger beside Demi's eye to steer her vision. "*That* one is where the former governor was murdered."

"A case solved by a very talented prosecutor, I've heard," Demi said.

As they rounded the top of the path, Nora pointed south across the water. "And, closer to our joint past, those needle skyscrapers are all along Billionaires' Row on Fifty-Seventh Street."

"Never seen them from this angle," Demi answered. "Really cool. I'm starting to understand why Jackie liked to jog here—pre–needle skyscrapers, of course."

They were quiet as they reached the southern end of the loop, and then Nora spoke. "Hey, speaking of getting an apartment here, I'm worried we aren't talking enough about where we're going."

"Meaning . . ." Demi responded.

"Meaning, it feels like we're a little stuck, seeing each other every week or two, when I come to Westport or you come here. It feels like we need to be *together* in one of those places. Not like tourists."

"I agree," Demi said, "but can we be realistic? And I don't mean for this to sound like a complaint—because it isn't—but isn't this really about when I'll quit my job and move here? 'Cause you're never going to live in Westport again, right? After everything?"

Nora didn't answer right away so Demi pulled at her hand to stop their movement and turned toward her. "Hey, I'm not blaming you. After everything you—and Sophie—went through, I get why you wouldn't want to move back. I get that. I just need to figure out how I feel about giving up the career I've built there."

Nora reached and pulled Demi into a hug, the shorter woman's cheek now pressed against Nora's collarbones. "Thank you for saying that. It would be really, really hard. But there's only one thing in the world that might convince me, and that's to be with you. I don't want you to give up what you love and I don't want to lose you."

As they broke the hug and continued walking, Nora chuckled.

"What?" Demi asked.

"Replaying what I just said, I come across manipulative as hell. 'I would do this horrible thing for you if you made me.' Ugh. I don't mean to be that way. I just want to be honest. And what I honestly hope is that you can find a job here that you really love, something that allows you to keep growing in law enforcement."

"Okay, so now you're crapping on my department?"

"No, no," Nora said quickly, "I also don't mean that. I just mean that you're a big fish and I think it'd be fun for you to swim here."

"I'm just messing with you," Demi said with a smile. "I know what you mean. It's just scary to leave a thing you know and do well for something that might not be either of those."

They walked on in silence and were almost back to their starting point when Demi stopped and burst into song, arms thrown back as she belted a Broadway classic about what she did for love.

Nora stood staring at her open-mouthed, before saying loudly, "Wait, you can *sing*? And *A Chorus Line*? How old are you?"

"My mom's favorite," Demi said as she began running, with Nora close behind shouting again, "You can *sing*?"

"Help!" Demi yelled in mock distress. "I'm being followed by a crazy person."

She slowed to let Nora grab her and spin her into a long kiss as runners squeezed past.

CHAPTER ELEVEN

Ashton Greenstone had come to the College of William and Mary from Columbia University, where he earned his PhD in political science based on his thesis, "The Political Economy of Systemic Racism in America's Immigration Architecture." His wife, a book editor who worked remotely, didn't love the change to the quiet, restored colonial town, but it was a rare chance at tenure for her husband, and he'd managed to get that several years ago. They shared two dogs and agreed they would bring no children into this polluted world. Greenstone was a popular teacher among the politically inquisitive student body, which bore little resemblance to the college's decidedly conservative alumni community or its Virginia state political overseers.

Greenstone's research focused on capital flows and corporate influence on American public policy, as well as the positive impact of immigration on economic growth. But that dry, data-driven work wasn't what had made him famous. Instead, he had become widely known on account of his regular appearances on cable news programs advocating for more liberal immigration rules, especially at the southern border. His frequent debates with immigration hard-liners had raised his public profile to the point that Samuel Buchanan had dubbed the eloquent professor, who had bushy blond hair and wore wireless glasses and tie-dyed T-shirts, "the hippie godfather of open borders."

Buchanan had been talking about him a lot lately, Greenstone had learned. So much that it had prompted a visit to his office on the second floor of Chancellors Hall from two FBI special agents out of the Norfolk field office's Peninsula branch office.

As the two women sat in front of his desk, Greenstone returned to his office chair and began opening the insulated foil package in front of him. "You mind if I eat? Got a class right after this."

He lifted one half of the long thin sandwich and used it to gesture toward them. "The Cheese Shop. Country ham and Swiss. You been? Always get it on the French bread with extra house dressing." He took an enormous bite, then asked through a mouthful, "So what's this about?"

The two women explained they were there to fulfill the FBI's "duty to warn" people who were targets of credible threats of violence. And he was such a person, they said, because Buchanan had been denouncing him and his influence on American public policy frequently in recent weeks.

"As you can imagine, I'm not a regular listener," the professor responded, "but it doesn't surprise me. What I don't understand is why it should concern me, or especially the FBI, an institution that has long protected a status quo in America harmful to disfavored groups, despite the more recent effort by the right wing to rebrand you as a cabal of deep-state leftists."

Greenstone chuckled at his own turn of phrase as one of the agents offered a tight smile and said, "What we try to protect, sir, is the lives of innocent people. The individuals Buchanan focuses on—such as yourself—frequently become the targets of violent attacks."

"I do big-data analysis on capital flow. That can't be what's upsetting these people."

"No, sir. We think it's your TV work concerning immigration, which is a topic of great interest to Buchanan and his followers. Again, we have no specific threat information to share, but we wanted to alert you to the possible danger."

Greenstone sniffed. "And what, exactly, am I supposed to do with that?"

"We have also spoken with the campus police and would urge you to do the same. They can offer you additional support as well as advice on ways you might reduce the risk of an incident."

"I doubt it," he replied. "We live in a country that is awash with angry White people with guns who are worried about being replaced by dark-skinned immigrants or some such nonsense, so I don't know that there is a way to reduce risk."

The second agent spoke. "Well, sir, I'm guessing you lock your car or your bike? We do all sorts of things to marginally reduce risks in our lives, and that's all we're asking you to do about this potential threat. We hope you'll speak with the campus police, but, at a minimum, we hope you'll be alert to your surroundings and vary your routes and your habits. By doing so, you will make yourself a more difficult target in the unlikely event someone wants to hurt you."

Greenstone exhaled sharply and lifted the remaining half of his sandwich. "Feels a bit like recommending they rearrange deck chairs on the *Titanic*, but no matter. I'll take your words to heart. Thanks for coming by."

As the agents stood to leave, he added, "And I confess to being conflicted by the sight of two female FBI agents. I'm pleased that you may represent some change to J. Edgar Hoover's patriarchy but also worry that your presence will be used to anesthetize the American people into trusting an instrument of state power that has never earned that trust."

"You have a good day, sir," the senior agent said as they walked out of his office.

◆

Every day for the last five years, Greenstone had left his office in Chancellors Hall, walked down the stairs, and gone out the front door looking forward to his daily walk through William and Mary's manicured campus. He would smell the freshly cut grass as he cut diagonally across the school's iconic Sunken Garden and through a small patch of woods to Crim Dell, a pond named for a former Manhattan federal prosecutor from the class of 1901. There, he followed the path across an arched wooden bridge where, according to campus lore, two people crossing it together while holding hands will be lifelong friends; if they kiss, they will marry and live happily ever after. The thought often crossed his mind that he should really kiss his wife on that bridge sometime—she loved it when he was romantic. He crossed the street from there into the school's "New Campus," weaving through the Arts Quarter to Jamestown Road and his neighborhood of modest single-family houses. He also made the fifteen-minute walk on afternoons when he had a cable interview scheduled because the college had asked him not to use a William and Mary backdrop for his increasingly controversial appearances—for fear of offending school donors. So he did his interviews by Zoom in his home office. Worked just as well.

Four days after the visit from the FBI, Greenstone made the walk for the last time. He didn't make it to the Crim Dell bridge and he never got to kiss his wife there. His body was found shortly after dark lying next to *Spring*, a statue depicting two students relaxing on the ground. He was on his back next to the reclined male figure, two bullet wounds in his chest and one in his forehead.

CHAPTER TWELVE

ecky kept tabs on her laptop open to a variety of news sources during every show. As Buchanan was working himself into a sweat—literally—condemning an effort by a Midwestern high school principal to regulate the placement of a cross on school grounds, she tuned him out and began clicking through her tabs, looking for news tidbits she could pass across the table electronically to senior producer Herb Cusak. The crawl at the bottom of one cable news website caught her eye: PROMINENT IMMIGRATION ADVOCATE MURDERED. She clicked on the link and read the short story frantically, covering her mouth with one palm. "Oh my God," she said, so loud that Buchanan stopped and turned to look at her.

"What is it?" he asked, before regaining his radio voice and saying, "One of my producers appears to have found something important enough to interrupt a *live* program. What is it, Becky?"

"They killed that Virginia professor you hate so much—Greenstone," she answered, not taking her eyes off the laptop screen. "He was shot on his campus last night. Executed, it seems."

Buchanan stayed in character. "Violent crime is everywhere in our new diversity-is-a-strength America, folks. Of course, thoughts and prayers to his family, but it sounds like the carjacking stories we read every day. Now—"

"No!" Becky interrupted. "Your followers did this," she said loudly, pushing her chair back, "because you *told* them to. Because you said he was a threat to America. And you only said that because they wanted you to."

She was standing now. "You killed this man! And I sat here watching it happen, but God help me, I know better now." Becky hesitated for a moment and then shouted "I quit!" before running from the room.

Buchanan paused and looked down, as if silently praying. After several beats, he slowly lifted his chin. He was glaring at the camera, a prominent vein bulging on his reddened forehead. He began speaking rapidly, the volume slowly rising with each word.

"I'd like to apologize to my live audience for that interruption, but we are going to leave it in the recording so all Americans can see the effect of the poison seeping through our *awokened* country. The voice you heard shouting about the unfortunate death of a truly awful man, Ashton Greenstone, was that of my junior producer, Rebecca Hubbard. Young Becky is a recent graduate of the University of Wisconsin, a longtime hotbed of socialist activism. But, kindhearted man that I am, I took a chance on young Becky. Thought maybe she was different. Thought she was a God-fearing daughter of the great American Midwest. But no. They got to her. They filled her head with all the usual nonsense. Then they used her to infiltrate my show, getting her into the very room where I alert Americans to the coming danger. She stood here and accused my followers of *murder*. You heard it. Said I told them to do it because Greenstone was a threat to America."

Buchanan was gasping for air but he pressed on, even louder. "Well, you know what? He *was* a threat to America, and so are the Becky Hubbards of the world that he and his like have corrupted. They all are. But I've never told anyone to kill anyone, even where the death of that person would be a blessing to this country, a godly act in defense of this shining city on a hill."

He seemed spent now, reaching for his water glass. After a long drink, he continued, much more quietly, "Look, I'm in the words business, the ideas business. And let me use those words to be candid: I don't like violence, I don't do violent things, but this country never would've been born if there weren't rough men willing to pick up a musket and stand the line, to come from the shops and the fields to stop the redcoats. I envy those brave enough to take a stand. I wish I had their physical courage. But that's not my role."

Buchanan smiled tightly before continuing. "So I wish Becky Hubbard well. May she have a long and happy life. Sure, she betrayed my trust, but the good Lord teaches that I should offer her the other cheek after she strikes me. So I'll do that, because it's the Christian thing to do, but nothing will stop me from warning Americans of the danger we face."

◆

Soaked in sweat, Buchanan finished his final monologue by signing off in the usual way. "Have a great day, my fellow Americans. Thanks to you, we may still have a country tomorrow. Until then, stay strong."

Cusak signaled that the taping was done. "Good show," he said, "although I'm afraid Becky's little meltdown was audible and it's going to cause some heartburn."

Buchanan sniffed. "Leave it. But let's make sure to get her keys and the doorman knows she can't come back. Oh, and make sure she left her computer and didn't take anything."

Cusak pointed to Becky's laptop, which was sitting in her chair. "Will do."

"And also make sure I'm involved in the hiring of the new assistant. Pain in the ass that we have to do it, but gives us a chance to upgrade, both philosophically and physically, if you get me."

"Agree," Cusak said. "My bad on Becky. There'll be some unhappiness about that one, but we'll get through it and do better next time. Will get you résumés and photos this week."

CHAPTER THIRTEEN

Benny paused in the doorway to Jessica's office, inhaling deeply. "Ahhhh. Best-smelling JTTF in the world. Still can't believe they let you be here."

"Here" was two floors of the enormous former National Biscuit Company building on Manhattan's West Fifteenth Street, between Ninth and Tenth Avenues. The FBI's Joint Terrorism Task Force had been there since shortly after the attacks of September 11, 2001. For years, the smell of fresh-baked bread made its way to the squads of agents and cops above, who were invisible to the hordes of tourists shopping and eating in Chelsea Market, which occupied the building's lower levels. Each squad was focused on a dimension of a terrorist threat, with I-squads dedicated to foreign terrorist groups like the Islamic State or Hezbollah and D-squads assigned to investigate dangerous homegrown American groups. Jessica's was D-6, whose specialty was a subset of the threat the FBI called "racially motivated violent extremists"—those conspiring to commit violent acts because they believed White people were under attack in America.

"Was chatting up one of your analysts," Benny said. "He told me this is the place where Nabisco invented the Oreo cookie. Wow. Now *that's* a historic site. I get why we make a big deal outta the Liberty Bell and whatnot, but *this* is holy ground."

Jessica couldn't tell whether he was kidding, so she ignored the cookie talk, pointing to a chair by her desk. "Have a seat. It's great to host you."

"My pleasure," Benny said, "especially now I know the history."

Again, Jessica wasn't sure how to react, so she asked, "I'm guessing this is your first visit?"

Benny nodded. "Yeah. The OC squads are all downtown at 26 Fed or out in Queens, as ya already know. Our friends in Cosa Nostra were kinda my life before this, but if I'd known, I'da come sooner."

Jessica laughed. "Same. When I got sent here from the Gambino squad, I thought I was being sent to Siberia but was pleasantly surprised to find out Siberia smelled like chocolate chip cookies."

"How's it bein' a boss?"

Jessica laughed. "Not sure we think of an acting squad supervisor as a 'boss.' Soon as the actual boss returns, I can work my cases and only *my* cases."

"Hey, you got agents and analysts and support reporting to you, even if it's temporary. That's bein' a boss. You gonna put in for a regular supervisor gig?"

"Maybe," she said, giving her head a slight shake. "There's openings because of the seven-year thing."

"They still got the seven-year up-or-out at the Bu?"

"Yeah. And all these years later, there's still a lot of pissing and moaning about it. But most agents agree it's healthy to get new blood in these seats. And a lot of good people need a push to move up in this organization, because moving up means moving your family. Moving up also means internal politics and, worst of all, DC and maybe getting known in the world of real politics."

"Ya think you're gonna climb that greasy pole?"

"Too early to say," Jessica answered.

"Well, I may be an old dog, but even *I* can see why it'd be a damn good thing to have more bosses around this place who know what they're doin' and who look like you—if ya know what I mean—and hope I'm not overstepping sayin' that."

Jessica suppressed a smile. "Thank you, Benny. That may be the nicest thing you've ever said to me."

"Well, don't get too used to it. Not my usual style."

Jessica was a thirty-five-year-old former Northern California high school chemistry teacher, with smooth dark skin and a soft Afro kept very short. Almost ten years earlier, she had been a happy teacher until a friend dragged her to an FBI Bay-area diversity recruiting event, where she found herself mesmerized watching the Bureau rep—a Black woman in her forties—challenge the audience to make a difference in an indispensable American institution. She felt the call, became a Special Agent, and got sent to New York, her forty-seventh choice.

"Just glad you signed up," Benny continued, "no matter whatcha look like."

"And I'm glad you're around too, and let me add that there's nothing wrong with big white men on the job, even though there've been way too many of you guys over the years—no offense."

Benny was smiling now, lifting both hands in the air, palms facing Jessica. "No offense taken. I get ya. You wouldn't believe how modern I've gotten."

Jessica ended the small talk. "Okay, moving on . . . What's your thinking on the Greenstone homicide?"

"Two in the chest and one in the head? Done by a pro. That ain't no mugger. And it also ain't no drunk Buchanan fanboy on his way from the bar shouting about being replaced by the swarthies. Gun musta been silenced too, right? Haven't been there, but they tell me there's students walkin' all around that area. Nobody heard a peep."

"Agree," Jessica said, "and I haven't seen any ballistics yet, but fair bet it'll be a twenty-two."

"Which would cinch it as a pro. No angry bubba would run around with a gun like that. They're too stupid to know it's the perfect way to kill your target without a lot of bullets flying through a body and out into the citizenry."

"I'll let you know as soon as I get more from the crime scene in Virginia. Our Norfolk Division is on it. In fact, we had two agents at his office just last week executing a duty-to-warn."

Benny lifted both eyebrows. "Seems it didn't take."

"No, it did not. He pretty much blew them off."

Benny shook his head and made a clicking sound. "He won't do that again."

Jessica grinned and shook her head. "You are a font of dark humor today, my friend."

"Yeah, sorry. I think I'm gettin' hangry."

"How close you think we are to getting DOJ sign-off on charging Buchanan?"

"Not sure. Carmen's been on the phone pushing them, but there's a lot of thumb-sucking going on in DC. Hoping this Greenstone thing will get 'em off the pot. I assume you're live-monitoring all Buchanan's public-facing accounts now, right?"

"Yes, *finally*," Jessica replied.

"Why'd it take so long? Don't need a court order. Just follow him on social media and stuff."

"You'd think," Jessica said, "but, this being the Bu, we are institutionally terrified of violating anyone's First Amendment rights and even more terrified of violating the First Amendment rights of some White guy who has the ear of wing-nut members of Congress."

"A large constituency, I understand," Benny said.

"When you follow the facts, political people get pissed, because facts are not their thing. So let's get on with it, do the work well, seek truth, and piss people off."

Benny was nodding in agreement. "If this was some Muslim dude saying the shit Buchanan's been saying—with bodies fallin'—FBI'd be on him like white on rice." He paused and grimaced. "Wait, is that racially insensitive?"

"No, it is not," Jessica said, chuckling. "Most rice is white. But I appreciate the question. I see the evidence of modernity you mentioned."

Benny swept a hand around Jessica's office. "So you're telling me this work is not the beating heart of the FBI?"

Now Jessica smiled broadly and pointed a finger at her own chest. "How do you think this child of God got to be acting supervisor of this squad?" She let that sink in before she continued. "And I'm not kidding. This is considered a career graveyard. Even by those who aren't angry-White-people adjacent—and if you've seen the news channels preferred in our workout rooms, you'd know we got plenty of those. Hell, getting some of our folks to help with the January Sixth cases was like pulling teeth. Unbelievable. But true."

"Yeah, I was sickened to hear some of that. Just do your job and shut the fuck up about politics, is what I always say."

"We even had somebody from another JTTF squad resign rather than cover leads out of January Sixth. Said we were being used to 'criminalize political differences.' Holy mother of God. Did he not see police officers being beaten near to death? How can they be that dumb and still find their car keys?"

There was a knock on the doorframe of Jessica's open door. An anxious-looking intelligence analyst was standing there holding a laptop balanced on one forearm.

"What's up, Ivan?" Jessica asked.

"Boss, I think we have a problem with Becky Hubbard."

"What?"

"She said on his show this morning that he had killed Greenstone, or caused him to be killed. You could actually hear it; she was yelling. On the spot, he then declared her a threat to America, of course saying the Christian thing to do was turn the other cheek."

"Damn," Jessica said, looking at Benny. "You heard from her?"

"No," he answered, reaching for the phone holster on this right hip, which was empty. "Course my phone's locked up."

The entire JTTF was a Sensitive Compartmented Information Facility, which meant devices with cellular or Wi-Fi capability were banned. Employees and visitors had to lock theirs in electromagneti-cally shielded boxes outside the SCIF entrance.

"What else?" Jessica asked Ivan.

"The fire ants are swarming. The online Buchanan-world is filled with comments and threats aimed at Becky. It's everywhere."

"Shit," Benny said as he hurried past the analyst and down the hall to the phone boxes.

◆

Benny was in the outside hallway, staring at his phone as it slowly powered up in his gigantic palm. After an agonizing wait, a small red

4 popped up in the corner of the green phone icon on the home screen. He had four missed calls, and four voicemails, all from Becky. The most recent was twenty minutes earlier.

In the first message, she was speaking while walking quickly, her breaths audible.

Benny, it's me, Becky. Hey, I have a problem. I lost my mind after I saw that professor was killed. I'm sorry. I've left Buchanan's and I'm going down Nineteenth, to get away from here, toward the FDR. Call me when you get this, okay? Thanks.

Five minutes later, she was breathing more heavily, sounding as if she was jogging.

Benny, it's me again. Hey, I'm just passing Ess-a-Bagel. Heading down Twentieth to the river. I actually think there's a guy following me, but maybe I'm losing it. Could you call me? Please?

In the next message, from four minutes later, Benny could hear highway traffic in the background. Becky sounded frightened.

Hey, there really is a guy following me. I'm still on Twentieth, almost to the FDR. Please, please call me.

Two minutes later, she was whispering.

I went into the lobby of a fitness place here at the end of the block. But the guy saw me. He's coming in.

She paused and he could just make out the garbled sounds of a male voice in the background. Then Becky was speaking as if to someone nearby:

Oh, hi. Oh, good. Thank you.

Becky's voice was close to the phone again, using a normal tone.

Never mind, he's one of yours. He says he'll take me somewhere safe and then we can call you. Thanks for watching over me. Talk soon, bye.

Benny immediately called Becky's phone, which went straight to voicemail. "Goddamn it," he muttered, throwing his phone back into the box. He ran to Jessica's office. "Do we have someone covering Becky?"

She shook her head. "No. No reason. Why?"

"Motherfuckers!" Benny shouted and turned toward the door, calling back over his shoulder. "Get the PD to Twentieth Street, the end by the East River. She's there and she thinks one of us is there to help her. Son of a bitch."

Chelsea Market was two miles away, but it still took Benny ten minutes with lights and siren to get there in his government-issued Ford Explorer, weaving in and out of crosstown traffic, shouting out the window at cars and pedestrians, banging an open hand on the outside of the driver's side door.

Police cars were clustered under the FDR at the Twentieth Street entrance to Stuyvesant Cove Park when he got there. The NYPD crime scene tape was already up, blocking the little path of wood chips that led into the bushes of sustainable native plants. He held up his badge and ducked under, but the scene was quiet. Rebecca Hubbard was no more. She was lying on her back in a patch of goldenrod flowers, two bullet holes in her chest, one in her forehead. Benny stood over her, staring, as if memorizing the scene. Then he turned, stone-faced, and walked quickly to his car. The tires smoked as he lurched away.

CHAPTER FOURTEEN

Benny's car skidded to a stop in the semicircular driveway of Buchanan's Nineteenth Street apartment building, and he jumped from the vehicle. "Sir, you can't leave that there," the uniformed doorman protested. Benny brushed past him, barking, "Government business."

The doorman followed him into the lobby, insisting that he stop and sign the guest register. Benny pressed the elevator call button and then turned, looming over the smaller man in the Pershing-style hat and blue tunic with gold epaulets.

"Look, pal, I never want to make a workin' man's day harder," Benny said, pulling his badge from his pocket. "I'm here to arrest one of your residents and ya don't want any part of what's about to happen."

As the elevator opened, the doorman took a step backward, nodding.

On Buchanan's floor, Benny took two long strides out of the elevator and used the side of his closed fist to pound on the apartment door, shouting, "Federal agent, open the fucking door or I'll break it down."

The door opened immediately and a familiar face greeted Benny. "Special Agent Dugan, please," Matthew Parker said calmly. "There's no need for raised voices or force. We'll be entirely cooperative."

Benny gave his head a hard shake, as if pushing out of a dream. He stared at the handsome man with blue eyes and combed-back silver hair blocking his way into the apartment. The man had no suit jacket on and wore a gold tie over his fitted, deep blue dress shirt with a contrasting white collar. Benny knew that toned frame was the product of hours in the pool and on a Peloton bike.

Fully awake now, Benny's voice came slowly, hammering the emphasis: "What the *fuck* are *you* doing here?"

Parker slipped a thumb behind each of his paisley suspenders and began running them up and down like a barber sharpening razors. "Well, my old friend, that's a question I've been asking myself quite a bit."

There was movement behind Parker and the bald head of David F. Lupo came into view, his eyes shielded by mirrored sunglasses.

Benny did a double take, then looked back at Parker. "Are you fuckin' kiddin' me? First you're in this dirt ball's apartment, then you're hangin' with this piece a' spoiled cheese? Didya lose your mind, or just your fuckin' sense of smell?"

"Nice to see you too, Dugan," Lupo replied.

Benny's eyes didn't leave Parker. "You know what that is, Matty, right?"

"A former member of both the FBI JTTF and the NYPD," Parker answered, using his courtroom voice. "A man familiar with the dangers of the modern world."

"'A piece of shit who *is* one of the dangers of the modern world' would be more like it," Benny said.

"Former Homeland Security Special Agent Lupo is providing personal security to my client, Mr. Buchanan," Parker said, "something he needs given that his words seem to irritate so many in the increasingly intolerant country in which we live."

Benny blew a pulse of air between his closed lips. "What've you been smokin', Matty? Thirty years I know you and you always had the occasional screw loose, but this is you comin' completely fuckin' undone. And I thought you were retired, anyway."

Parker dropped the formal tone and spoke quietly. "I was, Benny, I was. Tryin' to get used to golf, but I fucked up my shoulder, so I've been on the DL for a bit.

"Buchanan has a weekend place out by me in East Hampton. I've gotten to know him 'off camera,' if you will. Can't say I agree with everything he says, but I gotta be honest: a lot of it appeals to me. You yourself know this city has gone to shit being overrun by people who don't speak the language, people who have no business being here, people who jumped the line while the good ones who do what our people did long ago—follow the actual law—get taken for fools, stuck in some third-world hellhole waiting their turn like suckers. We gotta get control of our borders or we won't have a country left."

Benny pulled his mouth into a line and was silent for two beats. When he finally spoke, his words were quiet, coming through clenched teeth. "And so you're cool with killin' and beatin' people who see things different? You're cool with cappin' young girls who get crossways with your client, leavin' their bodies under the fuckin' FDR? That what you're into now?"

Parker squinted in confusion but didn't answer, so Benny pointed to Lupo. "You're cool hangin' with bottom-feeders like that? I knew him when he was just a dirty cop in Brooklyn."

When Lupo took a step toward him, Benny hissed, "Please give me a reason. Please."

Parker lifted an arm between the men and returned to his formal tone. "Now, now, there's no need for that kind of thing. Can you state your business here, Special Agent Dugan?"

"I'm here to arrest Buchanan for the murder of Becky Hubbard, his producer."

"And do you have a warrant?" Parker asked.

"I do not," Benny said.

"Then you have no legal authority to enter this dwelling, as you must already know. You can't enter a residence to arrest someone unless you have a warrant or are in hot pursuit of a suspect you saw commit the crime at issue. I'm guessing you didn't see Mr. Buchanan kill anyone, because he's been here all day. So I'm going to have to ask you to leave, Benny, and I do it with deep respect and a desire to avoid any kind of unpleasantness."

Benny paused, closed his eyes, and tilted his head back before taking a deep breath and then exhaling through his nose. Then he opened his eyes, leveled his head, and spoke. "This right here makes no fuckin' sense to me, Matty, but I'm gonna let it go for now. I *will* leave. And I will ask the prosecutors to arrange your client's surrender."

As Benny turned to leave, he could hear Buchanan's distinctive voice, but it was a strange, muffled version of the man. As Buchanan walked across the entry hall, Benny could see him looking down and shaking his head. "That poor girl, that poor girl," he muttered. "How, how could this be?"

When Buchanan disappeared from view, Parker offered Benny a strained smile. "A difficult day for all. Please ask someone from the office to get in touch."

CHAPTER FIFTEEN

"You didn't hit him?" Nora asked with exaggerated shock, rocking back in her desk chair. "What has the world come to?"

"Hilarious," Benny answered from the couch, "but I've been doin' some breathin' stuff your mo—that a friend recommended. And as I stood there, I realized anger was drivin' me and *I* needed to be the one in control. Plus, I didn't have a fuckin' warrant."

Nora worked hard to suppress a smile, bobbing her head in silence until Sean spoke, after he apparently missed Benny's near reference to the DUSA's mother. "Remind me who Matthew Parker is?"

"Chief of Violent and Organized Crime here, back in the day," Benny replied. "We worked a bunch of mob cases together before he left to do defense stuff—mostly white-collar, corporate fraud, big money. Nora brushed against him in a mob case she and I did a few years back. He was supposed to have retired after that shit show. Lives way out on the Island now, Hamptons."

"Of course," Sean said. "He represented Kyra Burke in the state case out of the former governor's murder."

"He did indeed," Benny said, "and got me in a hell of a crack with the IG when I made the mistake of sharing information with him."

Nora's smile widened as she turned to Sean. "The Department of Justice Inspector General can get all nitpicky like that when you tell old friends stuff about your investigation and it gets somebody killed."

"That was my bad," Benny said, tapping his chest with one finger. "Matty's a good guy. He didn't mean to get anyone hurt and I deserved the suspension that came with it. Plus, the guy who got dead was a piece of shit."

Nora turned serious. "Can't argue with that last bit, but if Matty's still a good guy, what's he doing standing in Buchanan's doorway? And standing there with Lupo—who you've described as very much *not* a good guy."

Benny brought a hand to his chin, shaking his head side to side. "Don't know for sure. Based on what he said at the door, he's been drinking some of Buchanan's Kool-Aid. Matty's always been, uh, less than what you might call 'progressive'—like many of us in this business—but it's hard for me to draw a line from him thinkin' we need to get our shit together on immigration or cut the nonsense about defunding the police to him actually helping Buchanan. Maybe he just wants back in the action, or maybe the Kool-Aid is stronger than I think. Bottom line: I don't know, but I still think Matty's earned the benefit of the doubt."

"Happy to give it to him," Sean said, "because it really doesn't matter who Buchanan's lawyer is. I don't think we arrest on a complaint, anyway. DOJ Civil Rights has the draft indictment and our memo. Carmen can call them and say we have to move now. How are we thinking about Greenstone and Becky?"

"Who the fuck else woulda done it but team Buchanan?" Benny barked. "That's why I went to grab the fucker."

"I don't know," Sean said quietly. "I'm sure it's connected, but it doesn't fit our theory at the moment. He mentioned her only once on air, and even then he didn't say his usual 'she's got to go,' like he did for Greenstone, for example. And he actually did the turn-the-other-cheek bit for her. Also, it's so fast; she's killed within an hour, so how do we argue it was one of his wing-nut followers? He got somebody motivated and with a gun at the east end of Twentieth Street that fast? And you told me it looked like a small caliber, like the twenty-two that did Greenstone, which is so different from all the others. I'm not saying we won't get him for it eventually, but I'd be inclined to leave both Becky and Greenstone out for now."

Benny started to speak, but Nora talked over him. "I agree," she said, turning to Benny. "We have trouble connecting Becky's death, but we also have issues fitting Becky into the hate crimes statute, which is the same problem we have putting Greenstone in the indictment. Even if we can connect the murders to Buchanan's words, neither of them is an obvious fit for one of the categories protected under the statute."

Nora put both forearms on her desk and leaned to look at Benny. "We'll get justice for Becky, but at least for now it'll just slow down the DC approval. And if we're going to detain Buchanan, the case has to look tight in the indictment. So maybe we use Becky—and Greenstone—in our bail argument, and say that once we fully investigate, there are likely to be more charges in the case."

When Benny didn't answer, Nora leaned back in her chair and continued. "I'll tell Carmen where we are and why we think we need to move now, before anyone else gets killed." To Sean, she added, "Shoot me the updated memo as soon as you're ready."

"Right away," Sean answered.

The two men got up to leave, but Nora called to Benny. "Hey, Mr. Rough, can I catch up with you on something else?"

"Sure," Benny answered, dropping heavily onto the couch as Sean left. "What'd I do now?"

Nora got up and walked to the office door, closing it quietly before turning back to Benny. "I just wanted to check in. That move at Buchanan's didn't seem like you. You know that, right? You can't go making an arrest like that, and in a case like this."

Benny exhaled audibly. "I know it. I saw Becky lying in the bushes with a hole in her forehead. She's a fuckin' kid, for heaven's sake. A good kid. Somethin' snapped, Nora, I gotta be honest. I'm sorry. We got her into this and we were supposed to protect her, ya know?"

When Benny looked up, Nora saw actual tears in his eyes.

Nora sat gently on the couch next to him and touched his shoulder. "I'm so, so sorry you had to see that. It's awful. I'm not gonna beat you up about what happened at Buchanan's. I also don't want you beating yourself up, 'kay?"

"Yeah. In a way, I'm glad Matty was there. Stopped me from doing something that mighta embarrassed you and Carmen and the office." Benny sniffed and blinked the tears away before continuing. "This one is hittin' me like nothin' ever did. I'm sorry. I gotta be better."

"Hey," Nora answered quietly, "this one is awful, just awful. The important thing is that nobody was embarrassed and we're going to do it by the book. I need you to move past this and work this case like a pro. We'll get justice for Becky."

When Benny nodded, Nora paused and then said, "Hey, I've kinda left the checking on you to my mom, but are you doing okay? Generally, I mean?"

He looked at her with a gentle smile. "Yeah, I'm doin' good. I appreciate you askin'. Been keepin' the demons at bay. I promise to let you know otherwise. But your mom's a big part of me being in a good place."

She knew what he meant. Four years earlier, as they prepared a mob case for trial, Benny hit bottom. Drunk and alone, he left his Brooklyn apartment at two A.M. to walk the streets, ready for a fight, hoping someone would attempt to rob him. Luckily for him, and any would-be robbers, an NYPD patrol car saw him staggering along the sidewalk and officers approached him. He was slurring his words as he held up his credentials, but they found Nora's business card tucked behind his badge and called her rather than arresting him for public drunkenness. He and Nora sat together in his little living room as the sun came up that morning, Benny leaning over the coffee table, holding his face in his huge hands. He'd done it before, he explained, ever since his beloved wife died, whenever he tried to drown the darkness with too much whiskey—wandering the streets looking for violence, to hit someone who deserved it, maybe kill someone who deserved it. He rejected her advice to speak to a counselor but promised he would call her if the darkness was descending again.

Now Nora smiled back at him. "Good," she said. "And I know you always keep your promises."

Benny grinned. "Copy that. Don't you worry."

Nora stood, looking down at Benny with a smile. "Plus you got the breathing thing now. From your *friend*. So that's good."

Benny smiled back. "It's very good. And my friend knows I'm a work in progress. But at least we're makin' some."

He pushed himself up from the couch. "Thanks for the talk and for givin' me a bit of a pass here. Won't let you down."

"Never a doubt," Nora said as Benny walked out the door.

CHAPTER SIXTEEN

A black SUV passed through the security checkpoint and stopped on Duane Street at the sidewalk to the employee entrance for 26 Federal Plaza. Matthew Parker stepped from the front passenger seat and stood several feet from the vehicle, waiting with hands clasped in front of his buttoned suit jacket. There were no reporters or photographers in the area, but he still waited. *Not gonna open the fucking door. I'm not security.*

After a long pause, David Lupo, wearing his usual sunglasses, came from the driver's seat and walked around the car to open the door. Sam Buchanan's unkempt head emerged, followed by the rest of him. After standing, Buchanan quickly brought his left hand to his waist and grabbed his pants, which were beltless on Parker's advice. Buchanan was wearing his usual horsebit loafers, so there were no laces to take before surrendering to the FBI. With his trailing right arm, Buchanan was holding the hand of his lawyer girlfriend, Riley Pond, who slid easily along the seat in her zip-up leather midi skirt and landed her black high-heeled shoes on the pavement without letting go of Buchanan. She paused briefly to tilt her head back and give it a shake, throwing her long black hair over the shoulders of her leopard-print jacket.

"You coming up?" Parker whispered to Lupo. "'Cause I didn't make arrangements to leave the car here."

With his back to the FBI building, Lupo pulled one side of his bomber jacket open to show a black Glock pistol in a shoulder holster. "Can't carry inside, so I'm with the car. Will find a spot to wait somewhere around Foley Square."

"Going to be a long wait," Parker answered. He turned to his client and said in a louder voice, "Okay. Here we go. Chin up, neither frown nor smile."

Parker led the way in his usual custom-made chalk-stripe blue suit, glancing left at one of his favorite contrasts in New York—the tall chain-link fence around the outdoor play areas for the 26 Fed's day care center, where FBI agents might be able to smile at their kids while dragging a handcuffed ne'er-do-well in for arrest processing. *What a world,* he thought, spotting Jessica up ahead. "Special Agent Watson," he said in a loud voice, "I appreciate the courtesy of the employee entrance."

Jessica shook his hand and nodded to Buchanan and Pond. "No problem. Please follow me."

As they rode the FBI-only elevator up to the area where Buchanan would be fingerprinted and photographed, Jessica explained the process. "Once Mr. Buchanan enters our space, you won't be able to see him again until we've transported him to mag court."

"Of course," Parker said as the elevator opened and Jessica gestured for Buchanan to move toward a solid steel door, which buzzed as he approached. Holding her hand up to stop the lawyers, Jessica pulled the door and gestured to Buchanan. "After you, Mr. Buchanan. You'll be able to see your lawyers over at the courthouse." With that, she followed Buchanan in and the door closed.

Parker and Pond rode the elevator down in silence for several floors before Pond spoke.

"Mag court?" she asked.

"So you've done a lot of federal work here?" Parker replied, not entirely hiding his sarcasm.

"I'm admitted to the SDNY Bar, if that's what you mean. I'm just not familiar with that term."

"Yeah, well, it means magistrate judge court. On the fifth floor at 500 Pearl, where defendants make their initial appearance in every criminal case. Bail gets set. All that jazz."

The elevator was silent again for several beats. Pond turned to look at him. "My work is primarily in the civil arena."

Parker continued staring at the closed doors. "That so? Well, that'll sure come in handy."

As Pond weighed how to respond to that, the doors opened and Parker walked quickly into the main lobby, then out the public entrance toward Foley Square. As he stepped from the building onto the marble plaza, he noticed two large clusters of camera operators—both photo and video—on either side of the stair railings from the plaza down to the sidewalk. He started laughing. "The fucking Bu," he said to no one in particular.

"I'm sorry?" Pond answered, her heels clicking behind on the marble. "Was that for me?"

"Nope," Parker said. "Just marveling at the FBI and its mysterious ways." He couldn't see the confused look on Pond's face because he turned right and made a wide circle to avoid the throng of media people.

◆

Thirty minutes later, a door opened in the FBI-only elevator bank and Samuel Buchanan, handcuffed behind his back, emerged, flanked by two young-looking agents in FBI raid jackets, followed by additional agents in FBI gear. Each gripping one arm, they led the defendant through the lobby, out the public door, and slowly across the plaza and down the stairs lined with media.

Unlike most perps experiencing a custodial walk in public, Buchanan didn't lower his head. Using the fingers of his handcuffed hands, he reached through the back vent of his suit jacket and held his beltless pants tight as he stood up straight, swiveling his face side to side in response to each request from a camera person, a tight smile fixed in place. And the cameras kept moving. The paparazzi paralleled the route across Foley Square—stopping repeatedly to shoot before moving quickly to set up for another angle farther down Pearl Street and then into the alley beside the courthouse. The public journey ended at the courthouse's front door on Worth Street, where Buchanan disappeared inside, passing under the outstretched arms of the large statue of Lady Justice.

◆

"Are you fucking kidding me? They did a perp walk? All the way across Foley Square? Like with mob defendants back in the day?"

Nora had never seen Carmen more upset. Without waiting for answers, because her questions were simply confirmations of what Nora had just told her, Carmen picked up her desk phone and dialed. "Yes, Carmen Garcia calling. Yes, I'll wait."

Nora knew she was calling the ADIC, downstairs in his office with one of the best views in Manhattan.

"Gene, it's Carmen. A fucking perp walk? In a case where the defendant's entire life is based on publicity and his claim that the government is out to get him? Are you kidding me? The FBI didn't walk Martha fucking Stewart back in the day—I'm told because the US Attorney personally asked them not to. And *she* wasn't trying to destroy our democracy. Oh my fucking God, Gene. Did I really need to call in advance and ask you not to light this on fire?"

Nora could hear the ADIC's smooth voice coming from the phone against Carmen's ear but couldn't make out the words. He was a nice guy, but slick. As Carmen once explained, "You don't get to the top of that slippery pole of Bureau politics without getting some grease on you."

Carmen waited for him to finish and then responded. "First, Gene, I hope you didn't hear me suggest *you* ordered it. I know you wouldn't. What I'm suggesting is that someone below you felt free to do it and it was a dumb fucking thing to do and if you really run New York, you should get a grip on your team. Second, there's enough weirdness around this case and the FBI that it's not beyond the realm of possibility that this was done precisely to fuck up the case and give Buchanan the martyr's moment he craves."

Carmen listened again and then said, "I'm not getting paranoid, Gene. What I'm getting is tired of the FBI acting like it isn't part of the Department of Justice. I don't want to embarrass you, but I'm so pissed about this I'm going to ask for an Inspector General investigation."

After a brief pause, she added, "Yes, I know they can be dumb finger-in-the-wind weasels, and masters of hindsight, and whatever. But there needs to be some accountability here and they're the only game in town. See you at the press conference."

Carmen hung up the phone and looked at Nora, exhaling loudly. "I hate to do that," she said, "I really do, but this shit is beyond the pale. And I meant what I said to Gene; I wouldn't put it past some January Sixth revisionist, closet Buchanan loyalists to have done this on purpose."

The room was quiet for a beat before Carmen continued. "And can I vent for a sec about the fact that I had to *call* him because to *see* him I have to ride the elevator down to the lobby and then ride another elevator up to his office just below mine and then ride it back down and back up again to return to my desk? All because the FBI has to have its own elevator bank? And can't let me into the goddamn stairwell? Wouldn't want to trust *us* with that kind of access. Give. Me. A. Fucking. Break. Okay, I'm done."

Nora ignored the familiar elevator complaint. "I talked to Jessica. She had no idea, and her squad has the case, for God's sake. She thought it was a self-surrender and that after processing, they would just drive him from their garage to the courthouse garage. She thinks somebody in public affairs did it."

"Well," Carmen responded, visibly calming down, "somebody did and three years from now the IG will tell us who, maybe, and that person will have retired already and everybody at the Bureau will hate me for siccing the IG on them. But whaddya gonna do?"

Nora grimaced in sympathy. "I was thinking maybe you should call the chief judge and apologize, but I really do think you're right—this helps Buchanan most of all, so I'm not sure what there is to apologize for. I don't know where you dug the Martha Stewart thing up from, but I've heard the same stories; the office was worried pictures of her in custody would seem cruel and make the government look like overreaching assholes."

She paused and sat heavily into a chair before adding, "Now *we* are those assholes."

"Awesome," Carmen said quietly. "We look bad for prosecuting a guy who *literally* calls for violence against his opponents. Why can't I just be going after the queen of home and hearth for lying about some stock sale? Be far less controversial."

"Because you, my friend, are a power-hungry lesbian libtard who hates America. That's why."

Carmen smiled. "I knew you could pump me up before the presser."

◆

The US Attorney's press conference was held in the biggest conference room the office had in its new space. Carmen stood on a wood box behind the podium, next to FBI ADIC Gene O'Meilia, waiting for the assembled media members to settle.

"Not much of a crowd," he whispered. "I think the real action is outside."

Because she was on the box, Carmen didn't need her tiptoes to reach his ear. "Oh, you decided to perp walk him back the other way?"

"Very funny," he answered. "No, I think his supporters have some sort of rally going on."

Carmen cleared her throat and began the press conference, describing the charges in the indictment, emphasizing the importance of deterring violent extremism, stressing that Buchanan was presumed innocent, and thanking the FBI for its help. In a departure from normal practice, she did not name the members of the prosecution team—an effort to reduce the amount of online hate and threats Nora and Sean would face, a gesture Nora described as "holding up a cocktail umbrella in a hurricane." Carmen also didn't offer a sound bite. As usual, her team had crafted something that the press could quote easily—"Today, hate meets the law"—but she struck it after the perp walk. She ended by noting that Buchanan's initial appearance was scheduled for three P.M. and then she introduced the FBI New York leader.

But if Carmen had angrily scratched out her staff's attempt at a sound bite, the FBI, as always, came well-equipped. During his turn at the podium, ADIC O'Meilia stressed that the case was the product of hard work by the FBI's Joint Terrorism Task Force and then looked down to read the lines crafted by his public affairs shop. "These charges are a reminder that terror knows no color," he said. "Today, the demon of radicalization is in the dock." For good measure, he read a third, which was his least favorite: "The FBI and its partners will not rest until our country is free of the scourge of political violence."

There were a handful of questions, but the press seemed in a hurry to leave to get to the real action outside.

CHAPTER SEVENTEEN

No fucking way. Matthew Parker was slowly taking tiny steps backward to move out of the cluster of people around the microphone at the top of the black granite stairs. *Never should have come up here in the first place.* Gwendolyn Harmon was at the mic now, pointing over the heads of the crowd, gesturing down Pearl Street to the courthouse entrance. And shouting.

"Right behind you, just back there, is where a great American patriot is being persecuted for being a champion of liberty, for standing up to tyranny on behalf of all of us!"

As the crowd, which was large enough to spill back onto Centre Street, roared—much to the consternation of the NYPD traffic enforcement personnel trying to keep cars moving north past the many courthouses on Foley Square—she took a breath before shouting again.

"We're standing on hallowed ground! *This* is Thomas Paine Park, named for the man who lit the flame of American rebellion, who gave ordinary Americans the inspiration they needed to throw off the shackles of a despot. Paine said, 'Tyranny, like hell, is not easily conquered; yet we have this consolation with us, that the harder the conflict, the more glorious the triumph.' Well, let me tell you: Sam Buchanan is going through hell now and we must let his example show us the way to a glorious triumph."

With a final slide-step in reverse, Parker hunched over and melted back into the group, wheeling to walk slowly across the stone platform, past the fifty-foot-tall abstract representation of a West African antelope resting atop a boat-like structure symbolizing the horrific Middle Passage that brought millions of enslaved Africans to America. He spotted Benny standing on the sidewalk in front of 26 Fed and walked toward the big man.

"Now I've seen it all," Benny said with a sour look on his face. "You, with a group of maniacs shitting on the rule of law."

Parker looked down and shook his head, his hands deep in his pants pockets. "Yeah, my bad, actually. Wasn't thinking. Even mob guys know when to show respect and keep their fucking mouths shut. And these assholes have no fucking idea where they're standing. Yeah, that's technically named Thomas Paine Park, but this ain't 'hallowed ground' for anybody except the thousands of Black people buried here—and then paved over."

Benny gestured with his head over his right shoulder toward Duane Street. "Over there, maybe. I've seen the African Burial Ground Monument."

"Not only there. That's just where they found bodies when they dug for a new building in the nineties."

Parker pulled one hand from his pocket and spun, sweeping his arm in a horizontal arc. "All around, from the courthouses to Broadway. Acres and acres. This whole area was a cemetery for those poor fuckers. All of this sits on their graves. Did you know there were more slaves in this city than any other, except maybe Charleston?"

"How the fuck you know so much about this?" Benny said. "Didn't take you for a Black history major, Matty."

"Well, I wasn't. Learned it all by accident. Back in the day, maybe even before I worked my first case with you, they made me the junior member of the committee to find a site to build a new US Attorney's office to replace One Saint Andrew's. I was supposed to represent the future or some shit. But no chance for a new building. Since the discovery of the burial ground nobody can dig a foundation anywhere near here."

He lifted his arm to point at the towering federal building behind them, then grunted and quickly dropped it. "Son of a bitch," he said, rubbing his shoulder, "there's no way something like that monstrosity will ever go up here again."

"The world's better off," Benny said. "And what's going on with your shoulder?"

"I fucked it up somehow—probably from carrying you all those years. Anyhow, I'll survive."

He turned back toward the crowd on the little island of land in the middle of the busy square. "This is a holy place for people who knew what actual fucking shackles felt like. Jesus. Not some dickheads who think there's too many gay books in a library or some shit. Unbelievable. What the fuck am I doing here?"

Benny sniffed. "Am I sensin' a loss of enthusiasm for your client and his cause?"

"No comment," Parker replied. "Guess I was getting bored and maybe I should have done more checking but the guy's a neighbor, and all he wanted was for me to sit and help his girlfriend—for an appropriately large retainer, I'll have you know—so I'm going to do what I was paid for and sit there quietly and see it through. Like a good lawyer. And also like a lawyer who doesn't want to lose his license by standing at a fucking microphone and yelling shit at the courthouse. Look, his nutcase girlfriend is up there now."

Across the street, the voice of Riley Pond bounced off the facade of the Thurgood Marshall courthouse. "I love a man named Sam," she said, her voice straining, "a man wrongly accused of trying to violate people's rights. A man who has dedicated his whole life to protecting the rights of Americans, rights that are under attack every day by the radical left. The leftists who are weaponizing our justice system. *They* are the people who should be in jail. *They* are the people who are conspiring to violate rights."

She raised her fist and shouted, "Stand for America, stand for America, stand for America."

As the crowd took up her chant, she stepped back to give the next speaker—an evangelical minister from Missouri—access to the mic for a planned final prayer. But when the crowd quieted and the minister moved forward, Pond shot an arm in front of him, grabbing the microphone and leaning close to the black foam bulb. "And one last thing," she yelled, "the government has assembled a collection of lying losers to say they attacked people because of Sam Buchanan. They're a plate of cockroaches, willing to say anything to save their own skins. Luckily, jurors don't eat cockroaches." With that, she stepped back and the minister bowed to ask God's blessing on the assemblage and their incarcerated brother, Sam.

Across the street, Parker turned to Benny with a red face and narrowed eyes. "That's it; that's *fucking* it. I gotta find a way to get away from this thing. I'm not going to jail with her. Goddamn it."

"Maybe it was the echo," Benny replied, "but I'm not following you. I thought you just said you were seeing this through, like a handsomely retained good lawyer would or some shit."

"Hah," Parker replied. "That dumbass just violated the local court rule on pretrial statements by lawyers. And she did it *in front of the fucking courthouse.* You can't say shit like that about potential witnesses. Lawyers go to jail for that crap." With that, Parker turned and walked angrily down the sidewalk, still muttering and rubbing his shoulder.

Benny smiled and called after him. "Good talk, Matty. Keep in touch."

Parker raised the back of one hand and kept walking.

Benny's cell phone began playing "Don't Stop Believin'" by Journey, and he answered with a smile.

"Hey T, what's goin' on?"

"Oh, nothing," Teresa Carleton replied, "just checking on you."

"Everything's under control, beautiful," Benny said cheerfully.

Teresa's tone changed. "Is it really? I just want to make sure you're okay. I heard you've been dealing with some hard things. You can talk to me, you know."

"You got informants, huh?"

"Don't deflect, Benny. She cares about you. And so do I."

"I know, I know," Benny said, "and I will tell you what's goin' on, but I can't right now. I'm on the street. But I promise. Tonight."

"Okay, I'll hold you to that. I love you."

Benny turned in a circle to be sure he was alone on the sidewalk. "Love you too," he said quietly.

"That was pretty weak," Teresa answered with a teasing tone. "Are you embarrassed by our relationship?"

"You're killin' me," Benny said, taking another look around before adding in a loud voice, "I love you."

"Better," Teresa said. "See you tonight."

Benny hung up and dialed Nora's cell phone. She answered on the first ring in a mock professional voice. "DUSA. How may I serve you?"

"You rat fuck," Benny said. "Just got off with your mother, who somehow heard I needed checking on."

"I hope you're kidding, Benny. You *do* need checking on. And as I said, I'm leaving that awesome responsibility to your girlfriend. But she has to know when she needs to check, am I right?"

Benny paused before answering. "Yeah, you're right. I shouldn't be breakin' your chops about it. Ya both care and I need all the help I can get. Sorry about the call. Go back to bein' you."

"A full-time job," Nora said with a laugh. "You do the same. I'll check in with you after court. You still going to see if you can talk to Cusak at the apartment?"

"Yup," Benny answered. "Headed there now."

CHAPTER EIGHTEEN

After the crowd was gone, Nora and Sean walked across Foley Square and down Pearl Street to the employee entrance for the Moynihan courthouse. Sean glanced to his right as they climbed the ten stairs. "I can't get used to this area being so quiet."

Along Cardinal Hayes Place, which rose steadily away from Pearl to meet Saint Andrew's Plaza, the federal prison stood empty after a series of health and safety crises, forcing Manhattan's federal defendants to be temporarily held six miles away at the Brooklyn Metropolitan Detention Center. And just up the gradual incline, next door to the vacant prison, their former office had been stripped down to its steel girders, awaiting rebirth as a building still too small for its mission.

"Ghosts all over the place," Nora replied.

They pressed their credentials against the entryway reader, nodded to the court security officers, and took the elevator to the fifth floor, where the hallway outside the magistrate judge's courtroom was packed with people. It seemed as though the entire crowd from the rally was now inside trying to attend the bail hearing. A Deputy US Marshal working the door saw Nora's tall head over the crowd and called out, waving them forward. After pushing through the group at the door, Nora and Sean emerged into a courtroom that was only slightly less crowded. Every seat in the public section was occupied.

The gallery was quiet as the prosecutors made their way through the little swinging door in the low wall—the literal "bar" of the court—until they took their seats at the empty table next to the one at which Riley Pond and Matty Parker were seated. Now the crowd knew who they were and an ominous grumbling began. Nora heard the word "fascists" before the handcuffed Buchanan was led into the room from a door next to the judge's bench. The grumbling immediately turned into cheering and shouts of "Go Sam!" At that, a huge deputy marshal with one hand still on Buchanan's handcuffs twisted to face the pews. "Hey, hey," he yelled. "That will stop *immediately* or this room will be cleared. This is a courtroom. Act like it or you won't be here. Fair warning."

The crowd seemed stunned into silence, during which a robed judge swept from a door behind the bench, accompanied by a clerk's calls that all should rise and then be seated and come to order. The crowd moved as instructed, making the surprisingly loud groaning, cracking, and rustling sound that dozens of silent humans make when rising and falling in unison. The deputy uncuffed Buchanan and steered him into the empty chair next to Parker, before backing to the side wall, where he stood with his hands tented together at his waist, staring daggers at the crowd. Other deputies stood at intervals around the walls, with two seated just behind Buchanan. As the magistrate judge began to speak, a man in the front row leaped to his feet and pulled open his green army surplus jacket, revealing a shirt displaying a large image of the Virginia state flag. He shouted, "*Sic semper tyrannis*," and was immediately grabbed by two marshals, who dragged him swiftly from the courtroom.

United States of America v. Samuel Buchanan had officially begun.

The magistrate judge, a judicial officer appointed by the court for a renewable eight-year term, did all the usual things: confirmed the defendant's identity, that he was represented by counsel, understood his right to remain silent, and didn't wish to have the entire indictment read aloud. He then received the defendant's "not guilty" plea to that indictment and announced that the case had been assigned to the Honorable Donovan Newton through the process of selecting judges from a lottery wheel holding cards bearing the names of each of Manhattan's three-dozen judges. The magistrate explained that Judge Newton had determined that he would handle all bail proceedings for this case, and not the magistrate, as was customary. It was something Judge Newton did regularly and was well within his authority. For that reason, he said, the parties should report immediately to courtroom 23A.

As the clerk began to call, "All rise!" Nora grabbed Sean's arm and pulled him to his feet. "Let's go," she whispered intensely, pulling him along behind her through the little swinging door and out of the courtroom just as the gallery was cracking and groaning its way to a standing position. They walked quickly though the hallway crowd, unrecognized by those who hadn't been in the room, and into the stairwell, where Nora began climbing quickly. "What just happened?" Sean gasped from behind.

"It was going to be nothing but ugly for us to get out of there. So we bolt. No direct elevator from five to twenty-three; gotta change at eight, so we get to eight before the mob and catch the elevator up from there. They'll all have to take the local elevator to eight, so we'll beat them."

"And we're gonna sleep on twenty-three until everybody goes home?"

"No, but Judge Newton will let us use the judges' elevator, in the back. Plus, I'll have Benny be there to keep an eye out for crazies. I should have had him here for this. My bad."

"Nah," Sean answered as they climbed, "it was a good idea to have him take a run at Herb Cusak at the apartment while everybody was down here. Any word from him?"

"Not yet," Nora answered, now breathing heavily.

CHAPTER NINETEEN

"**P**lease be seated, ladies and gentlemen," United States District Judge Donovan Newton said as he walked up the three stairs to the bench. The space was crowded, but the much larger courtroom of a district judge seemed to shrink the gallery that had packed the magistrate's courtroom eighteen floors below. He remained standing after the spectators were seated, towering over the cavernous room. In truth, he was even taller than he appeared, but his pronounced stoop lowered the top of his head to about six feet four. And the black robe exaggerated the roll and hunch of his shoulders, making it appear as if his kindly bespectacled face and thinning light brown hair were coming horizontally out of a mountain.

Now he swept that face from side to side, taking in the entire gallery as he spoke in a distinctive singsong voice, "I am only going to offer one reminder that this is a courtroom of the United States of America. No disturbances of any kind will be tolerated. There will be no further warning and I assure you the consequences of a breach will be life-changing."

A low murmur came from the public benches, but the group was otherwise quiet. The removal of T-shirt man was apparently still fresh in many minds and the unhappy-looking deputy marshals around the room served as a constant reminder. The judge sat and addressed the lawyers sitting in front of him at two rectangular tables—the prosecutors in their traditional spot, closest to the judge, with the defense directly behind them.

"Ms. Carleton, it's always a pleasure to have learned government counsel before the court."

"Thank you, Your Honor," Nora said, rising partway out of her seat to answer, although it wasn't clear an answer was needed.

"And Mr. Parker," the judge continued, looking at the second table, "it's a pleasure to have you before me. I have many fond memories of our association together in these halls of justice."

"Thanks, Judge," Matty Parker said, not bothering with the partial standing move and gesturing to his side. "But I'd like to introduce Riley Pond, who will be serving as lead counsel for Mr. Buchanan. I'm here only in a supporting role."

Nora rose completely. "And Your Honor, I apologize for not introducing Sean Fitzpatrick, the chief of our National Security and International Narcotics Unit, who will be handling this case with me."

"Yes," the judge said, "I'm familiar with Mr. Fitzpatrick, who has an excellent reputation as a skilled and careful lawyer, and I look forward to his participation in this matter."

Judge Donovan Newton was unfailingly polite and formal in his speech, so much so that newcomers often wrongly assumed it must be sarcasm. He was given to effusive praise of lawyers—all delivered with a kindly mix of emphasis and inflection, including what linguists would call "high rising terminal," in which the last syllable of a sentence is often lifted. With a tight smile, the judge looked back and forth between the two counsel tables.

"I certainly appreciate learned *coun*-sel, who I'm confident will represent their clients in the highest tra-*di*-tions of the ba-AHR."

Despite the up lilt, he was no Valley Girl, having grown up in the tony Westchester County suburbs of New York, where he was sent by his wealthy parents to the finest schools. A former federal prosecutor, longtime law firm partner, and proud member of the long-gone liberal Republican strain of New York politics, he was now approaching senior status in a job he had treasured for twenty-five years.

The judge stood and walked to the edge of the bench platform, where he bent over and began digging through a metal file box on the desk. He pulled a document from the box and returned to his big leather chair. With one hand he removed his glasses, and with the other he brought the document so close to his face that it almost touched his nose. After nearly a minute, he replaced his glasses and turned to face the courtroom.

"Ms. Pond, I don't believe counsel has had the opportunity to appear before this court. Is that correct?"

"Yes, Your Honor," she answered, rising to her feet and dropping her hands to tug her skirt into position. "This is my first time."

"Yes, well, despite that, I expect that Mr. Parker has informed you that this is a court that endeavors to scrupulously adhere to the federal rules and to the teaching of the Second Circuit Court of Appeals."

"Yes, Your Honor," she said.

"And, in that regard, I have come to believe that you engaged in conduct today that may have violated Local Criminal Rule 23.1, the so-called Free Press-Fair Trial Directives, which bind every attorney appearing before the court."

He removed his glasses and pulled the document close to his face again before continuing. "I will now read from the relevant portion of the rule, which forbids a lawyer, and I'm quoting now, 'to release or authorize the release of non-public information or opinion which a reasonable person would expect to be disseminated by means of public communication, in connection with pending or imminent criminal litigation with which they are associated, if there is a substantial likelihood that such dissemination will interfere with a fair trial or otherwise prejudice the due administration of justice.' And the rule goes on to offer examples of conduct that would presumptively violate its terms, including any statement concerning, and I'm again quoting, 'the identity, testimony, or credibility of prospective witnesses.' "

He put his glasses back on and leaned forward. "I tell you this, Ms. Pond, because, although we are not acquainted and I assume you are a talented lawyer, your public description this afternoon—in front of the very courthouse where I first learned to practice the law—of the government's witnesses in the case now before the court as a 'plate of cockroaches' is a presumptive violation of the rule and compels this court to issue an order to show cause why you should not be held in contempt and punished for those remarks by a fine or a term of imprisonment."

Pond began to say something, but he cut her off. "Please, Ms. Pond, do not speak. It is not in your interest to do so and the court does not wish this situation to become any more dire for you. Please be seated."

The murmur returned but one look from the judge silenced it before he continued. "The court's intention is to issue that order today and ask the chief judge to assign that matter to another judge so this court is not put in the position of adjudicating your guilt while trying to ensure your client, Mr. Buchanan, receives the fair trial to which he is entitled."

Judge Newton turned to Pond's client, who was sitting shadowed by two seated deputy marshals. "Mr. Buchanan, it may be that much of this is confusing to you, and on a day I'm sure has already been quite stressful. I'm going to ask your counsel, Mr. Parker, in whom this court has the highest confidence, to explain this to you privately and answer your questions to the best of his ability, which is substantial. Should you have questions of the court, we can address them the next time you are before me.

"And Mr. Parker, I gather from your opening remarks that you may have intended a subordinate role to your cocounsel, Ms. Pond, in this matter. Given these developments, even if she is able to remain as counsel in the case, I do not see how you can be other than lead counsel."

Parker dropped his head but didn't speak. The judge continued. "Let us now turn to the question of bail. Ms. Carleton, I understand the government intends to seek to detain the defendant. I can tell you, based only on the court's review of the indictment, informed by a lifetime of commitment to the law and the First Amendment, that the court has grave concerns about such a request. But, as ever, the court also has an open mind. Please proceed."

Nora stood. "Certainly, Your Honor. The government is seeking to detain Mr. Buchanan as a risk of flight and on grounds of dangerousness. As to flight, his constant expressions of admiration for Hungary as a place to live, his possession of a Hungarian passport and good standing with the current authoritarian government of that nation, his access to private air travel, and significant overseas assets all make him a serious risk of nonappearance. As to dangerousness, we believe that, given the way he is alleged to have committed these crimes—with his oral directions to coconspirators—there is no combination of conditions short of detention that will reasonably assure the safety of the community. And—"

Judge Newton cut her off. "I don't mean to interrupt counsel, but I wonder if there isn't a way to focus our inquiry this afternoon. I'm well aware of the factors the statute directs the court to consider, and of the excellent guidance provided to trial courts by the Second Circuit. To that end, I believe the risk of flight here is significant, but could be adequately mitigated by the kind of financial commitments and private monitoring of home confinement that the court has deployed in analogous cases. I will ask Mr. Parker to suggest a robust package.

"I think the obstacle to detention on grounds of dangerousness is, and I'm quoting from Title 18, United States Code, section 3142, 'the weight of the evidence against the person.' As I read the indictment, the government is not alleging that Mr. Buchanan personally engaged in any acts of violence, or even that he knew the persons who would engage in those acts. Instead, your theory is that he knew, or was willfully blind to the knowing, that persons unknown would engage in violence against those he had criticized. That is, he engaged in what would otherwise arguably be protected First Amendment expression but, because he must have known what the outcome would be, he is guilty of a violent hate crimes conspiracy. That strikes the court as a very thin reed on which to rest a prosecution and an even thinner reed on which to base a claim to detention. Please help the court."

What followed was an hour of spirited back and forth between Nora and Judge Newton. She used it all: the stochastic terrorism, the vulnerable victims singled out for focused and vicious verbal attack, the evidence from the attackers that they had been motivated by his exhortations, the idea that the government's case got stronger with each attack—that by victim number three or four, Buchanan actually *intended* to order violence against a target, the possible addition of two more murders. The judge was not persuaded.

For his part, Matthew Parker had not physically moved, sitting placidly with his hands folded on his lap, like a US Open tennis fan with great seats. When, at last, the court turned to Parker and asked what he had to add, he stood, buttoned his jacket, and said, "Your Honor, I believe the court has a firm grasp on the issues and I will be presenting a bail package," and sat down.

In the end, Judge Newton announced that he was denying the government's motion to detain Buchanan and would instead order him confined to his home with restrictions on public communication while the case was pending, with further details to be spelled out in a written order.

When the judge finished announcing his decision, Nora stood. "Your Honor, we very much appreciate the court's thoughtfulness, but we respectfully intend to appeal and would ask the court to stay the order while we do so on an expedited basis."

Judge Newton drew his lips in a tight line before speaking. "Very well. That is certainly the government's prerogative and while this court is frequently in doubt, it is also sometimes in error. I will stay the order pending your pursuit of an expedited appeal. We will set a control date, and I will exclude the time under the Speedy Trial Act."

He leaned forward and lifted a gavel from the bench, bringing it down with a single loud rap. "Good day. This court will stand in recess sine die"—which he pronounced *see-nay dee-ay*. His large hunched form then swept from the bench and disappeared through the door at the bottom of the little stairs. Deputy marshals quickly surrounded Buchanan, handcuffed him, and took him out the same door.

Parker stood and stepped past his cocounsel, crossing the short distance forward to the government's table, where he braced his hands on the wood surface and leaned down to Nora, speaking in a quiet, intense voice.

"Sorry, I can't bear to talk to her and I need all the mouth breathers married to their first cousins back there to know I'm on team Buchanan, so can we argue about something? Feel like I didn't do enough there, although I know to quit when I'm ahead. My momma didn't raise no fool."

Nora kept looking toward the bench so her smile would be invisible to the gallery. "Sure, Matty. What'd you want to fight about?"

"This sine die thing. What the hell does that even mean?"

"It's Latin for 'without a day.' Means the judge doesn't know when the next session will be because he needs to wait for the court of appeals."

Parker lifted one hand and brought it back down abruptly, slapping the table. "Why the fuck doesn't he just say that?"

"Not sure," Nora replied. "Maybe because Latin gets it done in two words."

By now, Riley Pond had joined the last of the spectators filing out of the courtroom. Parker banged the table again. "Okay, I think that covers it. I appreciate your time. And I'm guessing I'm going to need to say more at the circuit."

"I expect so," Nora replied. "I'll call you when I know the schedule."

Parker hit the table one last time, but gently, with his fingertips. "You're a pro. You too, Sean."

With that, Parker returned to his table, gathered his things, and walked toward the back doors, passing Jessica and Benny, who were moving toward the prosecutors. Jessica nodded. Behind her, Benny smiled. "Looks like ya got first chair now, bub."

"Fucking nightmare," Parker said, shaking his head as he continued walking.

"So how'd you make out?" Nora whispered to Benny when Parker was gone.

He gave her a wide-eyed look. "Ghost town. The place has been cleared out, literally. The doorman let us in. Apartment's empty. He said movers came yesterday. No sign of Cusak."

"Weird," Nora said. "Almost like Buchanan knows he's going to stay in the pokey."

"Maybe," Benny answered. "But we'll keep hunting for our boy Herb, and I'm gonna look up my old buddy Lupo to see what he knows. The dead professor and poor Becky are top of the list. Not gonna let this bone go."

CHAPTER TWENTY

The design of the Second Circuit's oral argument courtroom reflected the monastic culture of a federal appeals court whose vision for public engagement was straightforward: as little as possible. There was no jury box or door next to the bench through which ordinary citizens would file to sit in judgment or through which prisoners would move as defendants or witnesses. There were no handcuffs or jurors at all here on the fifteenth floor of the Thurgood Marshall courthouse; this was a quiet place where points of law were argued in carefully allotted time increments, assigned to advocates in advance and policed by tiny green, yellow, and red lights. The only door at the front was directly behind the horseshoe bench, displaying—when opened to permit the three judges who presided over each argument to come or go—a rose window with the scales of justice at its center. There was no "bar," no charming low swinging door to permit lawyers and witnesses to come forward and be heard. Instead, a chest-high dark wood wall crossed the entire space, separating the three judges on their horseshoe bench from lawyers and observers alike.

As if to reinforce that separation, marble busts of two serious-looking men sat on pedestals against the sidewalls, staring at each other across the room. They were former members of the court, long dead: Learned Hand—the one with the epic eyebrows—and Henry Friendly, both brilliant, anxiety-ridden Harvard Law School introverts, widely considered—at least in this courtroom—as the most talented judges never to be on the United States Supreme Court.

The attorneys participating in an argument sat at leather-topped tables built into the public side of the dividing wall. Lawyers spoke one at a time, standing at a massive podium at the wall's midpoint. Over the wall, a clerk would eye the lawyer rising to begin the allotted speaking time and press a button that would raise or lower the surface of the big podium.

Nora waited as the lectern's top slowly rose, accompanied by a low-pitched buzzing sound. When the clerk thought the height was right, he gave just the slightest nod of his head. Then Nora, having been reminded she was extraordinarily tall, began as appeals lawyers always did: "May it please the Court, I am Deputy United States Attorney Nora Carleton and—"

She got no further. This was what lawyers called a "hot bench," and it was evident the three judges were on her side from the start.

"Is it appropriate, Ms. Carleton," the first judge asked, "for a district court to essentially disregard a grand jury's finding of probable cause, as happened here? This indictment alleges, in great detail, that the defendant knew his words would bring about death or grievous bodily injury to five people and intended that result. I recognize that a court might have reasonable questions about where the boundaries of protected speech are, but can there be any doubt that this defendant's speech is across any line? You can't yell 'fire!' in a crowded theater and you can't yell 'go get him' to a crowd of deluded people with weapons."

Before Nora could answer, a second judge spoke. "And is a bail hearing ever the place to litigate legal questions, Ms. Carleton? Isn't it rather the place where the question is whether the defendant needs to be in jail to protect the community? And is that a close question here?"

The third judge jumped in. "I can't speak for my colleagues but, on the risk of flight issue, at some point we need to stop letting rich people stay out of jail because they have the resources to allegedly duplicate the security of a prison. By that logic, why don't we just let them stay in their mansions after they're convicted, so long as they hire somebody to make sure they don't go beyond the tennis court? Let the poor folks go behind those ugly walls and fences. At some point, don't you think the statute—and the very idea of justice—requires that we treat all defendants equally?"

Nora answered all the softballs carefully, knowing that Judge Newton would be listening to the live-stream audio of the argument. She explained that the district judge had obviously asked thoughtful questions in good faith about possible weaknesses in the case, but the prosecution agreed that the First Amendment issues were not fatal and the time for resolution of those legal issues was later, during any motions to dismiss that the defense might file. In light of the vibe from the bench, she decided she didn't need to touch the issue of rich people getting to stay home in their penthouses with private guards while the poor get locked up. She sat down before the little lights on the podium told her to.

Matthew Parker was visibly annoyed that the clerk made him pause while he lowered the podium slightly. He turned to Nora, who was seated at his left elbow and whispered, "Seriously? I'm *taller* than you."

Nora shrugged as the podium stopped and the argument began. Parker seemed energized with no client or cocounsel in the room—waving his arms, tapping the podium, his voice rising and falling—but he had no chance, so much so that Nora declined to use the two minutes she reserved for rebuttal. When the session finished, the three judges slid their chairs together behind the bench and whispered to each other. When they pushed back, the presiding judge announced from the middle seat that the court was reversing the district court's judgment and would promptly issue a written order detaining Samuel Buchanan. With that, the door behind opened, the presiding judge rapped his gavel, and the three filed out toward the rose window.

CHAPTER TWENTY-ONE

Nora slumped into the chair in front of Carmen's desk and sighed loudly.

Carmen frowned. "In one of those TV shows, I'd walk over to the cocktail cart and pour you a glass of brown liquid in an Old Fashioned glass."

"I'd love some," Nora said glumly. "You have a cart?"

"No, I don't. Also no alcohol of any kind. So just go ahead and tell me what crawled up your butt and died."

"Not sure that's the empathetic leadership I've come to depend upon."

"That's all I got in the tank today," Carmen said, offering a half smile. "So I'm guessing it went downhill after the longest perp walk in American history? Seems hard to imagine after my inspiring press conference."

Nora spoke quietly. "I don't want to depress Sean, but Judge Newton is normally a home game for us and he seemed to have major problems with the theory of our case. I'm glad we won the bail appeal, but I'm worried that Newton won't let us get to the jury with the stochastic terrorism, 'he must have known' theory. We still have a ways to go yet, but the closer we can get to 'he knew' and 'he intended,' the better."

"So how do we get there?"

"Not sure. We had hoped that poor girl Becky could get us to a place where Buchanan told her he knew, but that's gone now that she's gone."

"Any reason to think she was killed because he figured out she was cooperating?"

"No, but it's always possible. She was hit very quickly, and after she lost it with him on the air, which means thousands of his followers heard it live. Could be one of those crazies. But we don't want to rule out that Buchanan somehow learned she was working with us. We just don't know. We're looking for Cusak but he's gone missing. Look, we have time to tighten up our case and, at the end of the day, it's worth a swing anyway. He really is responsible for those attacks. It'll suck if we can't hold him *legally* responsible, but at least we have to try."

"No argument here," Carmen said. "This is what seeking justice looks like. You can't be afraid to lose when the cause is righteous."

Nora smiled. "Agree, but maybe I won't give the 'noble losing' speech to the team just yet."

"Good idea," Carmen replied, returning the grin.

◆

Nora grabbed the miniature Nerf basketball from the war room table and smoothly launched a left-handed shot at the little hoop taped to the far wall, holding the classic flexed wrist pose until the ball hit the wall and caromed through the net.

"Bam!" she announced, dropping her arm. "Still got it."

Benny looked up and frowned. "Seriously? You called bank? Musta missed it."

"Don't let the haters get you down," Jessica said. "The box score doesn't have a comment section. And you have a nice stroke, by the way."

"I had some game, back in the day," Nora replied. "Way back."

"The Hoboken Lisa Leslie is what I heard from a friend," Benny said, smiling now as he leaned over to open their little refrigerator. "You want a seltzer?"

Nora shook her head and plopped into a chair at the table. "There are so many ways this conversation could go wrong that I think we should just move on. But let me just say that your source may be blinded by maternal affection."

Before Benny could answer, Nora turned to Sean, who was staring at his laptop screen. "Trial partner, why're you so quiet?"

He didn't look up. "Because I know Judge Newton doesn't like our case and he's going to like it even less now that we got the circuit to reverse him on bail. We have to find some way to tighten up our proof of Buchanan's knowledge that people were going to get hurt, or Newton's never going to let us get to the jury. So I'm going back through our phone stuff to see if we missed any link between him and any of the attackers. Even if we can't read an encrypted message, it would help to show he was in touch with any of them beforehand."

Nora exhaled audibly through her nose. "Okay, so you see what I see. I was going to give the team an expectations-setting talk, but it seems you don't need it. I have to say, though, that I'm more optimistic that he'll let it go to the jury. The case is too important for him to Rule 29 it."

Sean looked up. "Maybe, but then he Rule 29s it after a jury verdict."

"That's obviously not great," Nora said, "but at least then we have a conviction and can ask the circuit to reinstate it."

"Translation, please," Jessica said, raising a hand. "Haven't done enough trials to follow this."

"Right," Nora answered. "Rule 29 of the Federal Rules of Criminal Procedure says a judge should acquit the defendant if the evidence is insufficient to convict—meaning no reasonable jury, following the law, could find the defendant guilty. The judge can do it *before* a jury gets the case or *after*. If it's after a jury convicts, we can appeal that. If he does it before, we're screwed and the case is over, forever."

Sean chuckled. "The fact that we're even having this conversation means we're in trouble. It's like talking about your will before you go in to have surgery. Not a great sign."

"Jesus, you people are some Debbie Downers," Benny said.

When he noticed Sean's stare, Benny raised both palms and said, "No, no, there's nothing wrong with that. It's from a *Saturday Night Live* thing a few years back."

Sean typed quickly on his laptop. "Yeah, two decades back, Benny, but you're right."

"Appreciate you fact-checking me in real time, Seany. Christ, this is a tough crowd."

"Sorry, Benny," Nora said gently. "Mom says that too."

"So I'm in good company," he responded. "Can I take us back to the case and ask whether putting Greenstone and Becky in the indictment now might help?"

Nora turned to Sean. "What do you think?"

"Assuming we could charge it as a hate crime, I think Greenstone could help us, although it's a little dicey because he's killed in such a different way. But I don't see how he fits the hate crime statute, given that he's a straight White guy. On balance, though, I think it would help to have him in there somewhere because Buchanan's attacks on him are so fierce and then, boom, he's dead."

"And Becky?" Benny asked. "Look, I hate to keep beatin' that drum, but she has to be a priority. Like, where the fuck is Cusak? His family says nobody's heard from him. What's that about? Maybe he's dead, maybe he ain't. We gotta chase that, hard. And Lupo is supposedly just security for hire, but I don't fuckin' know. We have to keep an eye on that weasel too. I just don't want us to take our eye off Becky."

"We're not going to," Sean answered. "I promise. But—and I hate to say this—I've come to think her case could actually hurt us. I mean, she's a sympathetic victim, for all the reasons we know, but Buchanan said so little about her and in an almost contradictory way, and then she's killed so quickly. Seems like it hurts our narrative."

"All fair," Nora said, "but if we don't charge it, doesn't it undercut us anyway? I mean, here's the government saying Buchanan is responsible for people killed after he attacks them, and here's someone killed after he says nasty stuff about her and in the same way Greenstone was, and we—what? Nothing?"

Benny jumped in. "Look, we all know he's responsible for Becky. We just don't know who actually did the hit. And if it's not charged, what happens to our theory?"

"Yeah," Nora replied with a grimace, "and I realize I'm about to argue against myself, but if we *don't* charge it, how does Buchanan use it to hurt us—really? He proves a murder in his defense case that we haven't mentioned just to say he didn't do it? How does that work out for him?"

Nora turned to Jessica. "You got thoughts on this?"

"I don't," she answered. "Again, I haven't sat through enough trials to have a feel for the strategy. Sounds to me like it could go either way. But we haven't talked about whether the bad guys might have found out Becky was working with us and that's what got her killed."

"We haven't," Nora said, tipping back in her wooden chair to look at the ceiling, "because we have no indication that might have happened. I suppose she could have told someone, but without something to go on, it just has to be something we watch."

After a long moment, she shifted forward and the front chair legs banged back to the floor. "I think, on balance, we leave Becky out of the indictment, at least for now. And we add Greenstone, but only as an overt act in the conspiracy because I just don't see how we can show he's a protected person under the hate crimes statute. But that'll allow us to prove six attacks at trial."

"Agree," Sean answered. "I'll draft it and get the grand jury time." He turned to Jessica and Benny. "And I'll use one of you as the witness to summarize the case as a whole and the Greenstone evidence in particular."

Benny pointed at Jessica. "You do it. Good to get you the at bats."

"Sounds like a plan," Nora said, jumping to her feet. "I have to go administrate or whatever it is the DUSA does."

"Hey," Benny called, passing her the Nerf ball just as she reached the doorway. Nora caught it and launched the long shot, turning away while it was still in the air. "Steph Curry!" she shouted as she disappeared from view, calling over her shoulder, "And don't even *try* to tell me that didn't go in."

CHAPTER TWENTY-TWO

The Metropolitan Detention Center occupied a full block near the docks in Brooklyn's Sunset Park neighborhood. It resembled the other giant warehouses that still dotted the area a century after Industry City, as it was called, was the largest shipping center in the country. Of course, the MDC was also the only warehouse in the area for humans, and it held far too many for its design, especially after the "temporary" closure of its Manhattan sibling, the Metropolitan Correctional Center. An inmate of Sam Buchanan's prominence would ordinarily be held in a special administrative wing, where single cells were designed to accommodate both ends of the prisoner bell curve—the vulnerable as well as the dangerous. But the MDC had no such luxury. There could be no single cells; the staff would simply need to be careful about assigning roommates.

Buchanan was given a gray jumpsuit made of paper with Velcro closures, an innovation in the wake of the suicide of wealthy sex offender Jeffrey Epstein and designed to avoid self-harm by high profile inmates. Two guards escorted him to his cell, which was a double—and apparently designed that way. But it seemed much smaller because of the man sitting on one of the two narrow platforms that served as beds. Buchanan was struck that Mike Gerardi had a very small head. Or at least it seemed that way, given that the rest of him resembled the Hulk, without the green. Gerardi was not wearing paper. Buchanan wondered whether that was because he wasn't a suicide risk or because the paper clothes manufacturer had simply not imagined his size.

"Hey, how you doin'?" Gerardi said in a gravelly voice, extending a huge hand. His accent rang of the New York metro area, although Buchanan couldn't tell Brooklyn from Jersey the way so many people claimed they could.

"I'm doing okay, considering," Buchanan replied, shaking hands. He said nothing else, which was not his nature. But Matthew Parker had specifically instructed him not to speak to anyone in the MDC beyond "hello" or "I'm being assaulted by my roommate."

"Believe me," he had explained, "that place, like all jails, is full of informants. You really cannot trust anyone. Don't forget that."

For his part, Gerardi seemed similarly careful and the two passed the early days and nights without sharing a word.

CHAPTER TWENTY-THREE

Special Agent Carl Wynne's cell phone buzzed on his desk. The caller ID read *Bureau of Prisons,* so he paused before answering. Nothing good came from a jail call. Anybody calling on a taped line was either full of shit or desperate, or some combination of those two toxic attributes. "Ah shit," he said out loud, reaching for the phone. "Hello."

A computer voice responded: "You have a collect call from a correctional institution." Then the computer paused to play a recording of the caller's self-identification. "Palace," said a gravelly voice. Then the computer returned. "To accept this call, press one; to reject this call, press three or simply hang up."

Wynne's finger hovered over the three on his phone keypad, as he silently debated the question—was there any part of the Bureau's values of fidelity or bravery or integrity that required him to take this call? Nope. He pressed three and put the phone down.

It buzzed ten seconds later and the drill repeated, except this time the caller's self-identification was replayed as "Palace. Urgent." Wynne's finger hovered over the three but with an audible "fuck it," he touched the one.

"Thanks for taking the call, Carl," Gerardi said.

"This is a recorded line, Mike," Wynne answered flatly.

"Roger that," Gerardi answered. "Need a low viz visit. MDC. Urgent. Over."

Wynne had never understood why Gerardi spoke like a military operative. He had never served in the military; what he *had* served was repeated stints in prison for most of his life as a violent criminal. But Wynne decided the prison's practice of recording all calls might serve a purpose. "You no longer have any relationship with the Federal Bureau of Investigation," he said, as if dictating a memo. "That relationship was terminated two years ago because of your repeated violation of the obligations of a confidential human source, namely, to avoid committing crimes and to keep your handling agents apprised of all activities that might be relevant to the relationship. This agency has no interest in further communication. Goodbye."

"Wait, wait, Carl! Don't!" came Gerardi's reply. "I know how much I fucked up. I got nobody to blame for that and I'm sorry. But you're gonna want to hear this, and not on this phone. Please."

"Don't call again," Wynne said, and hung up. He leaned back and loudly blew air between his closed lips. Across the double desk, his partner looked up.

"What the heck was that?" Adam Francis asked.

"Fuckin' Gerardi. He's at the MDC. Must be in a crack and has something we gotta hear. Urgent."

"Happens every time."

"Remind me why we code-named that piece of shit 'Palace'?"

Francis smiled. "Maybe 'Career-Ender' was taken?"

"Be funnier if that motherfucker hadn't come close to *actually* ending my career. *And* yours, if memory serves."

Francis didn't answer because he was distracted typing on his desktop computer. He talked to the monitor screen. "Oh, he's in a crack all right. Looks like he finally found his way back to the District of New Jersey for his probation violation. I bet they stuck him at MDC because half the criminals in Jersey know he's an informant."

"No, no, correction, my friend," Wynne replied. "*Was* an informant, at least for our beloved FBI. As you heard me remind Mr. Gerardi on the taped line, he was terminated as a CHS. Done. Finished. You can only stick up so many banks and terrify so many innocent people while working for us as a source before we cut you off. We have standards: once, maybe; twice, thin ice; three times and with a clown mask and a fucking bomb? Nope. We draw the line. We have standards in the FBI."

Francis chuckled. "It's good you can find humor in it now. Was hard to get you to see that a couple years ago."

"'Cause a couple years ago I was almost a private citizen because of that shithead."

Francis didn't seem to hear his partner's comeback because he was typing and leaning close to the monitor now. "Hah!" he shouted, pointing at the screen. "I'll bet that's it."

"What?"

"Just checking the BOP database. They have him rooming at MDC with one Samuel Buchanan, the recently charged voice of White America as I recall—and I, as your Black coworker, purposely leave it unclear whether I mean that as compliment or as sarcasm out of respect for both your whiteness and Republican leanings."

Wynne shook his head. "First, fuck you; I may be a Republican but I believe in the rule of law, so I'm against killing people you don't like. Second, they have *Gerardi* in with a podcaster? Are you fucking kidding me?"

Francis spun the monitor to face Wynne. "Hey, I don't make the entries in their records; I just read them."

Wynne squinted at the screen. "Ah, shit. Palace musta gotten something out of Buchanan and he's calling to try to cash it in. Son of a bitch. No way. Done is done."

Francis nodded toward their squad supervisor's office. "Not even gonna tell the boss? Maybe let Mags be the one to shut it down, so if it turns out to have been a plot to kidnap the Pope for blessing the gays or something you weren't the one who said no?"

Wynne rapped his knuckles once on his desk and then pointed at his partner. "That, my friend, is why you have a bright future in this organization. You have a graduate degree in ass-covering, a discipline I have come to appreciate only later in life."

Francis nodded solemnly. "Just here to serve."

CHAPTER TWENTY-FOUR

Carl Wynne knocked quietly on the doorframe to Margaret Kennedy's office. "Hey, boss, got a second?"

"Sure, Carl, what's up?" she said, gesturing to a chair.

Wynne sat and took a breath. "This is a weird one and requires some history from before your time."

"Okay," she said, "not the most enticing preamble of the day, but lay it on me."

"I had a productive CHS in the VCMO program"—he pronounced the name of the Violent Crime and Major Offender program in the usual FBI way, *vick-moh*—"who was also incredibly difficult. He gave us great stuff. He also gave us lots of heartburn. But we shut him down a couple years ago after a wild ride. He's trying to come back now, out of MDC, where for reasons I can't possibly explain, BOP made him roommates with celeb defendant Sam Buchanan."

"No shit. Okay, tell me about this guy."

Wynne took another deep breath and gave her the whole ugly story.

❖

Michael James Gerardi was born in working-class Belleville, New Jersey, Newark's neighbor just north up the sluggish and polluted

Passaic River. He was a huge kid, especially for someone of Italian heritage, and made bigger by the muscle he added to his tall frame with weights and steroids—topping out at 280 pounds. After finishing high school, he became a bouncer and debt collector, but he quickly graduated to being an armed robber. Gerardi at rest was frightening to behold, muscles bulging below a strikingly small head. He was even scarier while pointing a gun, which he did often.

He was also a creature of habit and his life was one long pattern. He conducted extensive surveillance of a bank or jewelry store, monitoring police radio frequencies to reduce the chances of a law enforcement encounter, typically scheduling his robbery for a police shift change. Then, wearing a bulletproof vest and a mask, holding his preferred .45 caliber semiautomatic pistol, and often joined by other really bad people, he marched into the targeted establishment, scared the life out of lots of innocent people, and departed with money or jewelry. If he stole jewelry, he often took it to New York, where he got to know major "fences"—dealers in stolen property. Sometimes they suggested jobs for him to do, and he would return to sell them the goods, at a steep discount.

That was the robbery part of the pattern. The rest of it was just as predictable: When Gerardi got caught, he would supply valuable information to law enforcement, which often got him out of jail. The deeper he got into life as a career criminal, the more valuable the information had to be, so the authorities couldn't refuse to listen.

He did early stints in county and state jails, but, at the age of thirty-nine, he became a *federal* prisoner for the first time after the FBI grabbed him for robbing banks in North Jersey.

After being sentenced to ten years in federal prison for the bank jobs, Gerardi chatted in the recreation yard with bad guys, many of whom were weight lifters awed by the powerful bank robber with the scratchy voice. During one of those conversations, an inmate expressed interest in killing a crucial witness against him. Gerardi said he could do that for him, explaining that he expected to be released shortly after a successful legal attack on his conviction. Gerardi then reached out to the feds and told them what was happening. He also offered a sweetener: he would also cooperate against his fences if he were released from jail.

The FBI in New Jersey decided the information about the murder of a witness was too important not to pursue. So, armed with an FBI recording device, Gerardi chatted his fellow inmate up again, confirmed that he had been hired to do the killing, and arranged delivery of payment on the outside to an undercover agent posing as Gerardi's associate. His fellow inmate was charged with soliciting murder and Gerardi was released, resentenced to five years of probation, and was to be handed off to Special Agent Carl Wynne of the New York FBI's major theft squad.

But before Gerardi's cooperation in New York could begin, he was sent to a New Jersey county jail cell after another judge revoked an old state probation. There, he struck up a conversation with his new cellmate, who was serving time for killing a two-year-old. The cellmate wanted to kill the police officer who had arrested him. Gerardi called the Jersey FBI, who put a recorder in Gerardi's cell and captured his cellmate confirming he wanted Gerardi to find someone to kill the police officer for money. Gerardi's cellmate was arrested and pleaded guilty, and Gerardi went free from the county jail as a reward for his cooperation.

With Gerardi finally back on the street, Special Agent Wynne and the New York FBI tried to confirm his relationship with a group of Brooklyn fences in a way that wouldn't require a jury to believe

Gerardi alone. Carrying a briefcase with a recording device built into it, he reintroduced himself to the criminals and announced he was out of jail and back in the robbery business, selling them a portion of a jewelry collection the FBI had given him. They said they remembered him from the string of armed robberies he had committed for them several years earlier and wanted him to bring them more stolen jewelry. Gerardi was going to slowly reestablish his relationships and get it all on tape. It was a good plan.

One night after reconnecting with his fences, Gerardi celebrated his freedom by inviting two escorts to a Manhattan hotel room for a party. When the women left that evening, Gerardi noticed that the remainder of the FBI's jewelry had also departed. Panicking, he chased them to the lobby, catching up as they stepped into a waiting limousine in front of the crowded hotel entrance. Grabbing the women and waving a gun, Gerardi piled into the rear of the limo, loudly demanding the return of his jewelry. Witnesses alerted the police. Gerardi ordered the terrified chauffeur to drive, and the limo led the NYPD on a wild chase through Manhattan, across sidewalks and the wrong way down one-way streets, until the cops finally cornered the vehicle and arrested Gerardi.

Incredibly, a New York state court released Gerardi on bail. He promptly called Agent Wynne to deliver the good news. He was still willing to testify against the fences, but would understand if, after the unfortunate kidnapping and limo chase situation, the FBI was no longer interested in using him as an undercover informant. He was correct.

Without the need to monitor any more meetings between Gerardi and the gangsters, the FBI arrested the fences and a trial date was set in Brooklyn federal court. After much debate, the prosecutors decided they could still use Gerardi as a witness because, as awful as he was, the tapes verified his relationship with the defendants, who clearly knew him and wanted his stolen goods. Defense lawyers could attack him on the witness stand, but every blow would bounce back on their clients.

But if he were to be a witness, the prosecutors needed to burn him and turn the tapes over to the defendants as part of the obligation to provide all evidence for the trial. They would know Gerardi had fingered them. The FBI concluded that would put Gerardi in danger and, as distasteful as he was, the government takes seriously its obligation to protect witnesses. Gerardi was not interested in WitSec, which was just as well because WitSec is all about disciplined adherence to the rules, something Gerardi had never demonstrated.

Instead, the FBI offered to pay Gerardi to relocate to Florida—where he had once lived—and to give him money for living expenses until he testified at trial. Without any federal involvement, New York had dismissed its charges after the escorts and limo driver refused to cooperate, so Gerardi was free to travel. The agents took him to the train station—his preferred mode of transportation—lectured him about not committing any crimes, including not possessing firearms, and urged him to just lay low until the trial, which was six months away. Enjoy the sun, lift weights.

Almost immediately, it went bad.

In Florida, Gerardi found himself at a Fort Lauderdale Holiday Inn, checking into room 225 as "Pablo Martinez." Two local FBI agents visited the next day to give him his first $500 in expense money. As they chatted with the huge man, they noticed the outline of a large-frame handgun in his pants' belt, silhouetted against his untucked Hawaiian print shirt. They left the hotel and called their New York colleagues to report the weapon. The next day, the US Attorney's office in Brooklyn convinced their Florida colleagues to obtain a warrant and

Gerardi was arrested for being a felon in possession of a gun. The New York agents also contacted the federal court in New Jersey to report a probation violation on his bank robbery conviction and seek a separate arrest warrant.

Gerardi saw the arrest as a betrayal, a sign that Wynne and the rest of the FBI didn't care that he was in danger and needed to protect himself. Up in New York, there was simply relief that he was off the street.

The relief lasted a couple hours. A federal judge in Fort Lauderdale dismissed the gun charge, concluding there was no probable cause because no actual gun had been found; agents had only seen what *appeared* to be a gun under Gerardi's shirt. She ordered him released. She also refused to hold him for the New Jersey federal probation violation, and merely directed him to report on his own to New Jersey.

So now he was out and angry and feeling betrayed. It went very bad. Over the next week, operating from room 225 at the Holiday Inn near the intersection of Powerline Road and Commercial Boulevard in Fort Lauderdale, Gerardi robbed three banks that he could almost see from his hotel. Donning a clown mask, carrying a .45 caliber semiautomatic pistol and a fake bomb, he plied his craft. As he walked from the third bank, a stack of bills preloaded with its own timed bomb of red dye—a "dye pack"—exploded, drenching the money in red ink.

When word of a giant bank robber in a mask reached the FBI, they immediately knew who the clown was. A SWAT team hit room 225, recovering the gun, the mask, money, and a lot of towels ruined by red ink. Gerardi was back in jail and stayed there this time—held pending trial for the bank robberies. For two years his case slowly made its way through the crowded courts of South Florida. While the case was still pending, he was transported to the District of New Jersey for a probation violation hearing and housed, for his safety, at MDC Brooklyn, where he made a collect call to his former handler.

◆

Squad supervisor Kennedy, who had not spoken or moved as Wynne recounted Gerardi's history, now blinked in an exaggerated way several times before saying, "So you're not making any of that up?"

"I wish I was, boss," he said, pointing to her computer. "It's all there in Sentinel if you want to read it. I spent six months answering Inspection Division questions about it."

She lowered her head, staring at the surface of her desk. "What. A. Clusterfuck. I've been around the block a few times before getting this chair, and *you*, my friend, are really lucky you still work here."

"Yup, I know that, which is why I hung up on the fucker a few minutes ago. We want no part of him."

Kennedy now looked to the corner and paused before turning back to Wynne. "I think that's right. Still, I gotta run this up the chain. Buchanan's too big a deal to shitcan this on my own authority."

Wynne looked slightly ill. "Oh, no worries," Kennedy said. "I'm sure it'll get shitcanned. I just think that decision should be made at a higher level. I'll let you know. Thanks for bringing it to me."

Wynne got up slowly and wandered back to his desk.

"So?" his partner asked.

"Gonna run it up the chain so she doesn't have to shitcan it personally, but thinks it should be shitcanned."

"See?" Francis said, smiling broadly. "That's Bu leadership at its best—achieve shitcanning while not being the actual disposer of the doo-doo. You made the right play, for sure."

CHAPTER TWENTY-FIVE

The US Attorney for the Eastern District of New York sat a mile and a half east of the US Attorney for the Southern District of New York, with most of that distance being the Brooklyn Bridge. It was all Southern District territory until 1865, when Congress created the Eastern District to serve the growing world across the forbidding East River from Manhattan, giving the new district the three faraway communities of Brooklyn, Queens, and Staten Island, and the farmlands of Long Island. But, of course, criminals didn't respect boundaries like that, especially after bridges, cars, and subways erased the distance. As a result, the two offices had cooperated—and fought—since the Brooklyn Bridge opened in 1883. And because many of the FBI's cases could be brought in either place, the New York office was not above playing the talented, aggressive siblings against each other, which only made the familial relationship more complicated.

"Their place looks old as dirt," Benny said, looking up at the facade of the 1892 old Post Office building on Cadman Plaza.

"At least they have a building," Nora replied, "and don't have to sleep in the FBI's spare bedroom like we do.

"Plus," she added, heading up the steps, "you'll be surprised how nice it is inside."

"And tell me again why we have to come over here?" Sean asked from behind.

"I told you—because Carmen asked us to. She says their US Attorney called and said they have something sensitive to share with us on Buchanan. So, like good neighbors, we cross the bridge to find out what might be important enough for their boss to call ours. Little mysterious for my blood, but here we are."

They pushed through the revolving door and began the process of putting belongings through the security screening.

"I've only been here one other time," Sean said, removing his belt. "Almost changed my life."

"Do tell," Nora responded as she pushed her bag into the X-ray machine.

"I made the mistake of applying to both districts at the same time when I was two years out of law school. Eastern called me first. It was just supposed to be a screening interview with some junior person, but during the half hour or whatever, the fricking US Attorney himself walks in, sits on the edge of the desk of the guy interviewing me, and starts looking at my résumé. Then he looks up, knocks on the desk, and offers me the job as an AUSA. I nearly shit."

They gathered their things on the far side of the checkpoint. "Smart move. So what'd you do?" Nora asked.

"Well, first, I panicked—a lot, obviously. I'm sure I turned all red and I stammered like a fool and told him that was awesome and I would get back to him as soon as possible. Then I called a friend who was already working at Southern to tell him what happened. He said, 'The pricks are trying to steal you. Stall them and let me see what I can do.'"

"And so how did you stall, exactly?"

"Well, I didn't answer their calls for a week, which was a starter. Then I told them I had some personal issues that I needed to handle and would get back to them when I could."

"How did I not know any of this?" Nora said. "I *interviewed* you."

"You did, as part of what I now know was a land-speed record for the SDNY process. But I didn't know whether they told interviewers my situation. Guess not. Anyhow, I got the job, blew EDNY off, and the rest is, well, the rest."

Benny had been listening and now laughed. "Good for us, but just think how much closer you'd be to your sad-sack apartment if you worked over here."

"And if I were here," Sean replied, "I would be upstairs knowing the mystery and waiting for you to come begging."

"Very funny," Nora said, turning for the elevator. "We aren't begging for anything; they asked to see us. Let's remember to be good neighbors, please."

◆

Nora was red in the face and nearly shouting. "You must be fucking kidding me! You've been running an *informant* at *our* defendant—who, I don't have to remind you, is a represented person who has a Sixth Amendment right not to deal with the kind of shit you've been doing. Of all the bullshit Eastern has pulled over the years, this has to take the cake."

Across the table, Nora's counterpart Lynne Regan—called the First Assistant US Attorney on this side of the Brooklyn Bridge—paused before answering and then spoke as if addressing a difficult relative at Thanksgiving dinner.

"Nora, look, you've known me a long time. I don't do cowboy stuff and I hate turf battles. That's not what this is. We approached this very carefully and we only did it because Main Justice asked us to. As I said, FBI headquarters took this to Criminal Division enforcement and operations at Main. And even *they* ran it up their chain. I think it went all the way to the Deputy Attorney General. So this is not some drunk dial. They thought this through in the usual DC way: meetings, memos, meetings about the memos—the whole nine yards before coming to us. And that's the important part for our relationship.

"They, not we—*they*—decided it was worth seeing what this informant had. They, not we, decided to set up a wall to protect your case from the legal issues. They decided to have our office run it on this side of the wall—because the MDC is here and because we had some prior contact with this Gerardi in the case against the fences—where we never used him, by the way. We didn't know a thing about the Buchanan case. And I should say right now that I think we handled it in a way where you won't have Sixth Amendment problems. And then *they* decided it was productive enough and important enough to your case that we should pass what we got over the wall to you, which is what we're doing today."

She waited a beat, looking from Nora to Sean and back before continuing. "Look, I'd be pissed too, if I found out stuff was going on with my case that I didn't know about. But if you take a minute, this was the right way to go. And now we're out. It's over to you, to handle as you want."

◆

Carmen had been silent during their briefing, but now looked across her desk at Nora and Sean and scrunched her face. "So the Bureau of Prisons puts this Gerardi—a violent career criminal who's a career informant *because* he's a violent career criminal—in with Buchanan. No prosecutor or FBI agent had any involvement in that placement?"

"Correct," Nora answered, "as far as we know. Just luck and stupidity. You may remember some years back the Bureau of Prisons put Jeffrey Epstein in with a quadruple murderer ex-cop, hoping, I guess, that the killer would keep Epstein alive."

"How'd that work out for them?" Benny asked from the couch.

"What's that old line?" Carmen answered. "Never attribute to malice that which is adequately explained by stupidity?"

"I gotta write that down," Benny said.

"Who says I don't add value?" Carmen replied with a smile before turning back to Nora. "So, Gerardi then reaches out to his old FBI handler, who wants no part of it."

"Check," Nora replied. "The agent actually hung up on him the first time, then told him NFW the second. We got it all on tape."

"But this still somehow makes its way to FBI HQ and then to Main Justice, where somebody decides it wouldn't hurt just to have a chat with Gerardi."

Jessica, sitting next to Benny on the couch, finally spoke. "It seems everybody at the Bu thought their *supervisor* should be the one to say this was a bad idea. So it got to the top and they decided to send it across Pennsylvania Avenue and have DOJ stop it. But somebody there thought it was worth a shot."

"Exactly," Nora said. "Lynne in Brooklyn said the thinking was, 'Important case, no harm in a conversation.'"

Carmen looked over at Jessica. "And they walled your squad off just like they did us."

"Yes," Jessica said. "First I heard of it was when Nora and Sean called me after the EDNY meet."

"So," Carmen continued, "because Jessica was out and Gerardi's handler was so done with this guy, they pulled a female agent from some white-collar squad and sent her in pretending to be a paralegal on his defense team."

"Correct."

"And she comes back with word that Buchanan and Gerardi have become buds and Buchanan has told Gerardi he absolutely knew all the victims in our indictment were going to be attacked. It's what he wanted, it's what he intended, although he never knew the particular attackers."

"That's right," Nora answered. "Gerardi basically wins our case for us, if he's telling the truth."

"And to see if he is, Justice gets the Eastern District involved to work with the FBI to put a bug—audio and video—in the cell. EDNY decides they don't need a warrant because the bug will only operate when Gerardi is present, making it a consensual monitoring."

"Correct," Sean answered. "They send Buchanan to the infirmary for a checkup and pull Gerardi out like he's meeting with his lawyers so they can secretly give him instructions to avoid a Sixth Amendment right-to-counsel problem. As you know, because Buchanan has a lawyer, the government can't directly or indirectly question him; Gerardi is limited to being a listening post. EDNY lawyers tell him what that means—that he absolutely cannot prompt Buchanan or nudge him in any way—and they have Gerardi sign a written acknowledgment and a consent to be recorded, and they send him back to the wired cell."

"And they wall us off in case Gerardi goes too far," Nora added. "That way, even if there's a constitutional violation, none of it splashes on us and jeopardizes the ongoing case. They can wait to see how the story ends before deciding whether to tell us."

"Okay," Carmen said. "And it must have a happy ending because they told us, right?"

"Well, maybe. First, yes, the tapes seem to be great. We haven't listened yet, but based on what we heard in Brooklyn a little while ago, Buchanan lays it out for Gerardi, without any apparent prompting. They're just lying in their bunks one night when Buchanan starts talking about feeling guilty that so many people got hurt and killed. In that context, he says exactly what Gerardi originally reported: I knew."

"So why the 'maybe'?"

"We have no idea what Gerardi might have said to him when they weren't in the wired cell. They didn't have much contact, but they could have spoken some other place and Buchanan might claim Gerardi pushed him *after* he started working for the government; if the judge buys that, all of this gets suppressed and maybe we also get sanctioned. And given Gerardi's sophistication as an elicitor of damaging statements, it's not a crazy thing to worry about."

"How do we deal with it?"

"Well, Benny had the idea to use BOP video surveillance and guard records to track the movements of the two of them during the period EDNY was running Gerardi. So we're gonna do that. We also have the FBI undercover—the 'paralegal'—who was meeting with him almost every day to debrief him on his contacts with Buchanan and to repeat the warnings. We'll talk to her and obviously prepare her to be a witness—for sure at a suppression hearing and maybe at trial."

CHAPTER TWENTY-SIX

The team was back in the war room. When Nora came rushing through the door, she caught the Nerf ball Benny threw at her, but rather than shoot it, she set it gently down on the table as she took her seat.

Benny made a face of mock disappointment. "Give the people what they want."

Nora ignored him. "Sorry to be late, guys. I hope I'm not screwing you up. It's harder than I thought to be the DUSA and a good trial team member."

"Worth it," Benny said, as Jessica and Sean nodded. "Plus we got an all-star," he said, pointing to a young woman at the table. "April Fugate, ace SDNY paralegal. Been here almost as long as I have. She'll be in charge of all the transcripts, discovery documents, and evidence exhibits. Everything, really."

"Oh, hey, April," Nora said with a smile. "So glad you're on the team. So where are we?"

Sean took that. "The FBI finished the draft transcripts for the cell convos between Gerardi and Buchanan. April is going through them now to finalize. We've also mapped the movements of the two of them for the days after Gerardi reached out to the FBI—from the moment he could conceivably be considered our agent. No evidence of contact outside their cell. And as you know, they pulled Gerardi right after the taped conversation; he's still up at Otisville. His Jersey lawyer doesn't love that, but, with traffic, it's not much difference from Newark. What else?"

"We've got no video or audio of Gerardi meeting with the FBI undercover," Benny said, "which we expected. Because she was pretending to be a member of his legal team, they were in the attorney conference rooms, which are not monitored. But we have her 302s, which she wrote after each meeting with him."

"How do you think she'll be as a witness?" Nora asked, looking between Jessica and Sean.

"I think she'll be okay," Sean said.

"I agree," Jessica added, "although, to be honest, she seems a bit off to me. No, maybe not *off*; naive or starstruck would be a better description. She's pretty new, New York is her first office, and she never worked anything besides bank fraud before this. She found this whole thing 'really cool'—her words. But I think she'll be okay. Her 302s of the meetings are well written and seem comprehensive."

"Okay, we'll need to be sure we prep her well, especially if this is her first dance. And when will we give Buchanan's team the discovery on all this?"

"Obviously they have all the discovery on the rest of the case already, including the Greenstone killing," Sean answered. "April will send them the Gerardi-related stuff . . ."

"Today or tomorrow," April said, "as soon as you sign off on the transcripts, which I just finished. And we've also got a lot of documents on Gerardi—guy's got more impeachment material than I've ever seen—which we usually wouldn't provide until closer to trial. You sure you want me to ship it all now?"

"Yeah," Nora said. "This is gonna be a shit show and we want Judge Newton to know we're going above and beyond here. No doubt there's going to be a suppression hearing and we don't want to be the cause of any delay."

"Got it," April answered. "So as soon as Sean signs off on the transcripts, it all goes."

"Sounds good," Nora replied. "And can I switch topics for a second? Where are we on tracking down Herb Cusak?"

"A work in progress," Jessica answered. "We've been going through his life—family, prior addresses, credit cards, phone records. We've got a better picture of his online history, but nothing on where he is. According to the doormen, he almost never left the apartment before they cleared out and there's been no sign of him since Becky was killed and Buchanan was arrested. His cell went dead and his family says they haven't heard from him, which apparently isn't unusual—they've been kind of estranged for years, except for his mother and she says he hasn't been in touch."

"Which we think is bullshit," Benny added.

"Right," Jessica continued. "He's not using any of his known devices, although we've seen one phone that may be a burner. It called his mother's house a couple of times, but it's almost never on, so we can't get a reliable location on it."

"So, bottom line," Benny said, "the dirtbag's either dead or gone really deep to hide. I know we've got a lot of pucks on the ice with the trial and whatnot, but I think we really need to find and squeeze Cusak, if he's still alive. I can't let go of the idea that he might be part of killin' Becky and the motherfucker's still out there."

"Squeeze him with what?" Nora asked.

Benny turned to look at Sean. "Has she not seen the kiddie porn?"

Sean reached behind him and picked up a file, but Nora held up her hand. "Spare me. Your words will do, and obliquely, please. I haven't had lunch."

He put the file on the table. "Sure. Bottom line is we got Herb doing all kinds of nastiness online involving kids. Pictures, chats, even ordering up some live sessions on the dark web. Bad, bad stuff, including—"

"Got it," Nora said quickly. "So maybe enough to hold life in prison over him. So how do we get close enough to squeeze?"

The team was quiet, shooting glances at each other.

"What?" Nora asked.

Benny pointed at Jessica, who grimaced before speaking. "Okay, and this is going to seem a little weird and aggressive, but we like it."

"Can't wait," Nora said.

"With a voice sample," Jessica explained, "our tech people can use AI to generate a message that sounds like a person. We have enough from an interview we did of Cusak's mother to generate a message from her to him. We're gonna leave it on the burner phone we think could be his. She'll tell him she's in real trouble, needs his help, and he has to come home to see her right away. She lives in Wilkes-Barre, Pennsylvania. About a two-and-a-half-hour drive from here."

"Two, if Benny's driving," Sean interjected.

"Right," Jessica continued. "We'll have a team set up on the house and grab him for the squeeze there. I mean, if you're good with it."

Nora grinned. "Honestly, I worried it was going to be something even more crazy. I'm good with that, although I'll never trust another voicemail from my mother. And because Main Justice may consider him a member of the media, we should get sign-off down there on this."

"You must be shittin' me," Benny said sharply.

Nora looked pained. "I shit you not. Anybody putting anything out on the internet falls within their definition of media, whether it's the *New York Times* or these sleazeballs. So we get sign-off. Which Sean will handle."

Sean nodded as Benny made grumbling sounds.

Jessica looked relieved. "Great. We'll move on it right away, as soon as Sean gives me the word."

"Okay, thanks," Nora said. "Let me know."

She turned to Benny. "Pucks on the ice, Mr. Rough? I had no idea you were a hockey person."

Benny smiled. "Beer and fighting? What's not to like?"

Nora shook her head. "Great description of the game. And speaking of fighting, you got time to join me on a call to your buddy Matty?"

CHAPTER TWENTY-SEVEN

Matthew Parker's voice was loud on the speakerphone. "You must be fucking kidding me! I know you're not a lawyer, Benny Boy, but the actual attorneys are gonna be in a heap of trouble for this. Running an informant in on an indicted defendant? You've haven't been able to do that since the sixties and I never—"

Benny interrupted. "Let me just alert you, Matty, that I'm in the presence of the Deputy United States Attorney, so don't be bad-mouthin' my attorneys."

"Hi, Nora," Parker said quietly.

"Hi, Matty."

"Seriously, Nora, what the fuck? This stuff has been verboten since TV was in black-and-white."

Nora shook her head and smiled at Benny, but spoke seriously into the speakerphone. "Depends upon what you mean by 'this stuff.' I agree that the Supreme Court held a long time ago that 'deliberate elicitation' of information by law enforcement from an indicted defendant about his case violates the Sixth Amendment's right to counsel."

"Okay then. Saved me the research. And we agree that you can't use an informant to do the deliberate eliciting either."

"Yes, I do," Nora said. "You can't do indirectly what you can't do directly. But the court has also said that it doesn't violate the Sixth

Amendment if the informant acts solely as a 'listening post,' where the government doesn't use him to prompt the defendant but only receives what the defendant voluntarily decides to say."

"Great, but it will not surprise you to learn that my client had all kinds of conversations about his case with your informant—who is a really bad guy, as I'm sure you know. And those conversations are a problem."

"Accepting what you say, Matty, the only relevant conversations between an informant and your client for Sixth Amendment purposes are the conversations that took place *after* the informant started acting as an agent for the government. And I think you'll see when you go through the discovery that there were no such conversations. The informant got instructions to do nothing but listen, and he followed them."

"I gotta tell you, Nora: It looks from the discovery material like you and my man Benny there had no role in this."

"That's right," Nora answered. "The Department of Justice walled us off and had EDNY run it with separate FBI people."

"Smart move on your part, I'll tell you, because this is the shit that gets your ticket pulled by the bar. I think they've handed you a flaming bag of crap."

"I actually don't think so, Matty. We didn't run it, but I think the people who did followed the rules. It's hard to thread a needle, but sometimes you actually get the thread through the little slit. I think they did here. But that's for the court to decide, if you move to suppress."

Parker laughed loudly. "Funny. You know I have to move to suppress this and to dismiss the indictment."

Nora paused before answering. "I know you have to zealously represent your client. See you in court, as they say."

"And maybe worst of all, I now have to explain all this to Ms. Pond, who is—and how do I put this delicately?—not the deepest body of water I have encountered."

"Very delicate, Matty," Nora said. "So she's staying on the case?"

"Yeah, the client wants her—in more ways than one—and he wants to waive any conflict from her concurrent prosecution for being an idiot. But he also wants me to be lead counsel because it seems love is not entirely blind to incompetence."

"Okay, we'll send over a sample conflict waiver colloquy the judge can use."

"Appreciate you, Nora," Parker said, then added, "Benny, still there?"

"Hanging on your every word, as usual," Benny answered.

"Fuck you."

"Fuck you too," Benny answered smiling. "Say hello home."

"You too. Bye."

Nora pressed the button to disconnect and began walking to the door, before turning to look at Benny. "You two have the strangest relationship."

"Love is like that," Benny said. "When you've been through it with somebody, like Matty and I have, the connection lasts forever. You and I'll be cursing each other someday too."

"Not if you're my stepdad," Nora replied with a smile. "I have too much respect for parents."

Benny shook his head. "You're a bad person, Nora Carleton."

Nora continued through the doorway, calling back, "And you, my friend, are a *good* person."

"Let's not start that," Benny shouted after her.

CHAPTER TWENTY-EIGHT

Nora had watched the video twenty times. In clear color, Buchanan could be seen lying on his back, speaking as he looked up at the cell's ceiling. "It wasn't always my idea to focus on a particular person, you see, but once I focused, I *focused*, if you take my meaning. I have built up a relationship with my followers over many years. They trust me and I trust them. These are people who feel, viscerally, the danger to our country from the godless, anti-family, globalist elites taking over this nation. And they are the kind of people who *act*, who *do something* in the face of danger. We've always been saved by brave people like them. I'm not brave, you see. I'm not tough, like you."

"You're tougher than you know, Sam," came Gerardi's gravelly voice across the little room.

"Well, you're very kind, Michael. But as I've said, I knew what my people would do once I focused on someone. I knew what would happen. The truth is I was focusing *because* I wanted it to happen, I was *committed* to having it happen. The tree of liberty must be refreshed from time to time with the blood of patriots and tyrants, as Jefferson said. And I confess that the initial guilt I felt was narrow. I felt badly that people who had done a noble deed because I asked them to refresh that tree were going to be punished, go to jail, have their lives turned upside down. They are the true heroes who, like me, are also being unfairly punished. I feel guilty because they are paying a high price for their heroism."

"Of course," Gerardi replied.

"Nights in here have broadened that guilt, as you know. I see the faces of the dead and injured. Yes, they were bad people, but they were still *people,* with lives and loved ones of their own. And I took those lives or at least ruined those lives. That's hard and, to be honest, my reaction surprises me a bit. I wonder if the farmers who shot redcoats at the North Bridge felt this pain, even though theirs was a noble cause as well."

He rolled on his side to face Gerardi, who was lying on his own bed platform across the small room. "I'm guessing in your career outside the law you have experienced this same unexpected sense of guilt from the pain and loss you inflicted on others."

Gerardi didn't answer, but drew his mouth into a line and waved the back of his hand at his cellmate.

Buchanan rolled onto his back and continued talking. "No matter, I know you're a private man. For me, what I did haunts me. Especially the young woman who worked for me, who attacked me on the air. That's the one I didn't expect, the one that surprised me. I didn't realize my own power with my people and that it could happen so quickly."

Nora lifted the remote control and stopped the video. She looked around the war room. "Has this thing changed how any of you think about including Becky's killing?"

"No," Sean said. "If anything, this, plus Benny seeing him upset the day she was killed, sure makes it seem as if he *didn't* want that one to happen."

"Agree," Benny added. "There's somethin' squirrelly going on with the Becky thing. He has no idea he's being overheard at the MDC, or he wouldn't be saying all that other shit, so I believe he didn't know it was coming and didn't want to make it happen."

Nora pointed at Jessica, who nodded. "I agree with all of that," she said. "And I keep coming back to something Becky said on the air right at the end of her last show. She said Buchanan went after Greenstone 'because they wanted you to.' What does that mean and who's 'they'?"

"I don't know," Nora replied before turning to Sean. "You think there's anything exculpatory about the Becky situation, even though we haven't charged it?"

He shook his head quickly. "No, but I'm glad we didn't, because this tape makes it weird in ways I can't fully explain. But as for whether anything about it tends to help Buchanan—that fucker knows everything we do about it, and probably a lot more. If he can figure out how any of this helps him, good for him. I can't."

"Okay," Nora said. She stood and walked to the whiteboard, which displayed pictures of key figures in the case. She tapped on one photo. "Now let's talk about Gerardi for a minute. Benny and I are going to drive up to Otisville to see him tomorrow. Honestly I would rather go see the Grand Canyon in the dark."

April made a confused face, but Benny leaned toward her, whispering, "Long story; fill you in later."

"I'm sure there are complex views about this in the Bureau," Nora continued, looking at Jessica. "I mean, his former handling agent didn't even want to speak to him. What are we supposed to make of that?"

"I talked to Agent Wynne," Jessica said. "Good guy—and, by the way, he did agree to meet you there tomorrow. He says there's good news and a whole lot of bad news. I'll start with the bad: Gerardi is a violent and bad guy, who has committed a lot of crimes and found ways to get close to other bad guys and get information he can use to go free. He looks like a monster from the Marvel Universe or something, but he's actually smooth and manipulative as hell and also a great liar."

Nora laughed and crossed her arms. "Can't wait for the good news."

"The good news," Jessica continued, "is that Wynne said Gerardi never lied *to him*. Whatever he said always checked out. And Gerardi always admitted when he'd gone sideways, like with kidnapping the women and the limo driver."

Nora squinted. "So *I guess* that's good news? Holy shit, *this* is our witness?"

Sean looked up at her. "And where are we with the cooperation agreement?"

"His lawyer says Gerardi won't sign it. Said it's a nonstarter because we require cooperators to admit to every bad thing they've ever done and Gerardi is not interested in giving us a list and he's especially not interested in confessing to the Florida bank robberies while that case is still pending."

"And so what happens when he's asked about it at our trial?" Sean asked.

"I guess he takes the Fifth and we run the risk Judge Newton strikes his testimony on grounds that he can't be sufficiently impeached. Or maybe we immunize him."

Sean chuckled. "All the shit that guy's done, it would seem to be enough impeachment for one lifetime. I think we'll be okay with the judge. So what's he want from us after his service as our witness?"

"He just wants us to promise to bring his cooperation to the attention of any sentencing judge in any case he requests it."

"Seems like a small thing," Sean said.

Nora stared at the wall and didn't reply.

"You okay?" he asked.

Nora shook her head, as if waking from a dream. "Yeah, sorry, it *is* a small thing, but the big thing is how this office—how *we*, honestly—feel about using someone like this as a witness. Our witnesses don't take the Fifth. A literal deal with the devil."

"To get a bigger devil," Benny said.

"I suppose," Nora answered quietly. "I really need to think on it."

◆

It was a two-hour drive to the Federal Correctional Institution at Otisville, New York, a tiny village tucked in the northwestern hills of rural Orange County, one of the eight counties making up the Southern District of New York. Benny drove while Nora reviewed Gerardi's extensive record on her laptop.

"Every time I come up this way, I remember why so many cops and firefighters live here," he said, turning his head to admire the tree-covered hills on both sides of the road.

"Because they can afford a tiny house here?" Nora said without looking up.

"I guess that too, but I was gonna say because it's so beautiful and so far from the suck of the city."

She looked up. "Aren't you the one who has taught me—and my child—that the suck—your word—is everywhere?"

Benny nodded and made a clicking sound before answering. "I am."

"And aren't we headed to a place that is one mile from where the ex-cop they once stuck in with Jeffrey Epstein buried four people he killed?"

"Yeah, sorry, it's a cesspool out here. Sometimes trees fool me. I may be losin' my edge. Please don't tell Sophie I said someplace is nice and safe."

"Secret is safe with me," Nora answered drily. "And speaking of your edge, do you think we should have brought more people, given Gerardi's history?"

"If we were gonna uncuff him, sure, but I ain't. Guy's huge and I don't need the problem. He stays cuffed."

"Fine by me."

"Plus, Wynne's gonna be there."

"Yeah, that's right, and we'll see which way that cuts. I know Jessica's team thought it would ease the conversation, but I'm not so sure."

◆

Nora had been warned, but she was still distracted by the tiny head. And the huge knuckles, which nobody had mentioned. But as the guard guided the front-cuffed prisoner to the metal table she couldn't stop looking at the prominent bumps crowning his gigantic paws. *Like boulders at Joshua Tree,* she thought.

Gerardi's eyes moved across Nora and Benny and stopped at Special Agent Wynne.

"Carl," he said flatly.

"Mike," Wynne said.

Nora was immediately reminded of a reality TV dating show, where producers throw two former contestants back together at some beach resort to spice things up.

"You hung up on me," Gerardi said.

"You nearly got me fired," Wynne replied.

"I always told you the truth."

"Same, which is why I didn't take your call and give you some kind of bullshit song and dance."

Nora cleared her throat. "Uh, Mr. Gerardi, I just want to confirm what your lawyer said: that you don't wish your attorney to be present and you don't want to enter into any kind of proffer agreement to cover our conversation today."

Gerardi talked like he was hiding a collection of metal BBs in his mouth but also spoke with an odd formality, using big words—the product of years of prison reading and trying to impress fellow inmates. "Affirmative. I've been around the legal process quite a bit. I know what I'm willing to talk about here today and none of it requires my attorney's presence or any kind of agreement. And let me just get to the heart of the matter, because I know what the issue is.

"When I ended up housed with Buchanan, it surprised me, but I also saw it as an opportunity. I remember reading about the case when he was first charged. I immediately went to the MDC library and read his indictment online and I also read what the judge said about the apparent weaknesses he perceived in the case. With that context, I could see the evidentiary value in potential expressions of personal responsibility. So I built a relationship with the individual. Over the years, I've been in a lot of therapy. I put that to use—I built trust, I listened, I reflected, I affirmed, I used unconditional positive regard. And it paid off. He started talking about his case, expressing remorse. I immediately called Carl here, and"—he made a sour face—"we know how that turned out."

"Seriously?" Wynne said loudly. "You lose thousands of dollars' worth of our jewelry, pull that shit with the hookers and limo, and I *still* look out for you, get you to Florida like you wanted. And you do what? Sunbathe? No, you rob fucking banks with a gun and bomb. Jesus, Mike."

"There was no real bomb, Carl. And you're leaving out a critical piece of causation—that you had me arrested for a gun."

"Because you *had* a fucking gun, Mike, as a convicted felon twenty fucking times over."

"Twelve. And nobody saw a gun, as the judge said when she released me."

"Christ," Benny said, swiveling his head between the two men. "Shame it didn't work out for you two, but at least there're no children to fight over. C'mon, let's focus on Ms. Carleton's questions. We don't care about any of that history right now."

Gerardi nodded. "Fine. After he hung up, I thought that was it, that this information was, unfortunately, not going to be valuable to the government, or to me. But then a few days later I got pulled to meet at MDC with an agent pretending to be a paralegal for my lawyers. I told her what I'd heard and she told me not to talk to Buchanan about his case anymore. So I didn't. Then I met with prosecutors, from Brooklyn I believe, who told me I can help, but only if I don't say anything, just listen. They used the term 'listening post.' I agreed. They put the instructions in writing. I signed. I went about my business, following the instructions, and meeting with the undercover agent every day. Nice person, by the way. As instructed, I didn't engage Buchanan about the case. A few days later, he just starts letting his guilt out again. I figured you folks recorded it, because I was pulled out and sent up here. End of story."

◆

After two hours, Nora looked up from her notes. "Mr. Gerardi—"

"Please, Mike," Gerardi interrupted.

I can actually feel the charm. Amazing. "No," she said, "and I don't mean to be rude, but I think it's important to keep our relationship entirely professional."

"Suit yourself," Gerardi said. "Just trying to be polite."

"Again, I appreciate that, but—"

"I get it. It's important not to get too close to a lowlife like me."

He wants me to explain why he's not a bad guy. He really is good. "It's important that prosecutors and witnesses maintain a professional relationship at all times. It's never a commentary on anyone, just a good practice."

"I appreciate you explaining it. Most people don't care enough to take the time. And I didn't mean to come across rude or unprofessional"

Nope, not being drawn in. I'm not in the unconditional-positive-regard business. "I'm going to try to do the suppression hearing without using you as a witness, but I'm certain you'll be needed for the trial, which will come right after that. The marshals will move you closer to court at the appropriate time and keep you in a WitSec facility. We'll meet again there before you testify."

"I'm grateful for the accommodation with WitSec," Gerardi replied. "I recognize I'm not a candidate, for reasons that are all my fault, but I'm grateful. And I appreciate the transparency. Again, most prosecutors don't take the time."

Nope, not falling for it. "Right. Be well until we meet again."

CHAPTER TWENTY-NINE

"What's wrong with my beloved deputy?" Carmen asked, looking up from her computer.

"I'm worried I'm losing track of what team I'm on," Nora answered quietly.

"Oh-kay," Carmen replied, drawing out the word as she came around from behind the desk and walked to the door, which she quietly pulled shut. "I still don't have brown liquor and a cocktail cart, you know."

Nora smiled weakly. "Ongoing leadership failure."

"But, seriously," Carmen said, "what's wrong?"

"This Gerardi is a seriously bad guy. I'm just worried we aren't doing the right thing using him."

Carmen tilted her head slightly. "Is he telling the truth about Buchanan?"

"For sure about the conversation in the cell, because we have it all on tape. God knows what kind of conversations they had before the Eastern District got involved."

"I thought you told me it really doesn't matter because he wasn't working for Uncle Sam then."

Nora grimaced. "No, that's right, although that requires us to slice the onion pretty thinly—because he knew if he got something good he could sell it to us. But whatever he said to get Buchanan to open up, there's no doubt we got the real Buchanan on tape."

"So it's something else then."

Nora was silent for a long time before answering. "Yeah, I think it's just that I feel icky using someone like Gerardi. I have a pretty good sense of how victims of violent crime or kidnapping feel, believe me. TV makes it seem like a flu you get over, but I know there are dozens of people who will never forget the day they met Gerardi and his gun and mask and whatever. I think we diminish ourselves by sponsoring his testimony, especially because he's been able to traumatize so many people simply because he knows how to play the system."

Carmen looked pained. "*Do* we diminish ourselves, though? Isn't our job to use lawfully obtained evidence to try to hold other bad people accountable? Sam Buchanan is responsible for the death or wounding of a bunch of people—and, honestly, the poisoning of our public square, although that's not a crime and I won't say that outside this room. You told me you think there's a good chance he walks without this Gerardi piece. Would we really feel better about ourselves if we passed on Gerardi and put Buchanan back on the streets and airwaves? I sure wouldn't."

Nora exhaled. "I suppose it's the combination of an aggressive legal argument and the awfulness of Gerardi. I have to ask myself, is there anybody I wouldn't use? Would I use Mussolini to get Hitler?"

"I sure as hell would. And the benefit Mussolini got from it would be up to a judge who sees the full picture. Isn't that how it's supposed to work?"

Nora shook her head. "I guess. It's just tough to be in the middle of that trade. I can't shake the feeling that Gerardi has been able to get out so many times by jacking people up to want to kill witnesses or cops or who-knows-else and then getting it on tape. Whole thing makes me feel like I should be wearing a hazmat suit."

"But that's not *this* case, right? Buchanan is talking about things he did *before* he met Gerardi. Maybe Gerardi got him talking about them, but no way Gerardi created the crimes."

Nora made a sucking sound in the corner of her mouth. "I suppose so."

Carmen stared at her. "Let me ask you a hard question: Is it the office you're worried about or yourself?"

Nora looked to the window before answering. "Both, I think, although maybe more about me than I'd like to admit. I just feel myself compromising because Gerardi is so valuable. We always insist our cooperators fully debrief and sign a cooperation agreement. Except here. We never do an initial meeting with a represented witness without their lawyer. Except here. We don't give somebody WitSec protection unless they go through the process to actually join WitSec, with all that brings. Except here, where we'll ask the marshals to protect him during trial. I worry all the exceptions are swallowing the rules."

Nora put her forearms on her thighs and leaned forward to look at the floor between her feet. "And, apart from me, I also worry that at some point a juror might be revolted by the whole thing and say, 'A plague on both your houses,' and refuse to convict."

"Ah, c'mon," Carmen said loudly, "where the defendant is a murderer like Buchanan? Honestly, Nora, I admire your scruples but I don't see a jury issue. You're not going to hug Gerardi; you're going to put on your big-girl pants and play the tape. That's it."

Nora sat up straight. "My big-girl pants? That seems kinda harsh."

"Yeah, I'm sorry I said it. I just worry you're overthinking this. You're a good person, dealing with a bad person to get a worse person. You're doing the right thing."

Nora pushed tiredly to her feet and walked to the door. "I sure hope so. Now I'm going to go hug Sophie."

CHAPTER THIRTY

I'm home!" Nora shouted as she came through the apartment door, dropping her keys on the little hallway table. When there was no reply, she added, "From saving America!" Silence. "Wow," she mumbled, "let's try to control our excitement about Mom being home."

In the kitchen, she found her mother wearing earbuds and cutting vegetables. When Nora waved, Teresa reached and tapped pause on her phone screen with a clean pinky finger. "Sorry," she said, "listening to this podcast called *Heavyweight* about people with unanswered questions that have come to dominate their lives, and then this show helps them find closure. I cry every time."

"Nice situational awareness, Ma," Nora said, "Maybe keep just one earbud in? I could've killed you. *Then* there'd be unanswered questions."

Teresa narrowed her eyes. "I'm in our kitchen, in our locked apartment, dear. I don't need my 'head on a swivel' or whatever it is you say."

"Fair enough," Nora replied, leaning over to hug her. "Just so long as it's on a swivel everywhere else. And so what unanswered question has dominated your life?"

"None, really," Teresa said. "This is about other people's questions. Although I suppose I'd love to understand how some people we've known could do bad things while pretending to be good."

"A question for which there is never a good answer," Nora replied, pulling a seltzer water from the fridge. "And why didn't my beloved daughter rush to hug her mother?"

Teresa gestured with her head. "She's in her room doing homework, probably with her earphones on as well. But she seemed grumpy coming home today. Quieter than usual. You might want to interrogate her a bit, maybe?"

"On it," Nora called, striding down the short hallway that led to their three bedrooms. She stopped and rapped gently on Sophie's door, gradually increasing the power of the knock until she heard Sophie call, "Come in!"

Sophie was facing away from the door and didn't look up from her desk. "It's your home too, and . . ."

"Yes, it is," Nora responded, crossing the room to Sophie's desk, "but I want us all to get used to you having space with a reasonable expectation of privacy." She kissed the top of her daughter's head and wrapped her in a bear hug from behind as she added in a deep voice, "Of course, I can get a warrant to search the place any time I want."

"Stop," Sophie answered in a slightly whiny tone.

Nora let go. "Hey, Bug. It's me. What's wrong?"

Sophie dropped her pen and pushed back from the desk as Nora sat on the edge of the bed. "Sorry, Mom. I just had a crappy day."

"Oh, I'm sorry. Who should we have Benny beat up?"

Sophie finally smiled. "Actually, I could give him a name. Audra Cofsky. If Benny needs more details, let me know."

Nora smiled gently. "What did Audra Cofsky—whom nobody is going to beat up, by the way; I was joking—do to my beloved daughter?"

"She said you were a 'taker.'"

"Well, I guess I could be," Nora said. "Should I be? Is that bad or good?"

"She told the class—the whole class—that there are two kinds of people in the world, takers and makers. Makers get money by creating things. Takers get money by living off the moneymakers who have to pay taxes. She pointed at me and said that my mother worked for the government and so she was a taker."

"And Audra's parents, I'm guessing . . ."

"Makers. Well, her dad. I don't know what her mom does."

"And so Mr. Cofsky is a farmer or a blacksmith?"

Sophie narrowed her eyes. "No, why do you ask that? He works for a hedge fund, Audra says, and 'creates value' or whatever."

Nora nodded. "I ask because only people who actually make stuff are 'makers' in my book. Mr. Cofsky is probably a fine person, but what he *makes* is money, by taking other people's money and investing it in companies where people actually make stuff: shoe companies, car companies, software companies. Mr. Cofsky's work may be valuable, but I'm not buying the labels."

"So are you a taker?"

"Maybe," Nora answered, "in the sense that people like me or Benny don't make a product and sell it. Although in a sense we do, I suppose, which is why those labels make no sense. We make public safety by going after bad guys and we get paid by the government for doing that."

When Sophie didn't answer, Nora added, "This stuff about trying to divide humans is a bad business, baby girl. We're all people, or we should be, who contribute to society and who benefit from being part of society. When Mr. Cofsky and I are old, I'm guessing we'll both take the Social Security checks the government sends us. We both benefit from the men and women willing to join the military and protect this country, all of whom are takers in his estimation, I suppose. And we both want the takers in the fire department to come when we call. But, believe it or not, I also appreciate the way his investing helps make financial markets healthier and that his taxes help pay my salary, but, by the way, I also pay taxes every year."

Sophie was quiet for several long beats before she nodded. "That makes sense. So we can't beat up Audra?"

"We cannot," Nora said softly. "In fact, we should have some empathy for Audra because I bet she has to deal with some stuff at home. When you hear people dividing the world into groups—with themselves of course in the good group—usually it's only one of two things happening: Either the person is afraid of something and being in the good group helps them feel more safe, or the person feels guilty about their own good fortune and so wants to make it about something more than luck. I saw this when I worked in Westport. It's hard for most people to recognize that they have a lot of money, at least in part, because they were in the right place at the right time, or had the right parents or mentors, or looked or sounded the right way, or so many other things that are accidents. Some of them deal with it by living a life of gratitude and humility while trying to help people who are less fortunate. But a lot of them deal with that by creating groups like this takers and makers thing. It helps them feel better about themselves and better than the groups they create. So just be kind to Audra; she's fighting battles we can only imagine."

Sophie grinned. "You okay if I use some of this at school?"

Nora smiled broadly. "Of course. We takers are givers too."

"And it's hard to hate up close. Only heard that about a thousand times in my childhood."

Nora got up and hugged Sophie, whispering, "And you shall continue hearing it, my dear. I'm proud of you, Bug."

"Me you too," Sophie said. "You're a good mom."

Nora released the hug, slipping her hands to briefly hold Sophie's face. "And you're a good daughter. No doubt we're in the good group there. All the rest of them are bad."

"Mom!" Sophie laughed. "What happened to—"

"Kidding, kidding," Nora laughed, walking to the door. "Nana will have the food ready soon. See if you can finish your homework so after dinner we can watch whatever takers watch on Netflix."

◆

Back in the kitchen, Teresa was pan-roasting the vegetables on the stovetop but still heard Nora's sigh over the sizzling olive oil.

"How's our adolescent?" Teresa asked over her shoulder.

Nora reached around her mother and plucked a green pepper from the pan. "Learning about human tribes, and I don't mean some group in the Amazon. I'm talking right here in the jungle of the Upper East Side. Some pain-in-the-ass rich kid in her class spouting about makers and takers and pointing at Sophie because her mother is—"

"Famously a taker."

"Right, and her finance-bro dad—"

"Obviously a maker."

"No doubt," Nora said, smiling at their banter. "I know people have to have their tribes, but I wish they could have them in a way that doesn't put others down."

"Tricky," Teresa answered, reaching to adjust the flame under the boiling water pot before lifting a pasta claw and gesturing with it. "A lot of tribes form *for the purpose* of putting people down, or at least keeping themselves up, especially when things are changing. Change scares people."

"Yes it does, Ma. And it makes those scared people vulnerable to someone who knows how to play on their fears. And then innocent people get hurt. Not to make it all about me, but that's what the Buchanan case is all about."

Teresa set the claw onto the spoon rest and turned to her daughter. "I think we need to make *more* things about you. I worry this case is keeping you from seeing Demi."

Nora chuckled. "I was wondering how we would get from tribal political violence to my love life. And, boom, you just did it, without even using your turn signal."

"Thank you for recognizing my move," Teresa replied. "And not a bad deflection by you, which I will now ignore. So where are we on the love front?"

Nora shook her head, smiling. "She's amazing, Mom, but you're right that we don't get to spend enough time together. This could be *the one*, but I don't know. I can't say yet. It's not early, but it's still *kind of* too early, if you know what I mean."

"I *do* know what you mean," Teresa said, turning back to the cooking. "I guess queer people are no different from straight people in that way. Though I continue to struggle to apply the word *queer* to my beautiful, amazing daughter."

"Doesn't mean what it did when you were a kid, Ma."

"So you've told me. Still, it has a negative association in my memory that makes me flinch. But as Benny would say, another growth opportunity."

The kitchen was quiet for a beat before Nora spoke. "And speaking of Benny, and love, where *are* you two? What are his intentions—and yours?"

Teresa turned her head and shouted, "Dinner time! Come on, Sophie. Food's ready."

"Ma!" Nora protested. "What's going on with you two? How serious are you guys?

Teresa smiled. "All's well, but I'm avoiding your questions for now. Grab that strainer, will you?"

CHAPTER THIRTY-ONE

Judge Donovan Newton looked silly with big black earphones clamped to the sides of his head. Glancing up at him from the government's table, Nora imagined the pincer arm of an alien spaceship had grabbed hold and was about to retrieve him as a sample earthling. But he didn't see Nora's small smile because he was studying the transcript while Sam Buchanan's voice spoke in his ears.

Benny was in his usual seat at the end of the prosecution table, sitting facing backward—as he always did—to watch the defendant and the audience. "Makes no sense to turn my back on people who might do bad things," he once explained to Nora. The courtroom was crowded but quiet because the judge had ordered all external monitors turned off, ruling that the potential prejudice to the jury pool from this evidence outweighed the press interest in reporting just what Buchanan said while staring at the MDC ceiling. If the judge found the government had violated the defendant's right to counsel by using Gerardi, the tapes would be suppressed and nobody would ever hear them and nor should they, he held. And if the government won the motion, the tapes would be played in open court at trial within days and the public would know. So the motions by various media organizations were denied.

The judge looked up when the conversation ended. Reaching a hand to each side of his head, he removed the spaceship probe and dropped it on the desk in front of him. "Well, Ms. Carleton, I can certainly see why government counsel has a keen interest in using this evidence. It addresses what the court itself noted during bail proceedings was the apparent weakness in your case. But the usefulness of the tape is not the issue, as the court understands it; the issue is whether Mr. Gerardi engaged in any activity that would qualify as 'deliberate elicitation' and whether any such elicitation is attributable to the government."

Nora stood. "That's correct, Your Honor. And—"

"I'm sorry to interrupt learned counsel," the judge said, "but I should have said, for the record, that I perceive no elicitation in the conversation I just listened to. In fact, I heard almost nothing from Mr. Gerardi, except the occasional word of affirmation or understanding—*uh-huh, sure, okay*—words to that effect. And in one place, the reassurance that *you're tougher than you know.*"

"That's correct, Your Honor, and I don't understand Mr. Parker to be arguing that there was elicitation in this conversation. He can speak for himself, but I believe his motion to suppress is predicated on his belief that the contact between Gerardi and the defendant *before* the government's involvement constituted the elicitation and that the unique status of Mr. Gerardi's historical relationship with the FBI means that it should be considered government conduct in violation of the Sixth Amendment."

Parker popped up from the defense table, where he was seated on one side of his client, with Riley Pond on the other. "Beautifully said by Ms. Carleton, Your Honor. Should have asked her to help write my brief."

Judge Newton moved his mouth to a position that was either a partial smile or a reflection of some pain he was experiencing. "I should note, because the court of appeals is often unable to discern and appreciate humor in the lower courts, that Mr. Parker is being facetious; his brief is excellent, as are all the briefs in connection with this motion. Please proceed, Ms. Carleton."

"Thank you, Your Honor. And while we're on it, I just want to confirm that Mr. Parker is stipulating that there is no evidence of any other conversation between Mr. Gerardi and the defendant *after* the government met with Gerardi and decided that he would serve as a listening post."

Parker stood again. "That's right, Judge. We've been through all the discovery and agree there's no evidence they chatted between the informant's first meeting with the government at the MDC and the taped conversation you just listened to."

"Thank you, Mr. Parker. Having quality counsel certainly allows the court to focus on the issues that matter. Although I should ask whether your client claims there *were* such conversations and they are simply not reflected in any of the material you received from the government, or whether your client agrees there were, in fact, no such conversations."

Parker grimaced. "Judge, I—"

The judge cut him off. "I see why counsel is manifesting mild discomfort with the court's inquiry. It is withdrawn. Your client has raised a colorable basis for a motion to suppress and has no obligation to say or do anything at this stage of the proceedings, and the court regrets asking the question. It falls to the government to demonstrate that its conduct was consistent with the law."

"Thank you, Your Honor," Parker said as he sat.

"Please call your first witness, Ms. Carleton."

"Yes, Your Honor. The government calls—"

"Again, Ms. Carleton, the court apologizes for interrupting, but I now realize there is one more matter where it would benefit the court to have clarity before the presentation of evidence. Does the government concede that, were Mr. Gerardi deemed a government agent *before* he met with representatives from the Eastern District of New York—a fine office, by the way, with a well-deserved reputation for excellence—that the conversation I just listened to would have to be suppressed?"

"We do, Your Honor. As you will hear from testimony this morning, Gerardi had a variety of conversations with the defendant prior to his initial effort to contact the FBI. For example, he asked him about his case and the nature of the evidence against him. Were he an agent of the government at that time, the Sixth Amendment would forbid those conversations. As Your Honor knows, the most an informant can do on behalf of the prosecutors or investigators is *listen* to a represented defendant, which is what Gerardi is doing in the tape you just heard. But it will very much be the government's contention that Gerardi was *not* working for the government until he met with the Eastern District and acknowledged the instructions they gave him."

"Thank you, counsel. Again, it is a pleasure to have this important matter litigated on both sides consistent with the highest traditions of this district, our nation's so-called mother court. Proceed."

"The government calls Special Agent Carl P. Wynne," Nora said, but paused as a deputy marshal leaned close to whisper to her.

Nora listened, nodded, and then spoke. "Your Honor, before we begin with the witness, could I be heard at sidebar with defense counsel?"

Judge Newton squinted. "Sidebar? But we have no jury."

"Yes, Judge," Nora answered, gesturing with her head to the crowded courtroom benches behind her, "but it's a matter of some sensitivity."

"Very well," the judge answered. "Briefly."

Nora and Sean joined Parker and Pond and the court stenographer at the side of the judge's bench.

"Judge, this is awkward," Nora whispered, "but the marshals have brought to my attention that the defendant has been rubbing his left leg against Ms. Pond's right throughout the hearing today and dropping his hand down to touch her thighs. They brought it to my attention in the hopes we could resolve it without them needing to take action."

Parker whipped his head to look at his cocounsel. "Seriously?"

Pond blushed. "Mr. Buchanan is a man of passion, Judge."

"Well, Ms. Pond," the judge said, "he is about to be a man of binding leather constraints and you are about to be out of this case if it happens again."

"Yes, sir," she answered.

The judge's face reddened as he continued in a whisper. "And I very much regret having to make this inquiry, but to ensure you are complying with the New York bar rules governing relationships between lawyers and clients, I'd like your representation on the record that whatever the nature of your relationship with Mr. Buchanan, it predates this litigation."

"It does, Your Honor."

"Very well," the judge answered, turning to look at Parker. "And, although I see no ethical issue, I expect learned counsel to assist the court in this matter in preserving decorum by changing seats and instructing your client."

Parker was shaking his head *no*, but said, "Yes, Judge. I will sit between my client and Ms. Pond, but I have to tell you—anybody rubs my thigh and we're going to have a problem."

Judge Newton tilted his head and narrowed his eyes in confusion. But before he could speak, Nora cut in. "That should handle it, Your Honor. Thank you for allowing us to resolve this quietly."

"I appreciate counsel," the judge said. "We will proceed with the witness."

Carl Wynne told the sordid story of Mike Gerardi's career as a criminal and an informant, including the fact that he was closed as a confidential human source in the FBI's records shortly after his arrest for the three Florida bank robberies. Wynne recounted being ordered to visit Gerardi at the federal detention center in Miami to inform him that the relationship was over.

"How did he react?" Nora asked.

"Not much at all, that I recall," Wynne answered. "He'd been around long enough to know it had to happen."

Riley Pond jumped up from her new seat on the other side of Parker. "Objection to testimony about Gerardi's state of mind."

Judge Norman shook his head slightly and began to say something, but Matthew Parker interrupted from his seat, speaking with his head turned slightly toward his cocounsel standing next to his chair. "The objection is withdrawn, Judge. *Some* members of this trial team are apparently unaware of Rule 104(a), under which the rules of evidence do not apply to a suppression hearing, except for legal privileges, which are not relevant here."

"Learned counsel is correct," the judge replied, beaming at Parker. "Please proceed, Ms. Carleton."

"And what was the next contact between the FBI and Mr. Gerardi?" Nora asked.

"There are no contacts reflected in our records until the collect call from the MDC on a recorded line about the Buchanan case."

After Wynne described the two calls, Nora asked, "And why did you hang up?"

"Because I wanted nothing to do with him. Still don't."

"And why is that?"

"What's that expression? There's no education in the second kick of a mule? The whole Florida gun and bank robberies thing was a difficult time for me professionally. And it's a miracle nobody was killed. To put it mildly, I wasn't excited about getting back involved with Gerardi."

Wynne turned to look at the judge. "Honestly, I didn't care what he was offering this time. I'd had enough. Others ended up feeling differently, Your Honor, but that's where I was. Still am, honestly."

Judge Newton looked puzzled. "Let me ask you this, Agent Wynne: Is that because of concerns about the trustworthiness of this individual?"

"No, Judge. His stuff always checked out. I mean, you couldn't trust him not to rob somebody if he felt like it, but he was a really good source, information wise. Did he maybe encourage some of the psychos he lifted weights with until they wanted him to go kill someone for them and then said so on tape? Maybe, but that was never the issue with my cases, or this one, near as I can tell. It's just that, at some point, it has to stop. At some point, we should no longer play his game, no matter what he's bringing to the table. Maybe you wouldn't want me running things, but that's how I felt, and still feel. Enough."

Judge Newton turned back to Nora looking both surprised and impressed by the testimony. "Ms. Carleton, do you have anything further for this witness?"

"I don't, Your Honor, although I feel like I should explain why the government disagrees with Special Agent Wynne in this case."

The judge waved with the back of his hand. "No need, no need. Given your track record, and that of your office, I always assume you have given careful thought to the difficult trade-offs that are sometimes necessary in pursuit of justice. It is not this court's concern, nor will it properly be the subject of evidence or argument with the jury at the trial.

"We'll go right into cross-examination. Mr. Parker? Or perhaps Ms. Pond?"

Riley Pond stood, shimmying her skirt down as she walked to the podium. "Sir," she began, "you said you are a special agent, is that right?"

"Yes," Wynne answered.

"What makes you special?"

"I'm sorry?"

"It's in your title, the word 'special.' My question is: Why do you think that?"

"It's the title for all gun-carrying federal agents—which the government calls the 1811 series."

"So there's nothing particularly special about any of you?"

At counsel table, Matthew Parker sighed so loudly that Judge Newton turned his head. "Mr. Parker? Something to add?"

"Sorry, Judge, no."

The judge turned back to the witness. "You may answer."

"Well," Wynne said, "I'd like to think so, personally, but career wise, all the armed investigators at the FBI are called special agents. They told us at the academy why that is, going back to early in our country's history, if you'd like to hear it."

"No, no," Pond said quickly, "I'd like to talk to you about what a bad man this Gerardi is."

She spent the next twenty minutes having Wynne repeat the Gerardi story. As she led the agent through the cycle of crime and cooperation,

Nora noticed Judge Newton's head starting to bob, his eyes fluttering. When at last Pond announced that she had no further questions, there was a pause of several seconds before Judge Newton abruptly sat up. "We'll go right into redirect."

Nora turned in her seat and whispered to Sean. "All she did was have him repeat his direct. You got anything?" When he shook his head, Nora stood. "No further questions, Your Honor."

The judge turned. "Special Agent Wynne, you are excused with the thanks of the court." He turned back toward the government table. "Call your next witness."

Sean stood. "The government calls Special Agent Janet Loftus."

A trim woman in her early thirties, wearing a navy blue pants suit and a plain white dress shirt, rose from the front row and made her way to the witness stand. She wore her light brown, shoulder-length hair in a ponytail and wore no jewelry or evident makeup. Sean had worked hard to prepare her for the first testimony of her career, even bringing her to Judge Newton's courtroom in the late evening to show her the scene, but her "I do" in response to the oath was still barely audible.

Sean began by asking her to keep her voice up and then started with her background. She worked as an auditor at a major accounting firm out of college, joining the FBI because she met a Bureau forensic accountant on a fraud case and his stories of unraveling complex financial crimes excited her; he urged her to go the special agent route so she would have more control over her own cases. She had hoped to be assigned somewhere near her home in Dayton, Ohio, after the academy at Quantico, but, as often happened in the FBI, she was sent to New York, where she was assigned to a financial crimes squad. The work was everything she expected until the day her supervisor told her she was needed on a temporary undercover assignment and she became Mike Gerardi's "paralegal."

In response to Sean's questions, Special Agent Loftus took Judge Newton through her involvement in the case. After meeting with the Brooklyn federal prosecutors, she went to her first meeting with Gerardi at the MDC. She went alone, she explained, because her supervisors thought that looked most consistent with a paralegal role. In an attorney meeting room, she simply asked Gerardi what information he wished to share with the government and took notes as he spoke. Gerardi told her he had been surprised to be housed with Buchanan but saw it as an opportunity to help himself. He said he had worked hard to cultivate a relationship so Buchanan might give him useful information. His investment paid off when Buchanan began to confide in him about the case, including about Buchanan's own culpability. Gerardi said he immediately attempted to reach Special Agent Wynne, hoping that the FBI might take steps to capture the conversations, removing the problems created by his own credibility issues. When that was unsuccessful, he stopped trying to cultivate Buchanan and was surprised when the FBI came back to him.

At the close of the meeting, she read him a direction: He was to have no further conversations of any kind with Buchanan about the case until further instructed. In fact, he should affirmatively shut down *any* conversation on that topic. Gerardi said he understood. Agent Loftus immediately afterward created a memorandum of the session on a standard form FD-302.

She testified that she returned each of the next two days to meet with Gerardi briefly, asking him whether he had had conversations with Buchanan and repeating the instruction that he was not to speak about Buchanan's case.

Her fourth visit to the MDC was with two EDNY prosecutors and they met with Gerardi again in an attorney visitation room. The prosecutors gave Gerardi "listening post" instructions and then had him read and sign a document laying out the instructions and his consent to have his cell wired for video and audio. He assured them he understood and would follow their directions. Loftus said she was aware the cell was being wired while Gerardi was away at their meeting. She said Gerardi asked the prosecutors to assure him that, whatever happened, they would bring his cooperation to the attention of a judge if he later requested it. They said they would. They left and, as usual, she created a 302 memorandum.

Loftus visited Gerardi two more times after that. The first was for the purpose of hearing whether he had any concerns or issues and to repeat his listening post instructions, which he acknowledged again. The second and final session was the morning after the recorded conversation in which Buchanan talked about his criminal responsibility. On this occasion, Gerardi was excited, saying repeatedly, "I hope you got it last night." She asked him to describe what he meant by "it," and he recounted Buchanan's words in a way that closely tracked the tape. She took notes and put it all in a 302. That was the last time she saw Gerardi. She returned to her regular squad the next day.

Matthew Parker dropped his chin to his chest when Riley Pond began her cross examination by calling the witness "Not-very-special Agent Loftus." But with a quick glance and smile at Buchanan, Pond went in a different direction.

"Were you afraid of Gerardi?"

"Not really," she answered.

"What does that mean? He's a huge and dangerous guy, and you aren't those things and you were alone in a room that isn't monitored by the guards."

"I was nervous, to be honest, but I also figured there was no way he would hurt me. His goal was to help the FBI and benefit from it."

"Did you find him intimidating?"

"At first, but then he actually was kind of charming."

Nora flinched at that and scribbled a note to Sean. *Charming? Can't have her with a jury.*

"What does that mean?" Pond asked.

"Formal, old-school, polite, like that."

"Did you tape record your meetings in the attorney room with Gerardi so we can hear that charm?"

"No," Loftus answered quietly.

"You don't have recording devices in the FBI? Like phones and such?"

"We do," she said in a whisper.

"Well, we heard how hard you worked to get your memos right, which is great, I suppose, but if you'd pushed a little button on your phone, we wouldn't need a memo, would we?"

Loftus blushed. "I guess that's right."

"So why didn't you? Tape it, I mean."

"Because we don't do that. We only record interviews of people in custody."

"Well, wasn't Gerardi in custody?"

Loftus paused at that one, then said, "Yes, he was a prisoner, but we weren't interrogating him. He was a witness, not a subject, so it was not a custodial interview."

"Why the difference?"

Loftus was looking down at her hands now. "Honestly, I don't know. I just know that's the way we're trained. Custodial interrogation is taped; other interviews are not."

"Is it to keep Deep Staters in jobs?"

Sean jumped up. "Objection, Judge."

"Sustained," Judge Newton said sharply. "Questions only, Ms. Pond, not insults."

"Fine. If you had taped all your meetings with Gerardi, instead of typing away at your little memos, wouldn't the taxpayers of the United States have been better off because you could have been out investigating actual crimes?"

Loftus looked stricken. "I don't know how to answer that, because I don't know the thinking behind our policy."

"Shouldn't you know the thinking?" Pond snarled. "I mean, aren't you supposed to be *special* people?"

The courtroom gallery was warming up now, with sounds of affirmation rippling through the crowd.

"Ms. Pond, please be seated," Judge Newton said loudly, before lifting his face to the audience. "And I will not repeat my warning about the consequences of disrupting proceedings in this courtroom. Is there redirect?"

Sean glanced at Nora, who subtly shook her head. "No, Your Honor," he answered.

Pond slid into her chair next to Matthew Parker. "Not bad," he whispered, "not bad."

"The witness is excused, with the thanks of the court. We'll take the lunch break now."

CHAPTER THIRTY-TWO

Matthew Parker came through the courthouse security checkpoint after lunch to find Sean bent over, studying the base of the statue of Lady Justice in the lobby.

"Hey, bud," he called, "sorry to keep you waiting—and what're you looking at?"

Sean stood upright and spun around. "Oh, hey, Matthew. No problem. I've passed this statue a hundred times and never read the base. Strange that it just says 'Justice.' They couldn't come up with something more inspiring than that? Even a verb would be nice."

Parker laughed. "No, no, my friend. Not in a two-for-the-price-of-one deal."

Sean turned so they were both facing the statue of the apparently sprinting, blindfolded Justice, in so much of a hurry that she had forgotten the beam of her pan balance scale and was holding one pan in each outstretched hand.

"Government got a deal on it," Parker explained. "The original is in Alexandria, the Eastern District of Virginia. That's the home of the 'rocket docket'—fastest courthouse in the land and all that. So when they built their new courthouse down there a couple years before this one, the government sprung for a custom statue with speed as the theme—Lady Justice sprinting forward, with 'Justice Delayed Is Justice Denied' written under her. And there were other parts to the theme sculpted into the front of the building below the statue—tortoise and hare, shit like that. When this place was finished, they just put a copy of the main statue here. They couldn't keep the 'Justice Delayed' thing because this place is the opposite of fast, so they went with 'Justice.' But it *was* cheap. And maybe *that's* some kind of parable."

Sean smiled. "I love that kind of stuff. Now, what can I do for you?"

"I just wanted to catch you before we go back up to see what's next for the United States of America."

"I think that's it for us."

"So not going to put Gerardi on?"

"We don't think we need to for this. He doesn't add anything on the legal issue, right? No doubt he wanted to get something out of your guy and talked him up, but we weren't part of it. And when we became part of it, it was done the right way. So no Gerardi. If you want to call him, let me know so we can make arrangements."

"Hard pass," Parker replied.

Sean nodded. "You gonna put Buchanan on?"

"Nah," Parker said, "for the same reason. Doesn't add anything at this point. Maybe different with a jury, but not now. You think Newton will just go ahead and rule? 'Cause I don't want to write another brief."

Sean laughed. "He usually does. See you upstairs."

◆

After hearing that neither the government nor the defense intended to call further witnesses, Judge Newton gave the lawyers one final opportunity to make their arguments. Nora and Parker both repeated in short form the issues they had argued in their written briefs. When they were finished, the judge lifted a document he had obviously written before coming back into the courtroom. He removed his glasses, held the pages close to his face, and began reading.

"The court is grateful to learned counsel for the excellent way in which this issue has been presented. What counsel have illuminated for the court is that this case is both unusual and turns upon a fairly narrow legal issue.

"The court finds that Mr. Gerardi had, at many times in his life, been an agent for the government. He had benefited enormously from his service as an agent for the government. Through that work and his own entanglements with the criminal justice system, he knew—despite being a man without formal education—a great deal about the criminal process and the kinds of issues and evidence at the heart of that process.

"To be clear, he acted like an agent for the government after discovering the good fortune of his roommate assignment, he thought like an agent for the government, and he very much wanted to be an agent for the government. But the court finds that he was not an agent for the government.

"Agency requires bilateral agreement and there was no such agreement until representatives of the government—in this case the FBI and lawyers from the Eastern District of New York—met with Mr. Gerardi at the MDC and formed an agency relationship. The court finds that, thereafter, he abided by the terms of his agency and served solely as a listening post, consistent with Sixth Amendment case law.

"That Mr. Gerardi may have prompted Mr. Buchanan, shaped Mr. Buchanan, or even manipulated Mr. Buchanan before establishing his relationship with the government is of no moment. The government did not use Mr. Gerardi to deliberately elicit statements from Mr. Buchanan, which is the extent of the inquiry this court is constrained to make. Perhaps there are those who wish the Supreme Court and the Second Circuit would change the governing law, but the contours of that law are clear to this court. The motion to suppress is denied. We will begin jury selection in the morning."

CHAPTER THIRTY-THREE

About one hundred fifty potential jurors were jammed into the spectator pews of the courthouse's enormous eighth floor ceremonial room, which Judge Newton had decided to use for the trial. Chosen randomly from the registered drivers and voters of the counties of New York (Manhattan), Bronx, Westchester, Rockland, Putnam, Orange, Dutchess, and Sullivan, many of them had traveled two hours or more to get to this spot. They were nervous, curious—and some a bit grouchy—waiting to learn why they were in this huge courtroom, with serious-looking Deputy US Marshals standing around the perimeter. They were about to find out, rising together—a symphony of knees cracking and coats rustling—as Judge Newton swept up the few stairs to his seat on the judge's bench. "Please be seated," the clerk called.

The clerk's announcement that this was "*United States of America v. Samuel Buchanan*" caused only the slightest stir. Apparently, despite the press attention, not many of them recognized the right-wing media star, even when the judge asked him to stand and face the audience with his lawyers. Then Judge Newton began by explaining how the selection process would work. They had each been given juror numbers, which they should use exclusively. At no time should any of them reveal their names or home addresses. "The jury in this case will be anonymous," he explained. "Not even I will know your names." This caused a modest ripple of murmuring in the crowd, as the smart ones figured out that they would only need to be anonymous if someone might mess with them.

Judge Newton said, "This case is expected to take about three weeks to try. Let me give you a brief summary of the case, because you will be asked questions about any knowledge you may have of this matter and about your ability to remain fair and impartial. This case involves allegations by the United States government that the defendant, a media personality, conspired to commit hate crimes against people around the country, who were killed or seriously injured."

That did it. Hate crimes. Murders. Media. Anonymity. An otherworldly moan came from the one hundred and fifty, as if a Gregorian chant choir were warming up.

Judge Newton tried to bring calm with a loud "Now, now, ladies and gentleman . . ." but the moaning continued. He grabbed his gavel and, with three loud bangs, managed to stop the choir. "We will have order and dignity in this courtroom at all times," he said.

Nora jotted a note to Sean, who sat beside her at the government's table. *Every one of them is going to try to get off this jury.*

Sean smiled and wrote back, *Yup, and those who can't get off will blame us. Good times.*

After his brief introduction, Judge Newton asked for a show of hands from any jurors who believed, based on what they had heard so far, that they would be unable to serve. Most hands went up. Newton told them to put their hands down and launched into a speech about the importance of jury service, the need for all citizens to sacrifice for the public good, and reminding them that juries were the bedrock of ordered liberty and the rule of law. He then asked his question again and the same number of hands went up. Judge Newton was now irritated.

He began calling jurors to a private conference at the side of the bench, one by one, to ask why they had raised their hands. Nora, Sean, Matthew Parker, Riley Pond, and a court reporter formed a lawyerly horseshoe around each prospective juror as the judge glared from his elevated perch just a couple feet away. Some said they had followed the case so closely that they couldn't be fair, although they couldn't explain in what way they would be unfair. Many professed to have childcare or eldercare issues or employment concerns.

Judge Newton didn't excuse anyone and slowly dropped his pleasant demeanor as he stared at the prospect of not having enough candidates from which to select a jury. After two hours of this, a sad-looking middle-aged man in business dress came to sidebar and whispered that his wife just left him for another man and he was in a mental health crisis and couldn't possibly serve. Judge Newton responded in a quiet, flat voice. "We all have problems, sir, and while I regret your difficulties, that isn't a basis for being excused. Please step back and take your seat."

The man leaned forward, still whispering, his voice full of genuine emotion. "Your Honor, my life has fallen apart. I am ruined. Please, sir, please. I beg you."

Newton glared at him and spoke in a loud voice, almost shouting, the sound bouncing off the back wall of the cavernous courtroom. "You don't *listen* sir! Maybe that's why your wife left you, because you don't *listen*! I told you to step back and resume your seat."

The man turned to Nora, ashen. "I have never been so humiliated in my entire life. This is outrageous."

As the potential juror turned toward the audience—who all now knew his wife left him and maybe because he didn't listen—Nora looked up at Judge Newton and whispered intensely. "Your Honor, the government would have no objection to excusing that juror, given the extraordinary circumstances."

"All right," Newton said with evident distaste, "I will accede to counsel's wishes, but we can't let people go for flimsy reasons or we won't ever get a jury. That juror is dismissed. Get the next one."

It didn't get any easier after that, but after three days of effort, Judge Newton had "qualified" thirty-two jurors after finding no basis for removal because of things like bias or hardship. Then it was up to the government and defense to cut it down until sixteen remained—twelve jurors and four alternates. Each side had copies of the jurors' completed questionnaires and heard their answers to questions from the court. Now they would decide how to best use their "peremptory challenges" to remove jurors without stating a reason.

Nora, Sean, Benny, and Jessica huddled together at counsel table, looking at the large wooden board the clerk shuttled between them and the defense. It was a process that demanded careful attention to seat position, because Judge Newton used the "struck jury method" common in Manhattan federal court. Clipped to the board were the numbers of all thirty-two "qualified" jurors—without names and identified only by their original juror number. The first twelve cards on the board were the presumptive jury and the next four were alternates, unless they were struck by the prosecution or the defense. The government could use up to six peremptory strikes and the defense ten. They alternated turns six times, with the defense having two strikes in each of the first four rounds and one for each of the final two.

When a juror was struck, the card was pulled, which meant all the cards following that one moved up. Once all challenges were used, the first twelve remaining on the board would be the jury; the next four, the alternates. But that meant the lawyers had to consider who would move into the top twelve if they pulled a card from the current top twelve. It was quite a game, which was why many federal courts didn't use the same method.

The board went back and forth through the rounds, with the early rounds featuring loudly whispered conversations between Buchanan's two lawyers as Pond reached for a card. "I don't like her," she whispered at one point, pulling the card of a thirty-five-year-old unmarried woman in management consulting. "Ivy league nepo baby."

"Maybe," Parker whispered back, "but she has about the same chance of being on this jury as you do. I told you, the way this works is that the twelve cards left at the end are the jury and the next four are the alternates. Sixteen seats is what matters. It's a waste of a strike to take someone who *mathematically* can't reach the top sixteen."

"Still don't like her," Pond whispered. "She's what's wrong with this country."

Parker turned away from Pond to look at his client, who was now in a suit and tie but still on the left side with Parker as the middle seat chaperone. "Please tell me you get this."

"I do," Buchanan said quietly. He reached in front of Parker toward Pond's hand. "Babe—"

"Nope," Parker interrupted, lifting his arm to block the contact. "We're not going to do that. Just tell her to let me pull the cards."

Buchanan didn't answer, but gave a deep nod toward Pond, who slumped back in her chair with an audible sigh.

Parker pulled two cards and passed the board to the prosecution table.

Only one card had caused controversy on the government team—a man of Irish descent who worked in a blue-collar job for the city of Yonkers, which bordered the Bronx, and had a variety of relatives in local law enforcement. "Definite keeper," Benny had whispered.

Nora gave him her confused face.

"Cop family," Benny explained. "They're always our people."

Nora made a pained face. "Are they, though? In a case like this? Fair number of off-duty cops were there on January Sixth. And I'm not naming names, but it's not a community known for a, uh, progressive bent. You feel me? And what's he doing spending what little money he has on Catholic school for his kids? Maybe something to do with the complexion of south Yonkers? Lots of immigrants are joining that community these days."

"Oh, that's not fair," Benny protested. "Lotta families send their kids to parochial school no matter what color the neighborhood, 'cause the sisters do a better job of educating the kids than our teacher unions do."

"Maybe, but why isn't he working harder to get off this jury?" Nora asked before adding, "Never mind. He's far enough outside the top twelve that we don't need to fight about it. Yet."

◆

After five turns, each side had just one strike left. Parker had made all his strikes from the top of the board, moving Yonkers guy to the fourteenth position. The twelfth card—currently on the jury—was a forty-three-year-old woman who worked for a nonprofit at NYU's law school that specialized in cases involving government misconduct. She also maintained, strenuously, that despite that work, she could be fair and impartial in this case.

"No brainer, right?" Nora whispered, her voice barely audible. "If we're going to call Gerardi, we can't have a juror who works at a place that will probably sue us someday for calling Gerardi."

Sean nodded in agreement. "Can't take that chance. Gotta get rid of her, but that leaves Yonkers as first alternate."

"We have no choice," Nora said. "I don't have a good feeling about him—and I know Benny's a fan—but maybe he doesn't make the top group."

They pulled the twelfth card. Feeling good, Nora handed the board back to Pond at the defense table. Parker snatched the board from her and smiled as he pulled the card in the fifth position, a juror they had assumed he liked. Yonkers guy moved from thirteenth position to twelfth and was now on the jury.

"Matty just did us a favor," Benny whispered.

Nora blew air between her closed lips. "Lordy, I hope you're right, Benny."

CHAPTER THIRTY-FOUR

"**M**ay it please the court," Nora said, buttoning her blue Brooks Brothers jacket and pivoting to look briefly at the judge. Then she turned back to the jury and gripped the small wood podium with two hands. "Members of the jury."

She paused briefly and looked down at her notebook on the podium's surface. Not because she didn't know what to say next but because she had decided to postpone the usual introductions and open dramatically—a technique New York's federal prosecutors called "pulling a dark and stormy." After the silence had brought all eyes to her, she looked up and began, not with a murder, but with an attack that would be narrated by the victim from the witness stand. Her eyes swept the jury box as she spoke, never looking away from the sixteen people in front of her.

"Friday was garbage day in Carla Rodriguez's neighborhood. So Thursday night after finishing work as a home nursing aide in Phoenix, Carla rolled the garbage can down the little driveway to leave it at the curb. Carla didn't notice the headlights of a pickup truck, but heard the squeal of its tires. The truck skidded to a stop and a man wearing a black surgical-type mask jumped out, shouting, 'Hey, Carla Rodriguez!' and proceeded to savagely beat Carla with a metal rod, breaking both arms and causing a severe head wound and lasting brain injury. Carla only survived because the police were on the block. They were nearby because Carla had been threatened."

Nora turned and pointed across the courtroom at Buchanan, speaking loudly. "Carla was threatened, and beaten, because of *that* man. Samuel Buchanan ordered the attack, using his voice on his podcasts, his videos, his radio show. He wasn't in that little Phoenix driveway that Thursday night, but he caused it to happen, he *made* it happen. And all because Carla Rodriguez was different."

Nora turned back to the jury and continued in a conversational tone. "Carla's preferred pronouns weren't what got Carla attacked daily on the defendant's broadcasts. What got Carla attacked was the audacity to try to help other people who didn't feel comfortable identifying as either a man or a woman. The publicity around that work made Buchanan tell his followers Carla was a threat to America and 'had to go.' He knew what would happen when he uttered those words. He knew one of his devoted fans would make that happen, even if Buchanan was hundreds of miles away. He intended for Carla to get hurt.

"This case is about the *six times* that happened to innocent victims across the United States. The *six times* Samuel Buchanan condemned someone to death or serious injury with his words. The *six times* he said someone 'had to go' and his followers followed his direction. Carla survived the attack, as did two other people, thank God."

Nora turned and pointed at the box and chair next to the judge's bench. "Those survivors will come to that witness stand to tell you what happened. But three other people can't come and tell you their stories, because the defendant's words ended those stories. They 'had to go' and so they went, out of this life, out of the lives of those they loved, forever. This case is about justice for the dead and the wounded."

Nora looked down at her notebook and turned a page. When she looked up, her tone was slightly lighter. "As Judge Newton told you, my name is Nora Carleton and I'm an Assistant US Attorney representing the government in this case. Working with me is Sean Fitzpatrick, another Assistant US Attorney, and obviously, we'll be helped by some other terrific people you'll see at counsel table: April Fugate, a paralegal in our office; Jessica Watson, an FBI special agent; and Benny Dugan, a special agent with our office. What I want to do now is briefly outline for you the charges in this case and the way in which the government intends to prove them. As you listen to me, I hope you'll bear a few things in mind.

"First, that the government bears the burden of proving Samuel Buchanan's guilt beyond a reasonable doubt. That burden never shifts and it's one we embrace. Second, nothing I say is evidence. The evidence comes from that witness stand and the things Judge Newton admits into evidence. And, third, there won't be a quiz after I'm done."

She smiled kindly. "What I mean by that is I'm going to try to give you an overview of the government's evidence, a rough guide, almost like directions to a trip. I'm sure you have friends who, even in the age of Google or Apple Maps, tell you how to get to their house by describing landmarks. A big church steeple here, an original set of McDonald's arches here, a duck pond with a big fountain there. You forget it all immediately—at least I do—but then you drive to their house and you see those landmarks and they're familiar. They assure you that you're headed in the right direction. That's what I want to do for a little while: tell you about the trip you're going to take in this courtroom over the next several weeks. Then you'll take the trip and we'll get a chance to talk to you about it when we're finished."

Nora then methodically walked the jury through the government's case—the nature of Buchanan's media operation, the "has to go" targets of his vitriol, the circumstances of the attacks, and the electronic evidence linking the identified attackers to his content. Judge Newton had ruled that postarrest statements by attackers blaming Buchanan's rhetoric would not be admissible, so Nora stayed away from those. She planned to finish with her last, best evidence—the MDC jail recording. And here she surprised herself by pausing.

◆

The trial team had debated endlessly about whether to call Gerardi as a witness. If he was going to testify, the usual practice would be for Nora to attempt to anesthetize the jury during her opening by talking about how bad he was and urging the jurors to scrutinize his testimony carefully, looking for corroboration. If she didn't do that, defense counsel would open by thundering about the awfulness and ask the jurors why the government hadn't even mentioned their sketchy witness, like some slick real estate agent describing a beautiful house but omitting the termite damage in all the support beams.

The team had argued about it up to the night before opening. Gerardi was already in the WitSec underground safe house near the court.

"I think we can get the recording in without him," Nora said. "We call the FBI tech who can say he installed it and monitored it while it was happening. That's enough authentication to get it in."

"Maybe," Sean replied. "Or maybe the judge smells a rat because we're twisting like a pretzel to avoid our own informant and he keeps it out unless Gerardi says that's what actually happened."

"I don't see him doing that, but, worst case, we call Gerardi then. All we lose is the chance to prepare the jury in opening. No biggie."

"Don't you think Parker calls Gerardi in the defense case anyway and the jury sees our stink no matter what we do?"

"Why would he do that?" Nora asked. "He's gotta put his client on to respond to the recording and Gerardi can only undercut whatever Buchanan claims in terms of manipulation or coercion. I actually think *we're* the ones most likely to call him—but in rebuttal after Buchanan says, 'Big bad Mike made me say those things.'"

"So if we're likely to call him, why not talk about him in opening?"

"Too much uncertainty. Too hard to see the future for us to be wrapping our arms around him in front of the jury. If we get the tape in and Buchanan doesn't testify, Gerardi will never come out of the basement."

◆

Nora glanced at her notes and then continued, without mentioning Gerardi. "You may be wondering how the government intends to prove that Samuel Buchanan knew about these attacks and wanted them to happen. Well, the most important way you will know that is because Buchanan will tell you so himself, on a recording the FBI made in his jail cell over in Brooklyn. You will hear him talk to his cellmate and express remorse for what he did, admitting that he knew it would happen and actually *wanted* it to happen to these victims. Samuel Buchanan's intention will not be in doubt by the end of this case."

Nora finished with the familiar government request for the jury to pay close attention, follow the judge's instructions, and use their common sense. But then she added something that few prosecutors did: she asked the jury to keep an open mind throughout the case— "Because no one witness or one piece of evidence can tell an entire story and both the government and the defendant are entitled to a fair trial." When she previewed her remarks for Carmen and the team—a "moot," they called it—Carmen asked her why she did it.

"Just feels right," Nora explained, "and I also want the jury to see us as caring about justice first and winning second."

"Makes sense," Carmen answered.

"And I don't mean to make it sound like I just want to *appear* that way; I want to *be* that way."

"Got it," Carmen said. "Remind me to have you do that for the new hires at one of our all-hands training sessions. I also like the directions-to-a-trip thing."

"Stole that from Sean," Nora said, pointing at her trial partner.

Sean smiled. "And I stole it from someone else. As you know, jury addresses are thefts all the way down."

◆

"Thank you, Ms. Carleton," Judge Newton said as Nora stepped away from the podium. "We'll go right into the defense opening. Mr. Parker?"

Matthew Parker stood and buttoned his usual tailored chalk-stripe suit jacket. "Your Honor, the defense intends to reserve opening, if it please the court."

Judge Newton blushed. "Oh, Mr. Parker, the court apologizes for its assumptions."

Sean was scribbling on a sticky note. *So Buchanan will definitely testify.*

Yup and Parker's smart to reserve, Nora wrote back.

The judge turned to the jury. "Members of the jury, let me explain that our rules offer defense counsel the option to speak to you in opening at the start of the government's case or at the start of a defense case. I should not have assumed Mr. Parker would speak now. He has elected to give his opening statement to you later, as is his right. We'll go straight into the government's evidence. Call your first witness, Ms. Carleton."

"Certainly, Your Honor," Nora said, slowly rising.

The prosecution team planned to present the evidence about the attacks in a consistent fashion. They would play extensive clips of Buchanan's verbal attacks on a victim, then present evidence about the circumstances of each physical attack—including crime scene forensics and the identity of any known attacker—and the electronic evidence showing how much the identified attackers consumed Buchanan's content. Then they would call the victim or a family member. But they agreed to change the pattern to begin their case with a memorable human face.

As Nora stood, the door behind the witness box opened and a short, slight person with dark hair limped through, dragging one foot. Nora waited as the jurors watched the clerk help the witness struggle up the two little stairs and come to an unsteady stop beside the chair.

Then, in a loud voice, Nora announced, "The government calls Carla Rodriguez."

The trial had begun.

CHAPTER THIRTY-FIVE

After Nora's tight direct examination, leading Carla through their story up to the horrific attack in the driveway and a grueling recovery, Matthew Parker's cross was brief and gentle, as he would be with the other victims and the surviving family members who took the stand to talk about their dead loved ones.

"Mx. Rodriguez," Parker began, using the courtesy title appropriate to a nonbinary person, "let me start by saying how sorry I am for what you've suffered." This was objectionable, but Nora let it go.

"Thank you," Carla replied.

"I only have one question," Parker said, turning to point at Buchanan. "Have you ever had any contact with my client? Ever met him or spoke to him?"

Nora let the compound question go.

"No."

"Thank you, and I wish you continued healing. Nothing further, Your Honor."

CHAPTER THIRTY-SIX

Because Parker's strategy was to stay away from the actual attacks, the government's evidence came in smoothly, like six short plays about the life of a person Buchanan made famous—in a certain way—for his or her or their involvement with causes that had become lightning rods to him and his followers. Parker even stipulated—the term lawyers used instead of "agreed"—to the government reading short summaries of what investigators would say about the identities of the known attackers—troubled White men in their twenties to early thirties—and their consumption of Buchanan's words and images. That avoided long testimony about those who had actually hurt or killed people.

All along, the strategy had confused Riley Pond. "I don't get why we don't force them to prove the case," she said while she and Parker sat with their client in a small conference room behind the courtroom as Deputy US Marshals stood outside the door.

"Because nothing good comes from extending the period of time a jury spends seeing how badly innocent people were hurt or how frickin' nutty and scary Sam's fans are. This case isn't about that. It's about whether they can prove he's legally responsible for what those idiots did."

"I just don't like our people seeing us agreeing with the government about anything."

"And by 'our people' you mean the crowd in the courtroom?"

"Them and those who are following this online—who are not all scary nuts, by the way."

Parker pointed at Buchanan. "Gotta be honest, Riley, with our pesky legal obligation to represent only *that* person, our client, I don't give a shit what everyone else thinks."

Buchanan spoke with a mouth full of turkey sandwich. "Well, I appreciate that, Matthew, and Riley, I also care what our people think. But my goal is to avoid spending the rest of my life in prison, where I can't be of any use to all those fine people. And I agree with Matthew that the more we make clear to the jury that all this violence has nothing to do with me, the better."

Parker looked at Buchanan. "This case comes down to whether you can convince the jury that the jail tape isn't what you really believed."

Buchanan swallowed and took a swig from his water bottle before answering. "Yes, I know that. It was because Gerardi made me think those things."

"Exactly," Parker answered before turning to Pond. "All of this is just the overture. The show begins when Sam hits the stand."

Pond looked confused by that but asked a different question. "So we're not going to present evidence that the country really is going to hell because of these people? We're not going to prove that Sam was right to raise the alarm, even if some of his followers went too far?"

Parker stopped just as he was about to bite into his ham and Swiss on rye. "So you want to argue that these folks deserved it? See if we can't get a Manhattan jury to agree that ol' Carla Rodriguez got what was coming to 'em? Are you out of your fucking mind?"

He dropped the sandwich back onto the butcher paper and turned to Buchanan. "Little help here?"

Buchanan spoke gently. "I have to agree with Matthew, my tupelo honey. We don't want to make this case about either the people who got hurt or about whether America faces an existential threat. Of *course* it does—you and I and millions of others see it—but the people here, in their gas-stove-hating, gender-is-a-construct, borders-are-immoral blue bubble are never going to see it that way. It's a fight we can't win here. Of course, it's a fight we *must* win as a country, and I'll stay in the fight, but not if I'm in a federal prison. You follow me, sugar?"

Pond slowly nodded her head in agreement. "And I still think you should let me do the opening or the summation."

They ate in silence.

CHAPTER THIRTY-SEVEN

Emily Hanshaw was a pleasant looking woman in her mid-fifties who had spent her career looking in dark places. As a researcher at Harvard's Kennedy School of Government, her specialty was online radicalization and the pathways through which individuals were drawn to ideologically motivated violence, both religious and political.

Matthew Parker rose as soon as Dr. Hanshaw sat down after taking the oath.

"Your Honor, I'd like to renew our objection to this testimony." He had already filed a motion to block the expert testimony, which Judge Newton denied, but Parker wanted to send a message to the jury.

Judge Newton looked mildly irritated. "Thank you, Mr. Parker, the court is aware of the objection, which has been overruled, but I think this would be a good time for me to offer an instruction to the jury."

He turned his chair to face the jurors. "Members of the jury, normally the only witnesses permitted to testify in a case like this are *fact* witnesses, people who personally saw or heard or found something that is relevant to the case. But our rules of evidence recognize that there may be times when a different kind of witness is appropriate. In certain circumstances, a witness may testify from his or her expertise in order to explain something to you that you might not otherwise know from your life experience. The government is calling this witness, who has studied, taught, and written about the way in which people become radicalized online, because they believe it will help you understand the evidence in this case. It is admitted for that purpose only and you should give it whatever weight you decide is appropriate. Please proceed."

Sean did the direct examination and, as with all good expert witnesses, he was soon almost invisible. After reciting her education, her honors, her areas of research, her countless hours trying to understand one of humanity's most disturbing impulses, she turned in her chair and spoke only with the jurors, who were mesmerized by her warm, friendly tone and plainspoken delivery.

All humans seek meaning and connection, she explained. We want to know we matter, that we are seen and loved. Most of us find those things through family, friends, church, school, or work—and usually a combination of those things. But there are those who, for a variety of reasons, don't find it and feel lost and unseen, without purpose. Those are people who are susceptible to messages that offer a sense of purpose through violence. Al Qaeda and 9/11 were largely pre-internet phenomena, but the Islamic State took full advantage of modern communication. During ISIS's peak in 2014 and 2015, the messages susceptible people heard and read online told them that the final battle between the faithful and unbelievers was at hand, that God had at long last established his prophesied caliphate on the Syria-Iraq border. The destiny of all believers was to come join the battle for the caliphate or, if they couldn't travel there, to serve the mission by killing unbelievers, the infidels, wherever they could be found. It was a noble calling, one with a divine mandate.

With a sad look, she explained that messages about violence always resonate more powerfully among young men. For a variety of reasons related to brain development and hormones, young men find violence more attractive as a source of meaning than women or older men do.

The most effective radicalizing messages are those that tell consumers, especially young men, that they are special, that they are under siege, and that the noble course is to fight back against their enemies. It's a message that has worked for all human history, she explained. The Middle Ages had no social media, but recruiters still managed to convince thousands to leave their homes and fight a holy war in far-off Jerusalem. Of course, she added, the power of social media is that the recruiter doesn't need to ride on horseback to your medieval village; he's in your pocket reaching you constantly through your buzzing phone. It's an order of magnitude more effective, she said, and more dangerous.

She stopped there. Sean had instructed her that Judge Newton would not allow her to offer an opinion as to whether the poison Samuel Buchanan spewed was fertile ground for radicalization. "Too close to the question the jury needs to answer," the judge said, a ruling that Nora willed herself not to smile about, because this subject was the only fight she and Sean had during preparation for the case.

◆

"We don't need her to tell the jury what's obvious," Nora had said during witness prep.

"It's not obvious," Sean had replied, his voice rising. "Ordinary people have a hard time believing that words on social media could get someone to kill. And weren't we worried about proving that Buchanan himself knew what he could accomplish with his words? Until we got the Gerardi tape?"

"Maybe," Nora answered, "but now that we have the tape, why take the risk that the court of appeals will think the expert testimony went too far?" *Jeez, what was that about brains and hormones and emotional regulation?*

Sean wouldn't back down. "It's reviewed under an abuse of discretion standard so they'll give Newton room. And, worst case, we argue it's harmless error because the other evidence was so strong."

"You do see how that actually supports my position, right?"

Sean went quiet, as he often did when angry. He was tired and worried. They all were. "Okay, Sean, you make the call," Nora said softly. *Judge Newton's never going to allow it anyway.*

◆

Parker began his cross-examination in an odd way. "Dr. Hanshaw, let me start by thanking you for the work you have done to help humanity understand the threat of online radicalization."

Sean started to stand and object, but paused and sat down.

"Remind me how many years you have studied this topic?"

"Since right after the attacks of September 2001, although my focus didn't become internet-based radicalization until a few years later, with the explosion of the internet as a tool."

"It's a complicated topic, is that fair to say?"

"I think so."

"Which is why we rely on experts like yourself to help us sort it out, people who have spent years doing research, thinking, studying."

"I hope I'm useful."

"Oh, you are, doctor, you certainly are. Because it's not obvious that words on a smartphone screen could move someone to go kill another human being, is it?"

"Not obvious, no, I suppose not. Although I think today people realize it more and more."

"Fair enough. But is it also fair to say that, despite the good work of experts like yourself, there are a lot of people today, including smart people, who do not understand the threat?"

"I think that's fair."

"And part of your professional mission is to help more people realize the danger of online radicalization."

"That's right."

"I'll bet you've even talked to senior government people who don't get it in the way they should."

"Yes, I have."

"I appreciate you staying after it, doctor. Important that people get educated. I have no further questions. Oh, I'm sorry, one: Have you ever met my client, Sam Buchanan?"

"I have not."

"Thank you, doctor."

Sean leaned over to Nora, whispering. "You think he opened the door to me asking whether it's obvious Buchanan was calling for violence?"

"I don't," Nora whispered back. "He's cute, but we'll handle it in summation. And we have the tape."

"Is there redirect?" Judge Newton asked.

"Briefly, Your Honor," Sean said, going to the podium.

"Doctor," he began, "when you open your front door and see that it's raining, do you need to consult an expert to decide if you need an umbrella?"

"Uh," the witness began before Parker cut her off.

"Judge, I have to object every time I don't understand a question."

"Yes, Mr. Fitzpatrick," the judge responded, "I have to agree with Mr. Parker. Sustained."

Sean paused, staring down at his notes for so long that the jurors turned to look at him. "Doctor," he tried again, "is common sense a useful part of your academic work?"

Parker stood and Judge Newton ruled before he could object. "Sustained. Is there anything else, Mr. Fitzpatrick?"

Sean was visibly angry, his face flashing red. He glanced at the government table, but Nora was motionless. He was going to try again. But as he was about to speak, he noticed Benny lean and place a Post-it note on the table corner nearest to him. Benny had never given him a note before.

In a solemn tone, Sean asked, "May I have a moment, Your Honor?"

"Of course," the judge answered.

Sean walked to the table and grabbed the note, cupping it in his palm as he walked back to the podium, where he pivoted and looked into his hand to read it. *Is there beer in the war room fridge?*

Sean slowly closed his hand on the note and looked up. "I have no further questions, Your Honor."

"Well, then," the judge said, "the witness may be excused, and I think that brings us to the end of the trial day. The jury will remember my admonition not to discuss the case or read anything about it and I will see you all here in the morning. Good evening."

As the courtroom emptied, Sean looked at Benny with a smile. "You fucker, you broke my rhythm."

Benny snorted. "Yeah, you had about as much rhythm as I do on a dance floor, Seany Boy. Plus, I looked at the clock and realized I didn't know the answer to that important question."

CHAPTER THIRTY-EIGHT

After the jurors were in their seats the next morning, Judge Newton looked at the government table and flexed his eyebrows, signaling that the day should begin. Sean immediately stood and announced, "Your Honor, the government calls Edgar Laturner."

The witness door opened and a slight man with thin brown hair cut short mounted the little stairs. He stood straight in a gray suit and white shirt with a blue tie held in place by an FBI tie clip.

After the witness was sworn and stated and had spelled his name, Sean asked where he was employed.

"In Quantico, Virginia, sir," he said stiffly. "I am an IT specialist in the Operational Technology Division, Technical Surveillance Section, Video Surveillance Unit."

Sean smiled. "Can you translate that for the jury?"

The witness visibly relaxed. "Of course. I work for the FBI installing video surveillance equipment."

"You said you were in Quantico. Is that where you do your work?"

"Some of it, but a lot of it is traveling around to support FBI field offices."

"How long have you been doing this work?"

"Since I joined the FBI out of Virginia Tech seventeen years ago. Actually, before that as a student intern. But seventeen years as a full-time employee."

"Did there come a time when you were assigned to install video surveillance equipment at the Metropolitan Detention Center in Brooklyn?"

"Yes."

"Video only, or audio as well?"

"Audio as well. All our installations have audio capability."

"And would you tell the jury about your execution of that assignment?"

"Sure. My boss told me to report to the New York field office, so I had to figure out whether to drive my own car or get a Bu car and—"

"I'm sorry, sir, maybe I can focus my question better. Did there come a time when you went to the MDC to install video capability in a cell?"

"Yes. Should I start there?"

"Please."

"I went to the facility. I had already reviewed the schematics, so knew it was pretty simple. I went to the fifth floor, where all the cells have a maintenance space that runs in the walls between rows of cells. They let me in there. I walked along until I found cell 5D, which they told me would be empty. I fed a fiber optic line into the air vent, anchored it, connected it to my transmitter and continuous power source, and confirmed I had a good signal. Because the prison is full of walls, as you would expect, I also boosted the signal with a separate local area network device. That allowed me to receive the signal at a significant distance. I viewed the image while in that little crawl space—which is a walk space, actually—and then I went back to Manhattan to 26 Federal Plaza and set up my monitoring station."

"What did that involve?"

"I was informed that it was a two-inmate cell—Thomas Buchanan and Michael Gerardi—and Mr. Gerardi had given consent to monitoring, which meant we could monitor and record when he was present. I set it up with a motion detector that would alert me whenever someone entered the cell so I could turn on the monitor. If it was inmate Gerardi entering, I would activate the recording equipment. If it was his cellmate alone, I would not. I would instead shut the monitor off and wait, checking only if the motion sensor alerted again. If that motion was Gerardi entering, I would activate the recording. If it wasn't or if Gerardi left, I shut it off."

"Did that mean you had to watch the monitor all night to see who came and went?"

"Oh no. The advantage of a prison—and I guess I shouldn't call it an 'advantage' because I realize not everyone would see it that way—is that the inmates are locked in their cells from evening until early morning. So once they were in there together, I could just leave it on all night."

"How long was the video monitoring?"

"Actually much shorter than I thought. I had gotten a room at one of those extended-stay hotels and—"

"Sorry, Mr. Laturner. I'm just asking how long in days or hours?"

"Right. We set it up by five P.M. and we shut it down that same night, around midnight. So about seven hours. Much shorter than I expected. I went in the next day and pulled the equipment."

"Why did you shut it off so quickly?"

"Whatever the investigators were hoping to get, they apparently got."

"Did there come a time that evening when Gerardi and his cellmate were together in the cell?"

"Yes, by about nine P.M."

"Were you monitoring it live then?"

"I was."

"Let me show you a disc I have marked for identification as Government Exhibit 45. Do you recognize that?"

"I do."

"How do you recognize it?"

"It has my initials and date on it from when I reviewed it."

"Is that a fair and accurate video and audio of a conversation you monitored the evening you first installed the equipment?"

"It is."

"And who are the participants?"

"The two occupants of 5D, Mr. Buchanan and Mr. Gerardi."

"Your Honor, I offer Exhibit 45 in evidence."

"It will be received," the judge said, turning to the jury, "and I instruct the jury not to consider in any way the fact that Mr. Buchanan was in a jail facility when this recording was made. That is irrelevant to your task."

◆

Nora and Sean decided to play the video while the technician was on the stand. Suddenly screens all around the courtroom, including small ones directly in front of the jurors, lit up and the viewers were peeking into cell 5D through the air vent. On the right side of the screen, an enormous figure smothered the slab that held his thin mattress. On the left side, Samuel Buchanan lay on his back, his right forearm bent behind his head as an additional pillow. He was studying the ceiling and baring his soul to his cellmate. The picture quality and sound were exquisite. Buchanan's southern accent filled the courtroom:

"I knew what my people would do once I focused on someone. I knew what would happen. The truth is I was focusing *because* I wanted it to happen, I was *committed* to having it happen. The tree of liberty must be refreshed from time to time with the blood of patriots and tyrants, as Jefferson said. And I confess that the initial guilt I felt was narrow. I felt badly that people who had done a noble deed because I asked them to refresh that tree were going to be punished, go to jail, have their lives turned upside down."

When the tape was finished, Sean announced that he had no further questions for the witness. Parker popped right up.

"Mr. Laturner, do you have other recordings of my client and Michael Gerardi?"

"Just from their time in the cell together that evening."

"So no other conversations, either in the cell on earlier days or outside the cell?"

"Not to my knowledge, sir."

"So you have no idea what Michael Gerardi might have said to my client before this recorded evening in the cell."

"I do not."

"You don't know whether Gerardi manipulated my client into believing he had done something wrong in connection with the actions of his followers?"

"I do not."

"You don't know whether Gerardi—"

Sean was on his feet. "Objection, Your Honor. The witness has explained what he knows. This is just argument."

"Yes," Judge Newton answered, "the objection is sustained. Are there further questions, Mr. Parker?"

"No, that'll do it, judge. Thanks."

"Call your next witness, Mr. Fitzpatrick."

Nora stood instead. "Your Honor, the government rests."

Judge Newton gave his head a slight shake, as if he had misheard. Then he slid his chair forward and looked at the jury. "Members of the jury, why don't you take the lunch recess a bit early today? The court has some legal matters to attend to and then we'll resume at one P.M, with Mr. Parker's opening statement, which you will recall he reserved."

When the jury was gone, Parker rose and made the usual motion to dismiss. Before Nora could respond, Judge Newton lifted a piece of paper close to his face and read the standard language of denial. "The court finds that, drawing all inferences in favor of the government, a reasonable jury could conclude that the government has proven guilt beyond a reasonable doubt."

The crowd audibly stirred, some of its members apparently confused by what they were hearing. The judge looked up and paused before continuing. "This is not to say the court has a view of the evidence or that the jury will find the defendant guilty. This is simply the court ruling on the Rule 29 motion, which requires at this stage of the proceeding that all evidence be viewed in the light most favorable to the government. The court will stand in recess until one P.M."

CHAPTER THIRTY-NINE

"I don't like to keep a jury waiting," Judge Newton said sharply from behind his desk. "And why did this need to be in the robing room, and where is the government?"

Because I'm living in hell, Matthew Parker thought. But he said, "Your Honor, I asked to meet in chambers to seek the court's guidance on a matter that relates to Mr. Buchanan's ability to receive effective assistance of counsel. The court reporter is here, of course, but Ms. Carleton has agreed that we can seek the court's intervention privately. If you like, the court could confirm that with her."

"No, no," the judge said, waving his hand. "If learned counsel represents it to be so, the court accepts that representation. What is the issue?"

Parker looked at his client and then at Riley Pond. "Your Honor, we have a disagreement about the defense's opening statement. Ms. Pond thinks she should do it; I believe I should. We have presented the choice to our client, who has asked us to split it. I told him that, in my experience, that's not done, is not in his interest, and he would need to make a choice. He said that, in that event, he would choose Ms. Pond, something I very much think is not in his best interest. That impasse is the reason we requested an ex parte meeting with the court."

The judge looked at Buchanan. "Mr. Buchanan, you recognize, I assume, that Mr. Parker is a skilled and experienced advocate who operates at the highest level of the legal profession?"

"I do, Judge," Buchanan replied.

"And that Ms. Pond is, well, both less experienced and laboring under a potential conflict in light of her own pending legal issues, a conflict I know you have waived, but one I feel constrained to raise in this context."

"I know all that, Your Honor, but I appreciate you raising it."

"You recognize further that Mr. Parker, experienced counsel that he is, believes it would be in your best interest to have him alone deliver the opening statement?"

"I do, Judge."

"And you know that you will not be able to later complain about the quality of your legal representation if the court should grant your very unusual request to have both your lawyers speak in opening?"

"Yes, Judge."

"Very well, then. Although I have never done it before, in these circumstances, to ensure that a reviewing court understands that the defendant was afforded the representation he desired, I will permit both of your lawyers to speak to the jury at the beginning of the defense case. This portion of the transcript will remain under seal until further order of the court. Now, let's not keep the jury waiting longer."

As the lawyers rose and the deputy marshals escorted Buchanan, the judge called after them. "Oh, Ms. Pond: Because you have previously shown some challenges complying with the court's rules, please be attentive to the proper purposes of an opening statement. There will be no further warning."

"Yes, Your Honor," Pond replied, turning for the door.

"And Mr. Parker?"

"Yes, Judge?"

"I would prefer you go second, in the unlikely event Ms. Pond fails to heed my admonition. That will give your client the benefit of experienced counsel batting cleanup, if you will."

"Got it, Judge," Parker said. *Just shoot me now.*

◆

Riley Pond stood at the podium and pushed the spread fingers of one hand through her long black hair to comb it into place. Then she reached both hands to the hem of her fitted leather jacket and tugged it down before turning to Judge Newton—"May it please the court"—and then turned back to the jury.

"Ladies and gentlemen of the jury. Let me say it again: *Ladies* and *gentlemen* of the jury. You might notice that I didn't say 'members of the jury,' like everybody else around here seems to. That's because there are only two kinds of people on God's green earth—ladies or gentlemen. Least that's what Sam Buchanan believes. Maybe you don't believe that, but he sure does. And he says it, all the time, on his shows. And he also says we can't be a Christian nation any longer if we let the United Nations decide how we should act. Or if we don't control our southern border. Or if we let people kill unborn babies whenever they want to. Or if we push God out of our schools, our homes, our communities.

"Now, you may have a different view of these things. That's all right. It's okay if you don't see what Sam sees. But he does *see* something. He sees a country dying from the inside out. He sees empty churches and drug overdoses and deaths of despair. He sees an emergency like we haven't had since the Japanese attacked us at Pearl Harbor. He sees the need for Americans to stand up and fight for their country. And that's the way he talks, as you've heard in this courtroom. He talks about fighting—a lot. He says that people who undermine our values, our faith, our independence, our borders—they have to go. They have to go."

Pond paused and moved her eyes across the jury box. "But he's not saying they should be beaten or killed. He never said that. He never meant that. He didn't know his followers were going to do that. He didn't want that poor mixed-up gal Carla from Phoenix to get all beat up. It doesn't matter what some horrible career criminal tricked him into saying on that jail tape. That's just garbage. He didn't know what would happen. Smart people with PhDs study this stuff. *They* know what can happen. But *he* didn't. And he feels awful about it."

She turned and stared at Buchanan for several seconds before looking back to the jury. "I love Sam Buchanan. He's a good and decent man, the love of my life—"

A loud voice cut her off. "That's it, Ms. Pond," Judge Newton thundered. "Sit down. Now. You will not testify during a jury address in my court."

Pond paused for several beats before turning and walking silently to the defense table, where she took her seat.

"Mr. Parker," the judge called, "would you like to address the jury on your client's behalf?"

Parker started to stand and then paused in his chair, looking up at the bench before slowly rising. "You know, Your Honor, I think we're good. I think we can go right into the defense case."

The judge looked at Buchanan. "That okay with you, Mr. Buchanan?"

"It is, Your Honor," Buchanan answered.

"Very well. Call your first witness, Mr. Parker."

Parker rose. "The defense calls Samuel Buchanan."

CHAPTER FORTY

Buchanan's direct testimony was predictable and went just as he and Matthew Parker had practiced it. Perhaps he should have realized that his followers would overreact to his words, he testified, especially given the very real and dire threats facing America. But he just didn't. Of course, as a man of faith, he had deep empathy for troubled souls and, once he understood the magnitude of what his followers had done, he carried a special sense of pain for the dead and injured. It was awful and a burden that weighed on him, especially when he was alone in prison.

But of course he wasn't alone. The federal government assigned as his roommate one of the most dangerous and manipulative creatures ever born. Day after day, Michael Gerardi talked about the need for him to process the trauma that had followed his words, to acknowledge and confront the pain he had caused. Gerardi counseled him, argued with him, and cajoled him, telling him he *must* have known what his followers would do. And the sooner he admitted it to himself, the sooner he could heal. That's what he was doing on that tape—trying to heal himself by forcing his spirit to accept that he was responsible for what had happened. The next morning, Gerardi disappeared, never to be seen again.

Shit this guy is a good liar, Sean scribbled to Nora. She just nodded and continued taking notes.

Judge Newton declared the afternoon recess at the close of the direct testimony. As the courtroom emptied out, Benny walked to the defense table, where Matthew Parker sat alone, staring at the wall behind the judge's empty bench and rubbing his shoulder.

"Matty, I'm really hoping you feel the need to take a shower," he said.

"No comment," he answered without turning toward Benny.

"Saw your man Lupo in the back. Douchebag sunglasses, even in court."

"You got no style, Benny."

"What's he doin' here?"

"He's a Buchanan supporter, does some security for him on the side. You know that. Probably just wanted to show it on the day Sam testified."

"Ya know he's a fuckin' corrupt scumbag, right?"

Nora looked back from her table. "Sorry to interrupt, but are you going to want Gerardi? After all that, I figured maybe you would call him."

"Nah," Parker said, "he's more useful to me as a caricature. I'll let you humanize the beast."

"Don't think I'm going to do that," Nora answered. "Feel like that would be gilding the lily."

Parker looked at her with a small smile on his face. "An expression I've never fully understood, honestly, but I'm guessing you think you can convict my piece of shit client without him."

Nora shook her head. "Easy, counselor. You gotta get in touch with some of that empathetic spirit or whatever." She handed Benny a note when he came back to their table. *Tell WitSec to ship Gerardi back to Otisville. Won't be going on.*

Benny nodded. "You gonna eat?"

"Yeah, I'll meet you in our trial room. My mom sent a bunch of sandwiches. But go ahead and get the creep shipped out now."

"Roger that. See you in a few. And I'm gonna see if I can have a chat with my man Lupo. Maybe he knows where Cusak is."

◆

"I'm so frickin' hungry," Benny announced as he came through the door of the trial team's dedicated courthouse workspace. "Perjury always does that to me. What've we got?"

Nora pointed to a tray of sandwiches on long Italian bread. "Teresa Carleton's chicken Parm or tomato and mozzarella with basil, all on unseeded semolina. You get Lupo?"

"Yeah, few words in the hall. I'm actually gonna follow up with him at his office—Wolf Eyes Security or some shit. Where do these assholes come up with these names?"

"That's what his name means in Italian."

"What is?" Benny asked.

"'Lupo' is how you say 'wolf' in Italian."

"Son of a bitch. Learn somethin' new every day. Thought it meant cocksucker."

"Lovely," Nora answered, shaking her head. "Gerardi gone?"

"Yup," Benny said, grabbing one of each sandwich. "They literally just drove off with him. Gone and, I hope, forgotten." He threw an envelope on the table. "Marshals said he left this and asked them to mail it. They're not the fucking Postal Service, so they gave it to me."

"What is it?" Nora asked, reaching for the envelope.

"Dunno. Addressed to that young agent who testified, Loftus. And he didn't seal it."

"Gerardi does nothing by accident," Nora said. "If he didn't seal it, that's because he wants us to look at it."

"You think?"

"I do. And it can't be personal. He's a federal prisoner and she's an FBI agent."

Nora pulled several pages of handwritten text from the envelope and began reading silently. After several minutes, she looked up. "Oh damn. Where's Jessica?"

"Back any minute," Sean answered from the corner. "Why?"

"This creep developed some kind of obsession with Special Agent Loftus. These read like love letters. He calls her his 'little bumblebee.' Goes on and on about how soft her lips are. Says he wants to lick her legs. Ick."

"Ick is right," Benny said, taking a bite of chicken Parm. "Almost enough to make me lose my appetite. Almost."

When Jessica returned, Nora told her about the letter and handed her the envelope. "Okay," Jessica said after she'd read them, "I'll stay back while you guys go to court. Let me give her a heads-up on this. Good news is Gerardi isn't getting out anytime soon."

◆

Nora opened her cross-examination by breaking an unwritten rule. But she only asked a question she didn't know the answer to because she didn't care what Buchanan's answer was. Whatever it was, she would stick it up his rear end.

"Mr. Buchanan, at what point did you realize that your followers were murdering or maiming the people you singled out on your show?"

Buchanan saw the trap and stalled. "I'm not sure what you mean."

"Well," Nora said, "over an eighteen-month period, you severely criticized Emilio Sanchez for two weeks; then he was killed and you stopped talking about him. A month later, you focused on Dr. Edward Fontenelle for ten days, until he was beaten nearly to death and you stopped mentioning him. You talked about Frederick Eton and he was killed and you stopped mentioning him. Then you started talking about Dorothy Davis, who was wounded, and you stopped talking about her. Then there was Carla Rodriguez, wounded by another one of your followers, and finally Professor Ashton Greenstone, shot dead."

She looked up from her notebook. "Do I really need to go through each of them?"

Parker stood but Nora quickly added, "Withdrawn, Your Honor. Let me ask you this, Mr. Buchanan: At what point did you realize that your followers were, to use your word, 'overreacting' to your rhetoric?"

"I don't know."

"Well, was it after the first person was attacked? The third? I mean, you figured it out at some point, right?"

"Objection," Parker called.

Judge Newton stirred. "The objection to the compound question is sustained. One question at a time, Ms. Carleton."

"Yes, Your Honor. When did you figure it out, Mr. Buchanan?"

"I'm not sure I ever did," he answered.

"Well, as part of your job you follow the news closely, am I right?"

"I do."

"And so you were aware that bad things had happened to people who had been featured on your shows."

"Vaguely, although I didn't connect that news to my work."

"Seems like you sure did lying there on your prison bed."

"That was the product of Gerardi's manipulation."

"Right, the bank robber who overcame your will."

"That's correct."

"So you said that stuff in your cell about the need to water the tree of liberty with blood because Gerardi worked some kind of mind trick."

"I don't know if I'd call it that, but he convinced me that I was responsible."

Nora nodded to her paralegal at the government table. "Mr. Buchanan, I'm going to play some excerpts from your show and then ask you questions about each of them. The first is from five days before Mr. Sanchez's death."

Suddenly the screens lit up with a video of Buchanan drenched in sweat, shouting, "This man is a danger to our country. It's him or us. The tree of liberty must be watered from time to time with the blood of patriots and tyrants."

"Is that you?"

"Of course it is."

"Had you met Michael Gerardi yet?"

"No."

Five more times, Nora nodded to April and the screens came to life. Five more times, Nora asked the same questions and got the same answers.

Nora then paused for so long that the jurors all turned to their left to see if she was still at the podium. Then she spoke.

"So when the jury heard you lying on your bunk saying you knew all along what would happen to these victims, *that* was entirely the product of Michael Gerardi's manipulation, is that your testimony?"

"It is."

"I have no further questions, Your Honor."

CHAPTER FORTY-ONE

Jessica was sitting waiting as Nora walked into the courthouse workroom.

"How'd it go?" Jessica asked.

"Okay, I think, although I'm biased," Nora answered. "How's Agent Loftus?"

"Yeah, about that. It's both not as creepy as we thought and at the same time creepier than we thought."

Nora dropped her files on the desk. "Okay, now I'm confused."

"Sit," Jessica said.

"Oh damn," Nora replied, dropping into a chair. "Tell me."

"They were hooking up during their private meetings in the attorney visitation room."

"You must be fucking kidding me."

"I wish," Jessica answered. "She says he convinced her that it would lend an air of reality to their meetings. He told her nobody would believe he was meeting on consecutive days with a paralegal. She needed to pose as a paralegal who was secretly his girlfriend or he would be in danger."

Nora's eyes went wide. "So she did it? Please tell me I'm wrong."

"She did it." Jessica looked down at her notes. "She says it was just kissing, but a lot of it. She said, and I quote, 'He didn't push. I think he is from the old Italian school. I think he really cared about me and I think he really respected me.'"

Nora was shaking her head from side to side. "Unbelievable. So what does Special Agent Bumblebee make of the caring, respectful letters from Mister I-want-to-lick-your-legs?"

Jessica looked down and read. "Quote: 'He fell for me, but I'm sorry. It was work for me. I had never been undercover before. I had never worked organized crime before. Maybe I should have handled it differently.'"

"You think?" Nora shouted before dropping her face into her hands. "Oh. My. God."

Benny came through the door, followed by Sean. "Well done, DUSA," he said cheerfully before noticing her hands over her face. "Wait, what did I miss? What's wrong?"

Nora spoke through her fingers. "Just the usual stuff. Special Agent Loftus sucked face with Michael Gerardi inside the MDC, repeatedly. He had a pet name for her: bumblebee."

"Stop," Benny said, then dropped his smile and turned to Jessica. "No fucking way."

"Way," Jessica answered.

"And now we need to figure out what to do with it," Nora said, still talking with her face covered.

"What do you mean?" Jessica asked.

Nora dropped her hands and looked up. "We have evidence that Michael Gerardi successfully manipulated an FBI agent into kissing him repeatedly inside the MDC. The heart of the defense is that Gerardi manipulated *Buchanan* inside the MDC. We have to disclose this, now."

"Whoa, whoa," Jessica said, lifting her hands. "That's going to cause major heartburn back at 26 Fed. I have to run this up the chain."

"Fine," Nora said. "I love you, so I'll give you the chance, but you better run it up fast. We're going to need to turn this over to Parker tonight so he can decide whether he can use it."

◆

Nora could almost make out the ADIC's words, even though Carmen had the phone pressed tightly to her head.

Carmen waited until he stopped speaking. "Gene, this isn't about anybody wanting to embarrass the Bureau. But *avoiding* embarrassment for the Bureau is never a relevant consideration in a situation like this."

Nora heard more garbled loud talking.

"Yes," Carmen replied, "I know you've gone out on a limb with this case. I know the heat your leadership is getting from wing nuts in Congress about criminalizing speech or some bullshit. I know all that. And I'm grateful for your leadership. But let me tell you what would be *truly* bad for the Bureau—and all of us: convicting Buchanan and then having it thrown out because we failed to turn over material helpful to the defense."

More talking.

Carmen gave Nora an exaggerated eye roll before speaking into the phone. "Yes, that's what Brady material is—information material to the defense, either because it's exculpatory or impeaching. And there's a hell of an argument that this is *both* because it supports the defense argument that Buchanan was manipulated and it undercuts the credibility of a key player in our case."

More talking.

"Yes, I know we haven't used Gerardi as a witness, but we should have provided this to the defense when Agent Loftus testified. And it actually should have gone to them when we still had Gerardi as a potential witness. We have all kinds of exposure for discovery fouls here, Gene."

Whatever the ADIC said next made Carmen's face flash red before she replied. "Well, let me make this easy for you, Gene. I am the United States Attorney, appointed by the president and confirmed by the United States Senate, and we are turning this over. It's the Bureau's fault for putting a new agent in that spot. And, yes, I'm sorry about what this will do to her career. But I run this office and we sure as hell are going to comply with our constitutional discovery obligations. This goes over to the defense, tonight. End of discussion."

Carmen held the phone away from her head and Nora could make out the words "bullshit," "uncalled for," and "unprecedented" in the string of sounds that followed.

"I'm sorry you feel that way. Good night."

Carmen looked at Nora after hanging up. "Well, that was fun. I'm guessing I won't be invited to the ADIC's July Fourth party this year. Just as well, with the pain-in-the-ass elevators."

"Thanks, boss," Nora said.

"Why I get the big bucks," Carmen replied. "Let's just convict this fucker."

"On it," Nora answered, heading for the door.

"Hey," Carmen called after her. "You think Gerardi did this thing with the letter because you didn't use him as a witness? To get even somehow?"

Nora paused. "With anyone else, I'd say not, but it's entirely possible," she said. "See you tomorrow."

CHAPTER FORTY-TWO

Benny was surprised to find a receptionist behind the door into Wolf Eyes Security. A pleasant-looking, middle-aged woman gave him a broad smile from her desk in the small but well-decorated lobby. "Can I help you?"

"Yeah, Benny Dugan to see Lupo."

She picked up a desk telephone that had a long column of intercom buttons and pressed one. "Mr. Lupo? Mr. Dugan is here for you. Certainly."

She hung up the phone and smiled again. "He's just finishing up. Won't be but a minute. Can I get you something to drink? Coffee, tea, water?"

"No, thank you," Benny replied. He was about to begin interviewing her when Lupo appeared in the lobby, not wearing his sunglasses. For the first time, Benny saw that he had hooded but striking hazel eyes.

"Benny, good to see you," Lupo said, extending his hand, which Benny shook. "Come on in."

As Lupo led him down a hallway, Benny counted five small offices, three of which were occupied by men seated at a desk on the phone or typing on a computer. "Gotta be honest," he said to Lupo's back. "I didn't expect this to feel legit."

Lupo laughed as he entered his office at the end of the hall and gestured to an empty chair. "I often have the same reaction," he said as he sat behind his desk. "I've got six people on staff now, counting Ellen at the front desk. Couldn't have imagined it when I left Uncle Sam a few years back. Still makes me nervous to have so many hungry wolves to feed."

When Benny didn't react to his pun, Lupo went on. "Look, Benny, I feel like I should clear the air. Yeah, we got history from the Brooklyn OC squad back in the day. You worked that investigation and no doubt those guys were dirty as hell. Truth is I didn't know it at first, but I figured it out, which is why I beat feet over to the federal side. Maybe that's a chickenshit way to be, and I should have had the balls to stand up and say something, but I didn't. So I ran. That's the truth. I'm not gonna piss on your leg and tell you it's rainin'."

"Appreciate that," Benny replied. "I'm not here to judge. But what's the story with you bailin' on the JTTF? Word I got was you didn't wanna work J6 cases, which seems kinda fucked to me—in keepin' with the whole not-pissing-on-your-leg thing."

Lupo smiled. "I like a direct man. There's some truth to what you say. I don't know your politics and I don't want to know. Maybe they're different than mine; maybe they're not. To me, what happened on January Sixth was bad and nobody should have laid a hand on a cop, but most of it was just a crowd of ordinary Americans gettin' out of hand. Thing is, they wanted us to work it like it was the British had just burned the fuckin' White House or some shit. You hit a cop, of course you should be locked up. But some husband and father with a full-time job who just wandered in there? Even if he took somethin' or pissed in Nancy Pelosi's ferns or some shit. We're supposed to hunt him like a terrorist? When we didn't do shit to people with actual criminal records who attacked cops *and* burned fuckin' cities as part of some George Floyd march or some shit? No, thank you. That's not why I signed up. So I left."

"Yeah, not the way I see it, but whatever. You do you."

Lupo extended his arms, palms up. "And I started all this, which has become a real thing. But let me be clear: I do this for the money. I miss the sense of mission that you have, that I used to have."

Benny paused and drew his mouth into a line before responding. "Some of this money seems kinda dirty, dontcha think?"

Lupo looked to the corner for a moment before answering. "This may surprise you, but yes, I agree. You can't always choose your clients, especially when you're starting out, and I'm not comfortable with some of the stuff Sam Buchanan's accused of. I hate what happened to that poor girl Becky, and to the rest of those people, to be honest. Look, I'm gonna honor my contract, but that's the reason I have my guys supporting his defense team and not me personally."

"So who's payin' Buchanan's bills, if ya don't mind my askin'?"

"Not something I can get into," Lupo answered. He paused, then added, "And not everybody who supports conservative causes is as nuts as Buchanan. But, for me, this is about keeping a business going."

"I appreciate that," Benny said.

"And if I can help you," Lupo continued, "I will, but I still gotta protect client info."

"Yeah, on that: Any idea where Herb Cusak is?"

"Ha," Lupo replied. "I was going to ask you the same thing. Buchanan's defense lawyers would love to find him, but I've struck out."

"Okay," Benny said, "let's stay in touch. You come across anything you think might be of interest, you hit me up."

"Agreed," Lupo said, standing to shake Benny's hand.

◆

Benny called Nora from the car to brief her on his visit with Lupo.

"So a zero," she said when he was finished.

"Yeah, except I may have judged the guy too harshly. He seems genuinely uncomfortable with this crowd."

"Wait, *you* may have judged someone too harshly? I find that hard to believe."

Benny laughed. "Okay, comedian. Get a good night's sleep. You gotta deal with Special Agent 'My Little Bumblebee' or whatever in the morning."

"Ugh, don't remind me. See you tomorrow. Oh, and where are we with the fake-mother message to Cusak? Anything on that?"

"Not yet. Took the Bu longer than they thought to create it. Should have it on the burner phone in the next day or so."

"Okay, thanks."

"No problem. And Nora? You got this bumblebee thing."

"Hope so. Really do. See you tomorrow."

CHAPTER FORTY-THREE

Matthew Parker was leaning forward in his center seat at the defense table, turning his head side to side as he whispered intensely to his client and cocounsel. "This has to be handled very carefully. We have a limited goal here."

"Yeah," Riley Pond whispered, "to show what fools these FBI Deep Staters are. I can't wait to rip her apart."

"Goddamn it," Parker replied. "No, that's not it. This isn't about the deep state or some shit. This is about showing what a manipulator Gerardi was." He lifted a finger to point to Buchanan. "It's about bolstering *his* testimony. That's it."

Buchanan was nodding. "Okay, got it," Pond replied, sitting back in her chair.

Parker leaned away from her to his client's ear. "You know she can't do this, right?" he asked quietly.

"I know," Buchanan said as they all rose at Judge Newton's entry.

When the judge said, "Please be seated," Parker remained standing and walked quickly to the podium by the jury box, loudly announcing, "The defense calls Special Agent Janet Loftus."

Riley Pond jerked her head toward Parker and began to stand, but Buchanan reached across Parker's empty chair and put his left hand on her forearm. When she stayed seated, he removed his hand, glancing back at the deputy marshal behind him and mouthing, Sorry.

Janet Loftus looked ill as she stepped up to the witness chair and took the oath. She was dreading this moment, but Parker's questioning was strangely reassuring—and also confusing. She was a dedicated public servant and a good agent, Parker established: smart, well trained, careful. She was relatively new, of course, but she had been taught that informants were a potentially dangerous threat to the FBI's commitment to integrity and they were to be handled with extreme care. She knew that was especially true of Gerardi, who had been a jailhouse informant many times over, convincing hardened criminals to trust him and tell him things he could use to reduce his own jail time. Yet, despite the training, the warnings, and the knowledge that good informants were always good manipulators, Michael Gerardi still convinced her to kiss him repeatedly in the attorney visitation room at the MDC. She was embarrassed by it, likely to suffer professional consequences for it, and it was entirely out of character for her. But she did it anyway—because he convinced her they needed to do it.

Nora was deeply uncomfortable listening to this. She knew Parker was making Loftus sound better than she was and Gerardi worse, but how could she object and look like she was trying to hide something or protect someone like Gerardi? So she stayed seated, scribbling notes to Sean. *Can't object here. Don't think I can cross her.*

I'll hit it in summation, he wrote back.

"I have no further questions," Parker announced, walking from the podium.

"We'll go right into cross-examination," Judge Newton said, looking at Nora.

She stood and began to say, "I have no—" but stopped and added, "I actually have one, Judge."

Standing at her chair, she asked, "Did Gerardi convince you to *kiss* him or to admit that you knew people were going to be *murdered*?"

"Objection!" Parker shouted.

"Sustained," Judge Newton answered, glaring at Nora.

"Nothing further," she said quietly and sat down to a note from Sean: *Learned counsel breaking bad!*

"Mr. Parker," the judge said, "call your next witness."

Parker stood and buttoned his jacket. "The defense rests, Your Honor."

◆

Judge Newton gave the jurors their usual midmorning break, but stayed on the bench so he could hear and deny Matthew Parker's renewed motion to dismiss. "You've done a good job of raising possible reasons for doubt, Mr. Parker, but, as you know, the court is constrained at this juncture to draw all inferences in favor of the government. The motion is denied and we'll go right into the government's rebuttal case after the break."

Nora rose. "Your Honor, there won't be a rebuttal case. The government rests."

The judge squinted. "I apologize, Ms. Carleton. I assumed you would be calling this Gerardi person about whom we've heard so much."

"No, Your Honor. Mr. Gerardi was available, but neither side called him. Which is why we object to Mr. Parker's request for an 'unavailable witness' jury instruction telling the jury they can hold it against us if we don't call him. It wouldn't be fair for the jurors to assume he was kept from testifying in the defense case."

"Mr. Parker?" the judge asked, flexing his eyebrows.

"Sure," Parker answered, "I could have subpoenaed him, Judge, and the prosecutors were kind enough to volunteer to have him brought into court for me. But I didn't need him. He was *their* informant, not mine, and *they* should have called him. You should still tell the jury they can draw an inference against the government from him not being a witness in their case."

Judge Newton lifted a document close to his face briefly and then continued speaking. "Ms. Carleton, as the court understands the teaching of the Second Circuit, such an instruction may be appropriate if the witness is not equally available to the defense—not just in the sense of being physically unavailable but also in the sense of being uniquely aligned with the government, in the way informants so often are. Here, as you say, I have no doubt that Gerardi was *physically* available to both sides and could have been brought to the witness stand during either the government or the defense cases. But I have serious doubts as to whether he was, if you will, *metaphysically* available to Mr. Parker. His motivation, as I understand it, was to help the government so he might obtain assistance with his own tangled criminal problems. It hardly bears stating that he would have little motivation to assist the defense."

Nora drew her mouth into a line before answering. "I hear you, Judge, and respectfully suggest that Mr. Parker's failure to even ask for an interview undercuts his request. But he has also failed to meet the second prong of the test—that the witness would elucidate issues in the case."

"Seriously?" Parker said loudly. "He's the guy my client says got him to talk about the things the jury heard on that tape. I confess I'm not one hundred percent sure what 'elucidate' means, but he could surely give relevant testimony."

"Then why *didn't* you interview him, Mr. Parker?" Judge Newton said quickly. "Not to be facetious, but this is not, as they say, the court's first rodeo. Might it be that you knew the interview would be less than valuable to your client? Might it be that by declining to interview him and now seeking the absent witness instruction, you are the proverbial orphan seeking leniency for killing his parents?"

Parker glanced at the table to suppress a smile at Judge Newton's uncharacteristic attempt at humor. "Judge," he said, looking up, "I knew this guy would twist every which way to avoid helping me. Same reason I didn't call him at the suppression hearing. It would have been a waste of time, and I respectfully request the instruction."

Judge Newton paused and looked down before ruling. "Very well. I'm sorry, Ms. Carleton, but the court will instruct the jury that they may draw an inference against the government for its failure to call Mr. Gerardi as a witness, and may, but need not, assume that his testimony would have been harmful to the government's case.

He paused and then added, "I'm going to send the jury to lunch early and we will begin summations in one hour."

◆

Nora looked up from her salad. "It was a mistake to push that so hard. I think the judge just saved me from myself. If we convict Buchanan, that would have been a huge issue with the court of appeals. Gerardi is *our* problem and *of course* we should get hit for not calling him. Although I still think we did the right thing by not putting him on the stand in rebuttal."

"No biggie," Sean said.

"Yeah, but still a mistake. I think I'm getting tired."

Sean blew a sharp burst of air—"Pfft"—before adding, "You still think we did the right thing by not calling him?"

"I think so," Nora said, "although I'm not certain. I just think we do better with the jury without wrapping our arms around that guy."

Benny's voice boomed from the back of the workroom. "Or letting him lick our legs."

Nora shook her head and smiled. "Or that."

CHAPTER FORTY-FOUR

S ean delivered the government's main summation. In a typical division of labor, Nora would do the rebuttal. His job was to bring the detail; she would bring the fire.

Sean took the jury through the charges in the indictment: five individual counts of hate crime—one for each victim except Greenstone—and one count of conspiring with the attackers to commit hate crimes, in which the Greenstone killing was alleged to be part of the overall violence conspiracy, even though Greenstone, as a straight, White, able-bodied, American-born male, didn't fit into any of the categories that would allow a federal hate crimes charge.

Sean told the jury that there were two ways they knew Buchanan was guilty: his words on the air and his words from his prison cell. Then he took them through the evidence.

He replayed Buchanan's verbal attacks, his exhortations for people to "go" and his repeated invocation of Jefferson's quotation about the need for blood to water the tree of liberty. "He knew what that meant and he got what he intended. His words to his audience convict him. You don't need any more.

"But if you want more, play the tape from the jail again during your deliberations. There's been a lot of noise about this supposed mentalist Michael Gerardi—and I'm sure there'll be more when Mr. Parker gets up here. I think we can all agree that Mr. Gerardi is not a good person, but that shouldn't be a surprise to Mr. Parker or any of us, because prison is not the place to make friends or meet good people. All I ask is that you watch that tape again and ask yourself: Does that really sound like the product of some kind of mind control? And as Judge Newton will tell you, you shouldn't look at pieces of evidence in isolation.

"Watching a trial is a little like watching autumn leaves fall in the park or your yard. They fall one by one or sometimes in small bunches, some over here, some over there. It's not until they're all raked into a pile that you have a full sense of what you have. Listen to Buchanan on his show all those times. Then listen to him in jail. It's the same man, and all he's doing is acknowledging the obvious. Of course he knew what was going to happen, of course he intended it to happen, because"—and here Sean raised his voice for the first time—"he ordered it! 'Blood for the tree of liberty' wasn't some fancy metaphor; he *literally* told his followers to kill those people! You know from the broadcasts alone that he's guilty, but when you watch the jail tape—when you pull the pile of evidence together—you know he's guilty beyond all reasonable doubt."

Sean paused, as if unsure whether to mention something. "You know, there's also another way you know he's guilty, at least of some of these acts of violence. Because even if you ignore what he actually said about getting rid of these poor people, and even if you ignore what he admitted from his jail cell, you know something else that Samuel Buchanan can't run from, something that Mr. Parker or Ms. Pond can't cross-examine or argue their way out of: After Buchanan singled someone out, after he gave people his special brand of nasty attention, those people started getting attacked. It happened *six* times. At some point he *had* to know. The second time? The third? Even if, for some reason, you want to believe he didn't know at the start, his eyes told him very quickly what was happening."

Sean continued with a sarcastic tone that was jarring coming from a quiet prosecutor. "So maybe the first was an unfortunate accident. I mean, all he did was suggest Emilio Sanchez had to go and the tree needed blood and whatever and, oh my gosh, Emilio got murdered. So unfortunate. But then it happened with Dr. Edward Fontenelle. Has to go, blood for the tree, and, oops, Edward is beaten within an inch of his life. Wow, who could have figured?"

Sean turned and pointed at Buchanan. "You know who could? *He* could. Because he's not blind, or deaf and dumb. Even if, for reasons I can't imagine, you cut him a break and decide Sanchez and Fontenelle are freebies, just accidents, by the time we get to poor Frederick Eton or Dorothy Davis—before we *ever* get to Carla Rodriguez or Professor Greenstone—Buchanan knows what his magic words do: they are orders to his followers that bring death and destruction. And when he keeps saying them, he's guilty of those crimes and of conspiracy, as guilty as if he had attacked those people himself."

Sean finished up with the usual government appeals to common sense and careful adherence to the judge's instructions and then returned to the prosecution table. As he took his seat, he noticed Benny nodding subtly, a tight-lipped expression of pride on the big man's face. Then Benny gestured with his chin to a Post-it note in his handwriting sitting just in front of Sean. *Deaf, dumb, and blind? Boom. I have both a Helen Keller and a Tommy joke for you at the break.*

◆

Judge Newton asked Matthew Parker whether he wanted to take a short break before his summation.

Jesus, the Irish kid is a beast. Who the fuck knew? "Yes, Your Honor, that would be great, thanks."

CHAPTER FORTY-FIVE

P arker stood at the podium and looked around. He could hear himself speaking the usual words of courtesy before a jury address—"Your Honor, government counsel, Mr. Buchanan, members of the jury"—but he was far away. *This really is the last time,* he thought. *God, how I've loved this life, this profession, these courtrooms. Now it ends, arguing for this guilty piece of shit. But the profession will get my best swing.*

When he came back to the moment, Parker felt his fingers buttoning his suit jacket and noticed the jurors were all staring at him. But he only looked at one of them. Juror number 12, Yonkers guy, was his best shot at a hung jury. His obligation was to do his best for his client and, in his professional judgment, the best possible outcome on these facts was a hung jury. He would ask juror number 12 to force a retrial—and then Buchanan could get another fucking lawyer.

"Samuel Buchanan believes this country is in crisis," he began, "that its very identity is threatened, that we risk losing everything that once made us a shining city on a hill. Maybe you agree, maybe you don't. What matters is something we all agree on—that the rule of law is the bedrock of our civilization. And at the heart of the rule of law are ordinary Americans serving on juries. Those citizens stand between the awesome power of the state and those who may be unpopular with the powerful, those who may be out of step with the fashions of the day, who may speak in a politically incorrect way."

He turned and pointed to his client. "*There* is one of those people. *There* is someone who is definitely out of step, especially in our metropolis. The things he cares about are not the things most people care about here. But being out of step, controversial, even outrageous in the eyes of sophisticates, is not enough to land you in jail. For that, the government must do something much, much harder. They must prove guilt by competent evidence beyond a reasonable doubt to a jury of twelve, who must agree *unanimously* that they have met their burden of proof. If even *one* of you disagrees in good conscience, the state may not take away my client's liberty. *That* is our protection against the tyranny of the majority, against the domination of the popular."

Holy shit, Sean scribbled, *he's going for a hung jury with #12.*

Nora gave just the slightest nod.

Parker locked eyes with Juror 12 as he parsed the words on Buchanan's shows, as he castigated Gerardi as a master manipulator the government wouldn't even vouch for as a witness. He stared at Juror 12 as he pleaded with the jury not to let one man's expression of unpopular, even outrageous, opinion become a criminal offense, not to let the government tar a prominent figure with the terrible acts of a misguided few.

And he finished by looking at Juror 12. "Be that bulwark against the state," he pleaded. "Represent the rule of law, which endures no matter the state of our borders, our neighborhoods, our families. Hold the government to its burden, which they have failed to meet. Ms. Carleton and Mr. Fitzpatrick are good people, but this case is filled with reasonable doubt. Please vote not guilty on all counts. Thank you."

Parker walked slowly to his seat, where he slid into place between Pond and Buchanan, who had been looking at his back the entire time and didn't know he had been looking at a single juror. Buchanan reached over and squeezed Parker's forearm. "That was inspirational. Incredible."

Yeah, and you're still gonna go down like a box of rocks. "Thanks," Parker whispered. "Let's hope it's enough."

"Really great," Pond whispered.

You can rub against each other all you want at the retrial. "Appreciate it," he said quietly.

"We'll take a brief recess," Judge Newton announced.

◆

Nora was too pumped to sit down in the workroom. "Damn," she said, "I have to do a rebuttal I've never done before. I've got to convince a juror not to violate his oath."

"Not gonna be easy," Benny said. "Matty was aimin' right at him. How the fuck did that guy get on the jury anyway?"

When nobody responded, he added, "My bad."

"He was coming on anyway, Benny," Sean said. "We had to pull NYU lady."

Nora wasn't listening. She was staring at the spot where the far wall met the ceiling. Then she lowered her eyes and turned to April. "Hey, do me a favor and print the section of the judge's jury instructions about the duty to deliberate, will you?"

April flipped open her laptop and began typing. "Got it. Two seconds."

The printer in the corner began whirring. When it stopped, April grabbed the page and handed it to Nora. "Thanks. Let's do this," Nora said, heading for the door.

◆

"Ms. Carleton will now deliver the government's rebuttal summation, and then the court will instruct you on the law and the case will be yours to deliberate. Ms. Carleton?"

"Thank you, Your Honor."

Nora stood and took two steps to the podium, which was set at the midpoint of the jury box. She took a deep breath and began, her eyes sweeping back and forth across the jurors. "Thank you all for your attention throughout this trial, and I'm grateful for just a few minutes to speak to you as the case ends. I'm not going to repeat what Mr. Fitzpatrick said or respond to all the points Mr. Parker made. Instead, I want to focus on one important thing."

She stared at the back left corner of the jury box, where Juror 12 sat, and spoke very quietly. "This case isn't about who's popular or unpopular, politically correct or controversial."

Then she stunned the room, looking at the entire jury and raising her voice almost to shouting. "It's about *violence*. It's about *murder*. It's about *vicious assaults* on vulnerable people. It's about death and disability, blood and broken bones. It has absolutely nothing to do with Samuel Buchanan's views of America. Nobody in America gets to kill and maim other people. Nobody gets to order that Carla Rodriguez be beaten to the point of brain damage. Nobody gets to order Emilio Sanchez's death. It doesn't matter how angry you are. It's against the law! You want to talk about freedom and the tree of liberty? There is no country, we aren't even human, if people are free to do that to others."

Then she lowered the volume slightly. "It's time to stop the clever word games, the subtle appeals to political beliefs. It is time for accountability under the law. And we all have responsibilities that we are duty bound to uphold."

She put her hand to the center of her chest. "I'll start here. The government bears the burden of proving guilt beyond a reasonable doubt. That burden never shifts. Hold us to it."

Now she almost whispered. "Because we've met that burden. We have gone *far* beyond that burden. There is no possible doubt about Samuel Buchanan's guilt."

Nora dropped her hand and took a step back before sweeping the same hand across the jury box and bringing her voice up to a normal level. "*Your* responsibility is to decide the case based only on the evidence and to listen to each other as you do that. Here is a part of what Judge Newton is going to tell you in just a minute."

She lifted a piece of paper off the podium and read from it. "You should make every reasonable effort to reach a verdict. In doing so, you should consult with each other, express your own views, and listen to your fellow jurors' opinions. Discuss your differences with an open mind. Do not hesitate to reexamine your own view and change your opinion if you come to believe it is wrong. But you should not surrender your honest beliefs about the weight or effect of evidence just because of the opinions of your fellow jurors or just so that there can be a unanimous verdict. You should give fair and equal consideration to all the evidence. You should deliberate with the goal of reaching an agreement that is consistent with the individual judgment of each juror."

Nora set the paper on the podium and fixed her eyes on Juror 12. "The rule of law depends upon people doing what they promised to do. There is only one just verdict in this case, one verdict consistent with the law and the evidence. Samuel Buchanan is guilty on all counts. Thank you very much."

CHAPTER FORTY-SIX

Jessica's voice came through Benny's radio. "Big man, what's your twenty?"

"Southbound on the Jersey Turnpike, Meadowlands, not far from the stadium. Motherfucker Lupo just pulled a U-ee through the guardrail and lost me. He's in the wind northbound someplace. You?"

"In my car, headed to the Holland Tunnel. The Wilkes-Barre team finally grabbed Cusak outside his mom's place. They're taking him to our Scranton office. Meet you there?"

"Copy that," Benny answered. "I'll hit Route 80 and run lights and siren the whole way. Looking forward to this."

"Okay, Speed Racer, but wait for me, 'kay?"

"Will do. Drive safe."

◆

Jessica dropped a Redweld folder onto the interview room table, where it landed with a loud bang.

"You're a hard man to find, Mr. Cusak," she said. "I'm Jessica Watson and this is Benny Dugan. I know you've been read your rights and I'm hoping we can have a brief chat."

Cusak's eyes darted between Jessica and Benny. "About what?" he asked nervously. "Nobody will tell me what this is about."

"It's personal—to you," Jessica answered. "Nothing to do with the Buchanan case, if that's what you're asking. But I think you're going to want to hear what I want to share with you."

Cusak's prominent Adam's apple bobbed up and down. "I'm not sure I want to be talking with you, at least until I understand what we're talking about."

"That's fine," she answered gently. "I need to tell you some things we've learned. But before I do, I need you to know something: It's going to be okay. We will find a way to resolve this situation."

Cusak's narrowed his eyes and scrunched his nose. "I'm not following you."

"You will, in a second," she answered, "but things like this can be emotional, so I wanted you to know up front that it's going to be okay. There's a way through it."

He still looked confused, but said, "Okay."

Jessica put her hand on top of the thick file. "Oh, and it's really important that you not lie to us, even a little, because that will make it hard to find a way through."

Cusak shrugged. "Okay, I still have no idea what you're talking about, but okay."

She used her open hand to push the file halfway to Cusak. "There's no easy way to say this, but you've been involved in online activities related to children that—"

He started to shake his head and interrupt. "I haven't—"

"Nope, nope," Jessica interrupted back. "As I said, it's really important that you don't lie to me or it's going to be hard to find a way through this. So please just listen."

Cusak continued shaking his head, but he was quiet.

Jessica nodded toward the file, which was still held down by her hand. "This file is full of printouts of some of that activity. I hope you won't make me show those to you, because I find it very upsetting. What's in this file will bring a federal prison sentence of many decades. You would never get out, except there is a way—"

Cusak was visibly sweating as he broke his silence. "I have no idea what you're talking about. I would never do things inconsistent with the values of the people I've associated with—"

Benny had been quiet for so long that the sound of his Brooklyn baritone surprised even Jessica. "See, that's the thing, Herb," he said loudly. "The people you're hooked up with got no fuckin' values at all and I pray, I pray, you don't listen to Special Agent Watson here. I pray I get to lock your motherfucking pedophile ass up for the rest of your miserable life. So *please*, tell us to get lost. *Please*. I'm beggin' you."

Cusak seemed frozen, staring at Benny for several beats after the room went quiet. Then he slowly turned to Jessica, looking stricken. He began to cry. "I won't make you show me the pictures. I have a problem, and I think people want to kill me like they did Becky. I need help. Please help me." He dropped his chin to his chest and started sobbing.

◆

"She flipped him like a fuckin' pancake," Benny said with a broad smile. "Seriously, Nora, you shoulda seen it. If there's an Oscar for Best Good Cop, she's up there givin' her acceptance speech."

Jessica tilted her head at Benny sitting next to her on Nora's office couch. "With an assist from Mr. Terrifying Cop here, who scared the daylights out of ol' Herb."

Benny nodded. "Thanks. It's a gift." He turned to Nora. "And thanks for giving us a hall pass so we didn't need to sit through the judge's jury instructions. This was much more fun."

"My pleasure," Nora answered. "So with all your fun, what'd you get?"

"A lot," Jessica said. "SparkNotes version: Lupo is the bagman for some mysterious guy named Bernard Epps—"

Benny interrupted. "Same name as the old fuck in Gwen Harmon's poolside cabana, by the way."

"—who funded Buchanan-world and a bunch of spin-offs. Lupo would call Cusak and tell him who or what Buchanan should focus on, and Herb would write it into the show. He actually hadn't met Lupo in person until pretty late; Buchanan just told him this guy would be calling and to do what he said. So Lupo would tell him to focus on Carla or Professor Greenstone or whatever, and that's who they would talk about."

"Whoa," Nora said, leaning back in her chair and shooting a look at Sean.

"I know," Benny answered. "Cusak says Lupo called him a few times when Buchanan was first locked up, trying to talk him into staying on the team, but he was too afraid. So it looks like Lupo picked up the job of online-idiot mantainer after Buchanan got detained and Herb went to ground—Lupo now tells all the wannabe Buchanans of the world what to talk about and gives them the script.

"And the latest obsession," Benny added, "is a big UN rally in September for global unity or some such. These nut bags are focused on it like you can't believe."

Nora didn't react to that, instead asking, "And what can our new informant tell us about this Epps?"

"Almost nothing," Jessica replied. "From Buchanan, he knows Epps is the money and the direction behind Lupo, but that's it. Doesn't know where he hangs out, how he works, what his motivation is."

"Ugh," Nora answered. "And so what are the next steps with Cusak?"

Benny took that. "He still denies knowing anything about Becky's murder, but he's scared shitless he could be next. He also admits knowing on some level that Buchanan's show was causing people to be hurt and killed. He wants a deal. He's got nowhere to go except with us. To test him, the Bu's gonna to try to connect him with Lupo on the phone and see what they can get, although that's a long shot."

"Okay," Nora said. "Good work on this, all of you. Let's just hope the jury does the right thing on Buchanan. Maybe we'll learn something when he's finally nailed. See you all in the morning."

CHAPTER FORTY-SEVEN

Benny looked across the courthouse workroom table at Jessica. "This is the worst part of a trial. Like waiting for a baby to be born, but without the fun part."

Nora looked up from her laptop. "The *fun part* of childbirth? I must have missed it."

"Yeah, I didn't mean it that way," Benny replied. "That whole thing sucks—for the woman for sure—but at the end you get a life, a child. You got Sophie. Here, the victims are still dead or fucked up. We're just waiting to see if we can put a guy in jail until he dies. There's no joy in it. Satisfying, for sure, but not fun."

Jessica turned to Nora. "And why haven't we heard from them? It's been three days."

"No way to tell with a jury," Nora said. "Everything on this side of the door is just guessing. Everybody has an opinion but—"

She was interrupted by a knock on the door, which opened, and Judge Newton's clerk leaned in. "We have a note. They have a verdict on two counts but are unable to reach a verdict on the rest. Judge wants counsel in the courtroom. He's going to give them an Allen charge."

◆

It was obvious when the jurors took their seats. As Judge Newton read the Allen charge—named for an 1896 Supreme Court case authorizing a supplemental instruction to urge a divided jury to make every effort to reach unanimity—Juror 12 sat with folded arms, leaning away from the others. The prosecutors passed notes to each other.

Parker got #12, Sean scribbled.

Not all the way, Nora wrote back.

Unless the two counts are not guilty.

FML, Nora answered.

Family and medical leave?

Seriously? Fuck my life. You gotta get out more.

Juror 12 scowled as the judge explained that another jury would be no better than they were, and the parties had invested time, effort, and trust in them, so they should go try harder. He nodded slightly when the judge added that, despite the instruction, no juror should surrender merely because he or she is outvoted. He glanced at the defense table as they filed out to continue deliberating.

◈

The jury gave it another day before the foreperson handed the deputy marshal a note saying they were in the same place: verdicts on two counts and deadlocked 11-1 on the rest. The judge would have to take a partial verdict; he definitely could not give further instructions to a jury that had revealed its numerical split.

After the jurors filed into the box with the same obvious body language divide, Judge Newton ordered Buchanan to stand and asked the foreperson to announce the counts on which the jury had reached a unanimous verdict.

"Yes, Your Honor," she said, standing. "We have reached a verdict on counts one and six."

The judge's courtroom clerk interrupted, not to be denied his usual dramatic role in taking a verdict. In his master-of-ceremonies voice, he said, "As to count one, conspiracy to commit hate crimes, how do you find: Guilty or not guilty?"

"Guilty," she answered in a strong voice.

The courtroom erupted with a series of angry voices. "Shame, shame!" a woman yelled from the back. "Deep state!" a man shouted from the middle.

The sound of Judge Newton's gavel echoed off the back wall. He was standing as he banged, and shouting, "Silence! Silence!"

The crowd went quiet, stunned by the judge's ferocity. "If there is another *sound* from the gallery, I will clear this room and jail those responsible." He turned his head from side to side, studying the entire audience, before sitting and saying quietly to his clerk. "You may continue."

The ring announcer's voice rang out again. "As to count six, the attempted murder of Carla Rodriguez, how do you find: Guilty or not guilty"

"Guilty," the foreperson answered.

When the audience murmured, Judge Newton lifted his gavel threateningly and held it until the sound stopped. Then he looked at the jury and the defense table. "Madam foreperson, Mr. Buchanan, you may be seated."

???, Sean wrote.

Weird but he'll still get life, Nora answered.

Matthew Parker stayed standing, but Judge Newton anticipated his request. "Poll the jury," he directed his clerk.

"Members of the jury," the clerk announced, "as I call your number, please answer yes or no. Juror 1, is that your verdict?"

"Yes," the foreperson answered.

"Juror 2, is that your verdict?"

Number two, a middle-aged elementary school teacher from the small town of Somers in suburban Westchester County, did not answer, instead giving her head just the slightest shake from side to side.

The clerk spoke more loudly now. "I will ask again. Juror 2, is that your verdict?"

The woman remained silent and looked down before raising her chin and saying, "Yes, it is, reluctantly."

Judge Newton intervened in a stern voice. "Madam, jury service is a heavy responsibility. But I need the record to be clear as to whether the jury is unanimous. So I ask you again, is this your verdict?"

"It is," she said quietly.

"Very well," the judge answered. "Continue the polling."

The clerk moved through the box until reaching the last juror, who answered loudly, "It very much is."

FML, Sean scribbled to Nora. *We were wrong on 12.*

Yup, she wrote back. *Never know.*

Judge Newton excused the jurors, explaining that he would have farewell words for them in the back.

CHAPTER FORTY-EIGHT

The trial team was seated in a semicircle of chairs in front of Carmen's desk at 26 Fed. "So how do we make sense of this result?" she asked.

"Always tricky with a jury," Nora answered. "Our current theory is that number 2, to our surprise, must have wanted to help Buchanan as much as she could. But she had to give in on Carla and the conspiracy for the reasons Sean argued in summation. Even if you throw out the jail tape and give Buchanan every benefit of the doubt, he *had* to know by Carla."

"Right," Sean added. "And if Buchanan knew what would happen to Carla and to Greenstone, 2 had to sign on for the conspiracy charge as well."

"And to take the guessing a little further," Nora said, "it's possible 2 didn't want to hit Buchanan with any actual murder charges because maybe she figured that would mean life in prison."

Sean chuckled. "Dumb shit doesn't know the sentencing guidelines for this are still gonna have Buchanan die in a cell."

Carmen smiled tightly. "Isn't it also possible, based on what you told me, that Juror 2 was reluctant because she wanted to convict on everything and Juror 12 was happy because he thinks he delivered a win for Buchanan? In other words, that you were actually right about 12?"

Sean grimaced. "Honestly, boss, I'm too tired to sort it out."

Nora just nodded, so Carmen continued. "Regardless, a win for justice, as I will now explain to the press." She looked at Jessica. "Will the ADIC be joining me for this victory lap or shall I handle the questions about leg-licking all by my lonesome?"

"Not sure," Jessica answered. "I can call."

"No, no," Carmen answered quickly. "Our press people will handle it. No sense you getting in the middle of a family feud."

Jessica looked visibly relieved. "Oh God, thank you."

◆

Nora stayed behind as the team filed out.

"How're you feeling, DUSA?" Carmen asked.

Nora scrunched her face before answering. "Good, I think. We got the bad guy."

"That's how I see it," Carmen answered. "Who will now spend decades in prison. That'll send a message of deterrence to the threatening voices at the edges of our democracy."

"That's *good*," Nora said.

Carmen smiled. "Yup. Been practicing that one. And the Bureau thinks they're the sound-bite experts. Hah."

As Nora turned to go, Carmen added, "And, hey, it was still the right thing to use the Gerardi tape—and to not use him as a witness."

"I hope so," Nora said quietly.

"I'm serious. I'll bet it's what helped the eleven stay strong, at a minimum."

"Maybe," Nora answered, looking at her phone. "Good luck with the presser. I have, like, ten missed calls from Matthew Parker."

In the hallway, she caught up to Benny. "Matty's blowing up my phone."

"Mine, too," Benny said. "Just got off with him. Says his client is still in the courthouse cellblock and wants to talk to us before they ship him back to MDC."

"That's strange," Nora said. "What do you think?"

"Hey, Matty's asking for the favor, and it never hurts to listen to a scumbag who now realizes he's going to die in jail."

"Maybe, but I don't want to do any kind of proffer agreement with this piece of crap."

"Matty says he doesn't want any kind of deal. Doesn't really want even a conversation. Just has something he wants to get off his chest."

"Okay," Nora said. "Meet you by the elevator. Let me tell Sean we're running over there."

Buchanan was handcuffed and back in his gray paper jumpsuit as a deputy marshal guided him into the cellblock attorney visitation room. Parker stood and pulled out an aluminum chair for his client, but Buchanan shook his head and looked at Nora and Benny sitting on the far side of the metal table. "I'm not here for a chat." He turned to the deputy, who had stepped back into the hallway. "Please don't go far. This will be but a moment."

Buchanan then stared across the table, his eyes shifting between Nora and Benny. "As I said to Matthew, I just want to tell you something—two things, really—in case my journey continues its uncanny parallels to Jeffrey Epstein's.

"You appear to have succeeded in using your system to silence me. So be it. Congratulations. I will, as they say, take it like a man, although perhaps my gender reference is unfashionable. But, first, please know that I am but a small cog in the machine of liberty, which will grind on and have its vengeance for our country's sins. You have no idea. And, second, I had nothing to do with the death of poor Becky. I pitied that confused child, but I never wanted harm to come to her. The machine consumed her, as it will all who sin against America. It is out of my control. Or yours."

With that, Buchanan turned into the hall and presented himself to the deputy marshal. "Ready to go," he announced loudly. The meeting was over.

"Too bad," Benny said loudly, "I was hopin' we could talk about your boy Epps."

Buchanan paused and made just the slightest turn before shaking his head and continuing down the hallway.

The room was awkwardly silent until Parker finally spoke, gesturing with his head toward his client, who was still visible shuffling down the hall. "Not a fan. Gotta be honest with you. Him, the girlfriend, the fuckin' machine of liberty or whatever. Not gonna miss it. Not one fuckin' bit."

With that, he also turned and left the little room.

Benny looked at Nora. "What. The. Actual. Fuck? That asshole is responsible for Becky's death no matter what fuckin' machine cog killed her. And I wanna personally find that particular cog and lock 'em up with the asshole cog who just left the room."

"My thoughts exactly, and we'll keep working the Becky angle," she replied. "But for now, let's go watch Carmen do her sound bites. Then to Sophie's game? I promised your girlfriend I would bring you if we could get there in time."

"Don't have to twist my arm."

CHAPTER FORTY-NINE

The traffic on the FDR Drive northbound was, as usual, crawling through the curves in the twenties, but Benny wasn't banging on the outside of his driver's side door accusing fellow drivers of being motherless fucks. He was deep in conversation with Nora.

"So what the hell did that mean? What's the liberty machine or machine of liberty or whatever? Is he sayin' it's not just him and his crazy listeners?"

"Don't know," Nora answered. "Buchanan's a bullshitter. Maybe he's bullshitting on his way out. Trying to spread the blame?"

"Maybe," Benny said, drumming his fingers on the top of the steering wheel, "but that's not the way it felt to me. Felt like a final 'fuck you.' Felt like he wanted us to know we missed the big thing that's still out there and there's nothin' we can do about it."

Nora looked out at the East River, swirling as it changed direction with the tide. "Yeah, felt that way to me too."

"So what do we do with it?" Benny asked.

Nora turned and looked at the side of his face. "I think you and Jessica keep pushing. We never did figure out for sure who was funding Buchanan and, if it *is* Epps, what his deal is. We still haven't found Becky's killer—probably the same person who killed the William and Mary professor. Whole thing moved too fast after Becky got killed. But

I think now that Buchanan's done, we take the time and dig harder. Sean can cut you the subpoenas you need."

"And you?"

"Oh, I'll stay around it, but I have so much management stuff to do that it'll be a relief to let you guys run with it. I am the DUSA, you know."

"I heard," Benny said, "I heard. Must be a burden with all the soup tasting and whatever."

◆

At 125th Street, Benny turned off the FDR and crossed the river to Randalls Island, a city-owned enclave at the spot where the East River received the Harlem River and then veered toward the Long Island Sound. "You said Field 90?" he asked Nora, peering at the signs guiding drivers among the maze of athletic fields, homeless shelters, fire training buildings, and psychiatric hospitals. "Jesus, if this spot doesn't capture New York in one place. Why the hell does a fancy girls' school play here?"

"Because this is New York City and the fields are here," Nora replied.

Benny pulled over by Field 90, deposited the placard declaring him to be on official fire department business, and followed Nora to the side across from where Sophie's team stood clustered on the sideline as the coach gave final instructions.

Nora waved to her mother, who gestured to the two empty camp chairs on either side of her own.

"Right on the fifty-yard line!" Benny said, leaning down to kiss Teresa on the cheek before slowly lowering himself into the L.L.Bean chair next to her, which appeared structurally sound.

Nora leaned across her mother. "It's called 'midfield,' Benny. Soccer, remember?"

"Yeah, I know nothing about this," he answered. "You two gotta tell me when and what to yell. And at who."

◆

After the game, Sophie ran across the field to hug her three fans. "You were awesome, kid," Benny said. "And I thought they got away with a lotta fouling and offsides or whatever, and you still won."

"Thanks, Benny. I'm so glad you were here." She turned to Nora. "Mom, I'm going to ride the bus back with the girls, okay? You or Nana meet me at the school?"

"Sure," Nora said. "And we won our case. You want to go out to celebrate with Nana, Benny, and me?"

"That's awesome, but I can't. I'm supposed to give my big presentation tomorrow about the rally for peace that's happening here next month. I really need to practice."

"Makes sense, Bug," Nora said. "See you at the school. We'll grab some takeout on the way home. Your choice."

After she ran off, Teresa turned to her daughter. "Did our little girl just tell us she has too much homework to party with the likes of us? Wow, either she's growing up or we're bad people."

"Ha," Nora answered. "Both, I think."

"Where's your car?" Benny asked Teresa.

"Car? I walked," Teresa answered.

"With the three chairs?"

"Benny, it's a half hour across the pedestrian bridge and these are light as a feather; they go over the shoulder."

"Rugged woman," Benny said with a smile. "You want a lift or what?"

"How about we give Nora the chairs and we walk?"

Nora laughed. "And have me drive Benny's car and claim to be with the fire department? Not on your life. And, not to be *that* person, but I also don't think Benny's supposed to be driving nongovernment people in his g-ride."

Benny shook his head and pointed at Teresa. "Okay, here's the plan. Nora walks and meets Sophie. The two of us take the chairs and how we get across the river is nobody's business. And maybe the two of us go out for a romantic dinner. How about that?"

Nora laughed and slipped the chair strap off her shoulder, dropping it to the ground before heading toward the walking bridge. "What I don't see," she called over her shoulder, "I don't see."

CHAPTER FIFTY

S ix weeks later the team was back in the trial conference room at 26 Fed. "This is making me all nostalgic for the days when I was an actual prosecutor and not just a manager," Nora said.

"That was eons ago," Sean said with a smile.

"A lifetime at the speed we move," Benny added, grinning at Nora. "While you've been administrating and shit, we've been out investigating bad people."

Nora kept a straight face. "I'm sorry—should I be handing out trophies, or did you want to brief the DUSA?"

"The latter," Sean replied as he got to his feet. "Jessica will jump in here, but we wanted to catch you up. We've been on this hard and something interesting is coming together."

He turned and faced the whiteboard, which was organized in sections with neat handwriting in different colors. "Oh," he added, nodding at paralegal April Fugate, "I know we said this isn't an award ceremony, but thanks to April for laying this out so well to help us talk you through it."

April blushed but didn't speak. After an awkward pause, Sean pointed at the left side of the board. "Anyway, Buchanan never took in enough money from his viewers to cover his lifestyle. We discovered from the case that his salary and Herb Cusak's and Becky's came from a

Delaware limited liability company, by the charming name of Freedom LLC. And that Buchanan's apartment was owned by a different one, also organized in Delaware, Liberty LLC."

"Right," Jessica said. "You know LLCs are a pain for us because under Delaware law they're private and don't need to disclose their ownership to anyone, which is why they're one of the state's biggest industries. But both of those were set up by the same law firm in Raleigh, North Carolina. So we got the bank records for the LLCs and also dug into this law firm. Turns out the firm is small, with basically one client: a privately held timber company—probably too small a word—a timber *empire* run by—wait for it—our mystery man, Bernard Epps. Owns thousands of acres of timberland in the southeast *and* the processing plants *and* the shipping. Really, the guy has the entire supply chain from seedlings to plywood and toilet paper. Amazing. And totally below the radar."

Sean tapped on a picture of Epps, who bore a striking resemblance to Arthur Slugworth from the original Willy Wonka movie—close-cropped receding dark hair with a narrow and bony bespectacled face ending in a prominent chin. "Okay, that's Epps. And it *is* the same guy Benny and I met alongside Harmon at The Boulders in Arizona. Keep an eye on him, because his money is all over this now."

He slid to his right and pointed at a section of the board labeled *Communications.* "I went back through the link analysis the Bureau did on all the phone, text, and email data we had collected around Buchanan. The only thing that jumped out at me was the amount of contact between Herb Cusak and David Lupo. They were in touch by phone at least once a week for more than a year before we charged Buchanan. The calls are all to Cusak from a phone owned by Lupo's security firm—the warm and fuzzy Wolf Eyes Security. All less than a minute. No texts, no emails that we can find. Consistent with what Cusak told us about Lupo calling with orders. And we have no contact between Lupo and Buchanan at all, although he was there the day Becky was killed."

"I remember that," Nora said, looking at Benny.

"Yup," Benny added, "just inside the apartment, standin' behind Matty Parker. Cusak remembers him coming one other time, when Harmon was there. And he came to the trial, you remember, his people provided security support for team Buchanan, and I had also had that chat with him at his office. He said it was all business and whatnot, didn't know nothin' 'bout nothin'. Pretty convincing, actually. Still, we decided we should sit on him, which I did a lot the last few weeks."

"Anything there?" Nora asked.

"Not much," Benny answered. "Lupo's got good OpSec and I'm sure we don't have a handle on all his comms. He works with a small team and no obvious clients outside Buchanan-world. I'm gonna stay on him."

Sean was now standing in front of a section labeled *Finances*. He tapped on the board. "*This* is the new part. Turns out that both the Freedom and Liberty LLCs are funded with money coming out of the Raleigh law firm, and Liberty also pays Lupo enough to cover his whole Wolf Eyes operation. It also looks like they're using the LLCs to fund other Buchanan wannabes around the country. Nobody with his reach, but the same vibe, if you take my meaning. Millions of dollars moving through these LLCs to Lupo and wing-nut American patriots."

"But wait, there's more, as they say," Benny added. "The wing nuts are all talkin' about the UN rally on Friday. Presidents of France, Ukraine, Mexico, lots of places, are supposed to be there. And the guy with the weird sunglasses from U2. I'd pronounce all the names but I don't want to show off."

Nora mostly suppressed a smile as Benny continued.

"Obviously, Buchanan used to crap all over the UN and he mentioned this rally a few times, but, of course, he got locked up before things got goin'. Now all his mini-mes are pickin' it up like it's gonna be the Antichrist and the Apocalypse or some shit. Dark and crazy stuff that's about to hit a big fuckin' fan right here in our beloved city."

Sean moved back to the *Communications* section of the board. "As Benny said, we're sure we don't have a full handle on Lupo's communications. The last couple months, he's still making short calls to different burner phones. And now we also have *Lupo* delivering messages to crazy podcasters around the country, which is the kind of thing Cusak used to do for Buchanan. Might be doing some kind of coaching or messaging."

The room was quiet for several beats before Nora spoke, gesturing at the board but looking at Benny. "You think this could all be the 'machine of liberty' Buchanan was going on about?"

"Don't know," Benny said, "but I'm startin' to think Buchanan was tellin' us he's just one player in a big fuckin' band. I mean, he mighta been the lead singer, but that sicko music is going on. And this dude Epps is backin' the band, through Lupo, I'm guessing."

"Any direct connection between Epps and any of the mini-mes?"

"Zip, but remember, we don't know much."

Nora nodded before adding, "Anything else I should know about this Epps?"

"We don't really have anything," Sean answered. "And not for lack of trying. He's totally below the radar. No political contributions, no memberships. We're not even sure where he lives. Everything anywhere near him is held in the name of some company, and those stack like Russian nesting dolls."

"Heck," Jessica added, pointing at the board. "That's his driver's license photo. We're using it because we could only find one other picture of the guy, from the day he killed a huge bear in North Carolina and some hunting guide snapped a picture and put it on Instagram. I'm guessing Epps didn't know the dude did it."

"Yikes," Nora replied. "The license photo is scary enough. So what are next steps?"

"We'll obviously push the threat info on the UN thing through the JTTF," Jessica replied, "and keep watching Lupo, which has become Benny's specialty."

"Yeah," Benny added with a smile, "I'm gonna put it on my LinkedIn page as one of my achievements. Nothin' unusual from him. But we'll stay on it."

"I forgot one interesting note," Sean interjected. "The trap and trace we have on Lupo's phone shows an incoming text, right around the time Benny lost him on the turnpike that day during trial when Cusak was grabbed at his mother's. The text came from a phone we think might be connected to Epps. Course, we have no idea what was in the text; just that they connected."

"Interesting," Benny replied. "And that's our only connection like that?"

"Yup," Sean said.

"Okay," Nora said. "Good work, everybody. Keep me posted."

As the group got up to leave, she called after Benny. "Mr. Rough, a word?"

Benny dropped back down on the couch and stretched his legs out, hands clasped behind his head. "Your DUSA-ness? How may I serve?"

"Seriously," Nora said, "about the UN thing. You know Sophie's class is supposed to go. She did the project about it. You think I should tell the school not to? Or just keep Sophie home Friday? I see lots of problems with either of those."

"I get it," Benny answered. "All I can say is that the nuts are focused on this like it's the angry White people Super Bowl. Lotta talk about 'threat to America' and 'patriots gotta rise up' and shit. Maybe it's all bull, but these are the same people who managed to get a bunch of people whacked, including poor Becky. So I think Jessica's doin' the right thing raising the alarm through the JTTF. Good news is that means NYPD will be out in force and they're good at that shit."

"And so you think that's enough to let our girl go?"

"I do not," Benny said, "but I wouldn't want Sophie goin' to the actual Super Bowl either. And I agree with you that you can't tell the school anything. But you could keep her home."

"And something terrible happens? How does that look? What does that do to Sophie?"

Benny grimaced. "Yeah, I don't know, which is why I'm glad nobody looks to me for parenting advice."

CHAPTER FIFTY-ONE

Benny began the warm Friday morning sitting in his minivan outside Lupo's apartment building in Jersey City. He followed him through the Holland Tunnel and up the West Side Highway to his office, on the second floor of a building on West Forty-Ninth Street in Manhattan. He watched Lupo park in front and go inside.

Benny knew the rhythms of the block after weeks of periodic surveillance in his beat-up minivan. The two White guys stood out, loitering in front of the building in dark baseball hats and wearing identical green backpacks, which Benny assessed to be heavy from the way the two stood. A few minutes later, Lupo emerged and spoke to the two. He gripped one by the shoulders, leaning in and speaking intensely before shaking the man with his hands and then releasing him. He repeated the move with the other man before the two men walked off, headed east, leaning slightly under the load of their packs. Lupo watched them until they reached the end of the block and turned south. He then got in his car and drove off, shadowed by a Chrysler minivan.

Benny reported what he had seen to Jessica. "Two White guys with backpacks?" she asked. "On foot in the area of Times Square? What are we supposed to do with that?"

"Yeah, I don't know," Benny answered. "I can only give you what I saw and I'm hoping maybe the hats and matching backpacks stand out. Right now I'm watching fucking Lupo drive in circles around Midtown. If he starts to do anything interesting, I'll hit you on the radio. How long till the UN thing kicks off?"

"I think the first speaker is at one, but people are already gathering there. The VIP area is locked down tight but the whole UN plaza is a mosh pit already."

"Gotta be honest, partner, the heavy backpack thing is really concerning. You don't think these assholes would go the jihadi route, do you?"

"Honestly, Benny, I wouldn't rule anything out. We haven't seen it with the angry White people crowd, but there are some mighty disturbed folks out there. And the Buchanan minions have spun up a lot of anger at this UN thing. I'm putting out the backpack intel to everyone. I'm at the south end command post, Forty-Second and First."

"Copy that. Back soon."

◆

"Mr. Rough!" came Nora's cheerful voice through the phone.

Benny spoke quickly and seriously. "Hey, you got a quick second?"

"Sure," Nora answered, sensing his mood, "what's up?"

"What'd you decide to do with Sophie and her school and the UN thing?"

"I didn't say anything, 'cause I really didn't have anything to say. I think her class was going to walk down. It's like two miles. They've probably left already. Why?"

"Yeah, here's the thing. I got a bad feeling. Been on Lupo all morning. He met with two White dudes with backpacks on Forty-Ninth. Gave them some kinda pep talk and then they headed off in that direction."

"Oh damn, Benny."

"Yeah, I know. Could be nothin', but could be really bad."

There was a long pause. When Nora spoke again, Benny could hear the anxiety in her voice. "So what do you suggest?"

"Maybe hit Soph on her cell and ask her to go back so you can pick her up for the dentist or something?"

"She doesn't have her cell at school, and what would that look like anyway? I save *my* daughter. Oh my God."

"Maybe call the school and tell them you can't say why but ask them to call the teacher and turn the class around."

Nora was struggling to control her emotions. "But I don't do that for other classes or other schools or other people? Oh my fucking God, Benny."

"Look, I'm sorry. I don't know what the right thing to do is. I just knew I couldn't live with not telling you. I'm on Lupo now. Jessica has passed this to everyone."

"Okay, okay," Nora said quickly. "Appreciate it. Stay safe. Bye."

◆

Twenty minutes later, Benny's voice came through Jessica's handheld radio. "Hey, Lupo has been slowly making his way in your direction. He just stopped at a Lumber Guys hardware store, Thirty-Eighth and Second. This whole thing feels like a surveillance detection run. Wait, wait, he's not going in. He's on foot now down Thirty-Eighth toward First. I'm getting out, but gonna hang back. I have a blending issue."

"You don't say?" Jessica answered. "Copy all. I'm on foot headed down First toward Forty-First to link up with you. Leave the channel open. I've got an earpiece in."

"Copy," Benny said, his breathing now louder in Jessica's ear. "He's turning up First. Lotta people moving that way, toward the UN."

A few minutes later, Benny was in her ear again. "I've lost Lupo in the crowd on First."

Jessica was whispering now. "Shit, the two backpack guys just came out of a park on Forty-First. They're midblock now, by the entrance to a little alley at the Midtown Tunnel ventilation building."

"Copy, coming your way." Benny turned onto Forty-First Street, hugging the south side of the road. He could see two men with backpacks ahead on the north sidewalk. They appeared to be facing the chest-high iron fence at the head of the alley. He could see Jessica ahead, crossing to his side of Forty-First. The two men appeared to be in intense conversation and the younger was visibly agitated, waving his arms angrily. Jessica and Benny were now within yards of each other. They turned and crossed Forty-First with weapons drawn, bracketing the men.

"FBI!" Jessica shouted.

Pop, pop. Two gunshots exploded just as the younger man with the backpack began shouting, "I can't!" and ran east toward the FDR, trying to shimmy the heavy pack off his shoulders. Before he could drop it, a thunderous explosion engulfed the block and the young man disappeared in a cloud of smoke. Jessica was knocked to the ground. Moments later, she sat up and noticed Benny on the ground, not moving.

Through the smoke, she could make out a figure moving away from her, up Forty-First toward First Avenue. She crawled to Benny. He had been shot in the right chest under his arm and was rapidly losing blood. "Fucking Lupo," he muttered and then laid back. Jessica pressed her hand against the dark liquid seeping from Benny's rib cage and noticed motion from the direction of the FDR. She turned to see an ESU officer running toward her through the smoke, his rifle leveled. With her free hand, she pulled her credentials from her pocket and held them high, shouting, "FBI! Jessica Watson, FBI! Agent down! Agent down!"

In seconds, an NYPD medic was at Benny's side and Jessica was robotically briefing the ESU leader, Sergeant George Burrell. "There were two," she said quickly but calmly. "My partner was shot just before the first bomber blew up. Second is White male, thirties, six feet, black cap, green backpack. It's gotta be another bomb. He's heading for the rally."

Sergeant Burrell ran off, toward First Avenue, followed by his team. As they turned onto First, the crowd was thick and slow-moving, as people moved to the right on the narrow piece of First Avenue that led to the UN Plaza as the left side of the roadway headed underground. "Move, move!" he shouted at the backs of pedestrians in T-shirts and crop tops, pushing his way forward, eyes searching for the hat and backpack.

There. As the mob of people surged across Forty-Second and began to spread out with the now-widening roadway, he saw the back of a man wearing a pack and a black hat. He began shouting, "Police, police!" and people between him and the target started to step aside, left and right, opening a wedge to the bomber. Burrell was ten yards away when the man with the backpack heard him and turned, frantically trying to drop the pack from his shoulders. Burrell fired two shots at the man's chest as the bomb went off, exploding fragments of metal into hundreds of bodies.

CHAPTER FIFTY-TWO

Nora's eyes were red rimmed from crying and lack of sleep. Carmen didn't look much better as she stared at her deputy across her office desk.

"You sure you should be working this?" Carmen asked.

"I have to be here," Nora said. "I have to be part of this. I couldn't live with myself if I didn't help."

"Okay," Carmen said quietly. "But I need you to check yourself. If it's too much, you have to promise to tell me."

Nora's response was barely audible. "I will."

Carmen switched to a more clipped tone. "Okay, well, I just got off the phone with the ADIC. The Director and the Attorney General just got back from the White House. Everything, and I mean *everything*, is to be on this. The president is going to speak to the nation in thirty minutes. 'America has been attacked from within,' he's going to say. The Bureau is going to let New York keep the lead, but any resources we need, we'll have them. Priority one is finding Lupo."

"Jessica?" Nora asked.

"Gene says she's going to be okay. Concussed, blown right eardrum, and obviously the trauma from seeing Benny go down. She's still at NYU Langone, where they took a lot of the wounded, but should get out in a couple hours. They can use the bed."

"I'd like to pick her up," Nora replied. "She doesn't have any family here."

"Good. Meantime, Sean's going to sit in the FBI command center and I'm going to send three other AUSAs. Need to make sure they have all the support they need on subpoenas and court orders."

◆

Even in her government car, Nora couldn't get anywhere near the hospital, so she parked and walked the last several blocks, passing crews already assembling the makeshift morgue tents beside the FDR Drive, the same spot where they'd been after 9/11. She found Jessica standing in front of the hospital entrance on First Avenue in the middle of chaotic streams of first responders and the family and friends of the wounded and killed.

They hugged and held the embrace as Jessica whispered "I'm so sorry" again and again.

"No," Nora whispered back, still holding tight. "You did a great thing. You saved a lot of people. You saved my Sophie."

Jessica leaned back enough to see Nora's face, which was streaked with tears. "I'm so glad she's okay, so glad."

Nora nodded. "They were walking down from their school, which is north. The bomb never got to the main area, because of you."

Jessica began crying again. "And because of Benny. What can you tell me?"

"It's bad, Jess. Lost a ton of blood. He's in a medically induced coma. They still don't know. Won't for a while. My mom is with him. His kids are on the way."

The two women walked slowly, arm in arm, to Nora's car. When Nora pulled away from the curb, Jessica spoke. "The last thing he said was 'fucking Lupo.' I don't know whether he saw Lupo—I didn't—or he meant Lupo ran this thing. But either way, finding Lupo's gotta be the thing now. He's the only connection we have to this."

"Whole world is working it. We'll find him. But you've got to rest now."

"I will, I will," Jessica said. She pointed to Nora's phone and added, "Can you hit Sean for a minute? Something came to me in the hospital."

"Sean," Nora said when he answered. "I have Jessica for you."

Sean's voice came through the speaker thick with emotion. "Oh, Jessica, I'm so sorry and I'm so glad you're okay."

"Thanks, Sean. Hey, let me ask you something. Don't know why this popped in my head as I was lying on a stretcher—maybe the concussion—but didn't we think we had a text between Epps and Lupo that came in right when Benny lost him on the Jersey Turnpike the day we arrested Cusak?"

"Yeah, I think that's right," Sean answered. "Why?"

"Long shot, but a maybe. Remind me what Lupo was driving."

"Beautiful new Ford F-150 pickup," Sean said. "I remember Benny's pictures and him joking about how only a commitment to honest work had kept Benny from having one."

"That's what I thought. And that's our long shot. That's what occurred to me. The F-150 has BlueCruise, the hands-free driving system. To make sure you don't sleep while it's driving, the car actually watches your face, using a camera on the steering wheel. If it catches you closing your eyes or looking away, it shakes the steering wheel and eventually stops the BlueCruise if you don't behave. My uncle has one. And—"

"And," Sean interrupted, "anytime there's a digital camera like that, the images it captures are somewhere in the system, no matter what the manufacturer tries to tell you. But I'm not getting how this might help. So what if we can get images of Lupo's face when he's driving, even when the text comes in?"

"That's the biggest 'and' of all—maybe," she answered. "You know how that jerk always wears his wraparound mirrored sunglasses?"

"I do," Sean said. "Benny called that his I-may-be-a-skinhead-but-I'm-a-cool-one vibe."

"If he was driving when the text came in—which we think he was—and moved his head to look at the message, the steering wheel would record him and tell him to cut it out. We might be able to see the text message in the reflection from his sunglasses. It'd be like reading it in a mirror."

The phone was silent.

Finally, Sean spoke. "Holy shit. I'm gonna hit Ford right now. They'll help us, especially after what happened. Son of a bitch, Jessica. That is so great, so great."

Jessica lifted both hands with her palms toward the phone. "Still a lot of ifs, ands, and buts, though," she said.

Nora turned to look at Jessica. "Sure, but we got hope we didn't have a minute ago."

◆

Nora looked up from her desk to see Sean coming into her office with Jessica behind him.

"Why are you here?" she asked, looking past Sean at Jessica. "You really should be home."

"You know I can't be," Jessica said, pointing at Sean. "Listen to this."

He was carrying an eight-by-ten photo, which he put on the desk in front of Nora. "Jessica was right. We got it."

Nora looked down at the photo, which appeared to be a screenshot of a text exchange. There were letters in a gray box, and more letters in a blue box below. "But I can't read the message."

"'Cause it's backward, a mirror image from his sunglasses," Sean said, "just like Jessica predicted."

He put another photo on the desk. "But we turned it around."

Now Nora could see that the gray box read: *Need you at Hyde. Jet at TEB now. E.*

Below that, the text in the blue box read: *Copy. En route.*

Nora looked up, scrunching her face in a confused expression, but Jessica answered her unspoken questions: "Teterboro," Jessica said. "Means Epps had a jet at Teterboro airport in North Jersey. Private planes only. And we already checked: A plane in the name of an LLC set up by the same Raleigh law firm took off an hour later for an airport in Hyde County, North Carolina—eastern part of the state, middle of nowhere. There's a gigantic chunk of land and a private hunting plantation owned by an Epps company. Plane came back the next day. It also went to North Carolina right after the UN bombing. That's gotta be where Lupo is now. And Epps."

"I know I should know this," Nora said, rubbing her face with one hand, "but what's a private hunting plantation?"

Sean shrugged, but Jessica answered. "Huge piece of land rich people keep for hunting. Usually a big house and staff to keep the land ready for killing whatever you intend to kill. That part of North Carolina, it's probably birds and bears, believe it or not. They have a ton of both. And very few people. That county is bigger than all of New York City and only has a couple thousand people."

Nora squinted. "How do you know all this, Ms. Bay Area Chemistry Teacher?"

"One of my squad-mates is a fanatical hunter. Talked about it constantly. Plus I googled it on the way here."

CHAPTER FIFTY-THREE

The group was too big to meet in Nora's office or the trial team room so they used the US Attorney's conference room. At Nora's request, they started the meeting by going around the big table so all the new people could identify themselves. The Special Agent in Charge of the New York office's Counterterrorism Division was there, as was his assistant SAC responsible for overseeing the Joint Terrorism Task Force. And Jessica's squad supervisor was back, along with a variety of other JTTF supervisors. A representative from FBI headquarters was there, along with two lawyers from the Main Justice counterterrorism section in Washington.

"Hello, everyone," Nora began after introductions. "As I said when I met each of you in the hall, you are welcome here and I very much believe many heads are better than one. But because this is a tactical meeting, what I propose to do, with great respect, is pretend you are not here so I can talk to the line people. But—and this is an important *but*—you are of course welcome to provide feedback or input at any time. And let me make you a promise that should relieve the pressure on you to be here: I will ensure that you are kept fully informed about the investigation, and in real time."

As heads nodded around the room, Nora looked at Jessica and Sean, who were seated closest to her end of the table. "Okay, so we use Cusak to reach out to Lupo, but to what end? And even if we could rely on him, there's no way he gets close to Epps. Are we really thinking we can get enough to flip Lupo and then use him to get Epps? Seems like a bit of a fantasy."

"Yeah, we gotta find somebody they would actually let in," Jessica said. "Somebody who could get to the hunting place, and we don't have time to build a backstory for one of our undercovers. Gotta be a CHS who fits."

"I'm guessing you already queried the source files," Nora said. The FBI kept a detailed index on all its Confidential Human Sources—a term that encompassed anyone willing to help the Bureau, regardless of motivation.

"We did," she answered. "We have a few business types we could call on, but none that are an obvious fit for a hunting plantation and none with a connection to Lupo or Epps that would let them get in quickly. Still looking."

Nora was staring off into the corner. "What?" Jessica asked.

"I have an idea." She picked up the conference table phone and dialed. The room heard her say, "Hey, Ma, how's it going there?"

After listening for a few seconds, Nora asked, "Is he still there?"

She listened for a beat and then said, "Good, good. Make sure he doesn't leave before I get there. Bye. Love you too."

When Nora hung up, Jessica tilted her head and squinted at her. "Too soon," Nora said. "Let me go check something. I'll let you know." Then in a louder voice she added, "Thank you, everyone, we'll talk soon," and walked quickly from the room.

◆

The ICU room was quiet, except for the constant beeping noises from the machines keeping the unconscious Benny Dugan alive and breathing. As Nora approached the door, she could see her mother on the far side of Benny's bed, reading quietly, inches from his left ear. At the foot of the bed, a man sat on a chair, leaning forward over his splayed knees, his silver-haired head staring at the floor between his shoes as he massaged one shoulder with his open hand. Nora nodded at her mother and spoke to the man.

"Hey, Matty, I'm glad you're here."

Matthew Parker dropped his hand and looked up, his face pained and pale, his eyes bloodshot. "Oh God, Nora, I'm so sorry. I'm so sorry."

"Me too," she answered. "Mom says you've been here a long time."

Parker gestured with his head toward the bed. "I'll never leave him. I owe my life to that guy."

Nora nodded. "Can I talk to you for a sec?"

Teresa stood. "Let me run down the hall and let you two be. It'd be good for you to talk here anyway. Doctors say hearing our voices is good for him. That's why I read to him." She paused and dropped her chin to her chest and began sobbing as Nora rushed around the bed to embrace her.

"You have to get some rest, Ma. He's going to need you."

"I know, I know," Teresa said quietly. "I'm just so afraid to leave him."

"We'll be here. He's never going to be alone."

Teresa gently pushed back from her daughter. "Okay, for a few minutes. But I'll be just down the hall. Maybe just rest my eyes in the lounge."

When she was gone, Parker exhaled loudly. "She's an amazing person, your mom. Our boy there is lucky to have her."

"And he's lucky to have somebody like you, Matty."

"I feel useless," he said. "And honestly, I feel like the crowd I was helping is mixed up in this somehow. They were just so obsessed with the UN. Look, I knew I'd made a mistake with Buchanan, but I saw it through. I just never imagined it could lead to"—he gestured toward Benny—"this."

He stopped speaking and stared at Benny lying frozen, the ventilator pushing his chest in and out with loud clicks as the air changed direction. "This, this," he began again, tears welling in his eyes. "I just . . ."

"Hey, hey," Nora said gently, "that's what I wanted to talk to you about. There may be a way for you to help, for Benny. You up for coming with me down to the office when my mom gets back?"

"Of course," Parker answered, wiping his nose on his sleeve. "Anything for the big guy."

CHAPTER FIFTY-FOUR

"Okay," Parker said, moving his head as he spoke to look at the team gathered around him in Nora's office. "So Cusak will get a message to Lupo that I have information that could be very helpful to him and his patron. If that works, Lupo reaches out to me, brings me to the fuckin' cabin in the woods or whatever. I meet this Epps and find out what I can find out."

"Yes," Nora answered. "That's it."

"And am I wearing a wire for this?"

"We don't think so," Sean answered, "at least not at the start. Lupo and Epps are pretty careful, so it would be too risky to go in there with any kind of device."

"Makes sense," Parker said. "I see if I can build something, then we get it on the record down the road and you snatch up Epps and Lupo."

"Well, let's not get too far ahead of ourselves, Matty," Nora answered. "First step is to see if we can get you in conversation with Epps, and we need any info on how hard a target the hunting place is."

Parker nodded. "Right. And so we're clear: You're good with me going in telling Epps I have information from my law enforcement sources, namely that the FBI has identified him and connected him to Lupo."

"Yes," Jessica said, "exactly that."

"Related question," Sean said. "You're good keeping the conversation away from anything they may later claim was privileged?"

"I am," Parker answered. "They trust me because I'm Buchanan's lawyer, but I'm not theirs and I'm not going to be. I'm just a true believer—in their eyes—with information that can help the cause. That's it."

"Right," Sean responded, "but what I want to be careful about is giving Lupo or Epps a basis to later claim they reasonably believed their conversations with you were for the purpose of obtaining legal advice. We got approval from Justice to do this, so long as we don't create an attorney relationship."

Parker grimaced. "Not my first rodeo, Sean. And, anyway, you got somebody else auditioning for this part?"

When there was no reply, he added, "Didn't think so. So we roll. Let me do my thing to help my friend."

◆

Under the FBI's close supervision, Herb Cusak used his phone—returned to him for thirty seconds—to type a cryptic message to Lupo: *Sam's lawyer says he has info your man is going to want to hear but please leave me out of it.*

It took several days, but Parker eventually received a similarly cryptic message from a number he did not recognize: *Tomorrow 6 pm Signature TEB.*

So early the next evening, with Teterboro airport blanketed by an FBI surveillance team, Matthew Parker walked up to the counter at the Signature private air terminal and identified himself. The receptionist directed him to a Bombardier Challenger 300 jet on the tarmac.

The two pilots asked to see his driver's license but did not identify themselves or speak to him after that, silently retracting the stairs and closing the cockpit door as he chose a seat on the empty plane. After an hour in the air, mostly over the Atlantic Ocean, the plane traced the gentle arc of North Carolina's Cape Hatteras National Seashore and then turned west, crossing the broad Pamlico Sound to land at Hyde County airport, elevation eight feet. Landing into a setting sun, Parker could see nothing but woods and swamps to the horizon in all directions. *They weren't kidding that nobody lives in this fucking place.*

An SUV driven by another silent man stopped at the foot of the jet's stairs and retrieved Parker for the drive to his destination. But before he got in the car, one of the pilots spoke again, calling, "Oh, Mr. Parker, we need you to leave all electronics on the plane, please."

Parker stopped and handed his phone to the pilot, then ran his open palms up and down his torso. "That's it," he said. "No laptop, nothing else."

"No Apple watch?" the pilot asked.

"Not that fancy," Parker replied, holding out his left wrist to show his Seiko.

"I'm afraid that counts, sir," the pilot said, extending his hand.

You paranoid cocksuckers. "Of course," Parker said, unstrapping the watch and handing it over.

He counted three sets of controlled security gates once they left the paved road, all adorned with prominent cameras and NO TRESPASSING signs. After driving what seemed like miles through dense brush and dark woods, the car arrived at a clearing dominated by a large and modern two-story black wood building with a steep peaked roof and long one-story wings stretching across the ground on either side like the arms of a bear. *I guess that's the intention. How Bond villain of you sick fucks.*

Standing at the bottom of the stairs leading to the center structure was a familiar bald head, with sunglasses on even in the fading light.

"No bag?" Lupo asked as the car drove off.

"Understood I wouldn't be staying," Parker answered.

"Correct. And sorry to do this, Matthew, but I have to pat you down before we go in. You're one of the good guys, but rules are rules with Mr. Epps."

Parker lifted his arms, wincing involuntarily as the right one went up.

"Shoulder's still bad, I see," Lupo said, running his hands over Parker's body. "You really need to get that fixed."

"Soon, my friend, soon." *Soon as you and your dirt-ball boss are in the pokey.*

"Okay, good to go," Lupo announced. "And it may sound like I'm kidding, but Mr. Epps is going to meet with you in the sauna."

Parker smirked. "Gonna get my suit a tad moist, David, dontcha think?"

"Yeah, that's the thing. It'll be the way you normally do a sauna. Birthday suit. I'll give you a towel."

For you, Benny, for you I'll do this shit.

Ten minutes later, Matthew Parker was naked and sitting on a towel in a large cedar sauna when the door opened and a thin man of about seventy-five with a prominent chin stepped in, wearing only round wire-rim glasses, which immediately fogged. He spread a towel next to Parker and sat.

Epps began by thanking Parker for his work defending Samuel Buchanan, speaking in a quiet, almost gentle voice with a hint of a southern accent. "I very much appreciate your work defending Sam. I know it was a difficult case, and in a challenging venue, but you did your best, which is all one can ask."

"You're welcome," Parker replied. "A great American patriot. It was my honor to defend him."

Those were the last words he spoke for the next ten minutes, as he listened to Bernard Epps share his thoughts about the decline of American civilization. It was eerily like listening to a right-wing Mr. Rogers, the soft words of apocalyptic prediction coming out of a wrinkled, sweaty, naked old man. Watering the tree of liberty, the whole playlist, but without the Buchanan bombast. And unlike Sam, Epps explained, God had blessed him with more money than one man should ever have, and with that came great responsibility. He was, he quietly explained, using his money to save the country he loved from heathens and foreigners so it could remain the Christian country God intended it to be.

When the monologue was finished, Parker nodded. *Fuck you, fuck your movement. I'm about to burn this shit down, you wrinkly old prick.*

"Couldn't agree with you more, Mr. Epps," he said. "I'm grateful you love our country that much. And I'd like to help you any way I can. I have some information you may find useful, but I want to be careful how you and I speak."

Epps nodded. "I appreciate that. And I'd like you to be my attorney so our conversations are privileged."

"Done," Parker responded, gesturing to the sauna walls. "Now we have an inviolable cone of silence around us in both a literal and a figurative sense." *And I'm about to stick it up your butt. What Nora doesn't know isn't going hurt anybody except you.*

"And the information?" Epps asked.

Parker explained that he had learned the FBI had identified Epps and knew Lupo worked for him and that the authorities were combing his financial empire, working to build a case against him.

"How do you know this?" Epps asked quietly.

"Because I used to work in that prosecutor's office and have friends there and in the FBI who tell me things. And obviously, I will continue to try to learn on your behalf."

"Well, I appreciate that, Mr. Parker. Should we discuss the financial terms of our relationship?"

"Oh no, sir, I wouldn't accept a penny for this. I'm doing this because I care about this country. This is on a handshake basis."

"We need more like you," Epps answered with a tight smile, extending a wet hand to grasp Parker's.

"Indeed we do, sir. And before I faint in here, if I have further information to pass along, shall I text the same number that made these arrangements?"

"Yes, do that," Epps said. "And I do hope you'll stay and hunt with me in the morning. No business conversation, of course—that's what I use the sauna for—but I think you'd enjoy the sport. You learn a lot about people by hunting with them. We'll outfit you fully and get you back on your way by lunch tomorrow."

"Fine, sir. I'd like that."

"Good night, then," Epps said, rising and stepping to the door. "I'll see you in the morning."

◆

It was dark when David Lupo rapped on the door of Matthew Parker's guest room in one of the wings of the big house. Parker was already awake and in the hunting clothes that had been laid out for him. "We'll get something to eat in the stand," Lupo said, directing Parker down the hallway toward the entrance hall.

Epps was waiting on the broad front porch with Gwendolyn Harmon, the Senate candidate, who looked like she just stepped out of a hunting gear catalog—formfitting matching camo top and pants and brown knee-high boots.

"Good morning, hunters!" Epps said with a broad smile. "It's such a pleasure to be with you all, and I do apologize about the early hour. Be good to get our day's work done before it's too warm."

He gestured toward Harmon. "Matthew, have you met the future junior senator from Arizona?"

"Haven't had the pleasure," Parker replied, gingerly extending his right hand, which Harmon took and shook vigorously. *Holy shit, lady, don't tear it off.*

"Nice to meet another fan of liberty," Harmon said. "Good huntin'."

Parker glanced at the rifle bags lying on the porch. "And what are we after this morning, sir?"

"The best thing about this area," Epps replied. "Bear. More of 'em here than any place east of the Rockies."

"Can you hunt bears before Thanksgiving, sir?"

That seemed to draw a rare rise out of Epps. "I can hunt whatever I please, whenever I please," Epps said. "My land, my bears. The government can't tell me how to live on my own land."

"But I thought the reason you don't hunt bears except late in the year is so the cubs don't lose a parent."

Epps sniffed. "Plenty of bears out there to look after them. They need to learn to make their way in the world, just like coddled American children do. So let's mount up."

With that, Epps climbed on his horse, a striking black Appaloosa with white-spotted hindquarters. Lupo directed Parker and Harmon to their chestnut-brown quarter horses and then mounted his own. A staff member picked up the rifle bags and put them in a mule-drawn wagon, which followed the horses as they walked slowly down a dirt road.

As they walked, Parker's horse drifted next to Harmon's. "First time for you too?" he asked.

She chuckled. "Oh no, many times. Been out here for birds, bears, you name it. No better hunting ground."

"Not real close to Arizona, though."

"That's for sure," Harmon replied, "but Bernard is a great friend and he has a plane. And we may be near the ocean, but the woke coastal elites couldn't find this place if their lives depended on it."

About a half mile into the woods, the group stopped and climbed ladder-stairs into a large hunting stand about ten feet off the ground. The staff member distributed some kind of beef jerky and black coffee in metal cups before setting up three rifles on tripods positioned so the shooter could sit in a camp chair directly behind the weapon.

Epps walked to the edge of the platform, fiddled with his pants, and began urinating over the railing in an arc onto the ground below. As he peed with his back to them, he gestured with his free hand to the far side of an open field in front, just visible in the predawn light, talking quietly while chewing jerky. "Big ones come out of that tree line in the morning and cross here to get to the fresh water we put in on this side. Especially when it's this warm, they need that water. So be ready."

Parker waited until Epps was finished doing his business—*Remind me not to shake hands*—and then asked, "And why use horses, sir?"

"Simple. Bears don't notice them the way they would something with an engine."

"Of course," Parker said.

Epps pointed to the rifles positioned in front of them. "Gwen, you take the right side. Matthew, the left chair and rifle are yours. Scope is dialed in to take the bears when they're about halfway across the field. No need to mess with it. And don't jerk the trigger, just squeeze."

"Got it," Parker said. "I should confess I'm a bit concerned about the recoil. I've got an issue with this right shoulder. Need to get it fixed soon."

"Lupo told me. Not an issue. Shoot left-handed. Tripod holds the gun. All you need to do is put your left shoulder to it and pull the trigger."

"Naturally," Parker said.

"Okay, light's coming up. Let's get in position," Epps said in a stage whisper, sliding into the center chair and leaning until his right eyeglass lens was pressed against the scope.

As he moved to his own chair, Parker noticed that Lupo had remained standing and was behind them, holding the fourth rifle across his body, the barrel pointing at the floor. *Great. The murderous psycho directly behind. What have I done?*

Parker awkwardly wrapped his left arm around the weapon and brought his left eye to the scope. He kept his left finger resting on the trigger guard as he waited. In just a few minutes, the field became surprisingly bright and he could see large shapes moving slowly out of the tree line, a group to the left side of their vision, and a single bear appearing fifty yards to the right.

"Here we go," Epps whispered. "Gwen, you take the right."

The group of shapes moved from the left into the light. It was two large female black bears, each leading several cubs across the field. Harmon's bear appeared to be alone.

What the fuck are we doing?

"Steady," Epps breathed. "Little farther, little farther. Now."

An explosion of rifle shots shattered the morning just a moment before Parker tilted his rifle slightly upward and fired. When he leveled the weapon again, through the scope he could see one female and her cubs sprinting back to the tree line. A black lump lay in the grass where the group had been standing, three cubs nudging the fallen form. Well to the right, Harmon's bear was rolling and appeared to be crawling through the grass, bellowing in pain.

"Got her!" Epps cried.

"Me too," Harmon shouted. "Think mine's a daddy, but he ain't done yet."

Epps turned to Parker. "You miss the other?"

"I'm afraid I did, sir," Parker replied, watching Lupo in his peripheral vision slowly lowering his rifle.

"Well, it's not easy to get used to your off hand. Next time you'll be better."

Parker looked up and noticed the staff member hurrying ahead through the tall grass, cradling a shotgun. He stopped just short of the moaning bear and fired twice. The bear stopped moving and was silent.

Harmon turned to Epps with a wide grin. "Took a couple slugs to put my bad boy down."

"He doesn't know who he's messing with, Gwen," Epps replied.

◆

"Well, at least it didn't taste like chicken," Parker said, lifting his glass to sip brandy.

"Your first bear steak, I'm guessing," Lupo said from the other side of the fire pit.

"Yup, not terrible, but I don't think it's going to make the menu at Peter Luger's."

Lupo laughed and took a long drink of his brandy, his third or fourth glass. "Listen," he said, "I really appreciate all you've done—for Sam, for the boss, for America, really."

"No big deal," Parker replied. "This country is worth fighting for."

Lupo held up his glass. "Amen to that, brother."

There was a long silence as the two men stared into the flames as frogs and cicadas called out in the dark woods all around them. Then Lupo spoke. "Hey, so you're our lawyer, right?"

Parker nodded. "For Mr. Epps, for you, for whoever Mr. Epps wishes me to represent. So, yes. You and I enjoy a privileged relationship."

"Then lemme ask you: You pick up anything from your sources about me?"

"Yes, in fact. They think you killed Rebecca Hubbard. They also think you engineered the UN thing. So you have significant exposure, which we should manage carefully."

Lupo took another drink before continuing. "They don't know the half of it. Sure, I did the girl, because it had to be done. She was a loose cannon. Totally unglued, making accusations on a fucking live broadcast. Would endanger Mr. Epps and the whole cause. So, business, not personal."

He stopped. Parker waited. *Give it to me, you motherfucker.*

When Lupo stayed silent, Parker prodded him carefully. "And the UN thing? Which, by the way, sent a powerful wake-up message to our confused country." He lifted his own glass, adding, "Bravo."

Lupo took another drink. "Yup, although it almost went totally to shit. I lined up two solid guys—or at least I thought they were solid. Backpack bombs. All they had to do was put 'em down in the crowd of woke-sters, just like the Boston Marathon. That's all. I handle the rest. Remote control, like a fuckin' garage door opener. Boom, lotta libtard legs go bye-bye."

When he didn't continue, Parker prompted again. "So how did it go sideways?"

Lupo snorted. "I met up with them for a final gut check about a block away. I had my old raid jacket on, using the alley next to the tunnel ventilation between Forty-First and Forty-Second so I could move freely. Nobody gave me a glance. Last second, one of them loses his nerve, starts givin' me a song and dance about how he can't go through with it. Nightmare.

"On top of that, two fuckin' feds come running up, guns drawn and shit. So from the alley, I popped one of them—actually that was both business and personal. Turns out it's a guy been up my ass for a long time. Big fuckin' bully, name a' Dugan. Fuck him. Anyhow, I put him down just as my chickenshit soldier is fuckin' runnin' away, so I gotta detonate him and send the other guy, who's still got his balls intact, up to the rally. I cut back through the alley to Forty-Second and up to the plaza. Course by now it's startin' to come apart. Cops are on my second guy, so I have to detonate him. But still: boom, message sent, and I beat feet here, thanks to Mr. Epps."

Lupo leaned back in his Adirondack and drained his glass as Parker stared into the flames.

CHAPTER FIFTY-FIVE

"**A**nd fucking Lupo shoots the bear *for* him," Parker said, eyeing everyone at the conference room table, "and everybody pretends that didn't happen and it's Epps's kill of some mama bear in front of her kids. And the wagon dude has to go kill Harmon's. Hooray. Fucked-up on so many levels."

"Sick people," Sean said, "but do you think you could get Epps talking business if you went hunting again?"

"Yes. The good news is that I could go there again and I think I could get him going. The bad news is that it's not gonna happen any place but the sauna, where I'm naked. Lupo will talk to me in other places, but not the boss."

"And any basis for him to claim he thought your conversation was between a client and his lawyer?"

Parker felt a twinge of guilt as he lied to Nora. "None. I made it clear this was just me as a fellow believer passing information along. Prick can say what he wants when this is over, but he can't claim he thought I was his lawyer."

"Good," Nora replied.

"But I'm not sure this goes any further," Parker continued, turning to Jessica. "Unless your tech wizards can figure out how to get a microphone into a sauna in the middle of that maniac's bear-killing retreat,

I'd say we're done. You're just gonna have to go down there and grab him."

Nora grunted. "On what evidence? We can charge Lupo based on his statements to you, and we can use Cusak as a witness against him as well. But Epps? We don't have enough to even get to probable cause; forget about beyond a reasonable doubt. Without a tape, we have nothing, which is why we're having this conversation."

"But we're not giving up," Jessica said. "We'd love it if you'd make another short trip and come with us to Quantico to help think it through."

Parker made a surprised face. "Quantico? Why do I want to go to your academy?"

"Oh, there's a whole lot more there than the training academy."

◆

It was almost too bright to sit outside, but Jessica, Nora, and Sean steered Matthew Parker to a table with an umbrella.

"You must be kidding," Parker said, setting his sandwich and chips on the table. "You have a Subway in the middle of the little fake town where you train new agents?"

"Yup," Jessica said. "Welcome to Quantico, where the Subway is real and we don't rob it." She pointed down the block in the mock town called Hogan's Alley. "Over there, of course, is the most robbed bank in America."

"Incredible," Parker said. "And as a taxpayer, let me say I'm pleased to see that Subway is not giving you any kind of deal on the sandwiches. The five-dollar footlong is long gone."

They ate in silence for a while until Jessica spoke. "Okay, listen, this meeting is going to be a little strange. We're headed over to OTD, the

Operational Technology Division. They're the wizards of the FBI. You remember Q from the James Bond movies?"

Parker nodded and grunted with a full mouth.

"That's fiction, but OTD is real, and better than Q in a lot of ways. And because this is the Bureau's highest priority right now, you've been given a temporary security clearance to go into OTD to help figure out how we might record Epps. They built a model of the whole place to facilitate the discussion. And there'll be other folks there. Please don't ask people about their jobs, okay?"

"Got it," Parker said.

❖

OTD was in a nondescript building that sprawled across the Marine Corps ground borrowed by the FBI to create the Bureau's huge Quantico operation. The group was buzzed through a series of secure doors and into a vast space that resembled the backstage of a symphony hall. In the center of the space was a big table holding a mockup of Epps's entire compound, including a detailed scale model of the black, bearlike building.

A strange mix of people stood around the table—half thin, pale-looking scientists and half large, muscular men with thick beards wearing green short-sleeve Under Armour shirts with American flags on one bicep. The group parted to let Parker approach the table, where he was prompted to use the model to narrate his visit and to answer dozens of questions from scientists and beards.

The scientists talked through a variety of technologies, from lasers to powerful directional microphones to nanobots, arguing with one another and checking facts with Parker as they talked. The beards wanted to know about gates, doors, vehicles, weapons, dogs, and people Parker had seen during his visit. After almost two hours, the lead scientist took Parker by the elbow and guided him to a couple chairs off to the side of the space.

"Mr. Parker," he said, "you've confirmed our belief that the only way this happens is with an extraordinary piece of cooperation on your part."

Feel like I'm already tits-deep in extraordinary cooperation, bub. "What'd you have in mind?"

"The only way we're going to be able to capture what goes on in that sauna is to use a small transmitter that will, essentially, pass the sound in the room to a drone flying overhead, which will serve as a relay and downlink. The drone needs to be nearby because the device must be small and can't beam a signal over a long distance."

"Okay," Parker said hesitantly. "Is this the part where you tell me you want to stick something up my ass?"

"We actually discussed that," the scientist replied flatly.

When Parker recoiled and lifted both eyebrows, the scientist went on. "We think that would be too unstable and you'd be literally sitting on it with other, uh, *matter* of unpredictable density in close proximity within your rectum, with uncertain impacts on the signal. So that won't work."

"Break my heart," Parker said with a small smile.

"Yes, well, we actually think our best chance is to implant it in your shoulder. We say that because we know from you and our colleagues that you are long overdue for a shoulder replacement. Our experts believe we could insert the device during that procedure. It will be stable in that position and, should you be wanded by a metal detector, the titanium and aluminum of the new shoulder would obscure the device."

"And it stays there?"

"No, no, it would have to be removed shortly afterward to minimize the risk of infection. So we would be asking you to run that risk as well as the risks associated with a second procedure to remove the device. But it would otherwise be a regular shoulder replacement. Nothing about this should affect that."

"You've done this before?" Parker asked.

"We have not. But we've done enough work to have reasonable confidence."

When Parker didn't respond, the scientist touched his arm and then pointed across the vast space. "Here, let me show you." He led Parker to a door that opened into what looked like a chemistry lab, but colder, and reeking of formaldehyde. "Sorry for the smell," he said as they walked to a long lab table on which sat a half dozen slabs of pink meat.

"Those look like—" Parker began.

"Yes, canned hams," the scientist answered, "because they are, without the cans, of course. We bought them at Costco to play the role of your shoulder."

As they came closer, Parker could see that several of the hams had what appeared to be incisions that had been sewn closed. "We've experimented with a variety of depths and angles on the transmitter so we can get optimal signal, especially with stitches so close to it. You're not a ham, but we have reasonable confidence that we know how to orient the device, because . . ."

The scientist gestured for Parker to follow him around a partition to another section of the lab, where three human cadavers lay on tables, covered in plastic sheets except for their shoulders, which had been cut open.

"These aren't from Costco," the scientist said flatly.

"They're dead to me," Parker replied.

The scientist paused and then nodded with just a trace of a grin. *You're welcome,* Parker thought. *And feel free to use that with your buddies.*

"As you can see, we've worked this up quite extensively, which is why we think it will work. Questions?"

Parker grinned. "Honestly, doc, I'm just so relieved nothing's going up my butt."

When the scientist didn't laugh, he quickly moved on. "I'll do it, but I want my surgeon at the Hospital for Special Surgery in Manhattan to do the shoulder. You could read him in or whatever for the implanting of the device. He's a solid citizen and can keep a secret."

"Fair enough," the scientist said. "You give us the information and we'll get the surgery set for the next couple days. Of course, you'll need to deploy with the device immediately afterward to preserve battery power."

"That's fine, Parker said. "I can tell Epps I have something urgent, so important, in fact, that I'm going to come even though my shoulder hurts like hell."

CHAPTER FIFTY-SIX

Parker sent the text from just outside the operating room. *About to have my shoulder fixed but have urgent info for the boss. Pick up TEB 7 pm today.* He handed the phone to an FBI employee in surgical scrubs. "Let's do this," Parker said, lying back on the gurney. "For Benny."

Two hours later, he was awake in recovery and unlocked his phone. The return text read: *Confirmed TEB 7 pm.* His surgeon was standing by the bed. "Okay, Matty, I confess that's the first one like that I've done, but the shoulder looks good. You and I should be back out on the course in six months. Short term, we loaded you up on an injected pain blocker, so you shouldn't feel much at that joint, or really in the arm, for another twenty-four hours. Just keep the sling on and don't move it, 'kay?"

Parker extended his left hand to grab the doctor's right. "Thanks, Dave. I can't wait to kick your ass at the club championship."

The surgeon smiled. "That'll be the day. It's a shoulder, not a miracle." He nodded to the FBI employees standing around the room. "These folks didn't tell me much except that you're about to do something important for our country and it relates to the UN attack. Godspeed, my friend. And get back here soon so I can get that little doodad, whatever it is, out of you."

◆

The shirt was easy because it had snaps up the front. The hard part was getting his pants off with one arm pinned against his sternum by a heavy black immobilizer sling, but Parker managed. Thank God for the pain blocker.

The hardest part was figuring out how to wrap a towel around his waist for the walk down the hall to the sauna. He finally decided to spread the towel on the bed and lie back on it, using his left hand to lift the ends and pinch them together at his waist. *Not gonna show these assholes my junk.*

Lupo was waiting by the sauna door when Parker got there. He pointed at the sling. "Not in there, sorry. Boss's rules. He read somewhere that Carlo Gambino died a free man because he only discussed Family business outdoors and when whispering. This is his version of that."

Parker squinted. "You can't be serious. Bet ol' future senator Gwen isn't bare-assing it in there with the boss."

"Well, she isn't here and, anyway, there are no exceptions," Lupo answered. "And towels are fine, as you know. The sling, please."

"Unbelievable," Parker said, turning to face him. "You'll need to pull it off so I can hold it still with the good arm." *Thank God they decided not to put the bug in the sling.*

Lupo stripped the Velcro to release the sling, carefully sliding it off as Parker cradled his right arm. When he was free of the brace, Parker turned and faced the sauna. "Little help on the door'd be great," he said.

"And the bandage," Lupo said. "*Nothing* means nothing."

Parker paused, but then said, "Fine, fine. You do it, but carefully so I can put it back on after."

"Whatever it is, must be important," Lupo said as he reached up and peeled the white rectangular dressing from the shoulder, exposing the six-inch incision arcing across the front of Parker's shoulder, the wound still raw and zigzagged with black stitches.

"Wouldn't be doing this if it wasn't," Parker answered, pausing to face the door until Lupo reached and opened it. Then he stepped into the sauna and sat, marveling that the towel stayed around his waist.

◆

There was no small talk. The naked Epps sat on the sauna bench, looked at him through fogged glasses, and quietly asked, "What is it?"

Jesus, I hope they can hear this. "Sir, the FBI knows that Lupo killed that professor—Greenstone—and the girl, Becky."

Epps was silent for several beats before asking in his usual soft voice, "How do they think they know that?"

"Not sure, sir. I think they may have flipped Herb Cusak, Lupo's connection to Buchanan."

There was another silence. Parker waited, then continued with the script he'd memorized. "And they know Lupo did it for you."

"How on earth would they prove *that*?"

"Again, sir, I'm not sure. I don't know what Cusak knew. I'm just here to warn you that they're onto you. No doubt they're going to grab Lupo. Not sure what the case on you looks like. But they seem certain Lupo was doing what you told him to."

"You think we could reach Mr. Cusak?"

"Very unlikely, sir. If I'm right that he's flipped, they'll have him fully protected."

Epps was silent, looking down. Parker's mind raced. *Is that enough? Did I get enough? Fuck, I don't think so.*

Epps stood and moved toward the door. "Okay, thanks for telling me."

Fuck, fuck, fuck, not enough. Parker took a breath and spoke rapid-fire before Epps could get the door open, going far beyond the script they'd given him. "And their theory is that you did it all because you hate America. That you're some kind of Russian agent."

Epps stopped at the door and turned back, the tendons on his wrinkled neck visible as he spoke, sounding almost hurt by the accusation.

"The FBI thinks *I'm* a Russian agent? Are they insane? I've devoted my *life* to trying to save America from tyranny. I *love* America. You know what I *hate*? People who don't understand that a nation can't exist without borders, can't exist without a common language, can't exist without common moral values."

Parker found that he was unconsciously turning his right shoulder to Epps as the old man spoke faster and faster.

"I've had to grapple with a hard truth—that it's too late, that America is finished, that the best course, the kindest course, is to put her down like some sick animal. So yes, it's all going down, but there'll be some of us around to rebuild, to lift a new country out of the rubble, one closer to the values of our founding."

Epps paused and shook his head angrily from side to side. "It kills me to do it, but I've put everything I have to short America, to bet that the collapse is coming. But I'm not betting against the real America. I'm betting against the globalist, amoral monster she has become, the unrecognizable beast that must be put down. Every penny I have is on the table through every market I can find. The money I make from her collapse will be used to build her again. You want to know why that Professor Greenstone died?"

Parker said a silent prayer as Epps paused for breath. *Please, please, God, let them be getting this.*

Two thousand feet overhead, a small black drone buzzed in the darkness as Epps filled his lungs with air. A mile away in a trailer in the woods, leaders of the FBI Hostage Rescue Team heard him begin to exhale a torrent of words.

"He didn't die because he was one of the fools we told Buchanan to talk about. Maybe Buchanan could have talked someone into killing him, like the others. I don't know. But Greenstone was a *special* problem for reasons Buchanan never imagined, because his real work was tracing money, especially short positions and options. Somehow, he and his too-smart-for-their-own-good students picked up on my bets. Maybe I piled too much into too few markets. I don't know. But Greenstone was going to ruin everything. So yes, he had to go. That's what Lupo is for. And the girl was just a loose end Lupo thought had to be tied off. I'm not sure I would have done it, but you've got to trust your people."

You, motherfucker, are now done, if the shoulder thing works. When Epps didn't say anything else, Parker took a chance. He was winging it. "I don't know whether they can prove you were behind the UN thing."

Three hundred miles away in the Strategic Information and Operations Center buried deep in the heart of FBI headquarters, the Director and his staff heard Epps blow air between his closed lips. He was sad now. "That was a hard one. And turns out only one of Lupo's people was reliable. But Lupo was right that something had to be done to push us toward the inflection point. The tree of liberty must be refreshed from time to time with the blood of patriots and tyrants. I very much regret the loss of life, but it's the only path to rebirth."

Five hundred miles away, Nora and Sean and Jessica and a crowded FBI New York command center heard the sound of Epps pulling the sauna door open and calling over his shoulder, "Good work. Keep me informed."

A mile away, the HRT commander keyed his radio, saying, "Blue team: execute, execute, execute," and dozens of armed men and machines began moving through the North Carolina night.

◆

Lupo was helping Parker into his shoulder harness when the sound of helicopters reached their consciousness. He dropped the strap and ran, leaving Parker holding the edges of the towel around his waist while the sling flapped against his numb right arm.

Lupo emerged from the front door holding a hunting rifle as the first Black Hawk helicopter flared in the front driveway to discharge six HRT operators and a canine. When he lifted the rifle toward the helicopter, an FBI overwatch sniper lying in the weeds one hundred yards away squeezed the trigger with the crosshairs of his nightscope fixed on Lupo's forehead. Two-tenths of a second later, Lupo died.

Parker could hear the sounds of HRT teams shouting clearance commands as the operators moved through the building. He also heard the terrifying bark of a Belgian Malinois and turned his head to speak directly into his shoulder. "I don't know who can hear this, and who's in charge of the dog and stuff, but I'm standing by the sauna with my dick in my hand. Please don't hurt me."

Five hundred miles away, Nora turned to Sean with a broad smile. "You know, I see why he and Benny got along."

CHAPTER FIFTY-SEVEN

"All rise!" came the clerk's familiar call as the hundreds of spectators and journalists squeezed into the ceremonial courtroom rose with the usual sounds as Judge Donovan Newton swept up the stairs to the bench.

"Be seated, please," the judge said as he looked around the courtroom, before adding to his clerk, "and call the case."

"*United States of America v. Bernard Epps*," the clerk said in a loud voice. "Counsel, please state your appearances."

Nora rose. "Nora Carleton and Sean Fitzpatrick for the United States, Your Honor."

"Riley Pond for the defendant, Your Honor." At the table next to Pond, a small, thin old man with glasses and a prominent chin sat with head bowed, his hands and feet shackled to a chain that wrapped around his waist and ran between his legs. Two deputy marshals sat close behind.

"Ms. Pond," the judge said, "I note that the defendant was detained by the magistrate judge in North Carolina following his arrest. Is that an issue the defense intends to revisit with this court?"

Pond stood. "Not at present, Your Honor. Given the nature of the charges and the government's intention to seek the death penalty, that seems like something not worth the candle, as they say."

"Very well," the judge replied. "And given that this will be a death penalty case, the defendant will need two attorneys, including one who is experienced in capital litigation, which I assume you are not."

"That's correct, Your Honor, and Mr. Epps is in the process of attempting to retain additional, experienced counsel to take the lead in this case, with me assisting."

"This case was assigned to me by the chief judge as related to *United States v. Buchanan*, which you handled with Mr. Parker, as I recall. Will he be appearing?"

Nora jumped to her feet. "No, Judge. We expect Mr. Parker will be involved in this case, but as a likely witness for the government."

Judge Newton looked mildly surprised but said nothing.

"Judge," Riley Pond said, "he won't be on our trial team, but we expect to make a motion to preclude any testimony by Mr. Parker on grounds of attorney-client privilege."

"With what client?" the judge asked.

Pond gestured beside her. "With Mr. Epps."

"Something that Mr. Parker denies," Nora said sharply, "and for which there is no evidence. But we'll wait for the motion." She sat down.

"Is the government ready—" the judge began, but he was distracted by movement to his left. The door beside the bench had opened and a large man was coming slowly into the courtroom, bent over, with his huge hands braced heavily on the handles of a walker.

The judge turned his head back toward the front. "If I could ask government counsel—" he started, but was stopped again, this time by the sight of tears streaming down Nora Carleton's face as she watched the man. Without speaking, Judge Newton turned back and waited as the man inched across the courtroom carpet until he reached a chair at the end of the prosecution table, where he rocked back off the walker, landed in a chair, and sat up straight in obvious pain.

Nora's eyes had never left him. She now mouthed, *Benny.*

"Wouldn't miss it for the world," Benny answered in a quiet, raspy voice.

Nora rose and faced the bench, her face wet. "The United States is ready now, Your Honor."

EPILOGUE

Teresa Carleton and her granddaughter walked arm in arm through a tunnel of trees, the only evidence that they were in a city provided by the woofers in someone's car stereo out on Flatbush Avenue.

"Have you been to Brooklyn before, Nana?" Sophie asked.

"Oh yes, baby girl, many times. This is where Benny grew up. In fact, we're close to where he was born. Prospect Park and this garden were what he considered 'the country' when he was a kid."

They turned and continued onto large flat stones that crossed a small stream. Ahead, they could see Benny's young grandchildren ambling through the grassy meadow.

"You nervous?"

"Not a bit; just incredibly happy," Teresa replied, before adding, "I'm also thinking a little of your grandfather, but I know he's happy too."

"I wish I'd known him," Sophie said.

"Me too," Teresa answered. She lifted her chin to gesture ahead as they turned the corner. "That amazing man is a lot like him."

There, in a clearing among the trees, at the head of an aisle created by rows of white folding chairs, stood Benny, in a tuxedo, watching his grandkids spread flower petals. Nora was standing angled toward him, with Carmen in the center, facing forward and holding a notebook. As guests began to notice Teresa and Sophie approaching, the audience rose and turned toward them.

Teresa reached with her free hand and squeezed her granddaughter's forearm. "Thank you for walking me down the aisle, Ladybug."

"Love you, Nana."

They were both crying when they reached the front. Teresa hugged Sophie, then handed Nora her small bouquet and turned to kiss Benny and take both of his hands. Benny's two sons stood beside him—bridal party bookends to maid-of-honor Nora and bridesmaid Jessica on the other side.

Carmen smiled and opened the officiant's notebook. "Dearly beloved," she said in a loud voice, "we are gathered here in the *Eastern District of New York* . . ." She paused to let laughter ripple through the gathering before adding, "with appropriate visas, I hope," to more laughter. The wedding of Teresa and Benny had begun.

"Mind if I join you, Mr. Groom?" Sean asked, "Or are you waiting for your spouse?"

Benny laughed and patted the surface of the stone bench next to him. "Nah, just gettin' off my feet. She's mingling, but I'm still not back to a hundred percent. Gettin' there, though."

"You look really good," Sean answered, before blushing and adding, "Don't mean to be weird."

"Weird? Not you, my nerdy friend." He gestured to the rectangular pool of water in front of them on the terrace. "Weird is Brooklyn havin' a giant lily pool and me sittin' here starin' at it a newly married man. Feels more than a little weird. But also pretty great."

They looked at the water until Benny spoke again. "How you feelin' 'bout the case, after all's said and done?"

"I feel good," Sean said. "I don't have Nora's issues about the death penalty, so it wouldn't have bothered me a bit if Epps got smoked. But he'll be dead of natural causes before all the appeals are finished. I'm good with where we ended up."

"Yeah, me too," Benny said, "I got respect for Nora's view that the government killin' him brings nobody back. And speaking of government killin', I won't be plantin' any trees for ol' Lupo. That motherfucker deserved an HRT bullet more than anybody I know."

"Agree," Sean replied, "but I would've liked to see that prick in chains."

"I suppose," Benny said, looking at the slate patio between his feet. "I still think of poor Becky all the time. After all the shit I've seen, that one stays with me for some reason. And then after that went down, I let the motherless fuck get the upper hand and shoot me."

There was an awkward silence before Sean spoke. "And speaking of not planting trees, no tears for Herb Cusak either. Got a small break for helping us, but he's still gonna do twenty and it'll be a hard stretch for him."

Benny blew a raspberry with his lips. "Dirtbag. Hey, while we're talkin', you think we pulled all the threads on the thing?"

"What do you mean?" Sean asked.

"Well, Gwendolyn Harmon is what I was thinking. She didn't get elected but she's still tryin' and I'd hate to think she's the one that got away."

"Yeah, good question, but the evidence just isn't there. We have her buzzin' all around, but sometimes that noise is just a fly—a little bug that likes to eat shit. And all the other wannabe Buchanans are on notice that they'll be held accountable for inspiring any violent attacks with their rhetoric and hate speech."

Benny chuckled. "Sometimes that noise is just a fly. That's some poetry there, Seany Boy. You got a bright future in songwriting if you give up the prosecution business."

Sean smiled. "And have to get a real life? No, thanks. I'm gonna stick with the national security and drug cartels stuff. Much simpler."

Benny looked up to see Teresa slowly making her way to them across the patio, stopping to greet guests as she came. "And speaking of that," he said, "did I hear right that we know a new FBI supervisor with the JTTF?"

"Yeah, yeah," Sean answered with a grin. "I'm drawing a blank, but I think she was standing up there during your wedding just now."

"I'm so glad Jessica decided to become a boss," Benny said. "That place needs more like her."

Teresa had finally gotten through the crowd. "May I borrow my husband?" she asked, extending her hand.

With a groan, Benny pushed himself to his feet and took the hand. "And now, Seany, me boy, I have to go be an adult."

"What's that like?" Sean called after him.

"I'll let you know," Benny laughed.

◆

Matthew Parker was drunk. Crossing the crowded dance floor of the Botanic Garden's Palm House with a drink in each hand, dark sweat circles staining his blue shirt, he stopped in front of Nora, who was slow dancing with Demi to the opening of Eric Clapton's "Wonderful Tonight."

"There's an open bar!" he shouted, too loudly.

"Yes, I know," Nora shouted back. "I'm helping pay for it."

Parker smiled broadly and continued on—leaning slightly—toward the head table, where he plopped into an empty seat next to Benny and handed his old friend a drink.

"To you, my man, to you," he said.

"Thanks, Matty," Benny replied. "Glad you're here. Don't know half of what you did for me, but thank you."

"Anything for you," Parker slurred. "Anything. And it's good you don't know. Got a little messy. Was a big puddle of shit, as they say, but luckily I had the shoes for it. And we ended up in the right place—Lupo's worm food and Epps'll die of old age alone, staring at a tiny piece of sky from his cell at ADMAX in Colorado."

He lifted his glass and added, "The trial was a pain in the ass, but that motherfucker Epps deserves what he's gonna get. Wish we weren't too civilized these days to give him a needle of poison in his skinny-ass arm. But life in solitary'll have to do."

Benny clinked his glass against Parker's. "Slainte," he said, just as Teresa appeared next to them. "Time to show my moves," Benny chuckled as he slowly rose and followed his wife to the dance floor.

◆

Nora stood near the dancers, watching Sophie and her four-year-old half sister. Little Amelia had one of her feet on top of each of Sophie's as they spun slowly in a circle holding hands. Nora turned to Sophie's father, next to her. "Nick, I can't believe how big Amelia is," she said.

"Yup," he beamed, "but what I can't get over is how grown-up Sophie is. Seems like yesterday she was a Hoboken baby."

"My mom likes to say that for a parent the days are long, but the years are short," Nora said, pointing at the dancing girls. "Too short."

Nick looked at her. "I'm so happy for your mom, and so grateful for all she did—and does—for Sophie. And for me, even having us here today. She was always great to me. And she and Benny seem perfect for each other."

Nora looked at him and nodded. "They really are. I've never seen either of them so—"

She was interrupted by the initial piano chords of "Don't Stop Believin'."

"This is their song!" Nora cried. "Time to dance!" She gave Nick a quick hug and hurried toward the dance floor, grabbing Sophie's hand and gently steering Amelia back toward her father. Snaking through the packed crowd, Nora looked up and saw Benny swaying with arms around Teresa and his eyes closed, mouthing the words to the song. Suddenly, Benny opened his eyes and smiled at Nora. "It does go on and on and on, don't it?" he shouted. Nora could only smile back and nod as she spun Sophie in circles.

ACKNOWLEDGEMENTS

I had to be nudged into writing crime fiction, and now it is my job and a source of great joy in my life. That job, that joy, and that life would not be possible without Patrice and our family, who make this—and me—better and more fun. I'm also very grateful to my loyal friend-readers—for their friendship even more than their valuable feedback.

As usual, my kind and talented agent, Kirby Kim at Janklow & Nesbit, made the book better, as did the team at Mysterious Press. Otto Penzler wouldn't want this to get around—so keep it to yourself—but he's quite nice in addition to being extraordinarily knowledgeable and hardworking. And everyone knows Luisa Cruz Smith is kind, but she's also a gifted editor who makes me a better writer. The rest of the MP team is as excellent—and as decent and warm—especially Charles Perry, Julia O'Connell, Will Luckman, and their partners at Norton. And copyeditors Kathy Strickman and Amy Medeiros bring attention to detail that is simply inspirational.

I stress kindness and decency because I'm writing at a time when those virtues seem in short supply, especially in our national town square. May these good folks be a reminder that one can be excellent and decent at the same time.